Deadly Communion

ALSO BY FRANK TALLIS
FROM CLIPPER LARGE PRINT

Mortal Mischief
Vienna Blood
Fatal Lies
Darkness Rising

Deadly Communion

Frank Tallis

W F HOWES LTD

This large print edition published in 2010 by
W F Howes Ltd
Unit 4, Rearsby Business Park, Gaddesby Lane,
Rearsby, Leicester LE7 4YH

1 3 5 7 9 10 8 6 4 2

First published in the United Kingdom in 2010
by Century

A CIP catalogue record for this book is available
from the British Library

ISBN 978 1 40745 539 6

Typeset by Palimpsest Book Production Limited,
Grangemouth, Stirlingshire
Printed and bound in Great Britain
by MPG Books Ltd, Bodmin, Cornwall

FSC
Mixed Sources
Product group from well-managed
forests, controlled sources and
recycled wood or fiber
SA-COC-1565
www.fsc.org
© 1996 Forest Stewardship Council

PART I

THE THESEUS TEMPLE

CHAPTER 1

Liebermann was seated on a wooden chair at the head of the rest bed. He had adopted an attitude which he found conducive to listening: legs crossed, his right fist against his cheek, the tip of his index finger resting gently on his temple. His supine patient – Herr Norbert Erstweiler – could not see the young doctor. In fact, Herr Erstweiler could see very little apart from the white ceiling and, if he dropped his gaze, a plain door in which a panel of opaque glass had been mounted. Herr Erstweiler's eyes were restless. Their agitated movements suggested unease, apprehension. It was as if – Liebermann thought – Herr Erstweiler was worried that someone might intrude.

'I am not expecting anybody,' said Liebermann.

'I beg your pardon?'

'We shan't be interrupted. No one will come in.'

'Good . . . I wouldn't want that.'

'You were saying that your sleep is disturbed.'

'That's right. I can't get to sleep any more. I get into bed, extinguish the lamp, and I am immediately overcome by terror. It's the darkness . . . something about the darkness.'

'Something *in* the darkness?'

'No, I wouldn't say that. I would say it was the *quality* of the darkness itself . . . its emptiness. I haven't been eating, either. My appetite has completely gone and my stools are loose.'

Liebermann noticed that Herr Erstweiler's hands were trembling slightly.

'Do you have difficulty breathing, Herr Erstweiler?'

'Yes – my chest feels tight . . . and my heart, I can feel it pounding all the time. There's something wrong with it. I know there is.'

Liebermann consulted the notes on his lap.

'No, Herr Erstweiler. There is nothing wrong with your heart.'

'I'm not sure the cardiologist I saw conducted a thorough examination.'

'Professor Schulde is an expert.'

Erstweiler glanced at the door.

'Well, that may be so . . . but even experts are wrong sometimes.'

Liebermann scrutinised his patient: early thirties, dark hair infiltrated with grey, a thin, drawn face, tired, bloodshot eyes, finger marks on his spectacles. Erstweiler's brow was scored by three lines: short, long and short. Their depth suggested indelibility. He had neglected his toilet and his chin was scabrous.

Erstweiler placed a palliative hand over his frantic heart.

The young doctor realised that discussing

symptoms was making Erstweiler more anxious. He decided to distract him by adopting a different line of inquiry.

'I understand that you have only recently arrived in Vienna,' said Liebermann.

'Yes. I settled here just before Christmas.'

'Where are you from?'

'Tulln – do you know it, Herr doctor?' Erstweiler's voice was hopeful.

'I know *of* it,' said Liebermann. 'Were you born there?'

'No, Eggenburg – but my family moved to Tulln when I was very young. Just a quiet provincial town,' said Erstweiler, 'but I'm a simple fellow and easily satisfied. Walking, fishing . . . a little rowing in the summer.' Erstweiler blinked and a faint smile softened his features. 'I was very happy in Tulln.'

'Why did you leave?'

'I was made redundant when my employer died. I was personal secretary to one of the councillors – Councillor Meternich – and worked in the Town Hall. It wasn't a very demanding situation – some correspondence, diary keeping, that sort of thing. Meternich died in the autumn of last year. His illness was quite protracted. He knew . . .' Erstweiler hesitated and stuttered. 'He knew he was g-going to d-die . . .' It was obvious to Liebermann that the poor man was struggling to overcome some private horror. Erstweiler took a deep breath and continued: '. . . And he wrote to

5

a friend – recommending me for a clerical post. He was a kindly old man – Meternich – and knew that I would have difficulty finding alternative employment in Tulln. Meternich's friend was Herr Winkler, a businessman who imports furniture and *objets d'art* from Japan. I now work at his warehouse in Simmering. The job doesn't pay very well, but I've been told I could be promoted shortly.'

Lieberman made some notes and asked: 'Do you live on your own?'

'Yes . . . no. What I mean is . . . I have taken a room – lodgings – in the house of a Czech gentleman and his wife.'

'In Simmering?'

'A short distance from Winkler's warehouse.'

'Do you have any family or friends in Vienna?'

'No.'

'What about back in Tulln? Did you leave anyone behind?'

'Both of my parents are deceased. I have an older brother . . . but we haven't spoken in years. He went to live in Salzburg. He's a railway official, of high rank. He wears a uniform like a general! We were never very close. He considers me . . .' Erstweiler grimaced, 'unambitious.'

Liebermann tapped his index finger against his temple, then wrote down the words *anxiety neurosis* and *anxiety hysteria*. But he was not satisfied with his putative diagnoses. Once again, he observed his patient glancing towards the door and added in parentheses: *dementia paranoides?* Liebermann decided to raise the subject of symptoms again.

'When did you first become unwell, Herr Erstweiler?'

'About a week ago. It came on quite suddenly.'

'Have you ever suffered from similar episodes in the past? Difficulty in breathing? Accelerated heart rate?'

'No, never. I've always been very healthy.'

'Then has anything happened to upset you?'

Erstweiler did not answer.

Liebermann persevered: 'Have you received any bad news? Witnessed an accident? Ended a relationship?'

'No . . . nothing like that.'

'But *something* has happened . . .'

Erstweiler closed his eyes. The mere thought of disclosure made him want to shut out the world.

'What do you think is the matter?' asked Liebermann softly. 'What do you suppose these symptoms mean?'

The patient opened his eyes again. They were glassy, unfocused, and the tone of his voice was nuanced correspondingly: 'They mean I am going to die.'

'But there really is nothing wrong with you, Herr Erstweiler. All the investigations and tests have demonstrated that you are in perfect health. Now.' Liebermann tapped his pen on the chair arm to capture the man's attention. 'There can be no doubt that you are currently troubled by anxiety

7

– hyperventilation, tachycardia, insomnia, and loss of appetite – but these symptoms are relatively benign.'

Erstweiler ignored Liebermann's plea.

'My fate is sealed,' he whispered. 'I am going to die. And there is nothing that you or any of your colleagues can do to save me. When death knocks on the door, you cannot deny him.'

Liebermann made another note.

'Herr Erstweiler?'

The patient seemed to rouse from his abstracted state. His eyes engaged with the material world again – the ceiling, the door.

'Yes?'

'Something happened to you.' Liebermann modulated his voice to counter the directness of his request. 'It is important that you tell me every-thing, if I am to help you.'

'I should never have agreed to this hospital admission. It was my general practitioner's idea – Vitzhum. He persuaded me . . . persuaded me that I was suffering from nerves and that I'd see things differently after a few weeks' rest. I was eager to believe him – of course – given the alter-native. At the time I thought he was right, I thought I might be going mad – but I'm not. Oh, if only I were! Dear God! If you declared me insane today – and could prove it – I would be greatly relieved.'

'What are you frightened of, Herr Erstweiler?'

'Dying. I don't want to die.'

Liebermann drew two lines under *thanatophobia*.

'Once again, Herr Erstweiler, I must ask you to consider the evidence.'

'Oh, believe me – I have.' Erstweiler was clearly not referring to the medical investigations.

'I cannot make a full assessment of your mental state,' said Liebermann. 'Unless you make me party to the facts. *All* of them. You say that a declaration of insanity would ease your suffering; however, I am in no position to provide you with such relief – albeit irregular – if you refuse to take me into your confidence.'

Erstweiler pulled at his bristly chin. A long silence ensued. Eventually he spoke.

'The first time it happened – I wasn't sure . . .' Erstweiler swallowed and his Adam's apple bounced up and down. 'I was walking on the Graben when a fiacre passed. I only caught a glimpse of the passenger – and thought it was my brother. We are of the same build and share many characteristics – particularly those typical of my father's side of the family. He was wearing a fedora hat. I should have realised.'

'You should have realised what?'

'We are very similar, physically, but we have always dressed quite differently. Unlike me, he has never – to my knowledge – worn a fedora hat. Besides, he rarely comes to Vienna. It *couldn't* have been him.'

'I am not altogether sure—'

'Please, Herr doctor,' Erstweiler interrupted. 'Let me continue. Now that I have started I wish to finish . . . That evening, I was quite restless. I couldn't sit down. I tried to read my book but found concentrating impossible. My table is close to the window and – for no particular reason – I pulled the curtain aside and looked out. My room is on the first floor and I found myself looking down at a gentleman standing beneath a gas lamp. He was wearing a fedora.'

Liebermann looked down at his notes again, smiled inwardly and underlined *dementia paranoides*.

'You were being followed?'

Erstweiler rocked his head from side to side. His expression was pained.

'There was something odd about him. I knew *that* immediately – but it wasn't until I had observed him standing there for a minute or more before I was really able to identify the cause of my disquiet.'

'Which was?'

'He did not cast a shadow. And it was at *that* moment – the precise moment when I realised he had no shadow – that he raised his head and looked up at my window. My heart was beating wildly and my bowels turned to water. His face . . .' Erstweiler's head rocked more violently. 'It was me, my doppelgänger – my double.'

'Could you have been mistaken? You were excited, night had fallen . . .'

'He was standing directly beneath the gas lamp!' For the first time a note of frustration had entered Erstweiler's voice.

'What did you do?

'What could I do? I poured myself a slivovitz and huddled on my bed until morning. I passed the night in a state of fearful agitation. You know what it means, Herr doctor, surely, when a man sees his doppelgänger? I am going to die – and nothing can save me.'

CHAPTER 2

Detective Inspector Oskar Rheinhardt stepped down from his carriage just outside the Court Theatre entrance of the Volksgarten. Two constables wearing long blue coats and spiked helmets stood either side of the gate. They recognised the inspector and clicked their heels as he passed. Hurrying along, Rheinhardt searched his jacket for a box of cigars and sighed when he found the pockets empty. He had left his Trabucos, he realised, on the desk in his study. Above the Hofburg, long flat clouds hung motionless in a temperate sky, the early-morning colours soft and muted.

Rheinhardt had not progressed very far when he heard the sound of someone running up the path behind him. He turned and saw his assistant.

'Sir!'

The youth's long legs carried him forward with a steady, confident momentum.

Ah, to be young again, thought the inspector (although, in truth, his own youthful athletic accomplishments had never been particularly noteworthy).

'Good morning, Haussmann.'

The young man slowed and came to a halt. He stooped, clasping his knees with his hands. When he had recovered his breath, they proceeded along the path until a grey stone edifice with triangular pediments and Doric columns came into view. More constables could be seen in its vicinity.

'Have you ever wondered,' said Rheinhardt, casually, 'why we have a Greek temple in the middle of our Volksgarten?'

'No, sir. I haven't.' There was a slight fall in Haussmann's voice. He knew from experience that such a question was usually followed by a didactic answer. His superior seemed to enjoy caricaturing the speech and manner of a schoolmaster.

'Well, my boy,' said Rheinhardt. 'It was built to house a famous statue – *Theseus and the Centaur* – by the great Italian sculptor Antonio Canova. That is why we call it the *Theseus* Temple. In fact, the building is a replica of an original that stands in Athens: The Temple of Hephaestus.'

'Hephaestus?'

'The god of fire and crafts, particularly those crafts which use fire – metalwork, for example.'

'Is the statue still inside, sir?' asked Haussmann, feigning interest.

'No, it was moved to the *Kunsthistorisches Museum* about ten years ago. It's on the main staircase – about halfway up. Have you never seen it?'

'I'm not a great lover of art, sir.'

'You've never been to the *Kunsthistorisches Museum*?'

'No, sir. I find old paintings . . .'

'Yes?'

'Depressing.'

Rheinhardt shook his head and dismissed Haussmann's remark with a wave of his hand.

'It's a fine statue,' Rheinhardt continued, undeterred by his assistant's philistinism. 'The mighty hero, Theseus, his club raised, ready to strike.' Rheinhardt suddenly looked anxious. 'I take it you know who Theseus is?'

'Yes, sir. I have a volume of the Greek legends at home. I won it in a poetry competition at school.'

Rheinhardt raised his eyebrows.

'I didn't know you wrote poetry.'

'I don't, sir. Not now. But at school I did.'

Their conversation was brought to a premature close when a constable, stout and with glowing cheeks, separated from his companions and came to greet them. He introduced himself as Constable Badem.

'Ah yes, Badem,' said Rheinhardt. 'It was you who discovered the body.'

'Yes, sir.' The constable's chest expanded and he stood erect, as if about to receive a medal. Rheinhardt, touched and amused by the young man's pride, reached out and gripped his shoulder.

'Well done! The security office is indebted.'

'Thank you, sir,' said Badem, his eyes glinting with emotion. Then, assuming a more detached attitude, the young man added: 'She's over there, inspector.' He raised his hand and pointed towards a row of bushes where his colleagues had assembled.

Rheinhardt left the footpath to investigate.

The woman was lying flat on the grass. Her hair pins had fallen out and dark, abundant tresses framed her face. The disposition of her limbs – legs apart, arms thrown wide – suggested abandonment. Her dress had ridden up over her knees, revealing a pair of striped stockings. Rheinhardt noticed that the soles of her ankle boots were almost transparent and closer examination revealed the presence of a small hole. Her coat was correspondingly threadbare, with frayed cuffs and the tattered remnants of a lining that had long since been removed. She was young, perhaps no more than eighteen, and the whiteness of her pale skin emphasised, by contrast, the artificiality of the carmine powder on her cheeks.

It was an interesting face, sensuous and attractive, but not conventionally beautiful. Her expression in deathly repose suggested disdainful indifference – perhaps even cruelty. Her lips were slightly uneven, twisted, and her nose was too generously proportioned. Yet there was something about these flaws that combined to create an arresting totality.

Rheinhardt kneeled down beside her and searched her pockets for identification, but all he could find was some small change, a handkerchief and two keys. The woman's hat was lying on the ground a short distance away, next to what looked to the inspector like an item of underwear.

'She hasn't been stabbed or shot,' said Rheinhardt, opening her coat. He could not see any bloodstains on her plain white dress.

'Strangled, sir?' Haussmann inquired.

Rheinhardt repositioned himself and looked at her neck.

'No, I don't think so. Smothered, perhaps . . .'

The inspector stood, brushed his trousers, and went over to retrieve the discarded item of clothing. As it unfurled, his suspicions were confirmed. He was holding a pair of red cotton drawers.

Haussmann frowned. 'Was she . . . used?'

'I imagine so.'

The drawers fluttered in the slight breeze. Rheinhardt, feeling suddenly disrespectful, folded the garment gently and placed it back on the grass.

'Inspector Rheinhardt?'

A man wearing a homburg hat and spectacles was looking over the bushes. It was the photographer. The man's companion – a teenage boy – appeared behind him, carrying a tripod.

'Ah, Herr Seipel,' said Rheinhardt. 'Good morning.'

'May we begin, inspector?'

'Yes, indeed. You may begin.'

Rheinhardt stood back from the corpse. Then he took out his notebook and recorded a few observations before addressing his assistant: 'Come, Haussmann.'

The two men set off in the direcon of the Theseus Temple.

On arriving at their destination, Rheinhardt and Haussmann ascended the wide steps.

The inspector rubbed his hands together and surveyed his surroundings. Directly in front of him he saw the white stucco walls of the Court Theatre and the steeples of the Votivkirche. Turning his head to the left he registered the Gothic spires of the Town Hall and the classical splendour of the Parliament building, on top of which two winged charioteers, struggling to control their rearing horses, faced each other across a tympanum densely populated with marble figures.

'Have you had breakfast?' asked Rheinhardt.

His assistant was surprised by the unexpected question, and replied cautiously: 'No, sir. I haven't.'

'Neither have I. Given that we find ourselves so close to Café Landtmann, it occurs to me that we might get something to eat there before we proceed to the Pathological Institute.'

'Yes, sir – as you wish.'

'Just a few kaisersemmel rolls.' The inspector paused, twisted his moustache and, finding the prospect of his imaginary repast inadequate, added: 'And a pastry, perhaps. I had a rather good plum flan in Café Landtmann only last week.'

They walked around the covered arcade that followed the featureless exterior of the Temple. Neither of them looked up to admire the new and delightful prospects revealed by their circum-navigation: the black and green domes, the baroque lanterns, the blooming flowers and ornamental hedge gardens. Instead, they kept their gazes fixed on the stone pavement, which had been worn by countless predecessors to a silvery sheen.

Haussmann suddenly stepped ahead and squatted down.

'What is it?' asked Rheinhardt.

'A button.'

He handed it up to his superior.

It was large, round, and made from wood.

'Any footprints?'

Supporting his body with his hands, Haussmann leaned forward and inspected the paving more closely. The position he had assumed – conveying a general impression of sharp corners and angularity – gave him a distinctly feral appearance. He looked like a rangy dog, sniffing the ground. His reply, when it finally came, was disappointing.

'Nothing.'

Rheinhardt held the button up and said: 'It's from her coat.'

CHAPTER 3

Where to begin, then? With a birth or with a death? And there it is, you see – the two, always together. When does a life begin? At conception? That is a beginning, but it is not necessarily the only one. Nor is there any reason why we should privilege conception. The colour of my eyes, for example, which I inherited from my mother, preceded my nativity. In a sense, the traits that eventually combine to become an individual are already in the world before he or she arrives. Conception is merely the point at which they converge. Therefore, when we are conceived we are as obligated to the dead as we are to the living. I existed – albeit in a rather dispersed form – long before a provincial priest splashed my forehead with holy water and gave me a name. There is no *fons et origo*. I have no beginning.

You want a history. You want chronology. But nothing is ever that straightforward. You see, even starting my story is fraught with philosophical problems. One thing, however, stands out. One thing I can assert with confidence. I killed my mother. Others see it differently, of course, but I can only see it that way. She died minutes after I was 'born'. Imagine – if you will – the scene: the doctor descending the stairs, my father, rising from his chair, eager, but suddenly confused by the medical man's expression. *Is the child all right?* The doctor nods: *Yes, a boy. A fine, healthy boy.* My father tilts his head. He knows that something is wrong. *Your poor wife* – the doctor mumbles – *I'm afraid there was nothing I could do to save her.* Swiftly, the doctor recovers his authority. Some technical talk follows. An explanation – but not one meant to elucidate. That is how doctors are – *you* should know that. He shakes my father's hand and leaves. My father, shocked, numb, hollow, ascends the stairs and enters the bedroom where the women are still removing the bloody sheets. His wife is dead. One of the women covers the corpse's face and makes the sign of the cross. She looks at my father and smiles, a merciful, sad, sweet smile, the smile that graces representations of the Madonna, and gestures towards the cradle. *Your son*, she says. My father steps forward and peers at the tiny creature wrapped in swaddling.

You will allow me to make an observation: I have since come to understand that my father's response to his misfortune was by no means typical. When women die during childbirth, it is frequently the case that loving husbands find consolation in their offspring because something of the beloved is preserved in their person;

however, my father seems to have been deficient in this respect. He did not see my mother in me. My presence in the world did not make him feel any closer to her. Quite the contrary. I would say that I merely reminded him of her absence, which made his loss even more painful.

A cheerless house, then. Blighted. Cold. Gloomy. Long silences – the clock ticking. That is the atmosphere in which I grew up.

There was a photograph of my mother on the mantelpiece. I still see it if I close my eyes – vivid – shining in the darkness: the repeated curlicue motif that flowed around the edges of the silver frame, the posy of little alpine flowers, the candle that was sometimes lit (but was mostly unlit). My father was in the habit of referring to my mother as an angel, and so it was that I came to think of her as possessing wings.

When I was alone in the house I would creep into the sitting room, take the photograph from the mantelpiece and study her face. My mother was a very beautiful woman: golden hair, big eyes, and delicate features. There was something in the background of the photograph which I mistook to be white feathers, folded neatly behind her back. Communing with my mother's image was a private activity. It had to be, because my father disapproved. He discovered me once and snatched the frame out of my hands. He was furious and said that I should be careful with such a precious object. If I dropped it the glass would break. It was irreplaceable and I should show more respect. I remember that he had a strange look in his eyes. I was frightened and thought that he was going to punish me. Recalling the incident now, I would say that my father's strange look was a jealous one – possessive.

The women of the village took pity on me. They brought me soup and shared their special dishes on feast days. I was always being invited to play with their children. And while I played with Hans or Gudrun or Dierk or Gerda, the women would watch and laugh. But I would sometimes catch sight of them as they exchanged glances and I would see tears of sympathy. Just before my departure, they would stuff my pockets with gingerbread, kiss me, and hold me close. All of these women had the same distinctive smell – a salty but sweet fragrance – a smell that combined perspiration with confectionery. I loved being enfolded in their plump red arms. But it was never enough. They could never replace my mother – they did not possess wings.

I enjoyed school. The other children hated it, but for me it was a welcome release from home and my father's black moods. I was fond of our little classroom: the whitewashed walls, the blackboard, the pot-bellied stove. My favourite subject was history, largely due to the lively instruction provided by our teacher, Herr Griesser: avuncular, bald but for two comic tufts that sprouted out from above his ears, spectacles, and prone to illustrate points with wild gesticulations. With the tip of his finger, he could trace an exotic horizon – pyramids, ziggurats – and transport us to Giza or Elam. Greek legends were brought to life with vivid descriptions of their heroism. Theseus was as real to me as the baker.

In addition to being an excellent teacher, Herr Griesser was also a keen amateur archaeologist. He once found a prehistoric axe-head in the Wachau and gave it to the Natural History Museum. They put it on display in a cabinet and it can still be seen today in the room dedicated to Bronze Age artefacts.

It was Herr Griesser who first told me about mummies. I was absolutely fascinated. And when he told me that there were mummies in Vienna – *real* mummies – I was eager to see them. I pleaded with my father, begged him to take me but, predictably, he refused.

My interest in mummies was curiously practical for a boy. I became preoccupied with the mechanics of preservation, how it was accomplished. The Egyptian method of embalming is actually described by Herodotus. It is a crude but effective process. After the entrails and brain are removed, the body is scoured with palm wine and purified with spices. It is then soaked in a saline solution for seventy days, bathed, and wrapped in strips of linen. Finally, the body is placed in a wooden case.

The Egyptians also took great care with respect

to the appearance of corpses, particularly those of women. The bust was preserved with stuffing and nipples were refashioned using copper buttons; wigs were worn; the body was painted in yellow ochre and the nails were tinted with henna.

Ingenious.

But I digress.

Such facts are of little interest to you. *You* want to know more about me.

CHAPTER 4

Professor Mathias stood at the foot of the autopsy table looking down at the body. He was an elderly gentleman with a tired, kindly face. His grey hair was uncombed and his general appearance was rather dishevelled. He was tying his apron strings behind his back while humming notes that never quite amounted to a melody. His dirge became even more tuneless as it sank to the bottom of his vocal range, where the professor was only capable of producing a sustained, rhythmic growling. In due course, he relinquished music in favour of speech: 'So, you think she was ravished?'

'Yes,' Rheinhardt replied. 'Her underwear had been removed. We found the garment discarded, not far from her body. Haussmann?'

His assistant produced the dead woman's red cotton drawers from a bag. Mathias took them and held them up to the electric light.

'No rips or tears. If they had been forcefully removed I would have expected to see some indications of violence. Perhaps she consented?'

'Or perhaps she was forced to undress at knifepoint.'

Mathias buried his face in the red cotton, closed his eyes, and inhaled deeply.

'Professor,' said Rheinhardt. 'What are you doing, exactly?'

The old man sighed and answered wearily: 'I am employing my nose – a somewhat under-estimated organ – to detect . . .' He paused before adding, 'Masculine *traces.*' The professor raised the drawers again and waved them under his flaring nostrils like a wine expert sampling the bouquet of a fragrant Bordeaux.

'Well?' Rheinhardt asked.

'Nothing,' replied the professor. 'A hint of ammonia, perhaps, but nothing else.'

He dropped the undergarment on a trolley and turned his attention to the corpse.

'I was told she was found in the Volksgarten?'

'By the Theseus Temple – behind a row of bushes.'

'No papers?'

'None.'

Mathias brushed his knuckles against the woman's cheek.

'*Death, you horror of nature, Ever-moving runs your clock: The scythe, when swung, glistens, And grass and blade and flower fall.* Well, Rheinhardt? Do you recognise it?'

'I'm afraid not.'

'*To Death,*' said Haussmann, doubtfully. 'By Christian Schubart.'

Rheinhardt looked at Haussmann and then to Professor Mathias for confirmation.

'Yes,' said Professor Mathias. 'Your assistant is correct.'

'Well done, Haussmann,' said Rheinhardt.

The young man smiled.

Professor Mathias continued in a declamatory fashion: '*Mow not on without distinction, here this little flower just abloom, There that rose, just half red. Oh, be merciful, oh, death!*' He shook his head. 'So young . . . and there is something rather aristocratic about her expression, don't you think?'

Rheinhardt remained silent. He did not really share Mathias's opinion.

The professor rearranged a lock of the dead woman's hair and addressed her directly: 'You will excuse me, madam.' Shuffling back to the foot of the autopsy table, Mathias removed her boots and stockings. The woman had painted her toenails purple and Mathias drew this to Rheinhardt's attention. Then he raised her dress, folding the cloth back onto her abdomen and thus revealing a delta of chestnut curls. He extended his right hand, parted the labia majora – employing his fingers like the blades of a speculum – and peered into her vagina. He then began to feel the dress material that lay directly beneath the woman's perineum. He dragged more material out from beneath her buttocks, and hunched over the table to examine it more closely. Subsequently, he picked up a pair of scissors from his trolley and cut out a small square of material which he rubbed between his thumb and forefinger before waving it under his nose.

27

Rheinhardt found the spectacle of the gnomish old pathologist engaged in such intimate study quite obscene.

'Well,' said Mathias. 'She certainly *received* a man. But I don't see any signs of ravishment. The dress isn't torn – no contusions, no signs of chafing or bleeding. Would you and your assistant be so kind as to remove her coat, inspector?'

Rheinhardt and Haussmann pulled the coat off the woman's shoulders and tugged it downwards. Once her arms were free it was relatively easy to complete the task. Mathias returned with an extra-large pair of scissors and cut a straight line up the front of her dress, from hem to collar. Using a sharp hunting knife, he then slashed through the laces of the woman's corset. The heavy canvas fell away, releasing her breasts.

'Gentlemen – your assistance again, please. Would you raise her slightly?' Mathias removed the clothing and put it on the trolley along with the red cotton drawers.

The three men stared at the naked body in silence. They did not look at each other, fearing that they might betray their thoughts. The woman was perfectly proportioned: delicate ankles, shapely calves, and hips that converged on a slim waist. Beneath the harsh electric light, the vivid contours of her body were strangely alluring. Rheinhardt closed his eyes and felt his cheeks become radiant with shame. The twist of her lip, he fancied, was no longer cruel but judgemental.

'May I smoke, professor?' Rheinhardt asked.

'Yes, inspector, of course.'

Rheinhardt took the box of cigars he had purchased on the way to the morgue from his pocket.

'Trabuco, Haussmann?'

'No, thank you, sir.'

His assistant's stare was fixed on the woman's exposed sex.

Rheinhardt lit his cigar. The familiar aroma was comforting, a timely reminder that he also had another, more agreeable life, one that awaited his return. He was already looking forward to his armchair and the sound of his eldest daughter Therese picking out the notes of a Mozart piano sonata.

Professor Mathias selected a magnifying glass and circled the table, inspecting the woman's skin.

'There are no rashes around the neck or abdomen, no signs of cynosis and no punctures.' He raised his head. 'Young man, could you help me to turn her over?'

The woman was heavier than Haussmann had expected and he grunted as he heaved her onto her side. He tried to complete the manoeuvre by rolling her forward slowly, but he lost control and her breasts made an unpleasant smack as they fell heavily onto the polished granite.

'Now,' said Professor Mathias, 'let's straighten her up.'

Haussmann released a trapped arm while

Professor Mathias parted the woman's legs. The pathologist continued to examine the woman's skin, occasionally pausing to press and probe with his fingers. When he had finished he drew back.

'Once again, nothing abnormal.'

'Then how did she die?' Rheinhardt asked.

'I don't know. I'll have to open her up. We can already exclude strangulation, stabbing, shooting, injection, and the ingestion of some – but not all – poisons.'

'What about suffocation?'

'She would have struggled.'

'Perhaps she did.'

'I don't think so.'

'Why?'

'Look how well manicured her fingernails are, not one of them broken. A woman thrashing around – doing her utmost to escape suffocation – wouldn't have nails in such excellent condition, inspector.'

'Do you think she died naturally?'

'It is certainly a possibility and, at this early stage, quite a strong one. You look doubtful, inspector.'

Rheinhardt flicked the ash from his cigar into an empty bucket and wrinkled his nose.

'Odd way to die, don't you think? In such very peculiar circumstances.'

'She looks healthy but you never can tell and she wouldn't be the first to die in such an undignified position. As for her lover – or client, more like – perhaps a married man with children, responsibilities and reputation – such a man would be reluctant to report the matter to the police. As soon as he realised his predicament, he would have made a swift – er – *withdrawal*.' Mathias looked to Haussmann. 'Young man, we must turn the body again.'

Haussmann reached over the table, choosing to haul the dead woman over from the opposite side. He had barely completed the movement when he suddenly pulled back, startled, and uttered a cry of disgust. The body remained face down.

'Come now,' said the professor. 'Don't be squeamish.'

Haussmann stared at the corpse, his eyes wide with alarm.

'I felt something.'

'What do you mean?' said the professor, slightly irritated. '*Felt* something?'

'I felt something hard, sticking out of the back of her head. Underneath her hair.'

Mathias put the magnifying glass down on the table and pulled the woman's tangled tresses aside. His actions revealed a metallic object that gleamed brightly under the fierce electric light. Rheinhardt dropped his cigar in the bucket and moved closer to the table.

It was a silver acorn, nestled neatly into the arched indentation where the skull and the back of the neck joined. Professor Mathias reached out and plucked at the object.

'It's stuck.'

He repositioned the woman's head and tried again. Eventually the silver acorn came away. It was attached to a needle – bent near the top – about twice the length of man's finger. Mathias held it up. The metal was coated with a film of pinkish residue.

'What is it?' asked Rheinhardt.

'I believe it is a hatpin,' Mathias replied. 'How resourceful!'

'Resourceful?' Rheinhardt responded. 'How is stabbing someone in the neck with a hat pin resourceful?'

'No, inspector – you misunderstand. This woman wasn't stabbed in the neck. It was her brain that was stabbed.'

'I still don't see what's clever about *that*.'

'Think, Rheinhardt, think!'

Mathias rapped his own head with his knuckles.

Rheinhardt frowned: 'I would appreciate a straightforward answer, Herr professor.'

'The brain is encased in the skull, inspector. It is the most well protected organ in the body.'

'Making ingress difficult?'

'Almost impossible.'

'However?'

'In the floor of the skull is an aperture – in the occipital bone to be precise – called the foramen magnum. It's about this big.' Mathias made a circle with his thumb and forefinger 'When the head is tilted forward, the foramen magnum is aligned with a relatively small opening above the uppermost vertebra. By taking advantage of this chink in the human anatomical armour, a sharp object, such as a hatpin, can be inserted directly into the medulla oblongata – a brain structure which very likely sustains the most basic bodily functions: breathing and heart rate. It is an extremely efficient and tidy way of killing someone. The pin itself destroys the critical brain centres and the head of the pin serves as a plug to stop leakage of blood and cerebrospinal fluid!'

Mathias handed the hatpin to Rheinhardt. The workmanship was not accomplished. It was made from cheap silver.

'Well, Haussmann,' said Rheinhardt. 'Where do you think a person might purchase one of these?'

'I don't know, sir.'

'Then perhaps you would be so good as to find out?'

He handed the hatpin to his assistant.

'Now, sir?'

'Yes, Haussmann. Now.'

CHAPTER 5

The sign outside the salon was simple and discreet.

A glazed tile, set into the wall; straight black capitals: HOUSE VOGL.

Beneath, in a small, cursive script, was the word *couturière*.

Kristina Vogl and her secretary, Wanda Wolnik, stood in the circular vestibule, looking expectantly out of the window. A servant had been posted by the door. The proprietor of the fashion house was an attractive woman, with dark hair and striking blue eyes. She was tall and wore a plain black dress; however, the pendant that hung from her neck was colourful – a silver rose surrounded by semi-precious stones of different sizes. Wanda was shorter than her mistress and was also dressed in black. She was pretty, with blonde hair and flawless skin, but there was something about the roundness of her features and her awkward posture that revealed a lack of sophistication. She had not yet acquired the air of arrogant detachment cultivated by most of her peers in the world of haute couture.

'Oh, *do* stand up straight, Wanda,' said Kristina.

'Yes, madame,' said the secretary. She inhaled and raised her bosom.

'Frau Schmollinger is a very important person. We must make a good impression.'

Kristina glanced anxiously at the wall clock. *Two minutes late . . .*

What if Frau Schmollinger didn't come? A note must be sent, obviously. A few lines expressing regret and concern: I am so sorry you were unable to keep your appointment and trust you are in good health. *No, too presumptuous.* It would be better, perhaps, to send a plain card with a new appointment time and eschew over-familiarity.

Kristina's misgivings were needless. The sound of clattering hoofs preceded the arrival of an impressive coach pulled by four horses.

'Is it her, madame?' asked Wanda.

'Of course it is. Now, for heaven's sake, remember not to slouch.'

Through the net curtains they watched the driver jump down from his box and help Frau Schmollinger out of the carriage. She was in her mid-fifties, wore a wide-brimmed hat festooned with exotic plumages, and a long sable coat.

Kristina called out to the servant: 'Karoline. Open the door. Slowly.' Then she glanced at her secretary, removed an errant gold hair from the girl's sleeve, and stood erect, assuming an expression of tranquil indifference.

Frau Schmollinger glided through the open door.

Kristina inclined her head and Wanda – over-awed by this vision of fur and feathers – produced something closer to genuflexion than to a curtsy.

'Frau Schmollinger,' said Kristina, adopting a languorous, refined accent. 'Welcome. We are honoured. This way, please.'

No introductions were necessary. It was assumed that Frau Vogl herself would receive such a distinguished client.

Kristina ushered Frau Schmollinger into the reception room, where Wanda took her hat and coat.

'Would you like some tea?' Kristina asked.

'No, thank you,' said Frau Schmollinger, looking around the room. Her expression was one of curiosity and surprise. The walls were lacquered white and decorated with mirrors, and from the ceiling lamps composed of hammered copper with glass spheres hung down on delicately wrought chains. Frau Schmollinger's attention was captured by a smart vitrine with metal fittings. Through the tilted glass she saw jewellery displayed on a bed of blue velvet: tourmaline brooches, agate earrings and a coral bracelet made in the likeness of linked salamanders.

'Please,' said Kristina. 'Do take a seat.'

Frau Schmollinger lowered herself onto a wooden chair, the high back of which was made up of rectangular 'hoops', the smaller being nested within the larger. The oak had been stained black and flecks of chalk had been rubbed into the grain.

On the table – just a cube with a square panel on top – were catalogues and magazines: *La Couturière Parisienne, La Mode Illustrée* and the journal of the Secessionist art movement, *Ver Sacrum*. Frau Schmollinger turned her grey watery eyes to Kristina. A smile made her powdered, papery skin wrinkle.

'You come highly recommended, Frau Vogl. I am a close friend of Countess Oberndorf.'

'The countess is one of our most valued clients.'

'You made an exquisite summer dress for her last year.'

'Indeed. A white and yellow smock with lace sleeves.'

'Yes, that's the one! She wore it when my husband and I were guests at Schloss Oberndorf. Sensational.'

'You are too kind.'

Frau Schmollinger raised her hand and performed an odd benediction in the air: 'I was wondering – my husband and I will be returning to Schloss Oberndorf this summer . . .'

'You would like something similar?'

'Yes.' She drew the syllable out. 'Something interesting. Something *new*.'

Frau Schmollinger's eyes narrowed. She didn't want something *similar*. She wanted something *better*.

'I'm sure we will be able to find something suitable for you,' said Kristina, 'in this year's summer collection.'

Frau Schmollinger smiled.

'Excellent.'

'Wanda,' said Kristina. 'Would you fetch my red book, please?'

The secretary crossed to a corner cupboard. She opened the doors, inlaid with sparkling tears of glass, and took out a big leather volume which she carried to her mistress. Kristina sat down beside Frau Schmollinger. The volume contained sketches and coloured lithographs gummed onto thick paper.

Most of the designs were loose-fitting and resembled kaftans. There were no furbelows and trimmings, but Kristina explained that the materials she used were of the highest quality – *peau de soie*, satins and organza. Moreover, all the patterns – some geometric, others floral – had been commissioned from artists of the Secession.

'The raised waist,' Kristina said, pointing to a typical example, 'renders the corset redundant, and affords the wearer unprecedented freedom of movement. My clients frequently describe House Vogl couture as' – she raised an attractive plucked eyebrow – 'liberating.'

There was something slightly subversive about Frau Vogl's vocabulary. Her choice of words sounded strangely political: freedom and liberation. At one point she even spoke of 'equality'. The older woman listened with keen interest. And as she did so, she became acutely aware of the tightness of the whalebone cage in which her torso was imprisoned. She remembered the previous summer, her breath labouring as she walked with the countess in the gardens of Schloss Oberndorf, and the copious bright fabric of the countess's dress billowing in the gentle breeze.

When they had finished looking at the summer catalogue, Frau Vogl invited Frau Schmollinger to view some of the designs that had already been made up. She led her into a wide corridor lined on both sides with glass cabinets. In each was a dressed mannequin. Couturière and client were followed at a respectful distance by Wanda. It was obvious from the tone of the conversation that Frau Schmollinger intended to order several garments.

About halfway along the corridor, Frau Schmollinger halted in order to study a gown that seemed to have been woven from spun gold. It might have been taken from the wardrobe of an angel.

'What is this?' she asked, her voice awed.

'Remarkable, isn't it?' Kristina replied.

'Made from gold?'

'A metallic yarn called lamé. It's by the Callot sisters . . . in Paris.'

'Would it be possible to have a summer dress made from . . .'

'Lamé? Yes, of course. It also comes in silver.'

Frau Schmollinger imagined herself stepping out onto the terrace of Schloss Oberndorf, the late sun catching the metallic weave, the men falling silent.

At the end of the corridor, double doors led into the changing room. It was a large space and included a chair – again, black, angular and simple – and a full-length adjustable mirror. The floor had been covered in grey felt so that wealthy customers could walk in comfort with their shoes off.

Above, the sound of industry could be heard: the rattle of sewing machines and the soft music of female voices. House Vogl employed a team of seamstresses and two cutters.

'Well,' said Kristina to Frau Schmollinger. 'Shall we proceed?'

'Yes,' said Frau Schmollinger.

'Wanda,' said Kristina. 'If you would get me a tape measure and my notebook?'

The secretary smiled and left the changing room. She was in a state of excitement. Frau Vogl always treated her to lunch at the Imperial when they secured a lucrative order from a new patron. Wanda was already contemplating what she would order: roast pork and dumplings followed by Topfenstrudel. Or should she have the Viennese Walnut-Apple Torte? She really couldn't decide.

CHAPTER 6

Rheinhardt looked across his desk at Arno Zeiler. Everything about him suggested deflation: lank hair, crumpled clothes and sunken cheeks. His eyes were dark and empty.

'Cigarette?' asked Rheinhardt.

The man turned and nodded.

Rheinhardt lit the cigarette and passed it to Zeiler, who took it awkwardly between his thumb and second finger. He drew on it once, coughed, and continued to stare blankly into space.

Zeiler had been brought to the Schottenring station directly from the Pathological Institute, where he had been taken to identify the body of his daughter, Adele.

'Herr Zeiler – forgive me,' said Rheinhardt softly. 'But may I ask: why didn't you report Adele missing last night?'

Zeiler shook his head.

'She often stays out.'

'All night?'

'Yes,' Zeiler rubbed one of his eyes with the heel of his palm. 'It wasn't until this afternoon that we started to worry. My wife said I should go to the police. Adele is usually back by midday.'

'Where did she go?' Rheinhardt pursed his lips before adding, 'All night.'

'I don't know.'

The inspector tapped his pen on the desk top.

'Forgive me, but am I to believe, Herr Zeiler, that your daughter was in the habit of staying out all night, and you never troubled to ask her where she'd been?'

'Do you have a daughter, inspector?'

'I have two.'

'Do you? Well, I have three.' Zeiler suddenly corrected himself. 'No, I have only two now. Adele is dead. The two I have left – Trude and Inna. Trude is sixteen and has bronchial problems. She's never been very strong – terrible phlegm that sits on her chest. Inna is thirteen and can't walk properly. It's something to do with her joints. Nothing can be done for her. I used to work in a timber yard in Favoriten, but I lost my job when the proprietor went bankrupt and I haven't been able to get another since. My wife gets occasional work at the laundry, but not very often. Life hasn't been easy, inspector. Adele was a sweet girl. She did what she could . . .' Zeiler bit his lower lip. 'She did what she could for all of us. We didn't like it but what could we do? We either accepted Adele's help, or we starved. What could we do?'

'Are you saying that she became a . . .'

42

Rheinhardt's sensitivity did not permit him to complete the sentence.

'A prostitute? No. She wasn't a prostitute. But she knew how to get a man's attention and gentlemen gave her gifts – never money, you understand – just gifts, and sometimes she didn't come home. Adele would take the gifts to the pawnshop. We needed the money. Inspector, I hope that you are never put in my position. No father should have to go through what I've gone through. That's why I didn't ask, you understand? I didn't need to ask – and in truth I didn't want to know.' Zeiler sucked on the cigarette and, looking towards the window, continued: 'She was stabbed. They said she'd been stabbed?'

'Yes.' Rheinhardt replied. He was reluctant to disclose the details of Adele's murder and moved the conversation on: 'When was the last time you saw Adele?'

'Yesterday afternoon.'

'Where did she say she was going?'

'To see Rainmayr.'

'Who?'

'Herr Rainmayr – he's an artist. She modelled for him.' As Rheinhardt was writing the name down, Zeiler added: 'But it wouldn't have been him, inspector. Not Herr Rainmayr.'

'Why do you say that?'

'She's been going to see him for years. Besides, he's a decent man. He once paid for a specialist to see Trude when she was very ill.'

Rheinhardt grimaced.

'I know this is difficult, Herr Zeiler, but . . .'

'You want to know if he had relations with her, if that was part of their arrangement?' Zeiler flicked some ash onto the floor. 'I don't know, inspector. Like I said, I didn't ask.'

'Did you suspect . . .' Rheinhardt's sentence trailed off. Zeiler was not going to share his thoughts on the matter. 'Do you know where Herr Rainmayr lives?'

'Yes. He has a studio somewhere in Lange Gasse.'

CHAPTER 7

Haussmann marched past caryatids holding up lintels and stucco façades crowded with putti. The roof tops seemed to be teeming with activity: statues of fabulous creatures, goddesses and legendary heroes disporting themselves against a darkening sky. He had spent all day searching the city for shops that sold the silver-acorn hatpin. Not one of the milliners or jewellers in the first district had recognised the design. Standing on a corner, Haussmann consulted his crumpled list of addresses.

How could he be expected to find all the distributors of hatpins in Vienna? Milliners, jewellers, stallholders, street vendors, junk shops – there were simply too many possibilities. Further, there was no evidence to suggest that the murderer had purchased the acorn hatpin recently. It might have been in his possession for years, a family heirloom belonging to his great-grandmother!

Haussmann crossed the Hoher Markt – an open square dominated by a massive fountain which commemorated the marriage of Mary and Joseph. The holy couple were protected by angels and a bronze baldachin resting on four lofty Corinthian columns. The entire edifice was finished with a radiant gilded sun, the upper spokes of which glinted with rays emanating from the sinking original.

In due course, Haussmann arrived at his destination: *Tassilo Jaufenthaler – jeweller*.

It was a modest establishment. A small shop space, some dusty display cabinets filled with unimpressive paste jewellery, moth-eaten drapes, and a counter behind which sat a diminutive balding man with unremarkable features and steel-rimmed spectacles. He stood as Haussmann entered.

'Good afternoon, sir.'

'Herr Jaufenthaler?'

'Yes.'

'Good afternoon.' Weary of trading pleasantries, Haussmann asked bluntly: 'Do you sell hatpins like this one?'

He placed the silver-acorn hatpin on the counter.

Herr Jaufenthaler picked it up and replied: 'Unfortunately, I haven't got any more of these, sir. Sold out. But I have something very similar about the same price. If you'd care to look in the cabinet by the door?'

Haussmann – disbelieving – repeated his question.

'You're quite sure?' Haussmann pointed across

46

the counter. 'The hatpins you sold were just like *that*?'

'Identical.' The jeweller looked at Haussmann suspiciously.

Haussmann showed his identification.

'Security office?' said Herr Jaufenthaler. 'I don't understand. I can assure you, the hatpins that I sold weren't stolen. I got them from Krawczyk, my Polish supplier. He's a devout Catholic – he wouldn't have accepted stolen goods.'

Haussmann raised his hand.

'I'm not accusing you of anything, Herr Jaufenthaler. I'd just like to ask you a few questions. Now, can you remember which customers purchased your acorn hatpins?'

Herr Jaufenthaler thought for a few moments before replying.

'I took five off Krawczyk. I didn't take *that* many because they're rather unusual. The pin is quite thick – see? They're really for very large hats, and I wasn't sure that there would be much demand. But they did sell – and faster than I'd expected. A few young ladies – oh yes, and Frau Felbiger – she's a regular – and a gentleman.'

'A gentleman?'

'Yes. A gentleman.'

'What was he like?'

'Tall. Dark hair. Well-mannered.'

'Would you recognise him if you saw him again?'

'Yes, I think so.'

'When did he buy the hatpin?'

'About three weeks ago. I can check my books if you want?'

'Have you seen him since?'

'No.'

'Did Krawczyk supply these pins to any other shops?'

'Well, you'd have to ask him.'

'Herr Jaufenthaler,' said Haussmann. 'I am afraid I must ask you to come with me to the Schottenring station in order to make a statement.'

'Statement!' Herr Jaufenthaler cried. 'You're acting as if someone's been murdered!'

'They have,' said Haussmann.

'What?' Jaufenthaler laughed. 'With a hatpin?'

'Yes,' replied Haussmann. 'The one you are holding.'

The smile vanished from Herr Jaufenthaler's face as he dropped the hatpin onto the counter, his face crumpling in disgust.

CHAPTER 8

'So,' said Liebermann. 'Has anyone else seen your doppelgänger?'

'You think I imagined it all, don't you?' said Erstweiler. 'You think I am insane!'

Liebermann was still considering how he might respond when Herr Erstweiler added: 'Forgive my impertinence, Herr doctor, but you are evidently trying to formulate a diplomatic answer. Please don't tax your brain on my account – it really isn't necessary. I am fully aware of how ridiculous everything I have said sounds. Indeed, I would think you a peculiar representative of your profession if you didn't think my doppelgänger anything but a figment of my imagination. As I've already said, I would be relieved to discover that I am mad. Oh, how comforting, to be assured that this creature, this devil in my own shape was nothing but a hallucination, and that this terrible sense of foreboding was a piece of harmless self-deception.'

'Then why respond to my question with a rebuke?'

'Because I cannot give you the answer you expect, the answer that would confirm your

49

medical prejudices and give me hope. Has anyone else seen my doppelgänger? The answer regretfully is yes. Herr Polster.'

'Who?'

'Herr Polster. He's the publican of a beer cellar in Simmering. A place called The Chimney Sweep.' Erstweiler paused, glanced at the door, took a deep breath and continued: 'On my way back home from work, I occasionally stop off at The Chimney Sweep for some light refreshment; however, I never go there on Wednesday nights – the reason being that it is on this day that we take deliveries at the warehouse and I must must stay late to check the stock, prepare an inventory, and write letters if everything is not in order. About two weeks ago, I was in The Chimney Sweep and Herr Polster came to my table and said something like: *Back again, so soon?* I thought nothing of it. But during the course of our conversation he kept on referring to things that I had no recollection of ever having said. I took this to be some kind of joke and did not react. However, Herr Polster persisted and eventually I became quite annoyed. I demanded: *When, when did I say that?* And he replied, *Last night, of course!* Which was, as I am sure you have already guessed, a Wednesday. I lost my temper and to my surprise Herr Polster responded with no small amount of embarrassment and confusion. He then made light of my reaction, reminded me that I had drunk rather more than usual and promised he would

50

be discreet. It became clear to me then that Herr Polster wasn't joking at all. As far as he was concerned, I really *had* been to The Chimney Sweep the night before. Which I realised could mean but one thing.'

'Your doppelgänger?'

'Indeed.'

'From your conversation with Herr Polster, were you able to ascertain what the double said?'

'I was left with the impression of a person considerably more ill-mannered than myself – a lewd individual.'

Erstweiler's face reddened.

'In what way?'

'Is it really necessary that I tell you everything, Herr doctor?' Liebermann allowed the silence to build. 'Oh, very well,' Erstweiler muttered. 'From Herr Polster's comments, I realised that my doppelgänger had made remarks about the desirability of Frau Milena, the wife of my landlord, Kolinsky.'

Liebermann leaned forward.

'What is she like? Frau Milena?'

'She is a very attr—' Erstweiler stopped himself from saying 'attractive' and continued, '*sweet-natured* person. Kolinsky really doesn't appreciate her. Indeed, I have to say the man is something of a brute. He comes home drunk and shouts at her . . . and sometimes I hear noises – as if she's being pushed around.'

'What do you do when that happens?'

'I go downstairs to ask if everything is all right. And Frau Milena says, *Yes, Herr Erstweiler, everything is well, I am sorry about the noise.* Or *Bozidar isn't feeling well,* or *I tripped and fell,* or some such nonsense. And old Kolinsky just sits there, grunting and waving his hand in the air. At least it settles down after I make such an appearance, which must be appreciated by Frau Milena. But I've often asked myself *What's the point of intervening?* – it only starts up again a few days later. They say it's unwise to get involved in domestic arguments and I can see why. Besides, marriage is supposed to be holy. We are advised not to come between a man and woman who have been joined together by God.'

Liebermann made a note: *Resists admitting Frau Milena attractive? Why?*

'Do you believe that?' asked Liebermann. 'That marriage reflects the will of God?'

'I don't know. It's what we're told. Or perhaps I'm just making excuses. Perhaps I should do more for Frau Milena? Perhaps I should have words with old Kolinsky.'

'Threaten him?'

Erstweiler sat up, his gaze suddenly fixed on the door. His hands were trembling.

'There's someone standing outside!'

Liebermann rose swiftly and approached the door.

'For God's sake, man,' cried Erstweiler. 'Don't let him in!'

The young doctor depressed the handle and pulled the door open, revealing a vacant corridor.

'You see? Nothing to be frightened of.'

Slumping back onto the rest bed, Erstweiler sighed: 'I could have sworn . . .'

'What?'

'I thought I saw a shadow, through the glass.'

Liebermann sat down again and picked up his notes. He immediately wrote: *Thought of threatening Herr Kolinsky triggers hallucination.* He wondered: *Why would that happen?* Struggling to understand the underlying psychodynamics, Liebermann turned over in his mind the facts of the case. Here was a man who desired his landlord's wife but disowned such feelings. Perhaps the notion of coming between man and wife had become associated with divine retribution. Did the hallucination represent a punishment for failing to respect God's sacrament of marriage? Liebermann glanced down at Erstweiler. The poor fellow certainly believed in God, but he was not devout or fanatical.

'Herr Erstweiler?'

'Yes.'

'Would you object to me speaking to Herr Polster?'

Erstweiler was still looking uneasily at the panel of glass.

'Do you think I made it all up?'

'No.'

'Then why do you want to speak to Herr Polster?'

'I think it will be . . .' Liebermann hesitated before selecting a suitably anodyne word '. . . instructive.'

Rolling his head to the side, Erstweiler closed his eyes and whispered: 'Do as you please, Herr doctor.'

He was evidently too exhausted to continue the session.

CHAPTER 9

Rheinhardt strode down Lange Gasse, hopping off the pavement to allow a perambulator to pass and hopping back on again to avoid a carriage. He was humming the *Andante con moto* from Schubert's B-flat Piano Trio, allowing his baritone voice to take on the expressive sonorities of a cello. The melody reflected his mood: subdued yet purposeful. In due course he came to his destination, a pair of tall wooden doors. He touched the peeling paintwork, pressed lightly, and entered a vaulted tunnel.

The inspector stepped over a rusting bicycle frame and an obstacle course of discarded items: a box of coat hangers, numerous empty wine bottles, and the statue of an angel (with weatherworn features and broken wings) lying on its side.

Beyond the tunnel was a narrow path which ran between two rows of identical terraced cottages. They had plain whitewashed exteriors and flat roofs. Someone, somewhere, was playing a Chopin prelude on an out-of-tune piano; however, Rheinhardt was impressed by the technical proficiency of the pianist. Raising his eyes, the inspector saw that he had entered a cul-de-sac. The path was truncated by a brick wall on which two large urns were precariously balanced. Behind the wall he could see the tops of trees and, some distance beyond these, the fenestrated rear of a high residential block.

Rheinhardt came to an open door and called out: 'Hello?'

A scruffy-looking young man appeared. He wasn't wearing a collar and his untucked shirt hung over a pair of dirty corduroy trousers.

'Yes?' His accent was almost aristocratic.

'I'm looking for Herr Rainmayr.'

'Ludo Rainmayr? Last cottage on the right; be that as it may, I feel obliged to inform you that he is presently engaged by his muse and he can't abide interruptions. It puts him in a foul temper. I assume you have come to settle a debt?' Rheinhardt did not answer. 'Well, if so,' the young man continued, 'you will – I am sorry to say – be disappointed. Ludo hasn't a heller left. He spent all his money last night. We went to see a troupe of comedy acrobats – The Dorfmeisters – at Ronachers.'

Rheinhardt was confident that he was speaking to an impoverished actor.

'Thank you for your assistance,' he said, raising his hat. 'Please accept my apologies for interrupting your busy day.'

'Not at all,' said the young man – oblivious of the inspector's irony. 'My pleasure.'

Rheinhardt ventured further down the path. A scrawny cat jumped down from a window ledge and ran on ahead like a herald. When the inspector reached the final cottage on the right he rapped his knuckles on the door.

A voice from inside shouted: 'Come in!'

The room that Rheinhardt entered was gloomy for an artist's studio; however, the absence of natural light was compensated for by several oil lamps hanging from the ceiling. There was an iron stove, some chairs stacked in the corner, an easel, and a table cluttered with rags, brushes, bottles, bowls and paint pots. Next to the easel stood a man in his late fifties. He was wearing a blue kaftan with yellow flowers embroidered into the fabric. His grey hair was exceptionally thick and long, as was his beard.

In front of the artist was a mattress covered with a white sheet on which two naked women were positioned. They were both very young and extraordinarily thin. One was lying on her front, the other on her back. The latter had underdeveloped breasts which barely rose from her chest. Her legs were slightly parted. She did not move or seek to cover herself when Rheinhardt entered. Indeed, her expression communicated only intense boredom. The other woman twisted her neck and glanced back over her shoulder but, like her companion, she seemed unperturbed by the arrival of a stranger.

'Yes?' said the artist.

'Herr Rainmayr?'

'Yes.'

'I am Inspector Rheinhardt – from the security office.'

Rainmayr was so absorbed in his work that he didn't bother to look up.

'What's it about?' he said gruffly.

'I am afraid I will need to speak to you in private.'

Rainmayr sighed, made a swift head-to-toe assessment of Rheinhardt, then addressed the women: 'All right, you two, get dressed. Go and have a coffee at Kirchmann's. But make sure you get back within the hour.'

The models stood up, exposing their bodies without a hint of self-consciousness, and stepped behind a screen over which their dresses and underwear had been thrown. A petticoat suddenly vanished.

'Can I offer you something to drink, inspector?'

'No, thank you.'

'Schnapps?'

'No, thank you,' Rheinhardt repeated.

'I'll be with you in a moment.' Rainmayr began cleaning his brushes with a rag soaked in turpentine; a simple task, but one which seemed to require his complete and undivided attention. The sound of giggling and whispering came from behind the screen. Then a slap, the unmistakable whip-crack of an open palm landing squarely on buttocks, followed by a hiss and a curse so obscene that it might have made a stevedore blush.

Rainmayr rolled his eyes and barked: 'Lissi, Toni. That's enough!'

A number of unframed but completed canvases were lined up against the far wall. Rheinhardt moved closer to take a look. The floor was covered with charcoal dust. All the paintings were of young women in various states of undress who all shared the same emaciated physique. The largest and most arresting image showed an adolescent girl standing by a mirror, wearing only black stockings and a neck band. The stockings were not held up by garters and hung loosely off her legs. The girl's right hand was held against her belly, the extended forefinger reaching towards the object of her attention (which Rainmayr had represented in the mirror with a vivid red daub amid the tangle of her pubic hair). She had large eyes, a full mouth, and her expression was provocative. It was a skilfully executed portrait, but Rheinhardt found the subject matter disturbing.

'Are you interested in buying one, inspector?' Rainmayr called out.

'No.'

The syllable was delivered with more vehemence than Rheinhardt had intended.

Rainmayr shrugged.

The two models came out from behind the screen. They were wearing calico dresses and wide-brimmed hats with decorative rosettes.

'Here,' said Rainmayr, scooping some coins out of a bowl on the table. 'Take this.' He dropped a few hellers into an outstretched hand. 'No longer than an hour. Understand?'

The women nodded and dashed for the door, suddenly laughing out loud on account of some private joke. Once they were out of the studio, Rheinhardt remarked frostily: 'Your models are very young, Herr Rainmayr.'

'All women look young,' the artist replied, 'once you get to a certain age. Besides, they're older than you think, inspector, and more worldly than you can imagine.'

'Do you always choose young women as your subjects?'

'An artist – like everyone else – must have food in his belly. My work reflects the tastes of my patrons. There are a number of collectors who have a weakness for the female form when it enters the transitional phase between adolescence and maturity.'

'I would very much like to see that list.'

'Indeed,' said Rainmayr. 'I'm sure you would – and if I wasn't bound to respect confidences I'd enjoy showing it to you. You'd be surprised to learn how many *art lovers* occupy positions of influence and power.'

It was obvious that Rainmayr didn't fear prosecution.

Commissions from judges? Rheinhardt wondered.

'I understand,' said Rheinhardt, 'that you employ a model called Adele Zeiler – is that correct?'

Rainmayr placed his brushes on the table.

'Yes. Although I don't use her as much as I used to. She only works for me occasionally.'

'When did you last see her?'

'Sunday afternoon.'

'How was she?'

'No different than usual.'

'What did you talk about?'

'A dance show that she wanted to see . . . the new fashion house on Bauernmarkt. At one point she asked me for more work, but I couldn't satisfy her request and she became a little petulant.'

'Would you say that you are well acquainted with Fräulein Zeiler?'

'Yes. I've known her for about three years.'

'You mean to say she started modelling for you when she was fifteen?'

'Sixteen. I saw her sitting on a park bench with her father and was intrigued by her face. She looked utterly indifferent. A child, yet already bored with everything life might have to offer. I approached Herr Zeiler and we came to an arrangement. He has two more daughters – one suffers from a terrible cough and the other's a cripple. I did some sketches of the one with the cough once: an engaging face – but not engaging enough.' Rainmayr shook his head. 'Herr Zeiler even brought the cripple here when he lost his job and begged me to use her too, but I'm not a charity.' Rainmayr paused and asked: 'Has Adele stolen something? Is that why you're here?'

Rheinhardt examined some drawings that had

61

been stuck to the wall: more naked women in positions suggestive of self-exploration. He responded with a question of his own: 'Did she say where she was going on Sunday?'

'After leaving here?'

'Yes.'

'Ahh,' said Rainmayr. 'I see. Run off, has she? Now that wouldn't surprise me.'

'Why do you say that?'

'I think she was getting tired of her situation. At home, I mean. She used to complain about it. She was supporting her family – more or less. You know how it is, inspector: an attractive young woman can always make money.'

'She didn't run away, Herr Rainmayr. Adele Zeiler was murdered.'

The artist smiled, as if Rheinhardt was joking.

'What are you talking about? Murdered!'

'On Sunday night. Her body was found in the Volksgarten. She'd been stabbed.'

Rainmayr touched the table to steady himself.

'My God . . . Poor Adele. Murdered . . .'

'Well, did she say where she was going?'

Rainmayr looked up.

'Yes, she said she was going to meet someone at a coffee house.'

'Who?'

'I don't know. I presumed a man.'

'Which coffee house?

'She mentioned Honniger's – by the Ulrichskirche.'

CHAPTER 10

They were nearing the end of their music-making and Liebermann found himself reflecting on Rheinhardt's choice of songs. His friend had demonstrated a distinctly morbid bias, favouring lyrics about gravediggers, sadness, partings and the moon. At one point, the inspector had been quite insistent that they should attempt an infrequently performed Schubert song titled 'To Death' and when Rheinhardt sang the opening line – *Death, you horror of nature, Ever-moving runs your clock* – Liebermann detected troubled nuances which made him suspect that his friend had recently paid a visit to the morgue. Years of service in the security office had not inured Rheinhardt to the sight of a corpse: the dead might decompose in the soil but in the medium of his memory they were preserved indefinitely.

'Before we finish,' said Liebermann, 'I would very much like to hear *this*.' He picked up another volume of Schubert and set it on the music stand.

'"Der Doppelgänger."'

Rheinhardt wasn't entirely sure that his tired vocal cords would be able to deliver a creditable performance. 'I'll do my best,' he assented. 'But you cannot expect very much from me. My voice is beginning to go.'

Liebermann paused, allowing a respectful silence to precede Schubert's mysterious introduction. He let his fingers descend and the keys surrendered under the weight of his hands. The contact produced dense harmonies, played softly like the tolling of a distant bell, evocative of darkness and the ominous approach of something strange. Rheinhardt began to sing:

'Still ist die Nacht'
Still is the night . . .

The narrator returns to the house where a woman he loved once lived. Outside, he sees a man, wringing his hands, racked by grief.

A dissonant note in the melody: a stab of anguish.

Rheinhardt's voice filled with horror:

'Mir graust es, wenn ich sein Antlitz sehe –
Der Mond zeigt mir meine eigne Gestalt.'

I shudder when I see his face –
The moon shows me my own form.

The inspector's rich baritone became powerfully resonant as he sang: 'You ghostly double, pale companion! Why do you ape the pain of love?'

For a few seconds the music seemed to find release from despair, but the insistent chords of the piano, fateful and benighted, guided the song to its desolate conclusion.

Liebermann did not lift his hands from the keyboard. He was deep in thought.

An interesting lyric . . .

The narrator sees his doppelgänger; however, his double is not a supernatural being but a vision of himself suffering the agonies of unrequited love. Liebermann wondered how such a hallucination might arise and what purpose it might serve in the psychic economy? Perhaps the narrator's inner torment was too much to bear, threatening his sanity, and some protective mechanism had been triggered? His grief – or the overwhelming part of it – had been displaced. If this was the case, then the doppelgänger might be construed as an elaborate defence: the custodian of memories and emotions that would otherwise cause mental disintegration. Liebermann thought of Herr Erstweiler and how he had spoken affectionately of Frau Milena, the young wife of his landlord, Kolinsky. As these ideas accumulated, the young doctor became dimly aware of something impinging on his consciousness, a sound which carried with it a note of frustration. It had originated in the vicinity of his friend.

'God in heaven, Max. Pay attention! You've gone into a trance!'

Liebermann turned. He had still not fully extricated himself from his cogitations.

'You haven't heard a single word I've been saying!'

Liebermann lifted his hands from the keyboard.

'I'm afraid not, Oskar. The music inspired a train of thought and I became utterly lost in a fog of my own speculations.' He closed the lid of the piano and stroked the glossy black lacquer. 'I'm sorry, what were you saying?'

Rheinhardt heaved a prodigious sigh.

'It hardly matters now.'

'Come, Oskar,' said Liebermann, standing. 'Let us retire. If I am not mistaken, we will have much to discuss this evening.'

The two men entered the smoking room and sat in chairs that faced a modest fire. Liebermann poured brandy and offered his friend a cigar. When they were both settled, Rheinhardt produced an envelope from his jacket pocket and handed it to his friend.

'As I expected,' said Liebermann, taking out the contents. The envelope contained photographs.

A young woman, lying on grass.

Coat open, striped stockings, ankle boots . . .

'Her name is Adele Zeiler,' said Rheinhardt. 'Age nineteen. She was discovered in the Volksgarten by a constable early on Monday morning. Her underwear had been removed and traces of dried semen were found on her dress. There were no signs to suggest that a struggle had taken place. Her fingernails were unbroken, there was no bruising, and no tearing of clothes. Moreover,

Professor Mathias did not find any significant' – Rheinhardt coughed into his hand – '*internal* indications of injury.'

A close-up of her face.

Another of her right hand – the long nails intact.

'She consented to intercourse?'

'So it would seem. I found one of the buttons from her coat under the eaves of the Theseus Temple. I imagine that she and the perpetrator had become intimate while sheltering beneath the roof of the monument. Perhaps he became intemperate in his excitement and began to pull at her coat – breaking the thread. Whatever, in due course she must have agreed to find a place where they would be better concealed and they chose a row of bushes close by.'

'How did she die?'

'She was stabbed.' Liebermann inspected the first photograph again and frowned. 'With *this*,' Rheinhardt added. The inspector reached into his pocket for a second time.

'A hatpin?'

'Precisely.'

Liebermann took the hatpin from his companion and studied the silver acorn. Then he ran his finger along the length of the needle and tapped the sharp point.

'We know that it was purchased,' Rheinhardt continued, 'from a small shop on the Hoher Markt called Jaufenthaler's. It was one of five supplied by a Pole called Krawczyk. Herr Krawczyk hadn't been able to persuade many jewellers in Vienna to stock them. In fact, only two outlets other than Jaufenthaler's bought these silver-acorn hatpins and I understand that, to date, they have yet to make a sale.' Rheinhardt paused and exhaled a vast cloud of cigar smoke. 'Herr Jaufenthaler, on the other hand, was able to sell all five of Krawczyk's hatpins, and, significantly, he recalls that one of these customers was a gentleman.'

'Did you get a description?'

'Yes, but not a very good one: dark hair, pale complexion – well mannered. Late twenties. No distinguishing marks.'

Liebermann placed the hatpin on the table and returned his attention to the photographs.

'Where was she stabbed? I see no bloodstains on her dress – particularly near her heart, where I would have expected there to be some.'

Rheinhardt remained silent.

'Surely,' Liebermann continued, 'Fräulein Zeiler wasn't stabbed in the back. Inflicting a fatal wound, or rather, an *instantly* fatal wound, from behind with such an inconsequential weapon would be virtually impossible. One could puncture the lungs, I suppose . . . but that would be so very inefficient.'

Rheinhardt derived a shameful degree of satisfaction from the sight of his friend floundering. It was an infrequent occurrence and he intended to prolong the pleasure for as long as possible.

'Professor Mathias was rather impressed by the killer's ingenuity,' said the inspector.

Liebermann, now evidently irritated by his own inability to solve the mystery, glared at his friend: 'Well?'

Rheinhardt took a leisurely sip of brandy.

'The pin,' he said – before pausing to delay his disclosure a few seconds more – 'was pushed through the gap between the uppermost vertebra of the spinal column and the skull, through the hole at the base of the skull – the foramen magnum, I believe it is called – and into the brain.'

Liebermann banged the side of his head with the palm of his hand.

'Of course, how stupid of me: and how very *interesting*.' He said the word 'interesting' in such a way as to suggest sudden illumination.

'Why interesting?'

It was now Liebermann's turn to be coy.

'Please continue.'

Rheinhardt knew that there would be little point in pressing his friend for an answer.

'Fräulein Zeiler was reported missing by her father who subsequently identified the body. She lived with her family – father, mother, and two sisters – in the sixteenth district. The two sisters are infirm; one suffers from a chest disease and the other is crippled. The Zeilers had become increasingly dependent on Adele for support, particularly after Herr Zeiler lost his job. She was able to provide subsistence for herself and her family by selling the gifts she received from gentlemen: gentlemen whose *friendship* she cultivated specifically for that purpose. Her father was insistent that Adele never accepted money, but most people would probably judge her to be not very different from a prostitute. She also supplemented her income by modelling for an artist called Rainmayr – a most unsavoury fellow whom I visited yesterday. I say unsavoury, largely on account of the work he produces. His oeuvre – if we can distinguish it by such a term – must appeal mostly to the kind of man one sees in Café Central, exchanging coins under the table for lewd postcards. He specialises in portraits of young women. *Very* young women.' Rheinhardt's expression darkened. 'Rainmayr claims to have patrons in exalted circles, a boast which I fear might very well be true. Fräulein Zeiler went to see Rainmayr on Sunday afternoon. She wanted more modelling work, which he says he was unable to provide. I suspect they might have argued. She then left the artist's studio for a small coffee house called Honniger's where Rainmayr believes she intended to meet one of her admirers. I went to Honniger's and one of the waiters recognised Fräulein Zeiler from a photograph. He was able to confirm that she had been there on Sunday night with a male companion. He provided a description broadly consistent with that of Herr Jaufenthaler: dark hair, tallish, thin, pale – but with the notable addition of blue eyes. The waiter supposed him to be some kind of professional.'

Liebermann picked up the hatpin and studied

it again. He seemed particularly absorbed by the bend – the small kink – close to the silver acorn. Once again, he ran his finger along its length.

A small shower of sparks erupted among the flames of the fire.

'It is tempting to assume,' said Rheinhardt, 'that Fräulein Zeiler's dark-haired companion is the perpetrator; however, the evidence is circumstantial. He might have purchased the hatpin as a gift, given it to Fräulein Zeiler, and then they could have parted. We should also remember that a woman like Fräulein Zeiler might easily arouse jealous passions. She was obviously unattached to her gentlemen friends, but who knows what they felt about her? Did she mislead them? And what if one of their number had learned that Fräulein Zeiler had been trifling with his affections? Could such a besotted admirer have stumbled upon Fräulein Zeiler in Honniger's – flirting outrageously with the dark-haired stranger – and become enraged? Could he have lain in wait, pretending, when the opportunity arose, that a chance meeting had occurred? And finally, could he have then persuaded Fräulein Zeiler to walk with him to the Volksgarten in order to enjoy her sexual favours one last time, before—'

'No, no, no,' cried Liebermann, waving his hand in the air impatiently. 'That is quite wrong! This murder isn't related to some cheap *demi-monde* melodrama. It has nothing to do with broken promises, dashed hopes and wounded pride!'

71

Rheinhardt – somewhat startled – raised an eyebrow.

'Jealousy,' Liebermann continued, 'especially in men, is indeed a common cause of retributive sexual violence; however, the individual who murdered Fräulein Zeiler is, I believe, quite different from the common herd of infatuated, intemperate, and vengeful lovers. His motives are as strange as the air of another planet. Indeed, I would go as far as to say that this man is unique in the annals of psychopathology.' The young doctor became feverish. 'Even the *Psychopathia Sexualis* with its exhaustive bestiary of lust murderers, necrophiliacs, fetishists, and sadomasochists, vampires and coprophiliacs, hermaphrodites and exhibitionists, does not include a comparable case.'

Rheinhardt's expression became increasingly sceptical as Liebermann's excitement mounted.

'Really, Max! This man *is* very interesting – I grant you that – insofar as he has recognised and exploited the murderous possibilities of the seemingly innocuous hatpin. But beyond this irregularity I see nothing singular or remarkable about his crime. If he is not a jealous lover then he is, at worst, a lust murderer. He availed himself of Fräulein Zeiler's favours and then he killed her.'

'I beg to differ.'

'I would have thought that much was indisputable!'

'Allow me to make some clinically relevant

observations. In cases of lust murder, the pervert kills to ensure compliance. A dead woman cannot reject sexual advances. The same is true – only even more so – of a necrophile. We know from Professor Mathias's evidence that Fräulein Zeiler gave herself willingly. Her murderer, therefore, did not need to render her insensible. He did not need to *take* her because what would otherwise need to be *taken* was already being freely offered!'

Rheinhardt looked confused.

'I'm not really following your argument . . . and I still don't understand your objection to my initial remark.'

'You suggested that intercourse occurred and then the perpetrator killed Fräulein Zeiler. This gives a false impression of what I believe actually happened. The perpetrator did not kill Fräulein Zeiler *after* sexual intercourse – he killed her *during* intercourse!'

Rheinhardt blew out his cheeks and let the air escape slowly. He motioned as if to speak, but immediately fell silent again.

'To drive a hatpin,' Liebermann continued, 'through the foramen magnum and into the brain is not an easy task. The head would have to be bent forward, widening the aperture between the final vertebra and the skull; however, sexual intercourse would have afforded the perpetrator ample opportunity to conduct such manipulations. He might have lifted Fräulein Zeiler's head – to kiss her, perhaps – while he positioned the hatpin in readiness for his . . . ultimate pleasure.'

'What do you mean by that? *Ultimate pleasure?*'

'I mean,' Liebermann replied, 'that he very probably *culminated* as he drove the hatpin home. You see, if I am correct he is in actual fact nothing like Krafft-Ebing's lust murderers and necrophiliacs, who find the dead arousing. He doesn't find the dead arousing – he finds *death* arousing, death itself! He is a thanatophiliac!'

Rheinhardt poured himself an extra-large brandy and gulped it down with uncharacteristic speed.

'You said that it wouldn't be easy to insert a hatpin directly into the brain.'

'Indeed.'

'Yet he seems to have had no trouble doing so.'

'In which case,' said Liebermann, 'he has had plenty of practice.'

CHAPTER 11

'I'm sorry to disturb you, sir,' said Haussmann, standing in the doorway. 'But there's a young woman downstairs who wants to see you. She's a bit agitated and she's very' – the young man assumed a woeful expression – 'insistent.'

'Why does she want to see me?' asked Rheinhardt.

'She says she has information that will be of interest to you.'

'What information?'

'I have no idea, sir. She wouldn't say.'

'Did you try to find out?'

'I did, sir, but my powers of persuasion proved insufficient.'

'Well, I take it, Haussmann, you persuaded her to divulge her name – that much at least, eh?

'Pryska Sykora, sir.'

'I've never heard of her. Even so, I suppose you'd better bring her up.'

Haussmann stepped back into the corridor but suddenly froze.

'Yes?' said Rheinhardt: 'What now?'

Haussmann's cheeks darkened. 'This isn't *very*

relevant, sir, but I think you should know. It says something about Fräulein Sykora's character. In addition to insisting that she should be allowed to talk to you, sir, she also suggested that I might want to consider taking her to the theatre one evening this week.'

'I see. And did you?'

'What, sir?'

'Consider it.'

'If I am to be perfectly honest, sir, I did. She is quite pretty; however, I was quick to point out that if I acted on her proposal this would very likely provoke your displeasure.'

'Haussmann,' said Rheinhardt, 'you are wise beyond your years.'

'Thank you, sir.'

'Not at all. Now, if you would be so kind as to fetch this *femme fatale* I would be most grateful. The day is already advanced and I regret to say I have done very little.'

After Haussmann's departure Rheinhardt opened one of the drawers in his desk and removed a cardboard box. It was full of his wife's *Linzer biscotten*. She had made them in the shape of hearts.

Rheinhardt was particularly fond of his wife's *Linzer biscotten* because she always coated them with a thick crust of sugary icing and cemented the shortbread together with a superabundant quantity of raspberry jam. The inspector wondered if his wife's baking (never stinting and conspicuously bountiful) betrayed something of her innermost nature. According to Liebermann, those things which were usually considered insignificant (for example, a person's choice of pastry cutter) often supplied the richest seams for psychoanalytic inquiry. The inspector picked up one of the biscuits and contemplated its dimensions, its telling shape and the extravagant applications of icing and jam. *Surely*, he thought, *all indisputable signs of a generous spirit.* He was overcome with sentiment but then laughed out loud. Professor Freud's *The Interpretation of Dreams* had received mixed reviews. What would the world make of *The Interpretation of Biscuits*? Perhaps it was better to leave the psychoanalysis to Liebermann.

Rheinhardt ate one of the *Linzer biscotten* and was contemplating eating a second when Haussmann returned with Fräulein Sykora. She was very young, perhaps no more than seventeen, small, and almost beautiful. Her face was flawed by a quality that Rheinhardt could only think of as 'hardness'.

'Fräulein Sykora,' said Rheinhardt, rising from his chair. 'Please, do come in.' He observed some crumbs on his blotter and discreetly brushed them aside. 'I am Detective Inspector Rheinhardt.'

Haussmann took Fräulein Sykora's coat and offered her the chair in front of Rheinhardt's desk. She did not make eye contact with the assistant detective and did not say 'Thank you.' Haussmann withdrew, hung her coat on the stand, and maintained a safe distance.

'Well,' said Rheinhardt, sitting down again. 'I understand you are in possession of some information which you believe may be of interest to me.'

'Yes,' Fräulein Sykora said. 'I am.' Her accent was rough, unrefined – but the timbre of her voice was pleasantly husky. 'You're the detective who's investigating Adele Zeiler's murder, aren't you?'

'That is correct.'

'I heard all about it yesterday.'

Rheinhardt registered that she had *heard* about the murder – and not *read* about it in the newspapers.

'From whom?'

Pryska Sykora swung around and glanced at Haussmann: 'I won't say anything while *he*'s here.'

'Haussmann is my assistant,' Rheinhardt replied. 'Everything I know, he must know too.'

'What I've got to say . . . it's *personal*.'

Rheinhardt sighed, then looked over at his assistant and said: 'Haussmann – would you mind waiting outside?'

'Not at all, sir.'

Haussmann bowed and left the office, closing the door with just enough surplus force to declare his wounded pride.

'So,' said Rheinhardt, steepling his hands and tapping his fingertips against his pursed lips. 'How did you learn about poor Adele?'

'From my friends . . . and it was them who told me about you.'

'And who might your friends be?'

'They were at Rainmayr's when you went to ask him questions.'

'Ah yes – Lissi and Toni?'

'Yes, that's them.'

Fräulein Sykora fell silent and she looked around the room. She then said: 'Do you pay for it?'

Surprised, Rheinhardt drew back a little.

'Pay for what, exactly?'

'Information.'

'Well, that depends.'

'You do pay, though, don't you? How much?'

'When citizens provide us with serviceable information, it is our practice in the security office to reward them – sometimes – with a small gratuity.'

'We used to talk,' said Fräulein Sykora. 'Adele and me – we were good friends.'

'And what did you used to talk about?'

'Things . . . Rainmayr.'

Pryska Sykora pursed her lips and rubbed her thumb and forefinger together.

Rheinhardt found two kronen in his pocket and placed them on his desk.

'Let us assume that I am interested in what you have to tell me,' said Rheinhardt. 'But you will have to be a little more forthcoming.'

Fräulein Sykora nodded.

'Adele was angry with Rainmayr. She wanted more work and he wouldn't give it to her. She used to curse him. She even threatened him.'

'How did she threaten him?'

'He's an artist. You know what artists are like with their models.'

'Fräulein Sykora, are you implying that Herr Rainmayr was intimate with Adele Zeiler?'

'He had his way with her, yes. When she was younger. And she told him she'd go to the police if he didn't give her more work.'

'Do you have any proof of this?'

'It's what she said to me.'

'When?'

'She was always saying it – I can't remember when.'

Fräulein Sykora leaned forward and picked up the coins. She examined them in her open palm.

'This isn't very much, inspector.'

'When did you last see Adele?'

'Friday night.'

'Where?'

'We bumped into each other on Lange Gasse.'

'Had she been to see – or was she going to see – Rainmayr?'

'She was going to see someone else. A gentleman friend.'

'Where?'

'A private dining room.'

'Which one?'

'I don't know.'

'Did she mention the name of this gentleman friend – or say anything about him?'

'No. She just said she was meeting him and that he'd promised to give her a gift.'

'What kind of gift?'

Pryska Sykora shrugged.

Rheinhardt picked up his pen and made some notes.

'I know other things . . . about Adele.'

The girl rattled the coins in her clenched fist.

'Where do you live, Fräulein Sykora?'

'Above Kirchmann's Coffee House.'

'With your family?'

'No.'

'May I ask . . . how do you pay for your lodgings?'

'I don't. Herr Kirchmann said I could stay in the attic room if I . . .' she paused and diverted her gaze before adding '. . . helped out in the kitchen.'

Rheinhardt doubted that the arrangement between landlord and lodger consisted of such an uncomplicated exchange of alms for labour.

'Tell me,' said Rheinhardt. 'How long had you been acquainted with Adele Zeiler?'

'About a year.'

'And how did you get to know her?'

'She used to come into Kirchmann's with some of the other Rainmayr girls. When it wasn't busy I'd join them.' Fräulein Sykora put the coins in her dress pocket and said: 'I really thought I'd get more than this.'

Rheinhardt scrutinised his guest.

'How old were you when Herr Kirchmann first offered you somewhere to live?'

Fräulein Sykora frowned.

81

'Look, I came here to tell you about Adele and Rainmayr.'

'If you've been living at Kirchmann's for at least a year you must have been rather young when you moved in.'

'Not that young.'

'How old are you?'

'Twenty.'

Rheinhardt smiled.

'Well, Fräulein,' said Rheinhardt, 'you must be a favourite of the gods of youthfulness. Twenty, indeed. Where do your family live?'

'I came here to talk about Adele and Rainmayr!' Pryska Sykora shouted, stamping her foot on the floor. 'Not about me! But if you're not interested . . .' She got up abruptly and turned to leave.

'Fräulein Sykora?'

Rheinhardt placed another coin on the desk. Pryska Sykora snatched it up and went to get her coat from the stand. Then she opened the door and barked at Haussmann: 'Take me down, I'm leaving.'

Haussmann craned his head around the door jamb and sought permission from his superior.

'Yes,' said Rheinhardt. 'The interview is over.' Then he called out, 'Good afternoon, Fräulein Sykora. You have been most helpful.'

CHAPTER 12

iss Amelia Lydgate had come to recognise that her knowledge of music was deficient. In most cities this would not have mattered; however, in Vienna the inability to engage in intelligent conversation about music was a significant social handicap. She was determined to rectify this deficiency and had asked Liebermann to recommend some concerts. He responded by offering to take her to a piano recital at the Bösendorfer Saal. On going to the venue to buy tickets he discovered a programme that seemed peculiarly apposite, given Amelia's temperament and nationality. It consisted largely of the *English Suites* by Johann Sebastian Bach. Liebermann was sure that Bach's 'logic' would appeal to the cerebral Englishwoman and hoped that the nominal reference to her homeland would create an illusion of comforting familiarity (an *illusion*, because there was nothing particularly English about these suites at all – other than the fact that they were supposed to have been commissioned by an English nobleman).

Liebermann and Amelia Lydgate had already heard the first and second suites, and were now listening to an energetic account of the third in G minor. The prelude and preliminary dances were vigorous and exciting; however, the mood established by the fourth movement – a saraband – was quite different: sad, reflective, and searching. The melody was ornamented and resembled a vocal improvisation over a strummed accompaniment. Occasionally, a chord change would affect Liebermann deeply. It felt like something inside him was being unlocked or undone. Bach – for all his ruthless proficiency – still had the power to move the young doctor. And yet, the music was never mawkish or sentimental. The venerable composer had dispensed with manipulative clichés, replacing them with something far more potent: ravishing ingenuity.

Liebermann stole a quick glance at his companion, curious to see if she had been affected by the music.

Pale skin, russet tresses, and eyes of an indeterminate blue-grey . . .

Her expression was typically intense and her brow was lined with concentration.

Amelia Lydgate confused him.

There had been moments when he had felt so close to declaring his love for her that he could barely resist the urge. And other times when her intellectualism and cool manner made him grateful that he had never succumbed to such impulses. Their relationship was complicated; Amelia Lydgate had once been Liebermann's patient and if this sobering consideration wasn't enough to make him question the propriety of making an amorous overture, he could always reflect on what he had discovered to be the cause of her hysterical paralysis: a repressed memory of a sexual assault. Liebermann had treated Amelia Lydgate and over time they had become friends. At first he had justified his continued presence in her life on medical grounds; then he persuaded himself that he was being altruistic, providing assistance and advice to a stranger who was alone in a foreign country; then he had recognised how her remarkable intellectual gifts and scientific skills (she was an expert on human blood and a talented microscopist) might be utilised by the security office. Rheinhardt had consulted her on several occasions. And so the justifications had accumulated, each one binding them closer together.

Earlier in the year Liebermann had stood on the Charles Bridge in Prague with his uncle Alexander and had confessed his attachment. Alexander had suggested that – apart from his mother – there were three women in every man's life: his wife, his mistress, and an unattainable object of desire. Clearly – Uncle Alexander maintained – Amelia Lydgate was Liebermann's unattainable object: a fantasy innamorata, best enjoyed not in the flesh but in the imagination – an ageless reminder of the youthful propensity for infatuation and desire. Actual consummation would be a great disappointment.

Another exquisite change of harmony . . .

Liebermann studied Amelia's hands, folded

together on the green velvet of her skirt. His uncle might well be right, but he still wanted to reach out and cover her slim fingers with his own.

The subsequent dances of the G minor suite jolted Liebermann out of his reverie, and the final movement – a lively gigue – brought the concert to a close. Insistent applause persuaded the pianist to give an encore – a delightful arrangement of 'Sheep May Safely Graze'. At its conclusion the pianist signalled his fatigue by shutting the piano lid, and the house lights came up as he was leaving the stage.

'Well,' said Liebermann to his companion. 'Did you enjoy it?'

'Yes,' said Amelia. 'Very much.'

They collected their coats from the cloakroom and walked to Café Central where Liebermann suggested that they should stop for coffee and cake. At an earlier point in their acquaintance he would have considered such an invitation impertinent, but their friendship was sufficiently established to render such scruples redundant. They entered the coffee house and found a table in the Arkadenhof, a courtyard decorated with small trees and covered by a glass roof. A curved balcony hung out over three arches and the seating area was enclosed between high fenestrated walls. Spherical gas lights seemed to hover in the shadows; however, closer inspection revealed the secret of their suspension – wrought-iron stands, painted black. A waiter emerged from the arches and escorted the couple to a circular table discreetly positioned behind a miniature orange tree. Liebermann ordered a schwarzer for himself and an Earl Grey tea for Amelia.

'And would you like a pastry?' Liebermann asked Amelia.

The waiter interrupted: 'Could I recommend the *Scheiterhaufen*? It really is quite exceptional.'

'Well,' said Amelia. 'I defer to your expert opinion. *Scheiterhaufen*.'

Her German was perfect, with the merest trace of an English accent.

'And for you, sir?'

Liebermann shrugged and smiled.

'The same . . .'

'A very wise decision, sir.'

They spoke a little about the concert, and Amelia remarked that music – being the most abstract of the arts – presented the uninitiated with a unique conversational challenge.

'Oh, I don't know,' said Liebermann. 'Music can be *felt* as well as understood. It is always possible to discuss its effects, even if one has little or no technical knowledge.'

'Indeed,' said Amelia. 'But I find conversations of that kind rather unsatisfying. A discussion of subjective impressions cannot progress very far: there can be no meaningful argument or resolution because the *sine qua non* of dialogue is a framework of agreed reference points.'

Amelia's eyes caught the lamplight and transformed it into something vital and mysterious.

Her companion was momentarily arrested by the flecks of electric blue that appeared in her irises.

'Then perhaps you had better take up an instrument?'

'Oh . . . I couldn't.'

'Why not?'

'I am far too absorbed by my medical and scientific studies. And without adequate time to practise I would play very badly.'

They talked a little about Amelia's courses, her continuing interest in diseases of the blood, and her growing enthusiasm for pathology. The latter was not so very surprising, as the medical faculty was famously obsessed with obtaining accurate post-mortem diagnoses.

'Yes,' said Liebermann.' Pathology is a fascinating area of study; however, when I was a student I could not help feeling that some of the professors believed that the job of healing patients was quite incidental to the practice of medicine, and that only autopsies mattered. A different generation, of course, but it is a sobering thought that in *their* student days treatment was actively discouraged because it might influence the natural progression of symptoms and mislead the pathologist. I was told – and I fear that this might not be apocryphal – that on some wards, the only medicament prescribed was cherry brandy.'

Amelia Lydgate tilted her head.

'That might be so, yet I cannot help but admire their singularity of purpose. The advances we enjoy today would not have been possible without their work. I believe that Carl von Rokitansky performed more than eighty-five thousand autopsies.'

The waiter returned with their coffee, tea and *scheiterhaufen*, which was served hot and exuded a potent fragrance of vanilla, cinnamon and rum. The thick slices of bread were sprinkled with raisins and icing sugar and were dripping with molten apple purée.

'I have heard,' Amelia continued, 'that there is a rather interesting pathologist favoured by the police. Professor Mathias?'

'Indeed.'

'Does Inspector Rheinhardt consult him?'

'Yes, although Professor Mathias is a rather unorthodox and intuitive pathologist. His critics describe him as eccentric. His enemies say he is mad.'

'I would very much like to see him at work.'

'Inspector Rheinhardt would not object to your presence at a police autopsy; however, I have no idea what the professor will say. He is somewhat unpredictable. Do you want me to ask Rheinhardt?' I can do that for you at least.'

'If it isn't too much trouble,' said Amelia. 'Thank you.'

Liebermann tasted the *Scheiterhaufen* and was glad that he had accepted the waiter's recommendation.

'I read the report concerning the murder of Adele Zeiler in the *Zeitung*.' said Amelia.

'Yes,' Liebermann replied. 'A dreadful business.'

'Is it one of Inspector Rheinhardt's cases?'

Liebermann nodded, his mouth still full.

'The article said that the perpetrator is expected to claim more victims.' Amelia hesitated before adding: 'I was permitted last year to help with a security office investigation. Would you consider allowing me to do so again?'

Liebermann felt uneasy. He instinctively wanted to protect her from anything associated with sexual violence. She seemed to read his thoughts: 'Doctor Liebermann, this crime represents a terrible abuse of my sex. As long as this fiend is free, no woman can walk the streets of Vienna without fear. I feel obliged to offer assistance, not only out of recognition of my civil duty but also from a deep sense of sororal sympathy. You will be so kind – I trust – as to inform Inspector Rheinhardt of my readiness?'

The young doctor smiled, touched by Amelia's courage but also slightly discomfited by the militancy of her language. She had obviously been immersing herself in the literature of the women's reform movement.

'Of course,' he replied.

Liebermann took another mouthful of *scheiterhaufen*, his enjoyment of which found a corresponding quintessence in Amelia Lydgate's satisfied expression.

CHAPTER 13

Kristina Vogl sat at her dressing table, looking through the day's post. The letters were mostly expressions of gratitude from friends and associates whom she had invited to the grand opening of her salon. Halfway through the pile she came across an envelope made of cheap, thin paper which she set aside. After reading her correspondence, she tied it all together with a red ribbon and placed the bundle in the lowest of her dressing-table drawers. Picking up the envelope she had set aside, she studied the handwriting and after a lengthy pause began to tear the paper into thin strips. She then tore each strip into little pieces, and sprinkled the resulting confetti into a wicker basket.

She caught sight of herself in the mirror.

The cast of light had placed shadows under her eyes. She tested the skin – pulling it down to make sure that the discoloration was an illusion.

Journalists had been generous in the society pages. *An attractive woman:* that was how most people – she understood – would choose to describe her. Neverthless, she was acutely aware of the ravages of time. An 'attractive' woman could become virtually invisible to the opposite sex within the space of a few unkind years. She had already marked the first signs of her falling stock. Kristina was a keen student of human behaviour and had learned to read men's minds by watching their eye movements. Even an immature girl like her secretary Wanda – with her bad posture and rounded features – could deprive her of the first admiring glances that she had formerly taken for granted.

Kristina looked into her basket and, on seeing the remains of the unread letter, screwed up some writing paper which she placed strategically over the waste for the purpose of concealment. It was an unnecessary precaution, but old habits were difficult to break. Diligence cost nothing.

Rising from her chair, Kristina crossed the room and got into bed. She reached out to turn off the electric lamp – the bulb of which was hidden by a floral shade – but her action was arrested by a gentle, deferential knock.

The soft percussion was coming from her husband's bedroom that adjoined her own.

'Come in,' Kristina called out.

The door opened, revealing the figure of Doctor Heinz Vogl. He was a man in his late middle years, with significant amounts of grey in his well-trimmed beard and moustache. He had taken off his jacket but had not removed his waistcoat. His gold watch chain was conspicuously bright against the charcoal-grey fabric.

'Ah, my darling,' he said. 'You are still awake.'

He entered and sat on the edge of the bed.

'Was there an emergency?'

'Yes, the old general. His breathing was terrible. I thought he was going to die. But he pulled through. I was delayed by his family. They had many questions – too many, if you ask me.'

'Oh?'

'His son was overly interested in the details of his father's medical condition. I strongly suspect that he is already thinking about his inheritance.'

'How dreadful.'

'The old general deserves better.' Vogl touched the collar of his wife's nightdress. 'Is this new?'

'Yes. I got one of the seamstresses to run it off.'

'Your design?'

Kristina nodded: 'We had a new delivery of Chinese silk. I couldn't resist it.'

Vogl smiled. 'It's very beautiful. You look exquisite.'

He placed his crooked knuckle under Kristina's chin and lifted her lips to meet his own. His tenderness acquired urgency and his free hand found the warm, acquiescing curve of his wife's breast beneath the slippery diaphanous silk. Kristina became tense.

'What is it?'

'I'm sorry, Heinz. I'm very tired.'

She felt a pang of guilt. Kristina had been unable to give her husband the children he had so dearly desired and she had come to regard it as her duty always to grant him his conjugal rights. On this occasion, however, the shredded letter in the basket was still on her mind: the cheap paper, the ugly handwriting.

'You have been working hard too. How foolish of me to forget.' Vogl showed no sign of irritation. He withdrew and, clasping Kristina's hand in his own, added: 'Any new customers?'

'Yes. Countess Kézdi.'

'How did she hear about you?'

'She's an acquaintance of Frau Schmollinger.'

'I see.'

Vogl mentioned that the medical director, Professor Hipfl, had invited them to dinner, and that Frau Professor Hipfl had expressed an interest in visiting the salon. They spoke for a few minutes more about their respective days, until Kristina stifled a yawn. Vogl kissed his wife chastely on the forehead and reluctantly let go of her hand.

'I'll sleep next door. I want to read a little. Goodnight, my love.'

Kristina turned the light off. The nightdress felt good on her skin. The perfumes on her dressing table scented the air with rose and lavender. She had worked hard for this life of hers. No one was going to take it away.

CHAPTER 14

Rheinhardt ushered Herr Jaufenthaler and Jochen Wetl (the waiter at Honnigers) into a large room. A row of soberly dressed men flanked by police constables stood against the opposite wall. The inspector did not really expect his two witnesses to recognise the 'black-haired blue-eyed' gentleman among their number but, he reasoned, even if the likelihood of a positive identification was remote it was not impossible. He had read of several cases in the police gazette where identity parades had brought cases to a swift and successful conclusion, avoiding months of painstaking detection. One had to be lucky, of course, but Providence occasionally sided with the law.

All the gentlemen standing against the wall were professionals with at least some knowledge of anatomy. Two were doctors, one was a physiologist, another a medical student, and the final member was a mortuary assistant. They had all been approached by constables who were patrolling the Volksgarten. Rheinhardt had issued an order that any dark-haired gentlemen with blue eyes observed loitering near the Theseus Temple should be questioned. Murderers – as every policeman knew – were often strangely compelled to return to the scene of their crime. Of those questioned, any with a medical occupation were to be recruited for inclusion in the identification exercise that was about to begin.

Jaufenthaler and Wetl moved up and down the row and looked closely at each individual. It became apparent that neither the jeweller nor the waiter had seen any of the men before.

They both shook their heads and returned to Rheinhardt.

'Thank you, gentlemen.' The inspector called across the room. 'You have been most patient. The Emperor and the security office are indebted.'

In the corridor, Herr Jaufenthaler said: 'I'm sorry, inspector.'

'There is no need to apologise,' Rheinhardt replied.

The jeweller seemed uncomfortable.

'Inspector?'

'Yes?'

'I discovered something in my ledger which may be relevant.'

'Oh?'

'I'd quite forgotten. The gentleman who purchased the silver-acorn hatpin . . .'

'Yes? What about him?'

'He didn't buy one hatpin – he bought two. You see, I had taken six originally, not five, as I told your assistant. I'm sorry. One can't remember everything.'

CHAPTER 15

Liebermann jumped out of the cab and told the driver to wait. He was standing in a cheerless road facing a decrepit terrace of low buildings. A crudely painted sign leaning up against railings directed visitors down to The Chimney Sweep. Liebermann adjusted his coat and descended a flight of concrete stairs which led to a green door. He rested his palm on one of the sunken panels and pushed – it yielded easily. A draught of warm air escaped, carrying with it a mélange of smells: alcohol, tobacco, paraffin and sweat. He stepped into the gloom and surveyed his surroundings. A low vaulted ceiling was supported by stone columns that were so wide and numerous that it was barely possible to see the furthest walls. Wooden tables were packed closely together, and around these sat a clientele of solitary, silent patrons. Paraffin lamps suspended on ceiling hooks did little to mitigate the gloom of the shadowy interior and somewhere, concealed in the darkness, was an invisible musician improvising a mournful lament on an accordion.

Squeezing himself between the tables, Liebermann made his way to the bar, which consisted of nothing more than planks supported by two trellises. A hefty man was standing behind this ramshackle construction, wiping beer steins with a cloth and hanging them on pegs that had been hammered into the wall. He had a wide, swollen nose, set in a broad face. His hair was brushed back from his forehead and his untrimmed beard hung over the top of his apron.

'Herr Polster?' Liebermann asked.

The publican stopped wiping the stein and squinted.

'Do I know you?'

'No. You don't,' said Liebermann. 'Permit me to introduce myself. My name is Liebermann. I'm a doctor.' The publican inclined his head. 'I was wondering whether you would be willing to answer a few questions concerning one of my patients who – I believe – comes here regularly: Herr Erstweiler?'

'Norbert?' said the landlord, 'I haven't seen him recently. Is he all right? What's happened to him?'

'Unfortunately, Herr Erstweiler is not very well. He has been admitted into the General Hospital.'

'Why? Nothing serious, I hope.'

Liebermann did not want to divulge the details of Herr Erstweiler's medical condition and, observing the redness of the publican's nose, diverted the man's attention with an obvious ploy. Placing a tower of silver coins on the makeshift

bar Liebermann said: 'Whatever you recommend
– and one for yourself, of course.'

'Oh, thank you very much, sir,' said the landlord. Herr Polster turned and filled two enormous
steins with a dark, frothy liquid that issued from
the tap of a small barrel.

'Bavarian,' said the publican. *'Prost!'*

They clashed their steins together and Herr
Polster took a long draught. He paused, smacked
his lips, and then gulped the rest down before
flicking the hinged lid of his stein closed.

'Wonderful, isn't it?'

Liebermann – who had drunk more temperately
– was nevertheless able to answer with sincerity:
'Yes, it is very good indeed.'

'Expensive. But you get what you pay for, eh?'

'Quite so,' Liebermann agreed, sampling again
the woody, aromatic beer. He then added casually: 'Herr Erstweiler told me he *never* comes here
on Wednesday evenings.'

'That's right. *Usually* he doesn't.'

'But he did once.'

'Yes.'

'And would you say he acted out of character
that evening?'

'I should say so!'

'In what way?'

'Norbert isn't a great drinker. He comes in, has
a few, and then leaves. But on this occasion, this
one Wednesday night, he got well drunk! Not
horribly drunk, you understand, but drunk

99

enough to say things he didn't mean to. And when I saw him next, he acted as if nothing had happened. I don't know whether he was just embarrassed, or whether he'd really forgotten everything. It happens sometimes – although, thinking about it, he didn't drink *that* much. Still, if you're not used to it, eh? You should see the state some get into. God in heaven! I have to pick them up off the floor and leave them outside in the gutter!'

'What did Herr Erstweiler say – that Wednesday evening?' The landlord looked a little uncomfortable. 'Will you have another one?' said Liebermann, nonchalantly pointing to the small barrel of Bavarian beer.

Herr Polster's troubled expression was erased by a wide, foolish grin.

'You're a gentleman, sir, a true gentleman.' Liebermann produced some more coins while Polster thrust his stein under the tap. 'And will you be wanting another one for yourself, Herr doctor?'

'Not just yet. You were saying . . .'

'Oh yes, that Wednesay evening . . .' Herr Polster raised the stein and poured half the contents down his throat. 'Well, he said a lot of things – but he spoke mostly about his landlord's wife. He went on about how beautiful she was and how she wasn't appreciated by her old husband. And then he got more drunk and said other things. And these *other things* became more earthy, if you know

100

what I mean? At the time we had a good laugh. When I saw him again – the next time – I reminded him of some of the things he'd said, and he reacted very strangely. And then he got quite annoyed . . . I suppose he was just embarrassed. I felt sorry for him. He doesn't strike me as the type to have had very much luck with women. He's a shy man. And he wouldn't consider going to a . . .' The publican winked in lieu of supplying a euphemism for *brothel*. 'It must be difficult for him. Naturally. Living in a house with an attractive young woman. He's only human.'

Liebermann finished his beer.

'Herr Polster, I have one more question, which at first you might think odd, but I would be most grateful if you would give it your most careful and serious consideration. My question is this: are you absolutely sure that the man who came here that Wednesday night was – without question – Herr Erstweiler?'

The publican frowned.

'I don't understand? What do you mean? Are you asking if it could have been an impostor?'

'Let us say someone who strongly resembled Herr Erstweiler.'

Herr Polster shook his head.

'No, it was Norbert! No doubt about it.'

CHAPTER 16

'**H**err Rainmayr,' said Rheinhardt. 'When we spoke last, you said that Fräulein Zeiler became petulant when you couldn't offer her work. But would it be more accurate to say that you argued and that subsequently she threatened you in some way?'

'Threatened me?' Rainmayr replied. 'I'm not sure what you mean.'

The artist was seated on a chair while Rheinhardt walked around the studio.

'She never mentioned that she might go to the police?'

'Why would she do that?'

'To accuse you of improper conduct: seduction of a minor, to be precise.'

'That is absurd, inspector.'

Rheinhardt turned to examine the artist's face. It showed no emotion.

'I recognise, Herr Rainmayr, that you are not fearful of the law. But I doubt whether your patrons or associates – whoever they are – would be able to give you an absolute guarantee of protection. Had Fräulein Zeiler made such an allegation, you would have been detained for questioning, tried, and the outcome – regardless of petitions and intercession – might have been a prison sentence lasting months, if not years.'

Rainmayr sighed.

'You've been talking to that stupid bitch Pryska, haven't you? Pryska Sykora?'

'I am afraid I cannot disclose my sources.'

'You don't have to. I know exactly what's happened here.' The artist shook his head and smiled, baring his teeth without good humour. 'It's like this: Pryska has got herself *involved* with Kirchmann – a local coffee shop owner. He's an ugly fellow and she's been trying to get out of his clutches for some time. Herr Kirchmann's charity is not without conditions, you understand? Now, a couple of months ago Pryska started coming here with her friends – models – and then she started coming on her own. It was obvious what she was up to. Needless to say, I didn't respond to her clumsy attempts at playing the temptress and she became very angry. In fact, she threw the most ridiculous tantrum. She actually put her foot through a commission I was working on. It took me days to repair the damage. Clearly, she's still smarting from the rejection. And now she's decided to make trouble for me by telling you a pack of lies. Did you pay her for them, inspector? I hope not.'

Rheinhardt twisted his moustache and considered the unfinished canvas on Rainmayr's easel. It showed a young woman lying on a divan. She was nude and her knees were spaced just far enough apart to expose a hectic stripe. Her skin was mottled and transparent, to the extent that the portrait was as much a study of the human skeleton as the naked body. Her ribcage was clearly visible and her breasts were shaded a putrescent green. It was a deeply troubling portrait, which managed to situate eroticism close to – if not in – the grave.

The artist observed Rheinhardt's expression change from curiosity to disgust. He sighed and continued in a more conciliatory tone: 'Look, inspector, I'm no angel – I'd be the first to admit it. But I do care about the girls who model for me. And when they're in trouble, I try to help them. I'm an artist. My way of life might not meet with your approval but I can assure you I have standards – *moral* standards. Different from yours, but standards nevertheless. I don't think I've been responsible for corrupting or harming any of the models I've sketched or painted. I'm not a child molester and I'm certainly not a murderer. Adele Zeiler was moody and we sometimes argued. But she never threatened to go to the police. That is completely false.'

'Did you have relations with Adele Zeiler?'

The artist paused before saying: 'Yes, I did.'

'And how old was she?'

'I don't know. I thought she was seventeen. She might have been younger. It's possible that her father lied about her age when we first met.'

Rheinhardt continued to question Rainmayr but he was already satisfied that the purpose of his visit had been accomplished. Fräulein Sykora's evidence was – as he had suspected – quite worthless. In due course, Rheinhardt crossed the floor and opened the door.

'Are you going already, inspector?'

'Yes.'

'I've told you the truth.'

As Rheinhardt departed there were no formal exchanges – only a heavy silence.

The inspector walked between the squat cottages, negotiating debris that had been strewn across the path. Above the vaulted tunnel that led to Lange Gasse he could see the upper storeys of apartment buildings. When he stepped out onto the main thoroughfare he was surprised to see his assistant waiting on the other side of the road. The young man hurried over.

'Sir.'

'What is it, Haussmann?'

'Another one, sir.'

'A woman?'

'Yes, sir.'

'Where?'

'Spittelberg.'

PART II

THE CARBOLIC STRANGER

CHAPTER 17

Liebermann was halfway through volume one of Bach's Forty-Eight Preludes and Fugues when a messenger rapped on the door of his apartment. Rheinhardt's brief dispatch had been scrawled on a page torn from his notebook. The ragged edge of the paper added an extra dimension of urgency to the words – a request for Liebermann to leave immediately for an address in Spittelberg. Taking his astrakhan coat from the hallstand, Liebermann ran down the stairs, past the concierge and out onto the street, just in time to stop a cab.

The gently flowing left-hand figure of the E minor Prelude repeated itself in Liebermann's head. This musical fragment, consisting of only the first four bars, would not fade. As images of Vienna flashed by, the mellifluous semiquavers continued, a peculiarly incongruent accompaniment to the busy life of the city.

Soon after entering Spittelberg, the carriage began to slow down. Liebermann opened the window and leaned out. The road ahead ran between eighteenth-century buildings that had fallen into a woeful state of disrepair. All of the façades were dilapidated, the stucco covered in patches of mould and the decorative window hoods blackened with grime. A constable was standing outside one of the entrances.

'All right, you can stop here,' Liebermann called.

The carriage halted and Liebermann stepped out.

'What's going on down there?' asked the driver.

'I don't know,' Liebermann said and shrugged, handing the driver some coins. Liebermann made his way up the road to the waiting constable and introduced himself.

'This way, Herr doctor,' said the young man, opening a large wooden door. On the other side was a vaulted tunnel which led to a spacious court-yard. It was surrounded by two-storey dwellings with plain walls and rectangular windows. Lower apartments were set back behind an arched arcade, beneath which several old carts with tarpaulin covers had been left. A balcony – supported by the arcade – provided those residing on the upper level with a railing on which to dry their laundry. Liebermann noticed that a horses' drinking trough had been filled with earth and planted with trees; however, this attempt to beautify the courtyard had not been successful. The trees had died and their leafless, twisted branches were afflicted by a leprous dark green moss. A pool of brown water had collected beneath the mouth of a drainpipe and a swarm of tiny flies hovered above its surface.

The balcony was reached by a staircase that

occupied one of the corners of the square. It was built against the wall of the building to the left and ascended to the first floor of the building facing Liebermann. At the foot of the staircase were a group of women and Inspector Rheinhardt's assistant, Haussmann. It seemed to Liebermann that the women were questioning Haussmann, not the other way round. Their chattering was shrill and excited.

Haussmann saw Liebermann and beckoned him over.

'Who's he?' Liebermann heard one of the women ask.

'That is no concern of yours,' replied Haussmann. 'Please stand aside.'

Haussmann herded the women away from the foot of the stairs, allowing Liebermann to pass. Liebermann thanked Haussmann and began to climb. At the top of the stairs was an open door. He entered the apartment and found himself in a dark, cramped kitchen. Pots and a ladle were suspended from a wooden beam that spanned the width of the low ceiling.

'Oskar?'

'I'm in here, Max.'

Liebermann pushed open a second door and saw Rheinhardt seated on a chair. The inspector's expression was glum. The flesh on his face seemed to sag and only the upturned points of his moustache contradicted the general impression of descent.

A young woman, entirely naked, was lying on a single bed. Her legs were spread apart and one hung casually off the side. The delicate foot at its end was tilted downwards so that the toes were just touching the floorboards. Her sex was exposed, the vertical lips folded back, offering the observer a disconcertingly frank view of her shadowy interior. She was very thin and her hip bones jutted out below an equally distinct ribcage. Her breasts were of such little substance that gravity had deprived her entirely of a bust, giving her torso a masculine appearance. She possessed a pretty face: harmonious, regular features marred only – perhaps – by overly thick eyebrows. Her hair was blonde and framed her face like a saintly aura. Although the fingers of her left hand were spread out, those of her right were contracted and claw-like. Liebermann also noticed something odd about the position of the woman's head. It seemed to be bent forward and slightly raised.

'The same method?' He spoke without looking at Rheinhardt.

'Not only that,' said the inspector. 'But the same hatpin. On Friday I learned from Herr Jaufenthaler, the jeweller on the Hoher Markt, that he had sold not one silver-acorn hatpin to the *gentleman* who visited his shop, but two. I knew immediately that it would only be a matter of days before . . .' Rheinhardt shook his head. 'But I never thought he would strike again quite so soon.'

'May I?'

Liebermann indicated that he wished to examine the body.

'Of course.'

The young doctor crouched by the bed and felt beneath the woman's neck. His fingers found the cold metal of the hatpin. He stood up and considered his surroundings: drab wallpaper and curtains, some mildewed and sentimental prints of animals, a wash table with a tilting mirror, a heap of discarded clothes.

'You will notice,' said Rheinhardt, 'that her dress is at the bottom of the pile, then her corset, then her drawers, and finally her stockings. It appears that she removed her garments in a leisurely fashion – casually dropping each item onto the floor.'

Liebermann opened a small wardrobe in which he found a coat and some more dresses. Above the horizontal rail was a shelf on which the woman kept her hat, underwear and gloves.

'Who is she?'

'Bathild Babel, a shop girl, aged eighteen. She came to Vienna six months ago from Styria.' Liebermann threw a quizzical glance at his friend. 'I've just finished interviewing Fräulein Babel's neighbour, Frau Prodoprigora.'

'How was Fräulein Babel discovered?'

'Frau Prodoprigora noticed that the front door had been left open and came in to investigate.'

'Interesting.'

'Why do you say that?'

'Well, the door must have been left open by the perpetrator.'

'So?'

'An open door is conspicuous and could only serve to hasten police involvement.'

'Which means?'

'A vestige of conscience still survives. Some part of him *wants* to be stopped.'

Rheinhardt sighed: 'Perhaps he simply departed in a hurry and neglected to pull the door hard enough to ensure its closure.'

'No action, however trivial it may seem, is truly accidental.'

'I don't know, Max,' said Rheinhardt wearily. 'If he wanted to be caught surely he would simply present himself at a police station and confess.'

'The human mind is not a unified whole,' Liebermann responded, 'but rather a community of parts, each with different requirements and objectives, and each possessed of varying amounts of knowledge concerning its accessories. Professor Freud has demonstrated that contradictory beliefs and desires are an essential feature of the human condition. In a sense, he has rendered the Greek aphorism *know thyself* utterly meaningless. There is no self – as we imagine it – to know. While one part of the mind attempts to execute an action another part resists. I have no doubt that the perpetrator *intended* to close the door; however, a remnant of his conscience exerted sufficient influence to arrest the action before it was completed.'

Rheinhardt pulled at his chin.

'Perhaps he feels invulnerable and left the door open out of contempt for the security office.

114

It might be translated as: *I do not need to be careful because I am confident you will not catch me.*'

Liebermann turned to look at his friend and smiled.

'Actually, both hypotheses might be true. The perpetrator might have left the door open, partly because of a desire to be stopped and partly out of conceit. Once again I would remind you that Professor Freud considers human behaviour to be the result of many – sometimes contradictory – impulses.'

Rheinhardt did not wish to delve any deeper into psychoanalytic theory and returned the conversation to the terra firma of conventional detection.

'Fräulein Babel was typical of her class. She had made the acquaintance of several gentlemen from whom she accepted small gifts and dinner invitations; however, she was not in the habit of bringing them home. Her assignations usually took place in private dining rooms and hotels.'

'Fräulein Babel discussed such intimate details of her life with her neighbour?'

'The two women were very close. When we spoke, Frau Prodoprigora was distraught – and not just because of the shocking nature of her discovery. She was clearly very fond of her young friend.'

'Where is she now?'

'On her way to the Schottenring station to make a statement.' Rheinhardt took a slim volume from his pocket. 'I found this.' He held it up. 'In the kitchen.'

'An address book?'

'Yes. It doesn't contain many names – but there are a few entries of interest.' Rheinhardt turned some pages. 'Here, for example. Velentin Frece. The address given is an accountancy firm called Fischof and Cerny on Singerstrasse. I doubt Fräulein Babel needed the services of an accountant. Presumably Herr Frece gave Fräulein Babel his work address to avoid personal correspondence falling into the hands of Frau Frece.'

Liebermann closed the wardrobe door and stood at the end of the bed. He dropped to his knees, leaned forward, and inspected the linen.

'We must suppose that, like Adele Zeiler, Fräulein Babel consented to sexual intercourse. She removed her clothes in a provocative manner before lying down in readiness to *receive* her guest. During their congress, he brought her head forward and inserted the hatpin – a new gift and readily at hand – through the foramen magnum of her skull and into her brain. Observing her death made him culminate.' Liebermann stood up and in less pensive tones asked: 'Where is the photographer?'

'He has already been. I was just waiting for you and the mortuary van.'

'Is Professor Mathias to undertake the autopsy?'

'Yes.'

Liebermann took his spectacles from his top pocket and began cleaning them with a handkerchief.

'Did you receive my note concerning Miss Lydgate?'

'She wants to see Mathias at work . . .'

'And assist in the investigation.'

'Well, I have no objection. You are welcome to invite her along, although it is a peculiar request for a young woman to make – to attend a police autopsy.'

'It might be advisable to leave that sentiment unexpressed in her company, Oskar.'

'Oh?'

'She is a medical student, accustomed to the dissection of corpses, and I believe that Miss Lydgate has strong views concerning equality between the sexes. I fear she might be offended were you to imply that pathology was not an appropriate interest for a young woman.'

Rheinhardt got up from his chair and sighed.

'Sometimes I feel lost in the modern world. All of the old certainties seem to have vanished.' He looked down at the naked form of Fräulein Babel and, clapping a hand on Liebermann's shoulder, said: 'Come, Max – let's wait for the mortuary van outside.'

Liebermann put on his spectacles and followed the melancholy inspector.

CHAPTER 18

You wanted to know more about my early life – and my first erotic experiences. I suppose that is to be expected under the circumstances. Well, I am happy to oblige. Indeed, I must confess that I am finding this exercise curiously satisfying. It is like the relief one feels after divulging a long-held secret. Even a small concealment becomes burdensome. It weighs heavily on the soul. The desire to share it with others mounts, until disclosure becomes irresistible. Imagine, then, how I must feel now. It is like some great catharsis – the untying of a Gordian knot. You have promised me peace when this history is complete. I must admit I did not believe you. But as I write more I can see there may be something in it.

Are you familiar with the folk customs of upper Bavaria and the Balkans? At funerals, food is prepared and laid on the coffin of the deceased. A person, known as the sin-eater, is summoned to the house, and by eating the food the sin-eater absolves the deceased of his sins. The food takes the form of bread, *dead-loaves*, or simple sweetmeats – *dead-cakes*.

You have an appetite for my sins. You are hungry for them. I can see it in your eyes.

But again, I digress. You wanted to know about the awakening of Eros.

Memory is unreliable, yet I am sure that in this respect my recollections are accurate. I was precocious. When those village women, full of pity and love and sorrow, pulled me close and I inhaled their salty, sugary fragrances I was aware of their physicality, the softness and warmth beneath the dirndls, and I experienced a curious sensation that I would later come to identify with desire. At first the sensation was very faint and located in my stomach. It was almost indistinguishable from anxious anticipation. But in due course the sensation matured, becoming stronger and more finely nuanced. Expectancy became a pleasurable tension and the fearfulness became guilt. Why is it – I wonder – that even the very first intimations of sexual pleasure are tainted with an undertow of shame?

My mind filled with images of nudity and a corresponding desire to be naked myself. The only opportunity I had to be naked was at night. I would slip off my nightshirt and run my hands over my body. If the moon was bright I would fold back the eiderdown and look upon my nakedness with eager satisfaction. Such was my guilty conscience – I have always suffered from scruples – that I became excessively anxious about disturbing my father. I imagined him bursting in,

119

catching me in my state of undress and meting out some form of retributive punishment. The idea that he might harm my manhood came into my mind. In this nervous state, every sound I made – every rustle of the sheets, every creak of the mattress springs – seemed horribly loud, and I formed the habit of remaining very still and holding my breath.

I wonder now whether the fear of being discovered became itself sexually exciting. When I consider my subsequent behaviour, this would seem to be so. I would steal away into the woods, alone, where I would take off my clothes and stand naked for hours. All the time I was fearful of being observed by someone from the village, but I could not stop myself.

The fluttering sensation that had formerly been in my stomach descended and settled in my loins. This transmigration coincided with my burgeoning interest in the anatomy of girls. I managed to persuade some of them to venture into the woods with me. One of their number – a simple-minded creature called Gerda – I persuaded to strip. I instructed her to stand very still while holding her breath. It was intolerably exciting. This was when I first experienced an adult *response*. The lick of fire on the thighs: animation of the flesh.

Of all the girls in the village the one I loved most was Netti. I adored her. She was sweet-natured, kind and beautiful. We played together – but she would never come walking with me. One winter she fell ill and became very weak. She had to stay in bed. The children in the village were not permitted to visit her. I can remember how the women spoke softly whenever Netti's name was mentioned. They looked at each other and pulled their little ones close. They feared infection.

Netti died just before Christmas.

My father made a point of going to pay his respects. It was in his nature to do such things. He could be contrary – and his black moods made him reckless. We marched through the snow, down the hill to Netti's house, where we were shown into the parlour to see the dead child in her casket. The room was filled with flowers. I can still remember the intoxicating scent. Long purple drapes covered the mirrors and a massive silver crucifix had been hung on one of the walls. Four candles, on large stands, filled the room with a fitful yellow light.

Netti looked exquisite. And so very still – a stillness and a breathless tranquillity that I had never seen before. In Vienna, you hear people saying that they hope to have a *schöne Leich* – a beautiful corpse. Netti was a *schöne Leich*. Truly.

My father said a prayer and rose to leave. I could not move. I was transfixed by Netti. I begged him to let me stay a few minutes longer so that I might say one final goodbye to my playmate. He squeezed my arm and left the room: big shoulders hunched – face grey and drawn.

I stared at Netti and felt the fluttering sensation below. It intensified until my loins were tense. I felt my flesh move.

But how to continue?

What followed is really inexpressible. Language is insufficient. I can offer you only an *approximate* description, a correspondent situation with which you will be familiar that reflects *something* of my experience. When a great cathedral organ is played, you hear music – but you can also feel the pew vibrating. What I am capable of expressing bears the same relationship to my *actual* experience as the vibrating pew does to the music. What I can express is only a small part of an ineffable whole.

This is what happened: *I felt as though I was being watched.* The impression was so strong that I turned round. But there was nobody there. Even so, this did nothing to mitigate the feeling. The evidence of my physical senses had become irrelevant. There was someone in the room – a presence. It did not cross my mind that this manifestation might be the ghost of my playmate, nor was I afraid.

I do not know how long I remained like this – watchful, curious – it may have been for some time. My father came back to collect me. Before we left, Netti's mother kissed my forehead. Her tears froze on my skin as we stepped out into the cold.

Christmas came and went. The villagers were

uneasy, fearful, and also ashamed after Netti's death. They had not been good neighbours. My only pleasurable memory that December is of a market. I was taken to a Christkindlmarkt by one of the women, who bought me some small gifts: a candle and a fir-tree decoration, a wooden angel painted gold and red. I touched its wings and thought of my mother.

January came and with it another death.

Gerda. Poor, simple-minded Gerda.

She went skating, the ice broke, she fell through and froze to death.

Once again, I stood at the foot of an open casket. How different Gerda looked: how dignified, how composed, how still. I stood with my back to the door – to ensure that I would not be surprised – and touched myself. The pleasure that I experienced was intense, violent and strange. I was too immature to achieve a release. Instead, I experienced a muscular convulsion, followed by pains.

And then, as before, I sensed that I was not alone. The presence I had felt beside Netti's casket had returned. Everything shifted and the next thing I can remember is waking up in my bedroom at home. I had passed out.

I was feverish and my father called the doctor. It was obvious that he was concerned about my health. I asked them if I was going to die – like Netti. The doctor said *No, of course not,* but he spoke without conviction. My condition got worse: sickness, weakness – I could not eat. At night I had such dreams – shadowy female figures and the sound of beating wings. I would wake in a sweat, trembling, delirious. It is impossible for me to say how long I languished in this state and I later learned that I came close to dying. And it was when my illness had taken me to the very threshold of oblivion that I saw *her* for the first time. Death does not come in the shape of a hooded skeleton, carrying a scythe. Death comes in the shape of an angel – and she is more beautiful than you can possibly imagine.

CHAPTER 19

Professor Mathias was standing by a trolley, arranging and rearranging his tools. He picked up a mallet, placed it on a lower shelf, and then positioned a knife so that it was exactly level with a small chisel; however, he was clearly dissatisfied with the result. The alignment was not quite right. Shaking his head, he picked up the offending instrument, carefully put it back, and nudged it several times until a final but barely perceptible shift met with his approval.

Rheinhardt had long since abandoned trying to fathom the scheme which Professor Mathias employed to determine the appropriate placement of instruments on his trolley. Liebermann had urged him not to try since, in the young doctor's opinion, Professor Mathias's preparatory ritual was symptomatic of an obsessional neurosis.

The old man took a small saw, reversed its orientation, and after a considerable pause placed it on the trolley's bottom shelf.

Mathias's ritual was not always so lengthy and, very occasionally, he managed to proceed without its performance. There was a strong relationship between the extent of Mathias's ritualising and his mood. The more he ritualised, the more likely it was that he would be irascible.

Mathias rolled up his shirtsleeves and moved a drill a fraction to the left.

'Professor?' ventured Liebermann.

'What?' Mathias looked up, his lips pursed. He did not like to be disturbed while making his preparations.

'I am acquainted with a medical student who chanced to hear of your reputation.' The professor sneered. 'She wanted to see you at work,' Liebermann persevered. 'I took the liberty of inviting her.' He studied the professor for a reaction and, when there was none, risked one more word: 'Today.' Still the professor did not react. 'I hope you will not object. Of course, if you do, that is perfectly—'

'She!' Mathias raised his eyebrows. 'What do you mean: "she"?'

'The medical student is a woman, Herr professor.'

Liebermann failed to see how he could answer Mathias's question in any other way, but he still felt foolish stating the obvious.

Mathias mumbled to himself and his expression changed from disgruntlement to weary indifference.

'Providing she keeps out of my way and doesn't say anything empty-headed, I have no objection.'

'Thank you, Herr professor,' said Liebermann, exhaling with relief.

Rheinhardt offered Liebermann a cigarette, and the two men smoked while Professor Mathias busied himself again with his tools. A large electric light was suspended above the autopsy table and twisting filaments floated across its powerful beam. Mortuary sheets had been laid over Bathild Babel's body, but her curled right hand had slipped out from beneath the coverings: it looked small and pathetic.

As Professor Mathias finally reached the conclusion of his ritual, there was a gentle knock on the door.

'Ah, that will be the student,' said Liebermann.

'Then you'd better let *her* in,' said the professor.

When Amelia Lydgate entered, Liebermann took her coat and placed it on the stand. She was wearing a grey skirt and a plain white blouse, and her hair had been compressed into a tight bun.

'Thank you so much for inviting me,' she whispered.

'Come – let me introduce you to Professor Mathias.' Liebermann guided her to the autopsy table. Gesturing towards his friend he added: 'Inspector Rheinhardt you already know.'

'Miss Lydgate,' said the inspector, bowing. 'I had hoped we might encounter each other again in more happy circumstances. But it seems that – as before – a terrible tragedy,' he nodded at the sheets, 'has brought us together.'

'And this gentleman,' Liebermann continued, 'is Professor Mathias. Herr professor, may I introduce Miss Amelia Lydgate.'

'Thank you, sir, for permitting me to attend,' said Amelia. 'I am most grateful.'

Mathias tightened the knot of his apron and looked from the newcomer to Rheinhardt.

'You too are acquainted with this lady?'

'Yes,' said Rheinhardt. 'Miss Lydgate is a talented microscopist and an expert on blood.'

'A pupil of Landsteiner,' Liebermann interjected.

'She was of considerable service to the security office last year,' said Rheinhardt.

Amelia blushed.

'Inspector Rheinhardt – you exaggerate . . .'

'English, eh?' said Professor Mathias.

'My father is English, my mother of German origin.'

'And you are studying medicine at the University?'

'That is correct.'

'Who teaches you pathology?'

'Professor Wangermann. He speaks very highly of you.'

'Wangermann!' Mathias chuckled. 'He was in my tutorial group over twenty years ago: it must have been 'seventy-seven – or 'seventy-nine, perhaps. A competent fellow – as I recall – but unimaginative.'

'Miss Lydgate,' said Rheinhardt, interceding. 'Would you care to stand here?'

Amelia came forward and Rheinhardt stepped back to allow her to pass. As he did so he bumped against Professor Mathias's trolley, displacing all

128

the instruments. A few fell onto the floor, clattering loudly.

An ominous silence preceded Professor Mathias's cry.

'God in heaven, Rheinhardt! Look what you've done! Do you realise . . .' The old man struggled for breath. 'Do you realise . . .' He found the sentiment he wished to communicate inexpressible.

'I am so sorry, professor,' said Rheinhardt.

'I'll have to start all over again now!'

'Surely not,' cried Rheinhardt.

'It is essential that everything is in its right place,' Mathias insisted.

Liebermann tensed as he saw Amelia Lydgate bend down to pick up the fallen instruments from the floor. He tensed even more when he saw her meddling with what remained of Mathias's meticulous arrangement.

'Miss Lydgate!' said Professor Mathias. 'Have you not caused enough trouble already? What exactly do you think you are doing?'

'Preparing your trolley,' said the Englishwoman, 'so that you may proceed.'

Liebermann saw her move a mallet and winced.

'Would you please,' Mathias's fists were clenched, 'leave my instruments alone.'

Amelia made one more adjustment and then, standing up, brushed her skirt.

Liebermann and Rheinhardt looked at each other. Their heads were lowered and their shoulders hunched, as though they were expecting the ceiling to collapse.

'Miss Lydgate!' said Professor Mathias. 'I am not accustomed . . .' He glanced at the trolley and his sentence trailed off. He looked back at Amelia – and then back at the trolley. This oscillation continued until he said: 'How did you do that?'

'I beg your pardon, sir?'

'Surely you couldn't have memorised—'

'I simply put the instruments in positions that I considered practical.'

Mathias examined the trolley more closely, his face screwed up with concentration. Quite suddenly, he laughed. It was a strained laugh, his disbelief introducing a note of hysteria into the outburst.

'That is very . . .' he said, returning his attention to Amelia. 'Satisfactory. Very satisfactory.' The professor continued staring at Amelia and by degrees his expression passed from bemusement, through curiosity, to something approximating respect. 'Well,' he said finally, 'shall we begin?'

Liebermann and Rheinhardt exchanged glances and sighed with relief.

Professor Mathias pulled back the mortuary sheets, revealing the naked body of Bathild Babel.

'She was discovered by her neighbour,' said Rheinhardt.

'In this state of undress?' asked Mathias.

'Yes. Lying on her bed – her clothes had been discarded on the floor. And she was killed in exactly the same way as Adele Zeiler.'

'Who is she?'

'Her name is Bathild Babel: a shop girl.'

Mathias stroked her forehead and said softly: '*To the quiet land. Who will guide us there? Who will guide us there with gentle hand: ah, across to the quiet land?*'

The old man looked up at Rheinhardt, his eyes liquid and luminous behind the magnifying lenses of his spectacles.

'Schiller?' asked the inspector.

'No,' said Mathias. 'How could it be? No – Johann Gaudenz-Freiherr von Salis-Seewis.'

Amelia looked quizzically at Liebermann, who shook his head as if to say: *it's nothing – ignore them.*

Mathias raised Bathild's head and pulled the hair away from the nape of her neck.

'Miss Lydgate . . .' The professor invited the Englishwoman to take a look.

'What is it?'

'The ornamental end of a hatpin,' said Professor Mathias. 'The pin itself has been inserted between the first cervical vertebra and the skull. It has been pushed through the foramen magnum and into the brain, thus damaging the fundamental life-preserving structures.' Professor Mathias pulled the hatpin out and held it aloft for all to see.

'In the newspapers,' said Amelia, 'it was reported that Adele Zeiler had been stabbed to death. I had assumed that the instrument used was a knife.'

'It is often necessary to withhold details of an inquiry for reasons of public safety,' said

131

Rheinhardt. 'It would be highly irresponsible to reveal ingenious and practicable methods of murder. Some readers might get ideas.'

Amelia nodded: 'I will respect your confidence.'

Mathias was still staring at the pin.

'You will notice,' he said, 'that there are two kinks: one close to the point, the other further down. The one near the point suggests that a first attempt at insertion failed. The point hit the base of the skull – instead of passing smoothly through the foramen magnum. This should not surprise us, as the manoeuvre is far from easy.'

Mathias dropped the hatpin into a glass retort, shuffled to the other end of the autopsy table, parted the woman's legs, and leaned forward. His nostrils flared.

'She has been used – by a man.' He glanced at Amelia. 'The male reproductive fluid has a distinctive odour. It intensifies, becoming pungent over time. If you wish to . . .' He gestured towards the woman's sex.

Liebermann was surprised by Amelia's response. She did not flinch or show any sign of disgust. Instead, she joined Professor Mathias, leaned forward, and inhaled.

'Like rancid oysters,' she said plainly.

'You will notice,' said Mathias, 'that there are no signs to suggest that this woman resisted ingress. The genital region is unscathed. Moreover, there is no bruising around her throat or abrasions around her wrists. When a woman is coerced, it is common for the assailant to ensure compliance by the threat of strangulation, or by tightly gripping her wrists. Observe: her skin is unmarked.'

Amelia listened attentively.

'You will also notice that her nails are unbroken,' said Mathias.

'May I inspect her hands?' asked Amelia.

'If you wish.'

Amelia lifted the woman's left hand and then her right.

'There is something under her nails.'

She reached up and pulled a hairpin out of her bun. Scraping the point beneath one of the corpse's nails, she dislodged a few dark grains which fell into her palm. She thrust her hand under the bright electric light and the grains became rubiginous.

'I think it's blood,' said Amelia.

Professor Mathias looked impressed. He nodded: 'She may have scratched her assailant before losing consciousness.'

'If this is the perpetrator's blood, then it may prove very useful,' said Amelia. 'Professor Mathias – do you have an envelope?'

'Useful?' asked Mathias.

'Landsteiner has demonstrated that human blood can be classified into three different types: A, B, and C. A fourth type – AB – was identified by Landsteiner's associate, Herr Doctor Sturli, only last year. It is possible to ascertain blood type from dehydrated samples or even a stain. According to Richter, the accurate identification of blood type is possible even if stains are up to two weeks old. If we know the perpetrator's blood type,' she turned to face Rheinhardt, 'you will be able to exclude certain suspects. Moreover, if when the perpetrator is apprehended he has the same blood type as this sample you will have a valuable piece of convergent evidence.'

Professor Mathias clapped his hands together. 'Excellent!' he cried. 'A splendid idea!'

CHAPTER 20

Kristina climbed the stairs. As she did so, her suspicions were aroused by the absence of any noise. The sewing machines were silent.

Her secretary, Wanda, had gone up to collect a garment some time ago but had not returned. Kristina had grown impatient.

The sound of voices . . .

Overcome with curiosity, Kristina tiptoed across the landing and placed her ear against the door.

'My mother has forbidden me to go out alone – not since the second one got killed.'

'There's no danger: not for the likes of us.'

'How can you be so sure?'

'The two that got killed: one was an artist's model, the other was a shop girl. She lived in *Spittelberg*.'

Now it was Wanda speaking: 'You think they were both prostitutes?'

'As good as.'

Another voice – rather low and ponderous: 'I'm not going out on my own, whatever you say. I'm frightened.'

'I'd get bored cooped up at home every night. It'd drive me mad.'

'I saw this man on the tram.' Again the low voice. 'He was staring at me.'

'I should be so lucky.'

Laughter.

'Albertine, you shouldn't joke about such things!'

Kristina opened the door and – miraculously – the seamstresses were all busy at work. The clatter of the machines and the girls' intent expressions suggested prolonged, concentrated industry. Wanda was standing, the dress that she had originally gone to collect hanging over her arm.

'I may not be as young as you girls,' Kristina shouted. 'But I can assure you, I am not going deaf!'

Guilty looks: burning cheeks. One or two machines slowed as the pretence of work was abandoned.

'We were talking about the murders, madame.'

'I know.'

'It's almost dark when we leave, madame. I don't want to walk home in the dark . . .'

'What are you talking about? Dark? It's getting lighter every day.'

'But, madame . . .'

Another girl, the one with the low voice, said: 'In my magazine it said the streets are no longer safe for young women, especially at night.'

Kristina looked around the room, up and down

136

the rows of expectant faces. The last machine slowed to a halt.

Silence.

'All right,' said Kristina. 'You can leave a little earlier – but only if you promise to work harder. We won't be able to deliver the new orders on time if you sit around gossiping all day.'

A chorus of thanks and promises.

Kristina beckoned Wanda.

'Come on. And please don't slouch so.'

'Yes, madame,' said the secretary, straightening her back and following her mistress.

CHAPTER 21

Rheinhardt entered Café Museum clutching Bathild Babel's address book. He did not find the ambience of the new coffee house very welcoming. It felt rather cold and the plain decor appeared unfinished. Shortly after Café Museum opened, Rheinhardt had asked Liebermann what he thought of it. The young doctor had insisted that the architect – Adolf Loos – was a genius, and spoke enthusiastically about the virtue of clear lines and simplicity. The inspector had not been persuaded by Liebermann's arguments and remained completely unmoved by the stark functional interior. He could not see beauty in emptiness, only a lack of invention. He hoped, as he sat at a table, that the cakes would not be as bland as the coffee house's design.

He ordered a Türkische coffee and a piece of Dobostorte. When the cake arrived – a baroque creation festooned with complex embellishments – he was grateful that the chef had not succumbed to the culinary equivalent of modernity. The pressure of his fork forced generous applications of chocolate cream to bulge out between the layers of sponge, and when he took the first mouthful of the Dobostorte the sweetness and intensity of the flavour produced in him a feeling of deep satisfaction.

When he had finished the cake, Rheinhardt asked to see the head waiter. The man who arrived was not unlike himself. A portly gentleman with a well-waxed moustache.

His name was Herr Heregger.

'I trust the Dobostorte was to your satisfaction, sir?'

'It was excellent. The consistency of the chocolate cream was particularly good.'

Rheinhardt showed the waiter his identification.

'Security office?' asked Herr Heregger, surprised.

'Yes – please take a seat.' The waiter lowered his large haunches onto a spindly chair, and Rheinhardt opened Bathild Babel's address book. 'I'm looking for a man called Griesser. He gave Café Museum as his address. Do you know him?'

'Yes, I do. He's a customer.'

'How long has he been coming here?'

'Actually, he's only been a few times.'

'Recently?'

'Yes, last week and the week before. He told me that he'd just moved to Vienna and was living in temporary accommodation. He asked if it would be possible for us to collect his mail, as it was his intention to breakfast at Café Museum when he was settled. I said that I had no objection.'

139

'Did any letters arrive?'

'Just one.'

'And did he collect it?'

'On his second visit.'

'And he's had no more since?'

'No.'

Rheinhardt offered Herr Heregger a cigar, but the man refused.

'Did Herr Griesser tell you what his profession was?'

'No.'

'What do you *think* he did for a living?'

'I have no idea.'

'Can you describe him to me?'

The head waiter scratched his chin.

'Tallish. Black hair.' His tone was cautious – as though he lacked confidence in the accuracy of his memory.

'Eye colour?' Rheinhardt prompted.

'Oh, I can't remember that, inspector.'

'Age?'

'Quite young.'

'What? Early twenties? Mid-twenties?'

'Yes. Mid- to late twenties, I should think.'

'Educated?'

'He spoke well.'

'Anything else you remember?' The head waiter looked across the floor towards the two billiard tables. His vacant expression changed suddenly, a glimmer of light appearing in his eyes. 'What is it?'

'Well, now that you mention it . . .'

'What?'

'I *can* remember something else about him.' Heregger smiled and a second chin appeared beneath the first. 'His smell.'

'His cologne?'

'No. It was something else. A sweet, tarry smell. Like carbolic.'

CHAPTER 22

Liebermann looked at his supine patient. For once, though, Erstweiler was not agitated. Liebermann made no assumptions about his mental state. Sometimes the apparent calm of anxious patients was actually exhaustion, and as soon as they had recovered their strength the agitation returned.

After a prolonged silence, Liebermann inquired: 'Did you sleep well?'

Erstweiler rolled his head from side to side.

'No. I woke up several times . . . one of the other patients on the ward became distressed. He was shouting something about the Hungarians coming. I managed to get to sleep after he was removed, but woke again from a bad dream.'

'Oh?'

'I say bad, but that's only how it felt at the time. Now that I think about it, the dream was really rather silly.'

'Were you frightened by the dream?'

'Yes.'

'What was it about?'

Erstweiler sighed.

'When I was very young, my parents had an English friend, Frau Middleton, who used to tell my brother and me fairy stories. Some of them were already familiar to us, but others were unfamiliar. I suppose these latter stories must have been of English origin. One of them concerned a boy without any money and some magic beans – have you come across it?'

'No, I haven't.'

'Well, the dream I had was very much like this English fairy story – except I was the boy. The dream was quite confused, though, especially the beginning.'

Liebermann remained silent, hoping that this would be sufficient to make Erstweiler continue. The strategy was unsuccessful. Erstweiler reverted to his earlier concern. 'What was wrong with that patient? The one who was taken off the ward? What did he mean by "*the Hungarians are coming*"?'

'Your dream, Herr Erstweiler? What happened in your dream?' Liebermann urged.

Erstweiler rotated his hand in the air for a few moments and then let it drop onto his chest.

'There were trams and large buildings and a man with a cow, who I spoke to – he might have sold me the beans – and suddenly I was the boy in the story and the beans had grown into a huge beanstalk which rose up into the sky. I climbed the beanstalk and found myself on a cloud, and on the cloud was a huge castle. I entered the castle but was frightened by the sound of an ogre, stomping around and crying out that he could smell the blood of an intruder – *my* blood. In one of the rooms I discovered mountains of treasure and a goose laying golden eggs. Not eggs the colour of gold, you understand, but eggs *made* from gold. I picked the goose up and ran from the castle, pursued by the ogre. I slid down the beanstalk and the ogre followed, but he wasn't as quick as me. When I got to the bottom I chopped the beanstalk down with an axe—' Erstweiler suddenly broke off, his forehead glistening with perspiration.

'Yes?' Liebermann prompted.

'And the ogre tumbled to the ground.'

'Did he die?'

'Yes, he . . .' Erstweiler paused before completing his sentence with a stutter '. . . d-d-died.'

'You escaped, then,' said Liebermann. 'And with the goose.'

Erstweiler showed no signs of relief.

'Herr doctor, why are we talking about a ridiculous childish dream? Surely there are more important things to discuss. I had hoped you would be applying yourself to the task of convincing me that the appearance of my doppelgänger was nothing more than a hallucination. At least then I might allow myself a glimmer of hope, the prospect of peace.'

'The two may be connected – the dream and the hallucination.'

'Impossible!' Erstweiler cried.

The anger invested in this explosive denial was sufficient to convince Liebermann that he was correct. After an extended hiatus Liebermann said: 'I went to see Herr Polster, at The Chimney Sweep.'

'Did you?'

Erstweiler twisted awkwardly on the rest bed in order to make eye contact with Liebermann.

'Yes,' said the young doctor. 'He remembered the conversation you referred to. But he didn't think he had spoken to your doppelgänger. He was confident that he had spoken to *you*.'

'That's hardly surprising, is it?' said Erstweiler, sighing. 'What did you think he would say?'

CHAPTER 23

Rheinhardt was shown into the accountant's office by a middle-aged woman wearing a high-collared blouse.

'Herr Frece,' she said: 'Inspector Rheinhardt to see you.'

'Ah, thank you, Anselma,' said the accountant. He was balding, red-faced, and possessed a large stomach that pressed against his waistcoat. 'Please, do sit down, inspector.' Rheinhardt caught sight of a framed photograph on Frece's desk, showing a matronly woman and two children. 'Would you like some tea?' Rheinhardt shook his head. 'That will be all, Anselma.' When the secretary had gone, Frece smiled and added: 'How can I be of assistance?'

'Herr Frece, I understand that you are acquainted with a young lady called Bathild Babel. Is that correct?'

Frece pursed his lips.

'Fräulein Babel . . . Fräulein Babel . . .' He muttered. 'No. I'm afraid that name isn't familiar to me.'

Rheinhardt sighed.

'You are mentioned in her address book.'

'Bathild?' said Frece, cupping his ear and feigning deafness. 'Did you say *Bathild* Babel?' He stressed the syllables of 'Bathild' in a peculiar way.

'Yes,' said Rheinhardt. 'Bathild Babel.'

The accountant shifted in his chair.

'Yes, yes . . . I *do* know someone of that name. I'm sorry, my hearing isn't very good.'

'And what is the nature of your relationship?'

'She is a client.'

'I see. Could I see her documents, please?'

'I'm afraid that won't be possible . . .'

'Why not?'

'Because . . .' Frece searched the ceiling for a convincing answer, but the cornicing failed to supply one.

'Herr Frece,' said Rheinhardt firmly. 'If you continue to be uncooperative, I am afraid we will have to continue this interview at the Schottenring station.'

'Please – no,' said the accountant. 'I'm sorry. That won't be necessary.' He opened a cigarette box with trembling fingers and struck a match. After lighting the cigarette, he drew on its gold filter. His exhalation dissipated the cloud of smoke that hung in front of his mouth. 'I'm sorry, inspector . . . a man in my position. It was a mistake . . . I never should have . . .' His voice trailed off.

'Where did you meet her?'

'With respect, inspector, why should my peccadilloes be of interest to the police? I don't understand.'

147

Rheinhardt glared at the accountant.

'Where did you meet her?' he repeated.

'In Frau Schuschnig's hat shop, behind the Town Hall. I was buying a hat for my wife. Bathild was very forward.' Rheinhardt listened as Frece spoke of his illicit meetings with Bathild Babel, in private dining rooms and cheap hotels. At its conclusion, Frece pleaded: 'Inspector, if my wife were to find out she would be mortified. She hasn't any idea. My marriage would be over.' The accountant reached out and turned the family photograph towards Rheinhardt. 'I have two children. Richarda and Friedo. I beg you to be discreet – if not for my sake, then for theirs.'

Rheinhardt chewed the end of his pencil.

'Did she ever speak of her other . . .' Rheinhardt thought *clients* was too strong a word and chose a less offensive substitute '. . . admirers?'

'I beg your pardon?'

'Her other gentleman friends,' said Rheinhardt.

The accountant looked indignant.

'I was her only . . .' Frece was unable to finish his sentence, given Rheinhardt's world-weary expression. He might as well have said out loud: *You can't possibly be that naive!* Frece's shoulders fell. 'No,' the accountant continued. 'She didn't mention anyone else.'

Rheinhardt made a few notes and when he looked up again Frece was staring into space.

'What is it?' Rheinhardt asked.

'I remember, I went to the hat shop a few weeks

ago, and Bathild was talking to a man. They seemed very familiar. After he had left, I asked her who he was. She was evasive and tried to make a joke of her flirtation. She said she flirted with all the men who came into the shop – it was good for business, according to Frau Schuschnig.' Frece scratched his nose. 'He was educated and wearing an expensive frock coat.'

'What did he look like?'

'Quite tall – dark hair.'

'How old?'

'Twenty-nine, thirty – perhaps.'

'What colour were his eyes?'

'I beg your pardon?'

'Think, Herr Frece. What colour were his eyes?'

'Blue . . . or grey . . . I can't be sure. A light colour anyway. He was buying a hat pin. And he smelt rather strange. A sort of hospital smell.'

'Could he have been a doctor?'

'Possibly.' Frece observed the tightening of Rheinhardt's facial muscles, the sudden intensifying of his expression. 'Inspector, why are you asking me all of these questions?'

'She's dead,' said Rheinhardt bluntly. 'Murdered – on Saturday.'

The accountant said something inaudible, and the colour drained from his ruddy cheeks. His hands shook so much that when he tried to light a second cigarette Rheinhardt was obliged to give him some assistance.

CHAPTER 24

Professor Freud tapped the ash from his cigar and consulted the pages of a manuscript. The writing was his own: regular and leaning forward, showing, perhaps, a certain impatience to proceed, ideas arriving more swiftly than his hand could comfortably transcribe. He opened his mouth, releasing a cloud of smoke that tarried in the air before losing definition in the already opaque atmosphere.

They had been discussing the professor's unpublished and unfinished work on sexuality, and Liebermann had – by means of subtle questioning – moved the conversation from more general considerations to the specific problem of deviance.

'The sexual instinct is, I believe, infinitely pliable with respect to its aims,' said Freud. 'Indeed, I am of the belief that all human beings are born with what might be described as a *polymorphously perverse* disposition: that is to say, a disposition that can be diverted into all possible kinds of sexual irregularity.' He was in full spate, glancing down at the text to remind himself of his conclusions. 'If one defines healthy sexual behaviour as that which is necessary for human reproduction, namely, heterosexual congress, it follows that all *other* forms of arousal-seeking behaviour are surplus, and therefore, in a literal sense, perverse. Their introduction into marital relations does little to further the primary reproductive purpose of the union between man and woman. Yet . . .' Freud sucked on his cigar. 'The human sexual instinct is so plastic that we find evidence of its Protean character everywhere – even in the most ordinary couplings. Take, for example, fetishism. The point of contact with the normal is provided by the psychologically essential overvaluation of the sexual object, which invariably extends to everything that is associated with it. A certain degree of fetishism is thus usually present in normal love, especially in those stages of it in which the normal sexual aim seems unattainable or its fulfilment prevented. May I remind you of Goethe's *Faust*, Part One, Scene Seven.' He looked at Liebermann expectantly.

The young doctor shook his head, indicating that he could not recall so precise a reference.

'*Get me a kerchief from her breast,*' Freud intoned. '*A garter that her knee has pressed.*'

The professor nodded, impressed by his own apposite example.

'When, then,' asked Liebermann, 'does the situation become pathological?'

'When the longing for the fetish passes beyond the point of being merely a necessary condition attached to the sexual object and actually *takes the place* of the normal aim, and, further, when the fetish becomes detached from a particular individual and becomes the *sole* sexual object.'

'Do you believe the polymorphous disposition has limits? Or do you believe that anything can become sexually arousing?'

'If you harbour any doubts,' said Freud, pushing the cigar box towards his guest, 'then you need look no further than the pages of Krafft-Ebing's *Psychopathia Sexualis.*' Freud stubbed out his own cigar, lit Liebermann's, and then took another for himself. 'Moreover,' he continued, touching the end of his cigar to the flame and rolling it between his thumb and forefinger. 'I am not so sure that Krafft-Ebing's cases – however disturbing – exhibit behaviours that are qualitatively different from those which might be observed also in the bedroom of a respectable household.' Freud glanced again at his manuscript: 'The most common and the most significant of all perversions – the desire to inflict pain upon the sexual object and its reverse – received from Krafft-Ebing the names *sadism* and *masochism*. As regards to sadism, the roots are easy to detect in the normal. The sexuality of most male human beings contains an element of aggressiveness – a desire to subjugate; the biological significance of it seems to lie in the need for overcoming the resistance of the sexual object by means other than the process of wooing. Thus, sadism would correspond to an aggressive component of the sexual instinct which has become independent and exaggerated and, by displacement, has usurped the leading position.'

'What you suggest implies that – given the right constellation of influences – any of us might have become one of Krafft-Ebing's monsters.'

'Indeed.' Freud toyed with one of the statuettes that stood next to the cigar box – a vulture with a worn, featureless head, perched on a pedestal. 'Binet was the first to maintain that the choice of a fetish is an after-effect of some sexual impression, received as a rule in early childhood . . .' He spoke these words dreamily, and Liebermann sensed they were more like a private afterthought than a conclusion. The tone of Freud's voice conveyed two rather contradictory meanings. On the one hand, he seemed glad that he was not the only person to entertain such ideas, but on the other, he appeared slightly resentful of the fact that he must concede intellectual priority to another theorist.

A silence prevailed, during which time the smoke haze intensified to such an extent that everything in the room acquired the flat colour-tones of a sepia photograph.

Liebermann had learned enough to give him confidence in his speculative diagnosis of *thanatophilia*. Freud's new ideas on deviance seemed to legitimise all possibilities. With respect to the erotic instinct, anything was possible. Wishing to make the most of his time with the great man, Liebermann resolved to test his views on another topic.

'I have an interesting patient,' the young doctor ventured, changing position to disturb Freud's reverie.

The professor looked up: 'I'm sorry?'

'I have an interesting patient,' Liebermann repeated. 'At the hospital: a gentleman who thinks he's seen his doppelgänger – and now must die.'

Freud waved his cigar, indicating that he wished to hear more. Liebermann adopted the telegraphic style of medical men when summarising a case history: 'Herr E. Born in Tulln: worked as secretary to a councillor in the Town Hall: lost his job when his employer died: came to Vienna – and is currently employed as an importer's administrator.' After sketching Erstweiler's background, Liebermann recounted his patient's descriptions of seeing his double.

Freud puffed repeatedly on his cigar until the smoke which he was producing became so abundant that he all but vanished behind it. Liebermann sensed that the great man was deep in thought and waited respectfully. Eventually, Freud cleared his throat.

'The idea that we possess a double most probably originates from our earliest experience of reflections. In a mirror, we see ourselves as something separate, removed; however, this illusion must have preceded the invention of the looking-glass. Our primitive ancestors would have viewed

154

their "doubles" in the surface of still water – or even as a tiny homunculus in the eyes of others. Thus, as soon as human beings could form the concept of self, experience of reflections would have suggested the existence of *another self*. We must conclude, therefore, that the idea of the double is deeply rooted in the human psyche.'

Freud seemed pleased with this initial exposition, and smiled before continuing: 'Now, let us turn our attention to religious teachings. In all cultures, the idea of the double appears in the guise of a soul – a spiritual doppelgänger. And wherever we find religion, we also find the terror of oblivion. So . . .' He paused to produce another volcanic cloud. 'It is possible that the double represents a defence against the destruction of the ego, as the soul – the first double of the body – is an insurance against anni-hilation. The operation of this defence is evident in the burial rites of ancient Egypt, where it was commonplace to make images of the dead in lasting materials.' Freud pointed to a tiny bronze box with the figurine of a bird on its lid. 'See here: this coffin for a sacred animal. Late period. Between about seven hundred and three hundred BC.' He was unable to resist stroking the falcon's beak. 'The desire for eternal life springs from the soil of unbounded self-love, from the primary narcissism which dominates the mind of the child and of prim-itive man. But when this stage has been surmounted, the double reverses its aspect. From having been an assurance of immortality it becomes an uncanny harbinger of death. It is in this form that the double is better known to the German-speaking peoples.'

The professor took another cigar from his cigar box.

'And there may be another process at work: it may be that material offensive to the ego – unacceptable fantasies, all the strivings of the ego which adverse external circumstances have crushed, and all our suppressed acts of volition – are projected outwards to something foreign. But such material cannot be disowned completely, and the object into which this undesirable material is incorporated takes the form of another self.'

Liebermann wanted to discuss this point further, but the professor had returned to an earlier theme: 'Doubling as a preservation against extinction also has its counterpart in the language of dreams. If one of the ordinary symbols for a penis – a tower, let us say – occurs in a dream doubled – thus, two towers – the doubling must be regarded as the warding-off of castration.'

Freud picked up another cigar and lit it. He was about to put the used match in his ashtray when he noticed that he had not finished the cigar he had been smoking. He had simply put it down for a few moments and forgotten that it was there.

'Mmm . . . two cigars,' he muttered.

His expression darkened, and with evident unease he stubbed out his old cigar and put the new one into his mouth.

CHAPTER 25

Rheinhardt was seated next to his wife Else, and further down the park bench his eldest daughter, Therese, was reading a book. His younger daughter, Mitzi, was deliberating with another girl whether or not to get on the merry-go-round (which had been commandeered by two boys wearing short trousers and flat caps). A group of mothers, dressed rather too finely for the occasion, were conversing in the shade of a tree, while two nursemaids rocked perambulators in order to keep the tiny occupants asleep.

'I was speaking to Frau Gaul this morning,' said Else. 'She went to the opera on Saturday to see Pagliacci. She said it was wonderful.'

Since the discovery of Adele Zeiler's body in the Volksgarten, Rheinhardt had had few opportunities to spend time with his family. The normality of sitting in the park with his wife and daughters was like a spiritual emollient.

'Would you like to go?'

'Yes,' Else replied, somewhat surprised by her husband's response. He was always so busy that it had not occurred to her that he might act on Frau Gaul's recommendation.

'Then we *shall* go.' Rheinhardt paused for a moment before adding, 'In fact, we'll all go – and to blazes with the expense. Would you like to see Pagliacci, Therese?'

His daughter looked up from her book, making heroic efforts to hide her excitement. In actuality she had not been reading at all, only pretending to do so while listening to her parents' conversation.

'Yes, father, very much.'

Therese's composure reminded Rheinhardt that his daughter was on the cusp of adulthood. Once the transition was complete, the child whose hair he had kissed and whose little hand had gripped his forefinger so tightly in front of the lion's cage at the zoo would be gone. It was a loss that he accepted philosophically, but to which a part of him would never be fully reconciled.

'Good,' he said decisively. 'I'll get some tickets this evening.'

Rheinhardt felt his wife's hand covering his own. She squeezed his fingers together and by means of this subtle gesture communicated more gratitude and affection than could ever be expressed using words. The fact that something so consequential could pass between them in a public place, without notice, was further evidence – as far as Rheinhardt was concerned – of the miraculous nature of his marriage.

'Is it a very long opera?' asked Therese, craning forward in readiness for her father's answer.

'No, my dear,' Rheinhardt replied. 'It is very short.'

Therese gave a curt nod signalling her approval and applied herself once again to the task of simulated reading.

On the other side of the children's enclosure, through the wooden struts and bars of a climbing frame, Rheinhardt noticed a man seated on his own. He was middle-aged, wore a long coat, and sported a shaggy moustache. He was looking at Mitzi and her play-friend, who were now enjoying the reciprocal motion of the see-saw.

Else had started to ponder the logistics of going to the opera, a string of considerations, not obviously connected. Rheinhardt was listening, but his attention kept on returning to the man opposite. Why, he wondered, was the man looking so intently in the direction of his daughter?

'Who is that girl? Mitzi's play-friend?'

Mention of her sister made Therese look up from her book.

'Her name is Eva,' Else replied, puzzled.

'And who is she with?'

'Her mother, Frau Kubauer. She's over there, wearing the yellow dress.' Else pointed out one of the women standing under the tree. At that moment, Frau Kubauer happened to look in their direction and Else was obliged to turn her indicating gesture into a polite wave. The woman in the yellow dress waved back. Rheinhardt raised his hat respectfully.

Else angled her head and awaited an explanation for her husband's inquiry; however, he remained silent. With an indifferent shrug of her shoulders she returned to her original theme.

Rheinhardt had stopped listening. He was working out which children were accompanied by which adults. It became evident that the man sitting opposite was alone. Rheinhardt studied the cast of his face.

Rainmayr's studio.

Images.

Two young girls, with skirts hoisted, proudly displayed their pudenda; a pair of disembodied skinny legs in loose stockings and garters . . .

Mitzi and her friend had abandoned the see-saw and were running towards the climbing frame. They began their ascent and as they did so the man's eyes narrowed: he was looking at their ankles – their shoes – and as they ascended, he seemed to slide lower down in his seat. His tongue moistened his lips. His right hand – thrust into the deep pocket of his coat – was conspicuously active.

'Excuse me a moment,' said Rheinhardt to his wife.

'Where are you going?'

'I want to be closer to Mitzi.'

'She's perfectly safe. She won't fall.'

'Even so . . .'

Rheinhardt crossed the play area.

'Be careful, Mitzi,' he said as he passed the climbing frame. His daughter smiled.

'I won't slip.'

'Yes. Well. Make sure you don't.'

He continued walking towards the man, whose face showed a flicker of apprehension as the inspector approached.

'Good afternoon,' said Rheinhardt.

The man mumbled a return courtesy.

Rheinhardt sat down next to him and scanned the enclosure. Else was talking to Therese, but unfortunately Rheinhardt had not fooled her. She had detected something odd in his manner and was stealing glances at him through the wooden cage of the climbing frame.

'Sir?' said Rheinhardt.

The man turned.

Rheinhardt grabbed the man's necktie and twisted it tightly. The man's eyes bulged and he began to make choking noises.

'I know *what* you are,' said Rheinhardt steadily. 'And I know what you are doing.' The man's tongue protruded between his teeth and his face became contorted. 'You will leave at once and never come back. Do you understand? Never. If I catch you here again, I give you my word, you will regret it.'

Rheinhardt released the man's tie. He coughed and loosened the knot, then got up and ran towards the gate, looking back anxiously over his shoulder. Rheinhardt sauntered back to Else and Therese.

'What happened?' asked Else, her eyebrows raised.

'I noticed that gentleman's tie was crooked,' Rheinhardt pointed towards the flapping coat-tails receding beyond the fence, 'and performed the small service of straightening it for him.'

'What gentleman?' asked Therese.

'That one over there.' Therese peered through the trees. 'He had to leave in a hurry – he had a train to catch.'

Else's expression was troubled.

As she started to speak, Rheinhardt touched her lips with an outstretched finger, tacitly banning further inquiry.

'Now, is anyone hungry?' he asked. 'I think we should find a bakery.' He brought his hands together to make a funnel and used it to amplify his voice: 'Mitzi! Would you like a strudel?'

CHAPTER 26

Amelia Lydgate sat in one of Landsteiner's laboratories in the Institute of Pathology and Anatomy. Having rehydrated the crystals that she had scraped from Bathild Babel's fingernails, she had mixed the resulting solution with samples of known blood types. The subsequent patterns of agglutination that she observed down the barrel of her microscope informed her that the man whom Bathild Babel had scratched before she died was a member of the group that Landsteiner had designated type-C.

As she leaned forward, Amelia felt her corset pinch. It reminded her of an article she had read in her *Ladies' Journal* about the 'new' fashion. The author had advocated abandoning the standard two-piece and corset in favour of a loose gown affording complete freedom of movement. Now that more women were entering occupations that had previously been the exclusive province of men, the limitations of traditional clothing were becoming increasingly apparent. Straining over her microscope, Amelia couldn't have agreed more. The wisdom of such reasoning was dramatised every time the stiff canvas that encased her body resisted her inclination and issued its creaky protests. The article had concluded with news of a fashion house on Bauernmarkt. Loose-fitting 'reform dresses' – as they were described – were made on the premises using fabric designs created by artists of the Vienna Secession. The prices, however, were quite prohibitive.

Amelia ignored her complaining corsetry, examined the slides one last time, and composed a note which she intended to send before attending her pathology class at the university.

Dear Inspector Rheinhardt,
I have completed the requisite procedures for the determination of blood type and can report that the sample I removed from beneath Fräulein Babel's fingernails is classified as C. No assumptions can be made concerning the origin of the sample, but I consider it reasonable to suggest that the dried blood was connected with the performance of an action made in self-defence. I sincerely hope that this new piece of information will serve some useful purpose as your investigation proceeds. The occurrence of two identical murders must surely suggest that this fiend – for I cannot think of a more apposite term – will act on his unnatural impulses again. The nature of his degeneracy, which demonstrates

164

such low regard for my sex, arouses a very particular disgust. If I possess such skills as might in any way help to ensure this foul creature's apprehension, then please do not hesitate to request my further involvement. Indeed, I would be honoured to continue my association with the security office. I trust you will inform Professor Mathias of my findings in due course.

Yours sincerely,

Miss Amelia Lydgate

CHAPTER 27

From earliest times men have known her. In the Sumerian and Babylonian myths she is called Ereshkigal. In Ancient Rome she was known as Naenia or Libitina, and was said to fall upon the living like a great bird of prey. The Etruscans called her Tulchulcha. To the Hindus she is Kali, the Black Mother. In Japan, she comes as the Snow Queen, who chills the dying with her cold breath and removes all suffering. In Norse mythology she is Hela and in Finnish folktales she is Kalma. The Poles call her the Bone Lady and the Celts call her the Morrigan.

I will not try to describe her. No purpose is served by attempting the impossible; however, I will make an observation that has not, to my knowledge, been recorded by others. When she appears she is enfolded by a dancing, purplish light. Her dark wings, which rise from her shoulders and curve forward, are bathed in an aurora of amethyst.

What is it like to be in the presence of such perfection?

I will tell you.

It is unbearable torment.

Her terrible beauty creates such yearning, such longing, that the soul immediately struggles to escape from its prison. In the throes of a strange ecstasy, it twists and turns within the heavy flesh – striving, desperately, to be free.

I reached out to her, lifted my wasted arms, and begged her to take me. But it was not my time. She began to fade, leaving only an afterglow. It was as if some alien sun had set, leaving in its wake a flush of colour on the low-lying clouds of the night sky, a vestigial trace of heliotrope – gentian violet.

Perhaps I cried out, because my father came into the room. I can remember his hand on my forehead, his hatchet face. He asked me what was the matter, but I could not reply. I closed my eyes against the candlelight, which seemed intolerably harsh and bright. I wanted to see her again: I wanted to follow her ghostly train into perpetual darkness.

The world was never the same thereafter. It seemed counterfeit – a hollow sham. When I recovered from my illness it was like waking up from a long sleep, in a foreign land. Everything had become flat – a crudely painted backdrop in a cheap theatre. Only things relating to Her were meaningful. The graveyard next to the church; the mummies of ancient Egypt; myths and legends of the underworld.

I remember little of that time. No, that is not

quite true. What I mean to say is that I remember little of what was happening around me. My inner life I can remember very well. I reflected on my experiences. She had made herself known to me as I stood by the open caskets of Netti and Gerda. Then she had revealed herself to me – when I was close to death.

Why?

I was chosen.

There is nothing more to tell of my life in the village. I grew up. I left and came to Vienna. I lived in warming-up rooms and hostels – and tried to find work. I visited the Kunsthistorisches Museum and admired Canova's *Theseus*. I went to the Natural History Museum and studied the mummies that I had longed to see as a child. I found Herr Griesser's prehistoric axe-head displayed in a case with others from the Wachau.

Now, let me tell you something. Not about me – but about you.

You are obsessed with death.

You Viennese relish a good funeral: the pall-bearers, with their splendid outfits; the liveries worn by the horses; the hearses; the sashes, lanterns and black flags. And where else in the world can one find a necropolis like the Zentralfriedhof? It is bigger than the entire Innere Stadt. Did you know that? Imagine, building a cemetery bigger than a town! It is a wonderful place.

I have fond memories of that first winter, in spite of the hardship, exploring the endless avenues of the Zentralfriedhof. I had never seen anything like it. Under the arcade I found the tomb of the miner, August Zang, with its fierce dwarves standing on roughly hewn pedestals, raising their torches, guarding the portal with sturdy shields. It was like a scene from the Norse legends. All of the statuary had been carved with such care. I remember a female figure – as large as life – with long slender arms and fingers of exquisite delicacy. The sculptor had worked a small miracle with his material, creating a gown for her that appeared to be semi-transparent. It was remarkable how a substance like marble could be made to suggest a garment that adhered to her curves like silk and collected in soft folds between her thighs. Sphinxes, lyres, urns and swans and, of course, pale imitations of Her – those great angelic wings open and ready for flight.

And did I feel her presence there, in the Zentralfriedhof?

I did – but only as a husband might feel closer to his wife when he contemplates a photograph. There was, however, one exception. Whenever I saw a funeral she seemed to come closer.

On rainy afternoons I would loiter by the open graves, in readiness. Then I would join the mourners as they arrived. No one noticed me or challenged me. I would close my eyes and be rewarded by a faint sense of her presence. And once or twice my heart leaped at a flicker of purple light.

It was after one of these funerals that I fell into conversation with an undertaker's assistant. He was very sanguine about his profession. Business was good. The population of Vienna was growing and, with it, increasing demand for his services: he mentioned that there had been talk of building a high-speed pipeline, running from the Innere Stadt to the Zentralfriedhof, for the purpose of transporting the great number of corpses. I asked him if he could offer me a job. He gave me his card and said that I should visit the company premises the following morning as they had a vacancy for a junior member of staff. I went and was interviewed by the funeral director who said that I could start work there the following day.

CHAPTER 28

Heinz Vogl accepted that he could do nothing more for his patient. If there was a God, then the old general's fate was very much in His hands now. The veteran soldier had coughed up blood and his lungs had made ominous noises that suggested their imminent collapse. Vogl remained at the man's bedside for two long hours, waiting for the 'attack' to run its course. Eventually the coughing stopped and the old general sank back against his pillows. He showed no obvious signs of discomfort and his shallow breathing became stertorous.

As Vogl left the hospital a flash of lightning turned night into preternatural day. A rumble of thunder released a shower of unseasonal hailstones that landed on his hat with casual violence. Such inclemency, thought the doctor, was downright inconsiderate – although he had no idea who he was blaming. This vague sense that the weather was being manipulated with spiteful intent was reinforced when the arrival of a cab coincided with the sudden cessation of the storm.

The journey to his house in the seventeenth district was not a long one. He hoped that his wife would still be awake, but when he finally got to his bedroom there was no light showing under her door. The doctor performed his ablutions, put on his nightshirt and got into bed.

It was impossible for him to estimate how long he had been asleep; however, he sensed that it had not been very long. He was awakened by Kristina, who had evidently risen from her own bed to join him.

'My darling,' he said sleepily.

She made herself comfortable, lying on her side with her head resting on her husband's chest.

They remained in this position for some time – exchanging body heat and caresses. A clock ticked loudly in the darkness. Vogl was on the brink of falling asleep again when the gentle ministrations of his wife's fingers on his upper thigh prevented him from descending further into oblivion. His subsequent engorgement attracted his wife's interest, and she shifted down beneath the bedclothes until her lips closed around his rigid organ.

The doctor let out a cry that suggested pain as much as pleasure.

Vogl was a man of the world. He had enjoyed relations with women before his marriage. He was, therefore, highly appreciative of his wife's readiness to give him such satisfaction. Most women – he had found – were repulsed by the idea.

How fortunate I am, he thought, as he gently encouraged Kristina with the palm of his hand on the crown of her head. *I adore her.*

Kristina dispensed with the eiderdown and mounted her husband with a swift, easy movement. She bore down hard and rotated her hips – maximising the extent of his penetration. Overcome with desire, Vogl reached up and grabbed her breasts. Kristina placed her hands over his and squeezed his fingers until her accommodating flesh was so compressed that it could yield no further. The hardness of her nipples proved too much for Vogl, who experienced the inevitable consequence of such intense excitement.

'Oh my darling,' he gasped. 'My beautiful darling.'

Vogl's buttocks rose from the bed, lifting his wife in the process. He felt himself pouring into her. Then, when his release was complete, he slumped back down onto the mattress. Spent. Drained. Empty. He was dimly conscious of his wife changing position.

'Thank you,' Vogl whispered into the darkness.

Kristina rested a finger against his lips, admonishing him for his gratitude.

Vogl inhaled his wife's perfume – a heavy, rich scent – that combined musk with subtle registers of lavender. Its soporific qualities ensured his delivery from the world. When he woke again it was the middle of the night, and he found that the bed was empty. Kristina had returned to her room. He turned his head into the pillow, inhaled the lingering perfume one last time, and slept soundly until morning.

CHAPTER 29

Liebermann was engaged in the preliminary examination of a woman suffering from abdominal pains which, according to her gynaecologist and gastroenterologist, had no obvious physical causation. He was approximately halfway through his assessment when a nurse knocked on the door, entered, and requested him to 'step outside' for a moment. Liebermann frowned and tilted his head, encouraging her to tell him more. The nurse's eyes warned him that in the interests of his patient he should not press for an explanation. The young doctor stood and followed her outside, where she directed Liebermann's gaze down the corridor towards the silhouette of a figure wearing a long coat and spiked helmet.

'Thank you, nurse.'

'Shall I wait with your patient?'

'Yes. That would be most helpful.'

Liebermann advanced towards his visitor.

'Herr Doctor Liebermann?'

'Yes.'

The constable clicked his heels.

'You are a difficult man to find, Herr doctor. I've been wandering around the hospital without success for some time – I got quite lost, in fact, ended up by the Fools' Tower. There must be more passageways in here than in the Hofburg! You wouldn't think so—'

'Did Detective Inspector Rheinhardt send you?' Liebermann interrupted.

The constable rolled back on his heels.

'There has been another . . .'

'Murder,' said Liebermann, helpfully.

'Yes,' whispered the constable. 'In Neubau.'

'I am afraid I cannot come at once. I am with a patient.'

The constable took out a notebook, wrote down an address, and tore out the page. Handing it to Liebermann he said: 'What shall I say to Inspector Rheinhardt?'

'Tell him I'll do my best to be there within the hour.'

The constable bowed, moved as if to depart, then stopped and asked: 'I'm sorry, Herr doctor, but . . . how do I get out?'

'Proceed down this corridor, turn left at the end, descend the first staircase, turn left again – then right – then left again.'

The constable repeated Liebermann's instructions, bowed once again, then took his leave, attracting curious glances from two nurses pushing men in wheelchairs.

★ ★ ★

When Liebermann entered the shabby parlour he experienced a jolt of surprise. Firstly, he had wrongly assumed that he would discover the body in the bedroom and secondly, he had not expected to see any blood. The sight of so much made him hesitate.

Rheinhardt was standing by a chest of drawers. He had obviously been examining the contents, removing papers and documents that were now piled between two iron candelabra. The inspector gestured towards the dead woman, his hand moving uselessly in the air beside him.

The parlour was situated on the second floor of an eighteenth-century apartment building. It was not a large room and the few items it contained created an impression of restricted space. In addition to the chest of drawers, there were two chintz sofas, several potted plants on three-legged stands, a glass-fronted cabinet, and a stove. The glass-fronted cabinet contained some chipped porcelain figures, tarnished silverwear, and an assortment of commemorative plates featuring images of the deceased Empress Elisabeth.

A distinctive rusty taint permeated the air and caught at the back of Liebermann's throat.

Between the two sofas, lying on the floor, was a woman in her thirties. She was wearing a simple low-cut blue dress, the bodice of which was stained almost black. The hilt of a dagger indicated the location of her heart. No part of the blade was visible. It had been pushed in deep, between her ribs and angled beneath the protective plate of her sternum. The hem of her dress had risen above a pair of scuffed boots and her white legs were spread apart, crooked slightly at the knee. Discarded on the floor beside the body was an undergarment: red silk bloomers with a trim of black lace.

Liebermann crossed the floor to the window, pulled the curtain aside and looked down into a tiny courtyard. The light was failing and the proximity of the opposite wall was claustrophobic. He noticed a walking stick resting against the windowsill.

'Does this belong to her?' asked Liebermann.

'Yes,' said Rheinhardt. 'She had a bad leg.'

'Who is she?'

'Her name is Selma Wirth. She was discovered by the landlord's agent – a Ruthenian gentleman called Shevchenko – around five o'clock. Fräulein Wirth owed three months' rent and Shevchenko had come to collect it.'

'Was the door open when he arrived?'

'No. The door was closed; however, it had not been locked.'

Liebermann let go of the curtain and his attention was drawn back to the corpse.

'What did she do for a living?'

'She was a laundry worker.' Rheinhardt lit a cigarette and dropped the blackened matchstick into a cracked glass ashtray. 'The undergarment seems to have been removed before she lay on the floor.'

178

'I wonder why she chose to *receive* her guest here, rather than in the bedroom? I presume there is a bedroom?'

'Yes, it's the next door along.' Rheinhardt waved his cigarette towards the corridor. 'One must suppose that Fräulein Wirth and her companion were so *overcome* that in the heat of the moment comfort was not a consideration.'

'Are you sure she was . . . taken?'

'It certainly looks like it.'

Liebermann knelt on the floor, lifted the woman's skirt, and shook it to displace the trapped air. He sniffed, wrinkled his nose, and shook his head.

'I can't tell. I don't possess Professor Mathias's nose for such things.'

'What do you make of the dagger? Was Fräulein Wirth killed by the same fiend who killed Adele Zeiler and Bathild Babel, or did someone else do this?'

Liebermann stood up.

'My thoughts go back to something Professor Mathias said concerning the hatpin used to kill Bathild Babel. You will recall that he observed a kink – near the sharp end – which suggested a failed first attempt to breach the foramen magnum. This blunder might have given Fräulein Babel an opportunity to retaliate – hence the blood discovered beneath her fingernails. Encountering resistance might have caused the perpetrator to review his modus operandi. A dagger pressed into

179

the heart is a less elegant but more efficient means of dispatch.'

Rheinhardt took some papers from the top of the chest of drawers and placed them in his pocket.

'I haven't been able to find an address book, which is a shame. Babel's proved very useful. It included the name of a man – Griesser – who gave Café Museum as his mailing address. He collected only one letter and hasn't been back since. The head waiter described him as educated and smelling of carbolic. One of Babel's *admirers* – Frece, an accountant – can remember her flirting with a customer in Frau Schuschnig's establishment . . .'

'Frau Schuschnig?'

'The proprietor of the hat shop where Babel worked. Frece gave a similar description, and also remarked on the man's *hospital* smell. That cannot be a coincidence. One must assume that the man who called himself Griesser and the flirtatious customer were the same individual. Taken together with previous reports, a clear picture is emerging: a young gentleman, educated, well dressed, with black hair and blue or blue-grey eyes. A professional man with a knowledge of human anatomy . . .'

'Frece saw this gentleman in Frau Schuschnig's hat shop. What was he doing there?'

'Buying a hatpin. He must have made the purchase before Fräulein Babel's sharp fingernails forced him to reconsider his procedures.'

Liebermann acknowledged the point with a curt nod and sat down on one of the sofas. Selma Wirth's face was deeply lined. Yet the height of her cheekbones and her well-defined chin suggested that she must have been beautiful once.

'Did the landlord's agent tell you anything about her history?'

'No. He didn't know her very well – and I haven't been able to glean much from her documents. He advised me to speak to her neighbour, Frau Lachkovics. She lives downstairs with her daughter. Apparently Frau Lachkovics and Fräulein Wirth were good friends.'

'She's not in yet – Frau Lachkovics?'

Rheinhardt shook his head.

There was a knock and both men turned to see Haussmann's head craning round the door.

'Sir. The mortuary van has arrived.'

'Very well – tell them to come up. Have we had a reply from Professor Mathias yet?'

'We have, sir. He said he was going to dine at Café Landtmann but would be back at the Institute by eight o' clock. He also said that he wasn't feeling very well and might need an assistant. He requested Miss Lydgate.'

Rheinhardt raised his eyebrows and addressed Liebermann: 'Do you think Miss Lydgate would be willing to join us at this late hour?'

'Such is her nature,' said Liebermann, sighing, 'I suspect that nothing in the world would please her more.'

CHAPTER 30

The morgue was particularly cold at night. Liebermann and Rheinhardt had kept their coats on, but Professor Mathias seemed comfortable in his shirtsleeves. The electric light suspended above the autopsy table shone down on the mortuary sheets, making them glow vividly. This artificial landscape of luminous hills and hollows was disturbed by a central peak, the summit of which was, by contrast, unnaturally sharp.

Liebermann was sitting on a stool, contemplating the mysterious contents of a jar filled with formalin. The preserved organ, which looked vaguely like a sea horse, was magnified by the curvature of the glass. It was pink with yellow pleats down one side, creating the illusion of a spine which curled to form a hooked tail. The young doctor thought it might be an unusually proportioned vermiform appendix.

Rheinhardt was pacing around the autopsy table and Professor Mathias, muttering softly to himself, was engrossed by the organisational possibilities of his trolley.

A knock roused the men from their respective states of self-absorption.

'Enter!' cried Professor Mathias.

The door opened and Amelia's voice floated out of the darkness.

'Good evening, gentlemen.'

She emerged from the shadows, her pale face and hands preceding the rest of her body like a ghost at a seance.

'Ah, Miss Lydgate,' said Rheinhardt, 'I would offer to take your coat, but the temperature in here is so low I would suggest you continue to take advantage of its benefit.'

Liebermann stood and inclined his head. As she approached, her hair drew the hard brilliance of the light and transmuted it into a ruddy haze. She glanced down at the mortuary sheets and a vertical crease appeared on her brow.

'So, he has struck again.'

'He has indeed,' said Rheinhardt, coming forward. 'This unfortunate lady,' he swept his hand over the covered body with its conspicuous peak, 'is his third victim.' Amelia stared at the salient irregularity that destroyed the gentle geography of the sheets. 'The hilt of a knife,' Rheinhardt explained. The inspector was about to say more but was cut short by Professor Mathias, who was tutting loudly.

'Miss Lydgate?' The professor looked up and beckoned. 'Would you be so kind as to arrange my instruments?' His voice sounded nasal and he took a handkerchief from his pocket. 'I have a head cold,' he added, as if this constituted sufficient explanation for his inability to complete his preparations.

'With pleasure,' Amelia replied.

Liebermann caught Rheinhardt's eye and their shared amazement brought them perilously close to laughter. Such an invitation was unprecedented.

Professor Mathias blew his nose and observed the Englishwoman's deft movements. When she was finished, she stepped back from the trolley and Mathias inspected her handiwork. His palpable relief was evident in the softening of his features.

'Very good,' he said, as if nothing remarkable had transpired.

He turned to face the autopsy table and folded the upper sheet back, revealing the corpse's face. He placed a finger on the dead woman's cheek and traced one of the lines that curved out from her nostrils and arced around her lips.

'Only distant death can heal the presence of such suffering; where the portals shall open, there shall I be healed again . . .'

Then he removed the sheets, exposing the dead woman completely.

'What is her name?'

'Selma Wirth,' Rheinhardt replied.

'And where was she discovered?'

'Neubau. In her apartment – lying on the parlour floor.'

'Was she found lying on her back?'

'Yes.'

Mathias picked up a large pair of scissors and cut vertically from the hem of the dress to the cinched waist.

'No undergarments?'

'Her drawers had been removed – voluntarily, so it would seem. We found them in the parlour beside her.'

Mathias examined the material that was bunched up directly underneath the woman's genitals. He pressed out the creases with the palm of his hand.

'I cannot see any traces. And there are no indications to suggest forced ingress.' Then he leaned forward, prised the woman's labia apart with his fingers and inhaled. The subsequent noise he produced was stertorous. The old man looked round at his companions. 'My nose is congested: I can't smell a thing.' His words were as much an appeal for assistance as a statement of fact.

While Rheinhardt and Liebermann were exchanging looks of alarm, Amelia took Professor Mathias's place between Selma Wirth's legs and breathed in deeply. She did so with the serious determination of a convalescent eager to experience the invigorating tang of a coastal breeze.

'I cannot detect anything . . .' she paused before adding '*distinctive*.' Then, addressing Professor Mathias, she said: 'Be that as it may, the question of her violation could be resolved – definitively –

with the aid of a microscope.' Mathias gestured towards a hefty optical device that stood next to the jar containing the mysterious organ. The tube was made of brass and it stood on three heavy iron legs. Amelia raised an inquisitive eyebrow and asked: 'Do you have any hematoxylin, Herr professor?'

Mathias shuffled over to a cupboard and returned with a flask of blue-purple liquid and a tray of glass slides and cover slips. He placed them by the microscope.

'I am happy for you to prepare the slide, Miss Lydgate,' said Mathias. 'Please proceed.'

The Englishwoman stood at the end of the autopsy table, folded her coat sleeve back, and insinuated her right forefinger into the dead woman's vagina. Her first metacarpal began to move from side to side, suggesting that the hidden digit was rotating. This image of Amelia Lydgate – so prim and controlled – exploring the internal anatomy of another woman (albeit a dead woman) aroused shameful feelings in Liebermann which he tried to suppress. He lowered his eyes and garnered some consolation from the sound of Rheinhardt nervously coughing into his hand and shifting his weight from one foot to the other. Curiously, Amelia showed no sign of embarrassment or discomfort, only the focused resolve of an individual utterly engaged in an important task.

Amelia withdrew her finger and turned it beneath the electric light. The cast of her face altered slightly – suggesting satisfaction – as the semi-transparent film covering her white skin glistened. Taking a glass slide from the tray, she rolled her finger over its surface, leaving a grey mucoid smear. She then dipped the slide into the hematoxylin, shook off the excess liquid and fixed the slide on the stage of the microscope. Finally, she wiped her finger on a grubby towel that was hanging from a hook under the bench and sat down on the stool.

With practised ease she altered the angle of the mirror, changed the objectives, and made coarse and fine adjustments.

'She was most definitely violated,' said Amelia.

The Englishwoman moved aside and let Professor Mathias look into the eyepiece.

'Come over here and see for yourself, inspector,' said the professor.

When Rheinhardt peered into the microscope he saw a luminous blue world populated by a swarm of bullet-headed creatures with long tails.

'Sperm cells,' said Mathias. He returned to the autopsy table where he completed the task of cutting off and removing Selma Wirth's clothes.

Her nakedness, brilliantly pale beneath the electric light, produced in the onlookers a respectful silence. In due course, the hilt of the dagger commanded their attention. It seemed monstrously large. An annulus of dark crystals had collected around the blade and the dead woman's breasts were marbled with blood. Professor Mathias filled a bucket with water and cleaned the body with a sponge.

'I do not see any bruises,' said the professor. 'But you will notice that her arms and hands are quite red – the skin is dry and cracked. What do you make of that, Miss Lydgate?'

'Did this lady suffer from a dermatological complaint?'

Mathias tilted his hand in the air and then reversed the movement. His expression communicated that although this was an acceptable answer, it was not the right one.

'The inflammation does not proceed up the arm,' said Mathias. 'Notice how it stops rather abruptly at the elbow.' Amelia frowned. 'Such an unusual pattern strongly suggests that Fräulein Wirth was a laundry worker. Am I right, inspector?'

'Yes,' said Rheinhardt. 'You are.'

The old man allowed himself a self-congratulatory half-smile. Mathias dropped the sponge into the bucket and then grasped the hilt of the dagger. He pulled – but the weapon resisted. He pulled harder and it came out, producing a slight rasp. The old man looked at Rheinhardt: 'You don't need a pathologist to tell you how she died, inspector.'

CHAPTER 31

It was early morning and a weightless sun hovered behind a screen of diaphanous cloud. Rheinhardt was making a wary descent down a slippery cobbled road towards a square-fronted building with a flat roof on which four cylindrical water tanks were clearly visible. A second storey, rising behind these tanks, presented an exterior comprised almost entirely of slatted shutters.

The drying room, thought Rheinhardt.

His speculation was confirmed when one of the shutters opened, revealing row after row of suspended undergarments.

A waste pipe, positioned next to the tanks, was expelling steam in sharp bursts. The sound it produced was oppressive and industrial, a repetitive mechanical cough, the unrelieved regularity of which had the potential, so Rheinhardt supposed, to induce a very bad headache. He watched the steam rise and wondered how the occupants of the building preserved their mental equilibrium. Perhaps they didn't . . .

When Rheinhardt arrived at the entrance he stopped and listened to the cacophony coming from

189

inside: raucous laughter, shrieks, whistles, a peculiar rasping noise, and snatches of popular songs issuing from the throats of brassy untrained contraltos. Rheinhardt advanced across a flagstone floor covered in shallow puddles. All around he could see soap bars, packets of soda and jars of bleach. He discovered an office, little more than a cubicle, created by the erection of flimsy partition walls. Peering through the tiny window, Rheinhardt caught sight of a woman sitting behind a desk piled high with ledgers. He rapped on the glass and the woman looked up from her paperwork. She had grey hair, tied back in a bun, and wore small half-moon spectacles. Indicating by a sign that she would come out, she rose from her chair and, emerging from a side door, introduced herself as the manageress, Frau Aehrenthal.

'Detective Inspector Rheinhardt: security office,' said Rheinhardt, bowing respectfully. 'I am looking for a laundry worker called Lachkovics.'

'That would be Viki Lachkovics? Not Jana, her daughter?'

'They both work here?'

'Yes.'

'Well, I may need to speak to both of them, actually.'

Frau Aehrenthal gave Rheinhardt a curious, doubtful look, the meaning of which escaped him.

'This way, inspector.'

The interior of the building was like an enormous shed, with cast-iron pillars supporting exposed beams that ran across the ceiling. Rheinhardt could

190

not see very far ahead because of a white mist that seemed to become more opaque as they progressed. Droplets of water fell from above like gentle rain, and the dank air contained a chemical sharpness that made his eyes prickle. The din that had first greeted him was now very loud.

Quite suddenly the fog lifted, and Rheinhardt found himself walking between two rows of washboards and washtubs. Each bay was occupied by a laundry worker. They were all female: sleeves rolled up, skirts hitched high enough to reveal coloured stockings and big thick-soled boots. Scrubbing, sloshing, shouting – the racket they were making was quite extraordinary. Yet Rheinhardt could still hear the unremitting cough of the waste pipe on the roof.

Halting at one of the bays, the manageress introduced Frau Lachkovics and left. She was evidently not interested in discovering the purpose of Rheinhardt's visit. Frau Lachkovics – a mousy woman whose hair was concealed by a waterproof bonnet – looked up at Rheinhardt nervously. He was considering how to proceed when a plump pink-faced woman with the collar of her dress pulled down to create a shockingly low décolleté plunged her hands into a tub, splashing everyone and everything around her.

'Frau Lachkovics,' said Rheinhardt, wiping the suds from his eyes and attending to the limp horns of his moustache, 'is there somewhere we can talk, somewhere private, perhaps?'

191

'Only the alley that runs round the back.'

'Very well,' said Rheinhardt. 'That will have to do.'

Frau Lachkovics left her bay and a young woman, no more than sixteen years of age and also wearing a waterproof bonnet, vacated the next position and fell into step behind them.

'My daughter,' said Frau Lachkovics. 'Jana.'

The girl had a peculiar shuffling gait. She walked with her right hand clasping her left wrist, which made her shoulder twist forward.

In the milky distance, a group of women armed with wicker implements shaped like tennis racquets were beating sheets that had been thrown over brass lines.

A door in a windowless wall led out into a narrow alley that separated the laundry from a warehouse.

'That's better,' said Rheinhardt, relieved to put the noise behind him. 'At least we can hear ourselves speak now.' He smiled at Frau Lachkovics and then at her daughter. The mother returned his smile but Jana's expression remained blank. 'Frau Lachkovics,' Rheinhardt began, 'may I ask why it was that you did not return to your apartment last night?'

'I was at my mother's,' she said with surprise.

'And where does your mother live?'

'Ottakring. She's old. Almost eighty now. I go to see her every Friday to wash her hair and cut her toenails. She wasn't very well last night. I was worried and stayed later than usual. I didn't want to walk home: not in the dark.'

'Of course,' said Rheinhardt. 'Very wise. Did Jana visit her grandmother with you?'

'Yes.'

He smiled approvingly at the girl, but again her expression communicated nothing but vacancy.

'Tell me, Frau Lachkovics, how long have you lived in Neubau?'

'A year or so. I used to live out in Ottakring with my mother but her apartment got too small for us.' Frau Lachkovics glanced at her daughter. 'Jana needed a room of her own. It's only right.'

'Forgive me – but is there a . . . a Herr Lachkovics?'

Frau Lachkovics blushed: 'My husband deserted us soon after Jana was born.'

She cowered slightly, as if the shame of her unsuccessful marriage was like a yoke bearing down on her shoulders.

'I'm sorry,' said Rheinhardt. 'That must have been very difficult for you.' The woman blinked at her interlocutor, more confused than relieved by his sympathy. 'Were you acquainted with your neighbour, Fräulein Wirth, before you moved to Neubau?'

'No.'

'You are good friends?'

'Yes. It was Fräulein Wirth who got me my job here at the laundry.' She paused and added. 'She isn't in today. Is she all right?'

Rheinhardt looked upwards. Steam from the waste pipe drifted across the thin strip of sky.

'Could I ask: when was the last time you saw Fräulein Wirth?'

'Thursday night.'

'The night before last . . .'

'Yes.'

'And how was she?' Frau Lachkovics appeared mystified by his question. 'Was Fräulein Wirth the same as she usually is? Or did you notice anything different about her?'

'She didn't look unwell, if that's what you mean.'

'Did she have any visitors on Thursday?'

Frau Lachkovics thought for a moment then said: 'Yes – she did. A friend.'

'Who?

'A lady. Frau Vogl.'

'Frau Vogl,' Rheinhardt repeated.

The name sounded vaguely familiar. He had an odd feeling that he had heard it only recently during a conversation with his wife.

'Yes,' said Frau Lachkovics. 'An old friend. They go back a long way. She's quite a well-to-do woman. I met her once, a very fine lady . . . and such clothes.'

She shook her head and looked down at her shabby dress.

'Do you remember what time it was when Frau Vogl visited Fräulein Wirth?'

'It must have been early evening. I looked out the window and saw her leaving. Her carriage came into the yard.'

'Tell me . . . did anything unusual happen on Thursday night?'

194

'No,' said Frau Lachkovics. 'Nothing unusual happened.'

Jana, who had been very still – almost absent – pulled at her mother's skirt. It was a peculiar thing for a girl of her age to do. Rheinhardt looked at Jana's face and realised that her void expression was probably the result of some defect of the brain. He thought of his own bright daughters and felt a stab of pity for Frau Lachkovics.

'What is it, Jana?' said Frau Lachkovics.

'I heard someone,' the girl answered. 'You'd gone to bed – but I was still up looking at one of Selma's books. I heard someone walking. I went out onto the landing and called: "Is anyone there?"' She cupped her hands around her mouth to demonstrate.

Frau Lachkovics's surprise rapidly turned to anxiety.

'Why ever did you do that?'

'No one answered.'

'Jana? Why didn't you tell me?'

The girl's face was blank again: an impassive mask.

'My dear,' said Rheinhardt, 'try to remember what you heard. It might be important and I would very much appreciate your help.'

'Footsteps,' said the girl.

'Loud, soft, slow, fast? What kind of footsteps?'

She paused and replied 'Footsteps' – as if, on reflection, no further qualification was necessary.

'Did you see anyone?'

'No.'

Frau Lachkovics put her arm around her daughter and drew her closer.

'Inspector, what has happened?'

Rheinhardt took out his notebook and began to write.

'Has Fräulein Wirth had any other visitors? A gentleman friend, perhaps?'

Frau Lachkovics shook her head, this time with considerable force. Rheinhardt suspected that she might be trying to protect her friend's honour.

'Come now,' said Rheinhardt. 'It is perfectly reasonable for a woman to enjoy the company of a gentleman. She must have had . . . admirers?'

'No. Not Selma. She isn't interested. She doesn't want anything to do with men.'

'Why ever not?'

'She is lame, did you know that? She can walk, but she gets tired and needs a stick. The muscles are weak. I think she is ashamed.'

'And what about you, Frau Lachkovics? Do *you* have any gentlemen friends?'

'No,' the woman said firmly. 'Not after Lachkovics.' Her hand rose up and she touched her face, as if the sting of a hard slap – administered many years ago – still tingled on her cheek. She shrugged. 'We don't need anyone else now. We can cope on our own – me and Jana. We have our little home – and our work – and our friends. We are quite happy – aren't we, Jana?' She shook the girl's shoulders and the movement placed a feeble smile on the young woman's face. 'But inspector – what are you asking me all these questions for? She is all right – isn't she? Selma?'

'Her rent has not been paid for three months.'

'Oh. I see. You've spoken to Herr Shevchenko.'

'I have. Why did she get so far behind?'

'She's always spending money on doctors. Trying to find a cure. She can't accept that nothing can be done. You're not going to arrest her, are you? It isn't a great sum of money and she'll pay it back.'

Rheinhardt looked into the woman's pleading eyes. He found that he had to force himself to speak: 'I have some terrible news.' Dismissing thoughts of impropriety he reached out and held her hand. 'I am afraid Fräulein Wirth is dead.'

Frau Lachkovics appeared stunned. Her mouth worked wordlessly until she finally managed to cry: 'Oh, Jana.'

Apart from a slight tensing of her brow, the daughter seemed indifferent to her mother's grief.

Above their heads the waste pipe continued to discharge steam into the atmosphere. Its beat had begun to coincide with a pulse of pain in Rheinhardt's head.

CHAPTER 32

Erstweiler appeared comfortable, but a muscle beneath his left eye was quivering. 'To be honest, Herr doctor, I didn't like my father. He was a domineering man who always thought he was right. I don't know how my mother put up with him. She was the opposite: a diminutive, genial creature, always prepared to listen to both sides of an argument. My grandfather – my mother's father – was somewhat impecunious, and I suspect that her family forced her into the marriage. Father was not wealthy, by any means, but he had a secure job in the railway office.' Erstweiler produced a crooked, sardonic smile: 'Although he never ascended as far up the bureaucratic hierarchy as my brother – and was never obliged to don the garb of a general!'

Liebermann waited. He could see in his patient's eyes that memories were surfacing.

'I remember,' Erstweiler continued. 'I once accompanied my father on a trip to Vienna. I forget why. Indeed, I've forgotten virtually everything that happened, except one thing. We were walking past the Stephansdom and my father said we should climb to the top in order to see the view. We began our climb, and almost immediately I felt apprehensive. I looked out of the narrow windows and it made me feel dizzy. I remember seeing the Habsburg eagle on the cathedral roof . . . the city below. I didn't want to go any higher: I thought the whole spire might tumble down. My father asked me what was the matter and I said: *I don't feel well.*' The memory was so vivid that Erstweiler's voice suddenly acquired the timbre of a frightened child's: '*Nonsense!* said my father. *There's nothing wrong with you!*' Again, Erstweiler's voice changed, becoming officious and unsympathetic. 'He dragged me up – higher and higher – and I began to cry. He lost his temper and called me *cowardly*, told me to be a *man* . . . told me to stop acting like a *milksop.* When we reached the viewing room at the summit I sat down on a bench and refused to look out. Even a glimpse of those rooftops, so far below, made my head spin. He pointed out a girl in a pink dress and said, *Look! Even she has more courage than you!* My father was disgusted with me. He left me there, on my own, full of shame and anger, while he walked around – enjoying the view. I longed for my mother. If she had been present, she would never have let this happen . . . After a while, I asked my father if we could go down. *No*, he said. *I want to hear the Pummerin.* He told me that the great bell had been made from the melted cannons that the *gutless* Turks had left behind when they fled the city. What did I care . . . about that?'

Erstweiler sighed and twisted his hospital gown in his hand until it bit into his skin like a tourniquet.

'He was always talking about honour – doing what was right. He always saw faults in others, never in himself.'

'Did you ever disobey your father?' Liebermann asked.

'No. Well, not in his lifetime, anyway.'

Liebermann leaned forward: 'I'm sorry?'

'He judged thieves harshly. He said that they should have their hands cut off.'

'You stole something?'

Erstweiler nodded.

'What?' asked Liebermann.

'A trivial thing.'

'Yes, but what was it?' Liebermann pressed.

'Actually . . .' Erstweiler hesitated before saying, 'It was a kimono for Frau Milena.'

How strange, thought Liebermann, *that this disclosure should be connected with reminiscences of his father.*

'Why did you do that?'

'I felt sorry for her. Kolinsky never buys her anything. He is a miser. Her wardrobe was pitiful . . . rags. I received a delivery of silk kimonos at Winkler's warehouse – a large delivery of thirty garments. It's my job to register the stock. I marked one missing and took it home.' Erstweiler shrugged. 'Was that so wrong?'

'Your father would have said so.'

Erstweiler released his hospital gown, allowing the blood to flow back into his fingers.

'I've had enough today.'

'Did Frau Milena like your gift?'

'Yes. She looked . . . She loved it.'

Liebermann noted the slip.

'Herr doctor . . . I'm feeling tired. Can we stop now?'

'Have you had any more dreams?'

'None that I can remember.'

Liebermann made some quick notes.

Spire – beanstalk. Ogre – father. Frau Milena – goose.
Hand cut off – punishment for masturbation? Desire?
Sophocles.
I've always doubted it. But perhaps Prof. F is right!

'The English fairy-story dream.'

'What about it?'

'Have you had any similar dreams since we last spoke?'

'No. Herr doctor? Can we finish? I really am very tired.'

CHAPTER 33

Liebermann and Rheinhardt were seated in Café Eiles. They had already finished their *bauernschnatterer* – a pork-and-bean stew, seasoned with pepper and chives – and were now studying the pastry menu.

'The *palatschinken*,' said Rheinhardt to the waiter. 'What are they filled with?'

'Curd cheese,' the waiter replied.

'I'll have two, then.'

The waiter turned to Liebermann.

'*Powidltascherln.*'

'Very good, sir,' said the waiter. He darted off, narrowly missing his colleague who was travelling in the opposite direction. Some civil servants at an adjacent table had drunk too much wine and one of their party – a bibulous gentleman with a large red nose – started to sing a jolly song from *La Belle Hélène*. He suddenly fell silent halfway through the second verse.

Rheinhardt was not distracted by the laughter and jibes that followed. He undid one of the buttons of his waistcoat and leaned forward: 'It was late and Frau Lachkovics had already gone to bed. The girl heard something: footsteps. But, given her mental deficiency, I am not convinced that the poor child's account reflects what actually happened, although it contains, I believe, a kernel of truth. It would seem that she was disturbed by the perpetrator's arrival *or* departure and that there is no way of telling which; however, I think the facts of the case are more consistent with the former than the latter. Jana Lachkovics heard Griesser – let us use his *nom de guerre* for convenience's sake – ascend the stairs to Wirth's apartment, *but she did not respond immediately*. Enough time elapsed for Wirth and Griesser to become intimate, during which interlude Jana Lachkovics finally reached her decision to investigate. She stood on the landing and shouted "*Is anyone there?*" and Griesser, on hearing her call and fearing discovery, stabbed Wirth through the heart. He may have already determined (on account of Fräulein Babel's final act of resistance) that he was going to use a dagger instead of the hatpin he had purchased at Frau Schuschnig's . . . or if there was any uncertainty in his mind, I have no doubt that the sound of Jana Lachkovics's voice resolved the matter. He subsequently chose the less complicated means of dispatch.'

Lieberman raised his coffee cup as if toasting his friend.

'That makes perfect sense, Oskar. Yet there is one thing that troubles me. You said that Frau Lachkovics was insistent that Fräulein Wirth did not entertain gentlemen friends.'

'Indeed.'

'Yet Fräulein Wirth admitted Griesser into her apartment and intercourse appears to have been consensual. She obviously knew him.'

'There are two explanations. Either Frau Lachkovics wanted to protect her friend's reputation or she was entirely ignorant of the association. I am inclined to believe that Fräulein Wirth's relationship with Griesser was clandestine.'

'Why would she wish to keep a relationship secret from her closest acquaintance?'

Rheinhardt shrugged.

'I have no idea.' The waiter returned with two lightly browned pancakes and a triangular pastry sprinkled with cinnamon and icing sugar. 'Fräulein Wirth,' Rheinhardt continued, 'was visited earlier on Thursday evening by a friend – a woman called Vogl. I understand that she is a famous dress designer.'

'Kristina Vogl?'

'Yes.' Rheinhardt drew back and produced an exaggerated, theatrical expression of amazement. 'I did not know you were conversant with the world of haute couture.'

'I'm not. But my sisters are. Vogl's name, if I am not mistaken, is associated with the *reform* movement.'

Rheinhardt transferred some pancake into his mouth. He closed his eyes and communed with the flavours: clarified butter, honey, vanilla pods, and grated lemon peel.

'Yes,' he said, opening his eyes again. 'Reform. Else explained it all to me. I had no idea that corsets were so political.'

'I don't like them.'

'What? Corsets?'

'No. Reform dresses.'

'You surprise me. You usually like everything modern.'

'They are shapeless . . .' Liebermann broke his pastry with his fork. The plum purée inside the folded parcel spilt out onto the white porcelain. 'They obscure the curves of the female figure. I am sure that reform dresses are very comfortable to wear – but I am not sure they are very pleasing to look at.'

Rheinhardt stopped eating for a moment: 'Be that as it may, I have some sympathy with the cause, don't you? It is a sobering thought – what a woman has to endure with respect to her wardrobe. The countless hooks and eyes that have to be fastened from waist to neck, the corset which has to be pulled so very tight, the petticoats, camisoles, jackets and bodices – layer upon layer – encasing her body like a suit of armour. Required to wear gloves, even on a hot day, bespangled in heavy jewellery and other adornments: stockings; garters; hair curled, braided, built up beneath the canopy of a monstrous hat, lush with vegetation and exotic fruits; perfumed, plumed, powdered. Really, Max. It's a wonder that any of them can move at all.'

Liebermann smiled at his friend, impressed by his humanity.

'You are quite right, Oskar. It is selfish of me to object to reform dresses on aesthetic grounds. I doubt if I could survive more than ten minutes in a corset!' Liebermann touched his throat. 'This collar is bad enough.'

'I'm going to pay a call on Frau Vogl this afternoon.'

'Really? Where does she live?'

'Not very far. The sixth district. Near the Theater an der Wien.'

'They say that she is greatly admired by the artists of the Secession. I wonder what sort of woman she is?'

'Why don't you come and see for yourself?' Rheinhardt recovered his fork and guillotined his pancake. 'I could do with some company.'

Their destination was a smart town house, three storeys high, with baroque window hoods and a balcony that bellied out above the front door. They were admitted by a maidservant and introduced to Kristina Vogl's secretary – an attractive girl whose elegance was undermined by an unfortunate stoop.

'Madame is unwell. She has taken to her bed. Even so, she is willing to receive you upstairs – if you don't mind . . .' The girl smiled, pointed at the ceiling, and remained in this position for longer than was necessary to achieve her purpose.

Rheinhardt indicated that he had no objection. 'This way, please.'

The secretary led them up a wide, somewhat ostentatious staircase, and down a corridor that led to the rear of the house. She knocked lightly on one of the doors.

'Madame?'

A muffled voice: 'Come in.'

The secretary ushered Rheinhardt and Liebermann into her mistress's bedroom and closed the door behind them.

Liebermann was impressed by the decor. It was decidedly modern. The furniture was black and boxlike, unencumbered by redundant detail. A beige carpet with a red grid pattern covered the floor and the wallpaper was enlivened by a subtle recurring motif of stylised leaves. The air was fragrant with rose and lavender.

Kristina Vogl was sitting up in a large double bed, surrounded by sketchbooks and fabric samples. Liebermann studied the famous couturière with interest. She possessed fine, regular features, and eyes of an uncommonly pellucid blue. Her hair was dark brown and fell down in loose curls to her slim shoulders, which were wrapped in the shimmering crimson swathe of a kimono. Gold dragons disported themselves across the silk. On a bedside cabinet stood a lamp which Liebermann identified as the work of Josef Hoffmann.

'You are Inspector Rheinhardt?'

Her accent was brittle.

Rheinhardt's bow was more florid than usual – almost foppish. He gestured towards his friend: 'And my associate, Herr Doctor Liebermann.'

Kristina tilted her head to one side, tacitly questioning why a detective inspector should be accompanied by a medical man; but Rheinhardt did not give her an answer. Instead, he clasped his hands together over his heart.

'Thank you so much for agreeing to see us today. I wish you a swift recovery. Permit me also to offer you our most sincere condolences.'

The woman coughed. Liebermann thought the action rather forced, like a hysterical patient with *tussis nervosa*.

'You are most kind, inspector. It was a shock, of course. I could hardly believe it. You read of such things in the newspapers but you never consider that your own life will be touched by such terrible events. Poor Selma.'

Rheinhardt took a step forward.

'I understand that Fräulein Wirth was a close friend.'

Kristina's brow furrowed. When she spoke, her delivery was hesitant: 'I wouldn't say that we were *close*. But I have known her a long time.'

'Since childhood?'

'Yes. But the nature of our relationship . . .' Kristina appeared a little discomfited. 'I think before we proceed any further it would be advisable for me to clarify a few points.'

'As you wish.'

'Selma was the daughter of my mother's laundry maid. We were very fond of each other as children and we corresponded as adults; but, naturally, our lives have followed somewhat different courses.' Kristina's expression became pained. 'We did not have a great deal in common. Further, I feigned a deeper affection than, in fact, really existed between us. You will ask why. Well, Selma was a proud woman and it was only by invoking our friendship that I could persuade her to accept financial assistance. I hope that God will forgive me this small deception which was practised only in the service of charity.'

'I see.' said Rheinhardt. 'I am sure that in the ledgers of heaven such an act of human kindness will not be counted against you.' Kristina dismissed the compliment with a languid flick of her wrist. 'You may not have been bosom companions,' Rheinhardt continued, 'but I assume you were familiar with Fräulein Wirth's general circumstances?'

'Yes – that *is* true.'

Rheinhardt nodded and checked the horns of his moustache.

'Then could you tell me if Fräulein Wirth had any gentleman friends?'

'She had many when she was younger. She was very striking. But as soon as her leg problems started she became markedly less interested in flirtations and romance.'

'What about recently? Did she mention meeting anyone?'

'No. But . . .'

Kristina shook her head.

'What is it?'

'Nothing . . .'

'Please,' said Rheinhardt. 'You were going to say something.'

'On my last visit – and the previous one – I thought there was *something* about her, something different, something changed. She seemed in higher spirits and more conscious of her appearance. And I must admit, it did cross my mind . . .'

'That she had begun a relationship?'

'Yes. But I cannot say for certain. She did not say anything to confirm my suspicions.'

'What *did* she talk about when you last saw her?'

'How much she disliked working at the laundry. I had – of course – offered her a good position among my household staff on numerous occasions, but she always refused. Pride again, you see. She talked about her leg; although she *always* talked about her leg. She wanted to go to a spa in Switzerland where she had read about a new miracle cure.'

'When you visited her on Thursday evening, did you see anyone else?'

'I saw her neighbour – looking out of the window. And there was a man in the yard.'

'Did you recognise him?'

'No.'

'What did he look like?'

'I wasn't paying much attention.'

'How was he dressed?'

'I think . . .' Kristina bit her lower lip. 'I think he was wearing a bowler hat and a long coat.'

'Did he have a beard? A moustache?'

'I really can't remember.'

'What was he doing?'

'He wasn't doing anything – he was just standing.'

'Waiting?'

'Possibly.'

'Did he see you?'

'I imagine so.'

'In which case, I would urge you to be very vigilant. If you see this man again, you must not hesitate to contact us.'

'But I took very little notice of him. He isn't someone I'd recognise.'

While Rheinhardt and Frau Vogl continued their conversation, Liebermann's attention was drawn to a series of lithographs. They were executed in a style that reminded him of illustrations he had seen in *Ver Sacrum,* the journal of the Vienna Secession. The female figures, in mannered stances, were greatly influenced by Klimt. Liebermann moved closer and examined the autograph: Carl Otto Czeschka. Each image showed a scene from the fairy story 'Ashputtel'. He followed the narrative: the ugly step-sisters, confiscating Ashputtel's fine clothes and giving her instead an old frock; Ashputtel, by the wishing tree, taking delivery of her 'magical' dresses – each more beautiful than the last; the handsome prince sliding a golden slipper onto Ashputtel's dainty foot as the stepsisters reel back in horror . . .

A gentle knock rescued Liebermann from the phantasmagorical world of the Brothers Grimm. On the other side of the room a door was slowly opening. The man who appeared was middle-aged and dignified. Before the newcomer closed the door again, Liebermann saw that the adjoining chamber was also a bedroom.

'May I introduce my husband,' said Kristina. 'Doctor Heinz Vogl. My dear, these gentlemen are Detective Inspector Rheinhardt and his colleague, Herr Doctor Liebermann.'

Heinz Vogl bowed: '*Doctor* Liebermann?'

'I am a psychiatrist.'

'And you work for the security office?'

'Doctor Liebermann is a psychological consultant,' interjected Rheinhardt.

'I see,' said the older man. 'Then I sincerely hope, Herr Doctor Liebermann, that your branch of medicine – controversial though it is – can provide such insights as lead to the swift apprehension of this . . .' his features screwed up in distaste '. . . monster!'

He inclined his head in modest deference and went to his wife, who reached out to him as he approached. Taking her hand, Vogl sat down on the bed beside her.

'Are you all right, my darling?' Kristina responded with a faint smile and then coughed.

212

Her husband addressed the visitors: 'A chest infection. She needs to rest.'

'Of course,' said Rheinhardt. 'We will not disturb you for very much longer.'

Heinz Vogl picked up one of his wife's sketchbooks.

'You have been working, my dear.' The tone of his voice carried a gentle censure.

'I was bored,' Kristina replied.

The physician shook his head and sighed.

'Were you acquainted with Fräulein Wirth, Herr doctor?' Rheinhardt asked.

'Yes, I met her once. Kristina wanted me to examine her – to give an opinion. I'm not really a leg man, so I arranged for her to see a colleague, Alvintzi. I met her briefly at the hospital.'

'What was wrong with Fräulein Wirth?'

'It was difficult to establish. Alvintzi wasn't sure whether it was a muscular or orthopaedic problem.'

'Frau Vogl must take great care,' said Rheinhardt. 'The man she saw outside Fräulein Wirth's—'

'What man?' Vogl cut in. He looked from Rheinhardt to his wife. 'You saw a man?'

'Hush now,' said Kristina.

'You didn't say.'

'It was nothing.' She made an appeasing gesture. 'Really, Heinz . . .'

'With the greatest respect, Frau Vogl' said Rheinhardt, 'I would not describe the observation of a man waiting outside Fräulein Wirth's apartment on the evening of her murder as *nothing* – particularly since he also saw you. If he was the murderer, then you may be in great danger.'

'My dear,' said Heinz Vogl, brushing a strand of hair from his wife's face. 'What did you see?'

'A man . . . in the courtyard. I thought nothing of it. He could have been anybody.'

'Frau Vogl,' said Rheinhardt. 'You cannot be complacent about such things.'

'It's just as well you haven't been out,' said Vogl to his wife.

'I intend to be at the salon tomorrow morning,' she replied tartly.

'But you are unwell.'

'I am feeling much better today.' A trace of irritation had entered Kristina's voice.

'My wife,' said Vogl, a little exasperated, 'is a dress designer of some reputation.'

'Indeed,' said Rheinhardt. 'Frau Rheinhardt is a great admirer of Frau Vogl's creations.'

'Ashputtel,' said Liebermann. All eyes fastened on the young doctor – the flow of conversation was halted by his exclamation. 'These lithographs,' he continued. 'They tell the story of Ashputtel.'

'Yes,' said Kristina, her voice dipping and rising – uncertain.

'They are very beautiful, and so apposite.'

'I'm sorry?'

'The dresses: dresses are so important in the story. And you – being a dress designer.'

Frau Vogl smiled.

'I had not thought of that. I bought them only because I admired the artist's style.'

'Czeschka.'

'Yes. He is young and very talented.'

Liebermann paused, then asked abruptly: 'Have you always kept in touch with Fräulein Wirth, continuously – throughout your life?'

The effect was jarring.

'No. We didn't correspond for a while. We stopped when I was about fifteen, and I didn't hear from her again until I was in my late twenties.'

A curious silence ensued. Kristina produced a lace handkerchief from the sleeve of her kimono and pressed it against her mouth. She coughed, this time more forcefully.

'Inspector,' said Vogl. 'My wife really should be resting.'

'Of course,' said Rheinhardt. 'Forgive me. You have been most helpful.'

As they walked down the Linke Wienzeile the sphere of gilded laurel leaves that surmounted the Secession building came into view.

'Odd,' said Liebermann.

'What was?' Rheinhardt asked.

'The whole thing.'

'I didn't think so.'

'Her answers . . .'

'What about them?'

'They were too perfect.' Liebermann frowned. 'Contrived. Everything fitting neatly into place.'

'You think she made it all up?' Rheinhardt looked at his friend askance. 'Why on earth would she do that?' Liebermann shrugged. 'Max, if anyone was acting oddly, it wasn't her, it was you! Why did you ask that question at the end?'

Liebermann stopped walking.

'Do you remember what she said: after you'd inquired about Fräulein Wirth and gentlemen friends? She said that Fräulein Wirth had had *many,* and that when she was younger Fräulein Wirth had been very striking. How would she have known that if they had lost touch as adolescents and not seen each other again in a decade or more?'

'Frau Vogl obviously learned these things after they had resumed their acquaintance.'

'But to say it in *that* way . . . *she was very striking.* She said it as though she could remember it.'

'She may have seen a photograph.'

'Were there any photographs found in Fräulein Wirth's apartment?'

'No. But that does not mean that such photographs have never existed.'

Liebermann shook his head.

'And why hadn't Frau Vogl told her husband that she had seen a man standing outside Fräulein Wirth's apartment?'

'She didn't think it important – or she didn't want to worry him. You saw his reaction. He is her senior by a considerable margin and probably prone to the anxieties more commonly observed in a parent than a spouse. I formed the impression that he was protective – perhaps over-protective.'

Liebermann walked a few steps further and stopped again.

'And another thing.' Rheinhardt's expression showed that he was losing patience. 'Didn't it strike you as strange that Frau Vogl had made no connection between Ashputtel's dresses in the lithographs and her occupation! She was genuinely surprised when I pointed it out. In which case, what was it about those pictures that appealed to her?'

'She told you. She liked the artist's style.'

'That goes without saying. But what – in addition to the artist's style – made her choose the story of Ashputtel?'

'Max,' said Rheinhardt, gripping his friend's shoulder and giving him a firm shake. 'Does it matter? She isn't a suspect, for heaven's sake!'

'So why was she acting so . . . strangely?'

'She wasn't!' Rheinhardt tapped the side of his friend's head. 'It was all in your mind! I am sure that Frau Vogl would make a very interesting case study; however, now is not the time and this street corner is not the place. Let's go to Café Schwarzenberg. I could do with another coffee.' Rheinhardt paused before adding, 'And something else, perhaps.'

CHAPTER 34

The photographs were spread across the top of Commissioner Brügel's desk. He selected three full-length portraits and laid them out in a row: Adele Zeiler, lying on the lawn of the Volksgarten, Bathild Babel, sprawled naked on her bed, and Selma Wirth, the hilt of a dagger sticking out of her chest. Brügel's gaze lingered on the central image. He sighed, opened a drawer and removed a ladies' magazine. He held the cover up for Rheinhardt to see. It was a publication concerned almost exclusively with society news and gossip.

'Have you seen this, Rheinhardt?'

'No. It is not a circular I subscribe to.'

The commissioner frowned, flicked through the pages and began reading: '"The dinner was given by Frau Kathi shortly before her departure for the Riviera. On this occasion, my fellow guests included Prince Liechtenstein; Marquis von Becquehem; the director of the Court Opera, Herr Gustav Mahler; Herr director Palmer; the court theatre actor Max Devrient and his wife. Frau Kathi was wearing the most beautiful pearls and was, as always, the perfect hostess. After dinner, she said that she wished all the women of Vienna could escape to the Riviera with her. Of course, our dear friend was alluding to the frightful spate of murders that have recently been the subject of so much speculation in the vulgar press."' Brügel closed the magazine and folded it over. 'You must have guessed the identity of Frau Kathi.'

Rheinhardt's mouth was suddenly very dry. He tried to swallow but found it difficult.

'Katharina Schratt?' the inspector croaked.

Brügel nodded. It was common knowledge that Schratt – a famous comic actress – was the Emperor's mistress.

'You know what this means, Rheinhardt? It's only a matter of time before I get a telephone call from the Hofburg. His Highness's aides will want to know what progress is being made. What shall I tell them?'

Rheinhardt motioned to speak, only to discover that when he opened his mouth he had no answer. He took a deep breath and tried again: 'We have made *some* progress, sir.'

Brügel patted a bundle of witness statements and reports.

'Have you, now? Permit me to précis what you have discovered so far. The perpetrator has dark hair, a pale complexion, and has knowledge of human anatomy. He smells of carbolic and once called himself Griesser. He owns an expensive frock coat and might wear a bowler hat.' The commissioner picked up the bundle and held it out towards Rheinhardt. 'You call *that* progress?'

Rheinhardt winced as the commissioner raised his voice.

'I am all too aware, sir, that the results of the investigation are disappointing.'

Brügel dropped the papers and they landed heavily.

'One more week, Rheinhardt.'

'I beg your pardon, sir?'

'After which I'm afraid responsibility for the case will have to be transferred to someone else. There's a specialist based in Salzburg, a detective with an academic interest in lust murder. He studied with Professor Krafft-Ebing. If I inform the palace that we're about to recruit an expert then that might pacify them, halt damaging talk.'

'With respect, sir—'

The commissioner was not inclined to listen to Rheinhardt's objection.

'Once the palace get involved, accusations of incompetence soon follow. I'm sorry, Rheinhardt. You haven't given me enough. I have the interests of the entire department to consider. One more week.'

PART III

THE SOPHOCLES SYNDROME

CHAPTER 35

In the dream he had been sitting cross-legged on the floor of an empty room where an oriental woman wearing a familiar scarlet kimono served him tea. Through an open door he had observed large dragonflies with opalescent wings hovering above a koi pond. The atmosphere was peaceful, the air redolent with exotic fragrances. A breeze disturbed a carousel of wind chimes suspended in the branches of a kumquat tree. He had watched the metal tubes colliding, each contact producing a tone of beguiling purity. As the carousel turned he noticed something odd about the motion of the chimes. They were swinging slowly, too slowly, as if submerged beneath water. The soothing silvery music became more sonorous and plangent, until the effect was similar to a gamelan orchestra. A man with a bowler hat and long coat ran past the doorway.

It was at that point that Rheinhardt was awakened by the harsh reveille of his telephone.

The driver had chosen to weave through the deserted back streets, following a concentric course in parallel with the south-western quadrant of the Ringstrasse – Josefstadt, Neubau, Mariahilf, Wieden – and the dream had accompanied his thoughts all the way. When the carriage finally slowed, Rheinhardt made a concerted effort to dismiss the Japanese room from his mind. He opened the door, stepped out onto the cobbles, and paused to consider the view: the gatehouse of the Lower Belvedere Palace. A lamp was suspended beneath the tall archway and the windows on either side were illuminated from within by a soft yellow lambency. In daylight, Rheinhardt would have been able to see a path ascending in two stages to the western tower of the Upper Palace. Now all that he could see was the flaring of torches in the distance.

Inside the gatehouse Rheinhardt discovered a constable sitting at a table with a much older man who was wearing overalls. They had evidently been sharing the contents of a hip flask. The constable started and attempted to stand up. His sabre became trapped behind the chair leg and he muttered an apology before straightening his back and clicking his heels.

'Inspector Rheinhardt?'

'Indeed.'

'Constable Reiter, sir. And this gentleman is Berthold Wilfing – the head gardener. It was Herr Wilfing who discovered the body, sir.'

Wilfing pressed his palms down on the table: rising seemed to require the strength of his arms as well as his legs. He was probably in his early sixties and appeared surprisingly frail for a gardener.

'It was a terrible shock – let me tell you.'

Rheinhardt addressed the constable: 'Has my assistant arrived yet?'

'No, sir.'

'Then who's up there?' The inspector gestured towards the rear window. 'I saw torches.'

'A colleague from Hainburgerstrasse, sir. Constable Kiesl. With the body, sir.'

Rheinhardt nodded and turned again to the gardener.

'Yes, it must have been a terrible shock. I am sorry; however, I am afraid I must ask you a few questions. I hope you will not find them too upsetting. Tell me, Herr Wilfing, at what time did you make your discovery?'

'About three-thirty. No, later.'

'May I ask what you were doing in the gardens at that time?'

'Collecting these.' Wilfing picked up a bucket from under the table. It was full of snails and slugs. One of the snails had climbed onto the rim, its tentative horns extended. 'Nocturnal creatures, sir, and at this time of year dreadful bad for the seedlings.'

'Do you always commence work so early?'

'No. But these last few weeks have been exceptional.'

'Why's that?'

'The Lord Chamberlain.'

'I'm sorry. What has Prince Liechtenstein got to do with it?'

'He's having a function, at eleven, in the Goldkabinett.'

'What? Today?'

'Yes. *Today*. If his guests step out into the garden and all the beds have been ruined by these fellows,' he flicked the snail on the rim back into the bucket, 'well, that wouldn't do, would it?'

'I suppose not.'

'They say that Prince Eugène was a keen gardener. He had rare shrubs and trees brought to the Belvedere from all over the world. You have to take care of a legacy like that. These gluttons,' Wilfing shook the bucket, 'will eat anything!'

'I'm sure that's true,' said Rheinhardt. 'However, if we could perhaps return now to the more pressing matter of your discovery?'

'Oh, yes. I was crossing one of the sunken lawns – and I very nearly trod on her. *What's this?* I said to myself. And there she was – just lying there . . . a pretty thing as well. Dead. But not a mark on her. She must have just keeled over. It happens, I suppose. The heart.' Wilfing tapped his chest authoritatively. 'What was she doing there, eh? That's what I'd like to know – out in the gardens after dark.'

'Did you touch the body?'

'You must be joking. It's bad luck to touch the dead.' The gardener shivered and lowered the bucket to the floor. 'I went straight to the stables.

226

I woke up one of the lads and sent him off to Hainburgerstrasse – told him to go as quick as his legs would carry him.' Wilfing's expression became anxious. He took a watch from his pocket and, glancing at its face, added: 'Can I get back to work now? If the beds get ruined and the prince's guests are displeased there'll be hell to pay!'

'Herr Wilfing, I suspect the prince's guests will be even more displeased if the body hasn't been removed by eleven o' clock. I am afraid I must ask you to wait here until my assistant arrives. You must make a statement. When this is done you can proceed with your duties.'

Rheinhardt left the gatehouse and walked up the path, heading towards the torches. He could see very little, but as he made his ascent his eyes adjusted to the darkness and he became aware of the Upper Palace as an elevated penumbra situated at the other end of the gardens. The distinctive line of the roof – suggesting a desert kingdom of tents and pavilions – was made just visible by the dull glow of the sleeping city beyond. Aiming for the feverish incandescence of the torches, Rheinhardt entered a mazelike arrangement of hedges. They enclosed a sunken lawn, in the middle of which was the conspicuous form of a supine female body. Next to her stood an anxious-looking constable, his hand gripping the hilt of his sabre, his tense posture communicating his readiness to use it.

'It's all right, Kiesl. Inspector Rheinhardt – security office.'

The constable let go of his weapon.

'Sir.'

Rheinhardt approached the body.

'Anything to report?'

'No, sir.'

'Where did you get these torches from?'

'Herr Wilfing – the head gardener. You've spoken to him?'

'Yes.'

'His paraffin lamp didn't give off enough light. I thought you'd be needing something better.'

'Well done, Kiesl. Commendable foresight.'

'Thank you, sir.'

Rheinhardt gazed at the dead woman. The scene evoked memories of the opera house: a shield maiden laid out beneath a starry sky, torch-bearers and a pyre. Crouching down beside her and falling on one knee like a vassal, he studied her face. Young. Early twenties, perhaps? A beauty spot beneath her left eye; coils of blonde hair complementing strong features; her chin, a little too broad – a dimple near its apex; long white lashes. The redness of her cheeks was borrowed from the flames.

Bracing himself, Rheinhardt slipped his hand beneath her occipital bone. He felt something cold and hard projecting out above the uppermost vertebra. When he tried to move it he found that it was fixed. He did not trouble to raise the body any higher in order to examine the object. He knew exactly what it was. The decorative head of a hatpin. To be exact: the decorative head of the hatpin purchased at Frau Schuschnig's shop by the man calling himself Griesser.

Rheinhardt positioned himself at the other extremity of the woman's body and lifted the hem of her skirt. There was no mistaking the pungent odour and – as he had expected – she wasn't wearing any drawers. He knew before he looked over his shoulder that the young constable's expression would be disapproving.

'Kiesl. I would be most grateful if you would search the area for a ladies' hat – and a ladies undergarment.'

'Yes, sir.'

The constable pulled one of the torches from the ground and disappeared behind a hedge.

Rheinhardt searched the dead woman's pockets. He found some money, a set of keys, a box of slim cigars, and a silk monogrammed handkerchief showing the interlinked letters C and R. He experimented with some possible names: *Clara Raich, Charlotte Ruzicker, Christel Rebane* . . . He thought of the other victims: Zeiler, Babel and Wirth. How many more women would this monster take? Rheinhardt was overcome by a wave of pity and hopelessness. The investigation had not progressed at all and it was *his* fault. It was his case, his responsibility – and what had he achieved? The collection of a few worthless facts, useless *scraps* of information. Commissioner Brügel had been right to admonish him. Guilt found a niche in Rheinhardt's gut. It settled somewhere in his lower abdomen, among the peristaltic mass of his intestines. Nausea threatened to empty his stomach. He stood up and made his way back to the path.

The broad staircase rising to the upper level of the gardens was inviting. Somehow the notion of ascent seemed to promise Rheinhardt the prospect of release from the despair that had suddenly seized him.

Higher ground, clarity, a longer view . . .

Rheinhardt climbed to the top, where he was confronted by one of the Belvedere's famous sphinxes. There was just enough light to make out her crouching, winged presence. The inspector approached and halted directly in front of her. The expression that she wore was one of supreme indifference, a blend of ennui and scornful disregard. She was wearing a cuirass, the design of which emphasised the fullness of her perfectly rounded breasts. Rheinhardt sensed her sisters, out there in the darkness – infinitely patient – a pride of sphinxes, incubating secrets.

'Give me the answer,' he whispered.

So, it's come to this, Rheinhardt thought. *Begging a statue for help!*

If the sphinx did possess supernatural powers, she showed no sign of willingness to employ them at Rheinhardt's bidding. Her centuries of disinterest and stony constitution had inured her to human misery: what could be more inconsequential than four human lives to a beast whose seasons were epochs?

'Sir?' Kiesl's voice floated up from below.

'What is it?'

'I've found something . . . an undergarment.'

'All right. I'm coming down.'

Rheinhardt descended the steps and negotiated the little maze of hedges. He found the constable – a torch held aloft in one hand, a pair of yellow drawers in the other – looking like a strange parody of the goddess Libertas.

'Where did you find them?

'Just here – thrown over this bush.'

Rheinhardt took the item from the constable.

'Now see if you can find her hat.'

Rheinhardt went back to the body. He patrolled the lawn, systematically searching the ground for anything that might have been dropped. While he was doing this he heard footsteps – the brisk, energetic stride of his assistant.

'Ah, there you are, Haussmann.'

'I came as fast as I could.'

'Indeed.'

Rheinhardt gestured toward the dead woman.

'Her initials are CR.'

'Cäcilie Roster,' said Haussmann.

'What?'

'That's her name. Cäcilie Roster. I recognise her. She's an entertainer. She does variety shows. I've seen her singing comic songs at Ronacher's.'

CHAPTER 36

In due course I worked for several undertakers; however, it wasn't until I secured a position at the Erste Wiener Leichenbestattungs-Anstalt Enterprise des Pompes Funèbres that I was permitted to assist Doctor Traugott Stohl – the embalmer. I had always been interested in embalming and considered myself fortunate to have this opportunity to study the procedures involved. Of course, I had seen embalmers at work before but, as you will appreciate, embalming is not common and observations conducted at a distance are no substitute for participation. I have no idea why embalming isn't more popular in Vienna, a city which has always appreciated the beauty of a corpse in eternal repose. The aristocracy are fond of laying out their dead – as are certain members of the bourgeoisie, such as composers and politicians. But other than among these elements of society, embalming is largely restricted to instances in which the deceased must be transported over a long distance to a final resting place. Indeed, in such cases where the transfer will take a week or longer, embalming is compulsory, as decreed by the Minister of the Interior on the third of May 1875. You see? My enthusiasm knows no bounds. Even the legislation surrounding death has a peculiar fascination for me. But again, I digress.

Herr Doctor Stohl – God rest his soul – was a remarkable man. He died some five years ago from a brain disease and is buried in the Zentralfriedhof. I often visit his grave – a modest peaked slab engraved with his name, dates, and a quotation from the Bible.

> *Seek him that maketh the seven stars and Orion, and turneth the shadow of death into the morning, and maketh the day dark with night: that calleth for the waters of the sea, and poureth them out upon the face of the earth.*

Amos, 5:8

Before he died, the good doctor was very insistent that this quotation – and no other – should be his epitaph. To this day, I am not entirely sure of its meaning.

Doctor Stohl must have been in his sixties when we met. He was a sagacious old fellow who never troubled to open his mouth unless he had something to say. Private, guarded, and occasionally brusque, but never rude or uncivil, it was his habit to quote Ecclesiasticus: *Let thy speech be short, comprehending much in few words; be as one that knoweth and yet holdeth his tongue.* He earned my respect immediately and I flatter myself that he recognised something of his own character in me. Doctor Stohl was dedicated to the advancement of his discipline, which he approached with the earnest disposition of a scholar. He had studied the preservative methods employed by the Egyptians and knew much about the procedures favoured in the medieval world. (The Crusades, you see. The bodies of the Christian Knights had to be embalmed before they were carried home.) He once showed me a preservative 'recipe' consisting of honey, red wine, and a mixture of rare herbs that he had found in a book written by a thirteenth-century monk and subsequently sent me out to purchase a hare from the butcher's shop in order to test the formula's efficacy. It worked rather well.

In passing, you might be interested to learn that the dye I use on my hair – a mixture of lead oxide and slaked lime – was first used in ancient Egypt. I discovered the method of preparation in one of the good doctor's books.

Stohl had a small laboratory in one of the outbuildings, where he experimented with various substances in order to discover a chemical compound capable of suspending the disintegration of human flesh indefinitely. The notion of *perfect preservation* had acquired for him some of the glamour that past generations have afforded the Philosopher's Stone or the Sangrail.

Herr Doctor Stohl was not a man whom one could get close to. He was always distant, monastic. Yet I know that we shared a certain affinity, a common bond. He had very particular views concerning education. *If you have a question*, he would say, *do not ask me. Just watch – and learn.* He taught by example, eschewing words in favour of demonstrations and surprisingly eloquent lacunae.

I remember with what great care he went about his work. He took such pains to do things properly, making sure that every crevice and crease was cleaned with disinfectant – eyes, mouth, and all other orifices: the way he trimmed beards, or shaved off stubble, never leaving the tiniest nick. Did you know that eyeballs have a tendency to sink down into their sockets after death? Doctor Stohl devised invisible supports to ensure that this would not happen. He taught me to tilt the head slightly so that mourners could see more easily the face of their loved one. Under his benevolent tutelage I was even inspired to learn a little Latin and Greek.

You have been wondering about my erotic life.

Did the stillness of the bodies arouse me?

I will be honest: Yes.

And did I succumb to the obvious temptation of their proximity?

The first time it happened was not long after I started my first job. The daughter of an American financier fell down some stairs and broke her neck.

She was removed to the undertaker's within a few hours of her death. As soon as I saw her I felt an electrical excitement that raised the hairs on the back of my neck. Her body was aglow with a faint purplish light. My Angel was close by.

I was supposed to lock up the premises after the others had left and then leave myself. I locked the door, but I did not leave, choosing instead to remain with the American heiress.

What was it like?

I must remind you that I am disadvantaged by language. There are no words that can express what I have experienced – and continue to experience. How can I expect you to understand? You, for whom this world is a sealed container, for whom the horizon and the sky are an absolute boundary.

Yes, there was satisfaction. But it was a communion once removed.

How can I explain?

It was like being intimate with a woman whom one does not love but who has recently brushed against the woman with whom one is infatuated. You detect a hint of the beloved's perfume on her skin – and it is maddening.

Are you familiar with *Faust*? *Get me a kerchief from her breast, A garter that her knee has pressed.*

The poet's words describe me well: a man discharging into a void while clutching a garter!

Yet I could not stop myself. When opportunities arose, I took them. Such was my desire for Her.

You cannot imagine how I suffered. The anguish and agony. Lying there upon the mortuary table: yearning, wanting, desiring. The inadequate comfort of a cold embrace – my virility reduced to a shrivelled *nothing* in a dry mouth. The fading violet of Her presence, teasing, tantalising.

It was never going to be enough. I knew that even then.

Two months ago I travelled to Paris. The western façade of the great Cathedral of Notre Dame has three portals, one of which depicts Mary as the Bride of Christ. The Virgin in Majesty is transformed from Mother to Empress.

I don't know why I have written this . . .

You said that I should write down whatever came into my mind – without any attempt to censor thoughts and memories. Well, there it is. Notre Dame. What of it?

No, there is a connection. I see it now.

I was at my lowest ebb. I thought that I could not endure separation from Her a moment longer and resolved to end my suffering. It would be easy enough. A sleep followed by eternal, blissful consummation.

On returning to Vienna I prepared a lethal tincture of opium. But I did not drink it.

As I sat in my bedroom, glass in hand, I began to doubt the wisdom of my actions. *To everything there is a season – a time to be born and a time to die.* Perhaps I was being impatient. I might become the instrument of someone else's fate, but I should

237

not wrestle my own destiny from the gods. Such presumption reminded me of so many Greek heroes, whose over-reaching ambition was ill-judged. It occurred to me: I did not need to die in order to summon Her. Someone else's death would do just as well.

CHAPTER 37

Rheinhardt had arranged to meet his assistant outside Ronacher's variety theatre. He had given Haussmann an hour to discover Liebermann's whereabouts. During that time, he had searched for – and found – a café, discreetly situated in a back street, where he could revive his spirits with a favourite prescription of strong Türkische coffee and a slice of poppy-seed cake. Emerging from the shadowy interior into the broad bountiful light of a crisp morning, he felt better prepared to face the day. When Haussmann finally appeared, however, it was clear from the young man's expression and gait that his mission had been unsuccessful.

'Herr Doctor Liebermann is not at home, sir. I telephoned from the Post Office. And the hospital said he wasn't expected until this afternoon. I even tried the little coffee house by the Anatomical Institute.'

'And did you get something to eat while you were there?'

Haussmann's eyes slid to the side.

'Yes, sir. But I was only there for a few minutes.'

'In which case, you made excellent use of your time. We have a busy day ahead of us and it is difficult to work on an empty stomach. Come now. Let us see if anyone is inside.'

They found the stage door, rang the bell, and were admitted by an attendant wearing a shabby uniform. Rheinhardt showed his identification and asked to see the manager.

'You're lucky,' said the attendant. 'He's not normally in this early.'

They ascended several staircases until they came to a door. The attendant knocked and opened it without waiting for an invitation to enter.

'Not now, Harri!'

'It's the police,' the attendant called into the room.

'What – for me?'

'Yes, Ralf.'

Rheinhardt repositioned himself and saw a balding man in a colourful waistcoat and shirt-sleeves sitting behind a desk. In front of him, on wooden chairs, were two gentlemen with long black hair and shaggy fur coats. Their shoulders were massive.

'I'm sorry, gentlemen.' The manager addressed his guests. 'You'll have to excuse me.'

'When shall we be returning?' The voice was deep, rumbling, and strangely accented.

'Later. I'll have the new contracts ready for you by then. I promise.'

The two men stood, and as they did so their

extraordinary height became apparent. They were immense: identical twins, with brown skin, black eyes, and wide features. The first stooped to get through the doorway and Rheinhardt was obliged to tilt his head back to greet him.

'Good morning,' said Rheinhardt, looking up into the round moonlike face.

'Good morning, sir,' the giant replied in stilted, grammatically compromised German. 'I am very glad to be having seen you.'

His brother followed, but as the second giant ducked beneath the architrave he glowered back at the manager and uttered something in a strange tongue – so venomous and sibilant that it was clearly meant as an insult.

Rheinhardt and Haussmann entered the manager's office. The balding man shooed the attendant away, rose from his chair, and bowed.

'Ralf Grosskopf. At your service.'

'Detective Inspector Oskar Rheinhardt and my assistant, Haussmann.'

'Please sit down, gentlemen. I'd offer you some tea, but my secretary hasn't arrived yet. Forgive me.'

As Rheinhardt lowered himself into the chair, he could not stop himself from glancing back at the closing door.

'Yes, *they* are a striking pair.' Grosskopf's hands travelled in opposite directions from a central point in the air, successfully conjuring an imaginary billboard headline: 'The Two Darlings: the largest brothers ever seen.'

241

'Where are they from?' asked Rheinhardt.

'Tibet. Well, that's what they claim – but who knows, really.' The manager laughed. 'They were a real draw last year. They can lift seven men above their heads, break iron bars in two, and juggle with three-hundred-kilo weights.'

'They didn't look very happy,' said Rheinhardt.

'Oh, they'll come around – a little misunderstanding over the terms of their engagement, that's all. It's their agent's fault. Nestroy. He's an honest man but not very good on detail. Now, how can I help you?'

'Cäcilie Roster . . .'

'Zilli? Dear Zilli? What about her?'

'When did you see her last?'

'Yesterday.'

'She performed here?'

'Yes. She sang some songs between The Osmond Troupe and Bastian Biedermeier, the illusionist.'

'Did she go home after the performance?'

'No. I think she said she was going to Löiberger's. He stays open late, you see. She often goes there after shows.'

'Was she meeting someone?'

'Probably.'

'Do you know who?'

Grosskopf shook his head.

'It's hard to keep track of her admirers. She's a popular girl.' The manager winked before leaning forward and lowering his voice. 'Last week I found her in The Two Darlings' dressing room. They were throwing her across the table as if she was a ball. She said she was developing a new stage routine with them . . .'

Grosskopf raised his eyebrows and pursed his lips.

The thought of the young chanteuse abandoning herself to the eccentric pleasures of the two giants robbed Rheinhardt temporarily of the power of speech. He imagined the arc of her trajectory: hair in disarray, skirts billowing – Cäcilie Roster, manhandled into the air by arms capable of shearing iron. It was some time before the image receded, with its troubling erotic implications.

'You are not painting a very ladylike picture of Fräulein Roster.'

'True. But I haven't said anything that would offend her. She abhors convention, its part of her charm.' Grosskopf wiggled his fingers in the air. 'She's a fascinating woman.'

'Does she have a following: gentlemen who always attend her performances?'

'Not just gentlemen,' said Grosskopf, producing a burst of suggestive eyebrow movements.

Rheinhardt produced a weary sigh.

'Would you recognise any of these . . . supporters?'

'Yes, some of them. There's a fellow who wears a fur coat and carries a cane – and another who looks a little like the mayor.' Grosskopf leaned back in his chair. 'Has Zilli done something wrong? If so, I sincerely hope you don't intend to arrest her. She's still under contract.'

'Tell me more about Fräulein Roster's supporters.'

'There's not much more to say. They come to see her sing and then they leave. Sometimes they wait for her by the stage door.'

'What do they want?'

'We sell postcards of our artists in the foyer. They like to get them signed. And some of them give her small gifts: bunches of flowers, jewellery.'

'Do you know if she was given a hatpin recently? Grosskopf shrugged.

'Look, my friend, if you want to know what Zilli gets up to after shows, I'm not the person to ask. You should talk to Löiberger.'

CHAPTER 38

Black smoke was rising from a factory chimney that towered over the roofs of a begrimed terrace. Further down the road and in front of some railings a group of children, barely out of infancy, were playing on a pile of rubble. One of the urchins noticed Liebermann's approach and stood up, observing the stranger with earnest curiosity. Liebermann acknowledged the boy's interest with a smile; however, this was not reciprocated. Instead, the boy's expression became more intense. Liebermann turned a corner and found himself in an avenue of better-maintained larger properties. A few trees added a splash of colour to the prospect, but not enough to relieve the atmosphere of pervasive gloom. The trees swayed in a breeze redolent with the dank fetor of the Neustadter canal.

In due course, Liebermann arrived at his destination – a two-storey house with four windows. The simplicity of the building reminded him of a child's drawing. The curtains on the ground floor were drawn and Liebermann could not see anything through the upper windows. He crossed the road to get a better view but gained no benefit from the change of vantage. Liebermann became conscious that he was standing under a gas lamp – presumably the very same gas lamp under which Erstweiler had seen his doppelgänger. The young doctor touched the cast-iron post as if to confirm the reality of its existence.

Liebermann returned to the other side of the road and knocked on the house's front door. He waited. No reply. He knocked again, knowing that there would be no answer.

A cart loaded with barrels passed by.

The young doctor stepped backwards and glanced at the upstairs windows one last time before deciding on which of the neighbouring houses he would try. The presence of a window box made him veer to the right.

As soon as he had struck the knocker, a dog started barking. He heard the sound of a woman's voice: 'Quiet. Be quiet, Prinz.'

The door was opened by a middle-aged woman who was accompanied by a lively Dobermann pinscher.

'Yes?'

'Forgive me for disturbing you. I am a doctor and need to speak with Herr Kolinsky, who I believe lives next door. He is not at home. Do you have any idea when he will be back?'

'I haven't seen him or his wife for weeks. I think they must have gone away.'

'Do you know them?'

'Not really. He's not very friendly . . . and *her*: she has a very high opinion of herself.' Liebermann nodded sympathetically. The woman was encouraged: 'I'm glad they're away. They make a lot of noise – arguments – and it upsets the dog.' She extended her hand and stroked the pinscher's head. 'Good boy, Prinz.' The dog licked her fingers.

'They have a lodger – is that right?'

'Yes. Herr Erstweiler. A very pleasant gentleman.'

'You are acquainted with him?'

'Well, I wouldn't say that. We met a few times when I was walking Prinz. I haven't seen him recently, either. He may have found somewhere else to live. It wouldn't surprise me. They can't expect to keep lodgers if they're going to carry on like they do.'

Liebermann smiled.

'Thank you for your assistance.'

'Shall I tell them that you called – if I see them?'

'Yes. If you see them.'

'And your name is?'

'Herr Doctor Liebermann.'

The woman nodded and closed the door. The dog started barking again.

Liebermann gazed at the street lamp on the other side of the road.

His conversation with Freud came back to him. It was possible for material offensive to the ego to be projected outwards onto something foreign.

But such material could not be completely disowned.

The object into which this undesirable material is incorporated might take the form of another self . . .

But what was the nature of that undesirable material?

Liebermann knew the answer. Herr Erstweiler's dream of the English fairy tale had been so very revealing.

CHAPTER 39

Amelia Lydgate had made an informal arrangement with Professor Mathias, the terms of which were dictated by Mathias's neurotic illness and satisfied by the peculiarity of Amelia's character. In return for tidying his instruments Professor Mathias was happy for Amelia to sit in the morgue and observe him at work. It was an arrangement that had been negotiated, for the most part, without the use of language. The Englishwoman and the old professor enjoyed a curious and unexpected rapport. Indeed, the understanding that they had reached could not have been achieved using words alone, with their hard edges and explicit meanings. The indelicacy of such a conversation would have required Professor Mathias to admit the severity of his condition, which was something he was not prepared to do.

When she entered the morgue Amelia found the professor sitting on a stool, contemplating the body of a young woman: too young, she thought immediately, to have died naturally.

'Another victim?' she asked.

The professor nodded and without taking his

gaze from the corpse, said: 'Cäcilie Roster. A singer. Inspector Rheinhardt found her this morning in the gardens of the Belvedere palace. This . . .' he picked up a retort containing a metal object '. . . had been inserted into her brain.'

'Another hatpin?'

'Yes. Although of a different design to those used by the perpetrator to kill Adele Zeiler and Bathild Babel.'

Amelia took off her coat, hung it up, and crossed the floor. The woman's body was covered with sheets but her head was still exposed. It was as if she was in bed, sleeping. The woman possessed an attractive face with well-proportioned features and a mane of yellow curls.

'When will it end?' said Amelia pitifully.

The professor sighed and presented her with a few sheets of paper. 'Here is my report. Read it if you are interested.'

Amelia sat down next to the professor and studied his findings. When she had finished, she discreetly rearranged the instruments on his trolley before positioning herself at the head of the autopsy table. Mathias joined her and lifted the dead woman's chin with a crooked finger.

'I liked that gay young wench, Her two cheeks so red, Her mouth and her handsome brow, Her hair, so blonde and curly . . .'

'A poem?'

'"Early Love" – by Ludwig Heinrich Christoph Hölty.'

'I am afraid, Herr professor, I am not familiar with his work.'

'He was the most gifted lyric poet of the Göttingen circle. You are English. I would not expect you to be conversant with our great poets.' Overcome with sentiment, the professor took a comb from his pocket and began to run it through the dead woman's hair. 'Hölty also wrote a rather lovely "Dirge to the Moon". The last verse is very affecting: *Soon, dearest friend, Oh, soon will beam, Your silvery sheen, Over the tombstone mine . . .*'

If Amelia was impressed by the lyric genius of Hölty, she did not show it.

Mathias finished styling the dead woman's curls but before returning the comb to his pocket he noticed that a few strands had become caught in its teeth. He began to pick them out. The routine ease of his movements came to a halt when he discovered a darker hair. He held it beneath the electric light.

'Black,' he said, flatly.

The professor and the Englishwoman looked at each other.

'Someone else's?'

Mathias pulled the extremities of the black hair to make it taut. Then, turning to Amelia, he made her party to his thinking by means of an impromptu lecture: 'The shaft of a hair is covered with a close-set layer of transparent scales – the cuticle – and beneath these are the differentiated cells of the cortex and medulla. The structure of

251

a hair shaft resembles that of a pencil. The paint or varnish corresponds with the cuticle, the wood of the pencil corresponds with the cortex, and the central column of lead corresponds with the medulla. Hair pigment, which gives the hair its colour, is distributed through the medulla and cortex.' The professor paused and his eyes appeared to expand behind the thick lenses of his spectacles. 'A head of hair is not always uniform with respect to colour. Take your own, for example. It is quite clearly comprised of many shades of red.'

'But a black hair among blonde?'

'It happens'

'Are there tests to determine whether two different-coloured hairs belong to the same person?'

'Indeed there are. Two hairs from the same head might be different in colour, but they will show marked morphological similarities – for example, breadth, scale pattern, or shape of tip. Further, one can observe the contours of transverse sections, together with the character and proportions of the various layers.'

'How very interesting.'

Professor Mathias touched the black hair very gently, bending the shaft. He then did the same with a blonde hair.

'The black hair is more bristly than the blonde.' His expression showed that he considered that black hair's resistance a promising indication.

'Miss Lydgate. Your eyesight is superior to mine.' He tapped the lenses of his spectacles emphatically. 'Would you set up the microscope and prepare two slides: black and blonde.'

Mathias passed her the black hair and one of the blonde hairs which she took with great, almost exaggerated, care.

Amelia did as she was instructed and switched on an electric lamp. She bent over the eyepiece of the microscope and rotated the turret until she had found an appropriate objective.

'Let us begin with breadth,' said Professor Mathias. 'What do you see?'

'The black hair is thicker.'

'And the tip of each hair?'

'The black hair is sharper – the blonde hair more rounded.'

'Now the cuticle. Can you see the scales?'

Amelia increased the magnification.

'Yes.'

'Are there differences in scale size – or distribution?'

'No.'

'Now the bulb. Although the bulb has fewer differentiating features than the shaft, it can also provide us with very valuable information. A plump bulb – and the presence of traces of the ruptured hair sheath – is typical of a healthy hair that has been detached by force, while a shrunken and wrinkled bulb – without any sheath – is typical of dead or diseased hairs.'

'Herr professor?'

Amelia's voice contained a note of excitement.

'Yes.'

'There is something rather odd . . . a reflection perhaps.' She changed the position of the lamp without lifting her head. 'No. It is not a reflection. How strange.'

'What is?'

'The black hair. The shaft is entirely black – but just above the bulb . . . it is blonde.'

'May I see?'

Amelia stepped aside and allowed Professor Mathias to look down the barrel of the microscope.

'It has been dyed.'

'Oh . . .' said Amelia.

'You sound disappointed, Miss Lydgate.'

Mathias turned to look at her.

'I was hoping,' said Amelia, 'that we had chanced upon a piece of useful evidence, a hair from the head of the perpetrator. But now we must suppose that this hair belongs to another female entertainer.'

'Must we?' said the professor.

CHAPTER 40

After attending Professor Mathias's autopsy Rheinhardt had returned to Löiberger's. He had visited the coffee house earlier in the day, but it had been closed and a sign in the window had informed him that the establishment would not be open again until six; however, it was nearly half past that hour when a man appeared, striding down the middle of the street, jingling a set of keys in his hand. He was a portly fellow, with a round face and snub nose, which, taken together with his black curly hair and steel-rimmed glasses, made him look very much – so Rheinhardt thought – like Schubert.

'Herr Löiberger?'

'Yes,' said the man. 'I'm Löiberger.' Then he laughed, for no apparent reason.

'Inspector Reinhardt – security office. May I come in?'

'Of course. My regulars won't be here for hours yet.' Again, the laugh. It didn't seem to be a nervous laugh but merely a welling-up of good humour.

Löiberger unlocked the door and pushed it open.

'Please sit down, inspector. I'll get you something to drink.'

'That won't be necessary.'

'No, I insist. You look as though you've been
waiting. You must be cold.'

For once, Rheinhardt didn't object. The day –
which had started so early – was beginning to
catch up with him. Löiberger disappeared through
a doorway behind a counter piled high with pyramids of Turkish delight and *punschkrapfen*.
Rheinhardt sat at a window table and looked
around the dark interior. It was a shabby little
coffee house. Yet it had a certain bohemian charm.
The walls were hung with Venetian carnival masks
and photographs of famous actors. A bust of
Goethe stood on a pedestal outside the toilets.

Löiberger returned with a tray on which he
balanced a bottle of schnapps and two shot glasses.
He took the seat opposite Rheinhardt and poured
the drinks.

'Thank you,' said Rheinhardt. 'You are most
kind.'

'*Prost!*' said Löiberger, raising the glass before
throwing his head back and emptying the contents
down his throat.

'*Prost!*' returned Rheinhardt.

It was good schnapps.

'So, inspector,' said Löiberger, refilling the
glasses. 'How can I help?'

'Do you know who Cäcilie Roster is?'

'Yes, of course. She's one of my regulars.'

'When was the last time you saw her?'

'Last night. She stayed late – as usual. And left just after midnight.'

'Was she with anyone?'

Löiberger laughed: 'Was she with someone? She's always with someone. She caused a stir last week by arriving with two giants. I'm not joking, inspector, two giants.'

'I believe you,' said Rheinhardt. 'But last night, Herr Löiberger. If you could try to remember who she was with last night?'

'A gentleman . . .'

'What did he look like?'

'A handsome fellow: high cheekbones and very bright eyes.'

'Blue?'

'I think so. Yes. I assumed he was a performer.'

'Do you remember the colour of his hair?'

'Black.'

'Did you serve him?'

'Yes.'

Rheinhardt paused.

'Herr Löiberger, I am sure that my next question will strike you as rather peculiar. But I would be most grateful if you would give it your most serious consideration. What did this man smell like?'

Herr Löiberger gave the question a moment's thought, and then burst out laughing. 'Really, inspector . . .'

CHAPTER 41

Frau Harrer arrived at Rainmayr's studio with her two daughters, Fränzel and Gusti. She was about to follow them inside when Rainmayr stopped her with a raised finger.

'I'd rather you didn't. There's no need.' Before Frau Harrer could object, he produced some coins and pressed them into her moist palm. 'You can expect more, in due course.'

She took the money and called after the girls: 'Fränzel, Gusti. Do whatever Herr Rainmayr says. Understand?'

Rainmayr had first seen Frau Harrer and her daughters in a queue, waiting to be given a free bowl of soup by workers from a women's charity, and had offered to buy them a more substantial meal in a nearby coffee house. Frau Harrer had not required much persuading and while she and her daughters were bolting down their food Rainmayr had made his proposal. He was never in any doubt that Frau Harrer would accept.

'Come back this afternoon,' said Rainmayr, closing the door.

The two girls stood awkwardly in the middle of

the studio. The eldest, Fränzel, was probably about fifteen. She had long straight hair and sharp angular features. Gusti, who Rainmayr judged to be a year younger, was obviously related, although her face was less severe.

'Now,' said Rainmayr, clapping his hands together. 'Go behind that screen and take off your clothes.'

'All of them?' asked Fränzel.

'Yes.'

'But it's cold.'

'Don't worry about that, I'll light the stove in a minute. Besides, you won't be entirely naked. I have some new clothes I want you to wear. Pretty clothes.'

He had learned from experience that a businesslike manner was more likely to produce compliance.

The two girls went behind the screen and Rainmayr rummaged in a bag for some garments and accessories. It was a condition laid down by his patron that the commission he was about to begin work on should feature 'partially clothed models of youthful appearance'.

Fränzel stepped out first, her arms positioned to cover her breasts and genitals. She glanced at Rainmayr nervously, before hissing at her sister: 'Come on – you have to.' Gusti appeared a few moments later. Her head was bowed and she was looking at her feet.

'Over here, you two. Don't be shy.'

They crossed the floor, leaving a trail of footprints in the charcoal dust. Rainmayr's eye was immediately drawn to their jutting hip bones and skeletal prominences. Their skin was perfect for his purposes: white and transparent enough to offer tantalising glimpses of internal structures. For Rainmayr, nudity was not simply about the removal of clothing. His aesthetic sensibility demanded a form of nudity that advanced one step further, satisfying a need for deeper and deeper levels of exposure. Not every model could be naked in the way that Rainmayr wanted. The opaque exterior of a well-fed woman held no interest for him.

Rainmayr opened the bag wide and showed the girls what was inside.

'See. Pretty things.' He then shook it for good measure.

He picked out a choker and placed it around Fränzel's neck. Then he found a stocking.

'Stand on one leg.'

Rainmayr knelt down, slipped the stocking on Fränzel's foot and pulled it up to her thigh.

'Now, the other one.'

The girl reached out to steady herself with the hand that she had been previously using to cover her genitals. Rainmayr glanced up and was pleased with what he saw.

CHAPTER 42

The dying human weakens the partition that separates *this* world from *Her* world. In Eastern religions it is said that the soul enters the body when the newborn infant takes its first breath. I believe this to be correct. The first breath creates an opening through which the eternal essence pours, filling the empty vessel of the flesh. A correspondent event occurs with the very last breath. The final exhalation creates the temporary corridor through which the soul must make its exit from the world, the very same corridor through which She enters to effect our liberation. Death is very much like a state of possession. In the moment of death, we are possessed by death.

You grasp, I hope, the significance of this?

Let me be plain.

It occurred to me that expiry during copulation would make communion with Her possible: as the Virgin in Majesty is transformed from Mother to Empress, so the Queen of Darkness is transformed from reaper to lover. She becomes attainable.

I searched for a fitting host but without success.

I tried the obvious places – the brothels, the Prater – but none of the women I encountered seemed right. Let us say that they struck a wrong note. In the end, it turned out that my nocturnal jaunts were entirely unnecessary. You see, I didn't *find* Adele Zeiler. Adele Zeiler found me.

I was sitting in the Volksgarten, admiring the Theseus Temple, when she emerged from a crowd, caught my eye, and sat next to me.

– *Good afternoon.*

– *Good afternoon.*

Pause.

An exchange of smiles.

– *It's very pleasant here, isn't it?*

Thus, with these simple words, she sealed her fate. She was flirtatious, engaging, yet at the same time oddly self-contained. Did you ever see her face? It was interesting. That said, it was perfectly clear what kind of woman Fräulein Zeiler was. We arranged to meet again and when we did I gave her the gift that she had been chasing. A hatpin. One of two hatpins, in fact, that I already possessed, having purchased them at Jaufenthaler's – a grubby little jewellery shop on the Hoher Markt – in readiness.

Ah yes. I am reminded that this is something that interests you.

You will appreciate that my task was fraught with logistical difficulties: guns are noisy, stab wounds bleed, and the time a poison takes to act impossible to calculate. By contrast, the method I chose

262

was silent, clean, and allowed me to determine precisely the moment of communion. Did I think of it myself? No, I didn't. I learned about it during a chance conversation with a gentleman by the name of Doctor Buchleitner. He was called upon to embalm the body of a twelve-year-old baron who had been accidentally killed by his older brother – a cretin – while writing a letter to his absent father. The cretin had come up behind him, picked up a freshly sharpened pencil, and had then thrust it into his brother's neck. Unfortunately, the pencil was not stopped by the floor of the skull but went through the foramen magnum and into the brain. Of course, the boy died instantly.

Fräulein Zeiler.

We met in Honniger's, a little coffee house in Spittelberg. I gave her the hatpin and promised her more baubles in due course. Our conversation was frivolous, but we both knew that a contract had been made and that she would honour her obligation. Therefore I was not surprised when she suggested that we go for an evening stroll in the Volksgarten. By the time we arrived there it was almost dark.

I will assume that you are not interested in our preliminary embraces and kisses. Such things, I dare say, you can imagine. You will be interested in what followed: communion.

CHAPTER 43

Professor Freud took a panatella from the cigar box on his desk. He had already told Liebermann two jokes that he had heard while playing tarock on Saturday night with Professor Königstein, and was about to tell a third.

'The villagers went to the cattle market and there were two cows for sale. One from Moscow for two thousand roubles and one from Minsk for a thousand roubles. They bought the cow from Minsk. It produced lots of milk and the people were delighted with their purchase. So much so that they decided to get a bull to mate with the cow. If the calves born of this union were anything like their mother, the shtetl would never be short of milk again. They scraped together just enough money to buy a strong, handsome bull and they put it in the pasture with their prize cow. But things did not go to plan. Whenever the bull approached the cow she did not respond to his bovine ardour. The villagers were very upset and decided to consult their wise rabbi.' The Professor lit his cigar before continuing. '*Rabbi*, they said. *Whenever the bull approaches our cow, she moves away.*

If he approaches from the back, she moves forward. When he approaches her from the front, she moves backwards. An approach from the side, she edges off in the other direction. The rabbi thought about this for a minute or so and then and asked: *Is this cow – by any chance – from Minsk?* The villagers were dumbfounded, as they had never mentioned the provenance of their cow. *You are truly a wise rabbi,* they said. *How did you know the cow is from Minsk?* The rabbi looked at them all with a sorrowful expression, shrugged his shoulders and answered: *My wife is from Minsk.'*

Freud allowed himself a sly chuckle, and looked to his guest for approval. Liebermann had anticipated the punchline and was only mildly amused. Undeterred, Freud continued: 'Jokes frequently contain a fundamental truth concerning human behaviour. Why is libido distributed unequally between the sexes? I have no ready answer. In the subject matter of jokes, we find a very worthy agenda for psychoanalytic inquiry.'

Ever since Erstweiler had told Liebermann about his beanstalk dream the young doctor had been reflecting on a particular passage in *The Interpretation of Dreams*. The passage, perhaps only four or five pages long, was concerned with the origin of the psychoneuroses and made many references to Sophocles' great tragedy *Oedipus Rex*. Liebermann succeeded in steering the conversation away from jokes and towards theories of aetiology. Freud did not resist the transition. He seemed to welcome the opportunity to talk about this aspect of his work.

'I had been thinking about this possibility many years before the publication of my dream book.' He counted off the fingers of his left hand with the thumb of his right. 'Since 'eighty-seven, to be precise. I can remember sharing my thoughts with Fliess and recounting an incident from my early years. I was two – or perhaps two and half – and travelling on a train with my mother from Leipzig to Vienna. An opportunity arose to see her,' he paused, embarrassed, and ended his sentence in Latin, '*nudam.*' Freud's eyes glazed over with memories. He puffed on his cigar and the action seemed to pull him back into the present. 'In the intervening years, since writing to Fliess, I have become increasingly confident that love of the mother and jealousy of the father are a general phenomenon of early childhood.'

'General?'

'Yes. That is why I introduced the notion in my chapter on "Typical Dreams". It is remarkable how frequently the same themes emerge: for example, death of the parent who is of the same sex as the dreamer. Such dreams are very common among children aged approximately three years and over. They reveal – I believe – a wish to eliminate a rival. In Sophocles' drama, King Oedipus kills his father and marries his mother. The Greek myth seizes on a compulsion which everyone recognises because he has felt traces of it in himself. Every member of the audience was once a budding Oedipus in phantasy, and this dream-fulfilment played out in reality causes everyone to recoil in horror, with the full measure of repression which separates his infantile from his current state. Oedipus' destiny moves us only because it might very easily have been ours – the oracle has laid the same curse upon us before our birth as it has upon him.'

'Are you suggesting that, ultimately, there is no escape from neurotic illness?'

'Allow me to clarify.' Freud drew on his cigar again and stared through the dissipating cloud with penetrating eyes. 'I am not suggesting that this general phenomenon of childhood is the cause of the neuroses. But rather it is the failure to resolve these issues of love and hate which can be pathogenic: if prohibited desire and rage linger in the adult unconscious, then mental equilibrium *will* be disturbed.'

Freud caressed one of the statuettes on his desk: a little bronze Venus admiring herself in a mirror. A diadem circled her head and her legs were covered by a hanging garment. Her shoulders were narrow, her torso long, and her breasts pert.

'Most mothers would be horrified,' Freud continued, 'if they were made aware that their affectionate gestures were rousing a child's sexual instinct and preparing it for its later intensity. A mother will regard what she does as innocent – carefully avoiding excitation of the child's genitals;

however, we now know that sexual instinct is not only aroused by direct excitation. What we call affection will unfailingly show its effects one day on the genital zones as well. Be that as it may, an enlightened mother – conversant with psycho-analysis – should never reproach herself. She is only fulfilling her task in teaching the child to love. After all, he is meant to grow up into a strong and capable person with vigorous sexual needs and to accomplish during his life all the things that human beings are urged to do by their instincts.'

Liebermann changed position and as he did so Freud pushed the cigar box towards him. The young doctor declined.

'This *Sophocles syndrome* . . .' said Liebermann tentatively. 'When unresolved, does it always produce neurotic disturbances? Or do you think it might also be associated with more severe forms of mental illness, for example *dementia praecox*?'

'It is impossible – as yet – to say.'

'And how is the syndrome resolved?'

'The process of resolution must require the detachment of sexual impulses from the mother and the forgetting of jealousy for the father. But how this is achieved and by what mechanism I cannot say. The dissolution of this syndrome presents us with complex problems, and our burgeoning science has yet to furnish us with a comprehensive answer.'

Liebermann smiled inwardly. The professor had

exhibited a peculiarity of speech with which he, Liebermann, was now very familiar. Whenever Freud could not explain something he tended to blame psychoanalysis for the deficiency – never himself.

On his way home Liebermann thought deeply about his conversation with Professor Freud. Had he ever hated his father as a rival? Hate was too strong a word. No, he had never *hated* his father; however, he had to admit that their relationship had never been entirely satisfactory. He had always been a little uneasy in his father's presence and this subtle underlying tension – which had no obvious cause – had persisted, taking different forms, throughout his entire life. Did this underlying tension have an Oedipal origin? Although Liebermann was prepared to accept Freud's theory – at least provisionally – with respect to his father, he just couldn't do the same with respect to his mother. He had never loved his mother in that way!

Suddenly, he was disturbed by a realisation that the converse might be true. His mother adored him, of that there could be little doubt . . .

The dramatis personae abruptly changed position, discovering – in the process of reconfiguration – a new way in which their emotions could be triangulated.

An uneasy question rose up into Liebermann's mind.

What if his father, Mendel, secretly hated him for stealing his wife's love? What if his father had an unresolved Cronos syndrome and, like the mighty Titan, wanted to kill his usurping child? If such a desire was lurking in his unconscious, was it any wonder that they had never been entirely comfortable in each others' company?

A carriage passed and the curtain was drawn aside by a gloved hand. Liebermann glimpsed the face of a stunning young woman who was wearing a tiara. The vision of her beauty rescued him from the quagmire of his own self-inquiry.

He had never intended to consider the *personal* relevance of Freud's theory. He had only wished to discuss the Sophocles syndrome with Freud for one reason. Liebermann had sensed that within the tortured family dynamics of the Greek drama was the key to understanding Norbert Erstweiler.

CHAPTER 44

The carriage followed the Ringstrasse around the western edge of the Innere Stadt before turning into Rennweg and heading south towards Simmering. Rheinhardt opened his bag and handed Liebermann an envelope. The young doctor tipped the contents out onto his lap.

'She was discovered in the gardens of the Belvedere Palace,' said Rheinhardt, 'in the early hours of Monday morning.'

Liebermann studied the first photograph: a long shot of a woman lying in the middle of a sunken lawn.

'Who found her?'

'The head gardener. He was out early collecting slugs and snails.' Liebermann sifted through the photographs until he came across a close-up of the woman's face. 'She was stabbed with a hatpin,' Rheinhardt continued, 'just like Fräuleins Zeiler and Babel. In the relative isolation of the Belvedere gardens the fiend was once again emboldened to use his preferred technique. Remarkably, when Haussmann arrived he was able to identify the body.'

271

'They were acquainted?' said Liebermann, surprised.

'No,' said Rheinhardt, shaking his head. 'He had seen her performing at Ronacher's. She's a variety singer. Cäcilie Roster.'

Liebermann noticed the beauty spot under her eye and the dimple on her chin. He imagined the sound of her laughter – loud and life-affirming.

'Haussmann and I went to interview the theatre manager, who suggested that Fräulein Roster was an inveterate flirt. He also directed us to one of her haunts, Löiberger's, a coffee house patronised mostly by actors and poets and which is situated a short distance from the theatre. Herr Löiberger remembered serving Fräulein Roster on Sunday night. She was in the company of a gentleman with black hair and blue eyes. It must have been Griesser.'

'Did Herr Löiberger smell anything on the gentleman's clothes?'

'No.' Liebermann slipped the photographs back into the envelope and handed it back to Rheinhardt. 'Professor Mathias,' Rheinhardt continued, 'with Miss Lydgate's assistance made an interesting discovery. He found a black hair on Roster's body. Under the microscope, it proved to be a blond hair that had been dyed. Of course, we don't know that it belongs to Griesser . . .'

'But it seems likely.'

'Indeed. The combination of blue eyes and black hair is rather unusual.' Rheinhardt dropped the envelope into his bag. 'If the hair does belong to Griesser, I wonder why he does it – dyeing? He isn't assuming a disguise to avoid recognition. Vanity, perhaps?'

'Nothing so mundane,' said Liebermann. 'By dyeing his hair black he is associating himself with darkness, oblivion. It is a psychological phenomenon that Professor Freud calls *identification*.'

Rheinhardt considered his friend's comment and frowned. He did not ask Liebermann to elaborate. He had already heard enough of Liebermann's psychoanalytic theories at the start of their journey.

'Haussmann is going back to Ronacher's today,' said Rheinhardt, returning the conversation to routine police work. 'I've asked him to interview some of the performers, people who were acquainted with Roster.'

Liebermann nodded and turned to look out of the carriage window.

'You should probably be there too.'

'Well, not necessarily. If you are correct . . .'

'Yes, if I am correct, then you will be able to justify deserting Haussmann. But I can see that you are far from convinced that my speculations have a legitimate basis. Moreover, I appreciate that, given how matters stand with you and Commissioner Brügel, I cannot make excessive demands on your patience.'

'Forgive me, Max, but all your talk of doppel-gängers, dreams, and Sophocles *was* a little confusing. How was Herr Erstweiler this morning?'

'His condition is unchanged. I've told my colleague Kanner to medicate him if he becomes agitated.' Still looking out of the window, Liebermann asked: 'What was Miss Lydgate doing at the morgue?'

'Professor Mathias and Miss Lydgate seem to have developed some form of . . .' Rheinhardt's hand revolved in the air as he searched for the right words, '. . . *serviceable relationship*. He refers to her as if she is his protégée. I would never have predicted it. Would you?'

The streets outside were beginning to look shabby. Liebermann recognised the factory chimney, belching its black smoke into the sky, the railings, and the pile of rubble in the road. On this occasion there were no children scrambling up its sides. The carriage turned sharply into the adjoining avenue and came to a halt outside Erstweiler's residence.

They disembarked and Liebermann noticed that the house looked exactly as it did before: ground-floor curtains drawn, upper-floor curtains set apart. It was just as he had expected.

Liebermann crossed the pavement and grasped the knocker. His three strikes were comfortably absorbed by a yawning silence.

'Are you going to try again?' asked Rheinhardt. 'There's nobody in.'

The inspector smiled and, taking the knocker,

reproduced the insistent rhythms of Rossini's overture to *The Barber of Seville*.

'Just in case, eh?'

Rheinhardt waited for a few moments before searching his pockets. He withdrew a bunch of skeleton keys and began to insert them, one by one, into the keyhole. His efforts were rewarded by the noise of the lock-cylinder turning. Rheinhardt pushed the door and watched it swing open. 'There.'

The two men stepped inside.

'Hello?' Rheinhardt called out.

Tilting his head to one side, he listened for sounds of occupation.

Nothing stirred.

To their right was a parlour, and to their left a kitchen through which access could be gained to a walled garden. A staircase of uneven stone sank into the ground and terminated at a cellar entrance.

They returned to the kitchen and Rheinhardt began opening the cupboards.

'No bread, no cheese, no meat or vegetables. Only grains and pulses . . .'

When he had finished, Rheinhardt pointed at the ceiling.

'Shall we go upstairs?'

Liebermann consented with a curt nod.

The first room they entered contained a double bed, a wardrobe, a washstand and a chest of drawers. Liebermann opened the wardrobe. Inside, he found a gentleman's winter coat and a brightly coloured kimono. He lifted the garment from its hanger and held it up for Rheinhardt to see. Golden dragons flashed against a crimson background.

'Isn't that—?'

'The same kimono that Frau Vogl was wearing? Yes, it is.'

'What a coincidence.'

'Erstweiler works for a businessman called Herr Winkler who imports objets d'art from Japan. He told me that he stole it for Frau Kolinsky. Herr Winkler must also supply Frau Vogl with kimonos for sale in her salon.'

Liebermann put the garment back in the wardrobe and turned his attention to the chest of drawers. The top drawer was filled with men's clothing: socks, undergarments, shirts and trousers. The two lower drawers were empty.

'Herr Kolinsky's clothes are still here,' said Liebermann. 'But Frau Kolinsky's are gone. It is interesting that she took all her clothes *except* the kimono.'

'Why? What does *that* mean?'

'She didn't want to be reminded.'

Liebermann closed the empty drawers, stood up, and stepped out onto the landing. Rheinhardt followed.

'Erstweiler's room?'

'It must be.'

Liebermann turned the handle and entered. Whereas the Kolinskys' bedroom was cramped,

Erstweiler's was more spacious. The single bed and narrow wardrobe took up less floor space. A table and chair were positioned by the window and a large white bowl and razor showed where Erstweiler conducted his ablutions. On a stool beside the bed was a small pile of books. Liebermann examined the spines. The first was an anthology of fantastic literature, and the other two were slim volumes of romantic poetry.

Rheinhardt placed his hands on his hips and surveyed the room.

'Something's going on – I grant you. But, clearly, it isn't what you've been thinking. I would suggest that Frau Kolinsky packed her bags, departed, and, shortly after, a distraught Herr Kolinsky ran after her.'

'Without his coat?'

'Perhaps he has two coats.'

'Stopping – as he rushed out the door – to clear the kitchen of perishable foodstuffs?'

Rheinhardt twisted one of the horns of his moustache. Then, after a moment's consideration, he sighed.

'Yes, it is very peculiar. But the fact remains . . .'

Liebermann shook his head.

'The fact remains that Erstweiler's symptoms, his peculiar dream, and Freud's notion of a universal Oedipal syndrome, suggest – very strongly – that something bad has happened here.'

'But look around you.' Rheinhardt began to turn. 'Where's the evidence?'

Clicking his fingers, Liebermann said: 'The cellar. We haven't looked in the cellar yet. Come, Oskar.'

Liebermann launched himself out of the room and hurried down the stairs, dashing through the kitchen and out into the garden. Rheinhardt caught up with the young doctor as he was about to open the cellar door. Liebermann took a deep breath and lifted the catch. As the rusty hinges groaned, Rheinhardt saw Liebermann's shoulders sag. The interior was empty.

Rheinhardt slapped his hand against Liebermann's back.

'Never mind, eh?'

'But I was so sure.' Liebermann ducked beneath the low lintel and stepped into the vault. 'I'm sorry, Oskar.' His voice sounded particularly dejected in the closed space. 'It appears I've wasted your time.'

'The disappearance of the Kolinskys is indeed suspicious. It will merit a report.'

Liebermann bit his lower lip.

'There's always the attic. Was there one? I wasn't looking.'

'Max – we would have smelt something!'

'Yes, of course.'

Rheinhardt threw his head back, looked at the curved ceiling, then stared down at the space between his feet. He circled Liebermann, keeping his eyes down, before squatting to inspect the surface of the tiles. He ran a finger across the glaze.

'Mmmm . . .'

'What?'

'These tiles . . .'

'What about them?'

'They're very clean.'

'So?'

'And there's nothing in here. Nothing has been stored. Doesn't that strike you as odd?'

'I don't see—'

'Max,' interrupted Rheinhardt. 'Be a good fellow and get me a jug of water and a knife from the kitchen.'

'I beg your pardon?'

Rheinhardt was now on all fours, crawling towards the nearest wall, his nose alarmingly close to the floor.

'A jug of water and a knife.' Rheinhardt repeated. 'I saw a striped green jug standing in the sink. The knife needn't be sharp, but the blade should be strong.'

Liebermann left – somewhat bemused – to do Rheinhardt's bidding. When he returned, the inspector was standing in the middle of the cellar, deep in thought.

'Oskar?'

Rheinhardt took the knife from Liebermann, put it in his pocket, and then showed his readiness to receive the jug. It was heavy and some water swept over the rim, splashing his shoes.

'If you would stand by the door, please?' said Rheinardt.

Liebermann took a step back.

Rheinhardt tipped the jug and a thin braid of water twisted to the floor. When he had created a small puddle, he stopped and observed how under the influence of gravity the water sought the path of least resistance. A silver tendril thickened and flowed towards the groove between two adjacent tiles. Rheinhardt canted the jug again and watched as the rivulet accelerated down the channel, diverting abruptly into another as it obeyed the discipline of the floor's gradient.

'What are you doing?' asked Liebermann. He sounded a little irritated.

'Determining the lowest point in the cellar.'

'To what end?'

Rheinhardt poured more water and smiled.

'Have you heard, by any chance, of Gustav Macé?'

'I'm afraid not.'

'Over thirty years ago a man called Désiré Bodasse was murdered and dismembered. His body parts were discovered washed up on the banks of the river Seine. Gustav Macé – the detective involved in the case – suspected one of Bodasse's friends, a man called Pierre Voirbo. Macé believed that if he was correct and Voirbo was the killer, then the villain had most probably committed the murder and dismemberment in his own private lodgings. When the great detective arrived he found no traces of blood. Everything was spotlessly clean. *Too clean*, Macé thought. He subsequently asked for some water, which he proceeded to pour onto the floor. If Bodasse had been dismembered in Voirbo's lodgings, then his blood would have drained beneath the tiles, accumulating at the lowest point in the room.'

About half a metre from the wall, the rivulet had begun to feed a second puddle. The water collected, revealing the presence of a slight depression.

'There it is,' said Rheinhardt. 'The lowest point.'

Rheinhardt placed the jug on the floor and, kneeling by the second puddle, he brushed the water away with his hand and removed the knife from his pocket. He pushed the blade between two tiles and worked one of them loose. Turning it over, he inspected the underside. A layer of pale adhesive was caked with dried blood. He held it up to show Liebermann.

The young doctor came forward.

'You were right, Max,' said Rheinhardt. 'Something very bad did happen here. Something very bad indeed.'

CHAPTER 45

The carriage deposited them outside the Schottenring police station. Rheinhardt and Liebermann entered the building and without exchanging words or glances ascended the stairs to the inspector's office. Rheinhardt sat behind his desk and removed a stack of forms from one of the drawers. He picked up his pen and prepared to take a statement from his friend, but was distracted by the sweet fragrance of his wife's baking. Reaching to the back of the drawer, he found the box of *Linzer biscotten*, which he took out and pushed towards Liebermann.

'Else made them.'

'In which case . . .'

Liebermann bit through the thick, brittle crust of icing. The shortbread crumbled and he had to perform some complex manoeuvres to stop jam from dropping onto his trousers.

'She makes them in the shape of hearts. Do you think that says anything about her character?'

Liebermann drew back a little.

'Are you *really* asking me to analyse your wife's choice of pastry cutter?'

'I was just wondering – that's all.' Rheinhardt acknowledged his friend's censorious look and, pushing the final quarter of his own biscuit into his already crowded mouth, picked up the pen again. 'Let us begin. However, I trust that when expressing the ideas that guided your thinking – the ideas that we discussed earlier – you will make allowances for the layman.'

'Of course.'

'Moreover, I think that it would be preferable if you avoided the use of certain technical terms. Such as . . .' Rheinhardt's tired eyes made a tacit but eloquent plea '. . . *infant sexuality*?'

'Rest assured, I will do my best to eschew language that might cause offence.'

'Thank you.'

Liebermann loosened his necktie.

'Herr Norbert Erstweiler is currently a psychiatric inpatient at the General Hospital. He was referred to the department by his general practitioner, Doctor Vitzhum, after reporting insomnia, agitation, and feelings of dread.'

'A little slower, please.'

'Oh, I'm sorry.'

Rheinhardt looked up from his writing.

'Go on . . .'

'I saw him for the first time during a ward round with Professor Pallenberg on Friday the fourth of April and undertook my own assessment on Sunday the sixth of April.'

Liebermann continued, but was obliged to stop

when Haussmann appeared. The young man's head craned around the edge of the door.

'Sir?'

Rheinhardt produced a prodigious sigh.

'What is it?'

'Herr Löiberger's downstairs – just arrived. He wants to see you. He says it is a matter of the utmost importance.'

'Herr Löiberger?'

'The gentleman who—'

'Yes, yes,' interrupted Rheinhardt. 'I know who he is!' After a pause of considerable length, during which the pouches of loose skin beneath Rheinhardt's eyes seemed to sink yet further down his cheeks, the inspector said: 'Oh, very well. Go and get him.' Turning to address Liebermann, he added: 'You might as well stay here.' He offered his friend another biscuit in order to justify taking another one himself. 'When Löiberger arrives, take a good look at him. He bears a striking resemblance to Franz Schubert.'

After the biscuits had been consumed a silence ensued, which Liebermann relieved by humming.

'Not *that*,' said Rheinhardt, brushing some crumbs into a bin. 'If Herr Löiberger hears, he'll think you're mocking him.'

Liebermann suddenly realised he had been humming the introductory theme of Schubert's B minor *'Unfinished'* Symphony.

'I'm sorry, Oskar' said Liebermann. 'The melody just came into my head. It was quite unconscious.'

Rheinhardt moved the biscuits out of view as soon as he detected the steady beat of approaching footsteps. The door opened and Haussmann ushered Löiberger into the office. Rheinhardt stood to greet the coffee-house proprietor.

'Herr Löiberger. Haussmann, please get Herr Schu— do get Herr Löiberger a chair.' The inspector covered his mouth in an effort to convince everyone present that his slip was nothing more than a cough. 'Please take a seat,' he added, clearing his throat, and anxious to carry the conversation forward. 'Permit me to introduce a colleague, Herr Doctor Liebermann.'

Löiberger bowed and lowered himself into the chair that Haussmann had provided.

After the exchange of pleasantries, Rheinhardt made a steeple with his hands, peered over the pinnacle created by his touching forefingers, and waited for Herr Löiberger to speak.

'Inspector. Forgive me for this intrusion – but . . .' Herr Löiberger suddenly looked less confident. 'I *think* I am in possession of information that could possibly be of some use to you.'

'Please proceed.'

'My wife's cousin died yesterday.'

'Did she? I am very sorry.'

'There is no need to be. The familial bond was not particularly strong. Indeed, I must confess that my wife didn't really like her cousin.'

'I see.'

'She was a valetudinarian, completely preoccupied by imaginary illnesses.'

'That is a very peculiar thing to say of someone who has just died, Herr Löiberger.'

'None of us are immortal, inspector. Even valetudinarians must die of something . . . eventually.'

'You were saying: your wife and her cousin were not close.'

'Quite so. Be that as it may, the responsibility of arranging the funeral has fallen upon my wife. My wife's cousin's estranged sister lives in England and the cousin's brother – I regret to say – is something of a ne'er-do-well. He lost all his fortune at the gaming table and escaped his debtors by going to America. He is still in America, but God only knows where.'

'I am sorry, but how – may I ask – is this information useful to me?'

'When you came to my coffee house you were asking questions about the man whom I had seen with Cäcilie Roster. Do you remember?'

'Yes, I remember our conversation very well.'

'Today, I accompanied my wife to Schopp and Sons – the undertakers. They are situated near the old Town Hall. Our meeting with Herr Schopp was rather protracted on account of my wife's cousin having left behind rather elaborate instructions for the church service and her interment. I have no idea why, because she was an atheist. It was as we were leaving that I saw *him*. He emerged from a door at the back of the reception area and immediately made his exit through another door.'

'*Him* – being the man?'

'Indeed.'

'You are quite sure,' said Rheinhardt slowly, 'that it was the same man – the man with black hair and blue eyes – whom you saw with Cäcilie Roster on Sunday night?'

'Quite sure.'

Rheinhardt leaned forward.

'Could he have recognised you?'

'No, I don't think so. He didn't look over.'

'And when did this happen?'

'About an hour ago. I came here directly.'

'Thank you, Herr Löiberger,' said Rheinhardt. Then, calling over to his assistant, he added: 'Haussmann. Would you be so kind as to organise a carriage?'

CHAPTER 46

Liebermann, Rheinhardt and Haussmann said very little to each other as the carriage rattled past the Stock Exchange, up Wipplingerstrasse and towards the Old Town Hall. It was a short journey and completed in a matter of minutes. Before getting out, Rheinhardt reached into his coat pocket and produced a pistol – a gleaming Luger P08. He made some final checks and indicated his readiness to proceed.

They stepped down from the carriage and walked to the entrance of Schopp and Sons.

'Haussmann, you wait here. If he runs out – tackle him.'

'I'll do my best, sir.'

'Good man.'

Rheinhardt opened the door and entered, Liebermann following behind him. The vestibule of the funeral parlour was large and austere. Apart from a crucifix, the ubiquitous portrait of the Emperor, and a vase of fragrant flowers, there were no other decorative features. A roll of black carpet encouraged visitors to step forward to a walnut reception desk which was at that moment unattended. One of several doors located behind the desk suddenly opened, and a gaunt grey-haired man, dressed in a long old-fashioned frock coat and wearing half-moon glasses, advanced to greet them. He seemed to have mastered the skill of soundless locomotion and glided forward silently, like a ghost. His hands were clasped in front of his chest and his shoulders were slightly hunched.

'Gentlemen. Herr Wiesner – at your service.'

He bowed and remained in this submissive attitude for longer than protocol required. When he straightened up again – or at least straightened up as much as his wilting spine would allow – Rheinhardt showed him his identification.

'I would like to speak to the director,' said Rheinhardt.

'One moment, please,' said Wiesner.

After a brief absence, he returned and guided them down a long windowless corridor lit by flickering gas lamps. On either side were pedestals supporting ornate cinerary urns and statues of sphinxes. The effect was rather dreamlike. They arrived at a door on which Wiesner tapped with the knuckle of a crooked finger, producing a knock so faint that it was barely audible. Then he opened the door and extended his arm, inviting Rheinhardt and Liebermann to enter.

'Good afternoon, gentlemen,' said a man standing by a tall window. He was gazing up at the sky which sagged with the promise of imminent rain.

'I am Detective Inspector Rheinhardt and this is my colleague, Doctor Liebermann.'

'That will be all, Wiesner.' Schopp was completely bald but for two tufts of white hair that fanned out from behind his ears. His beard and moustache were also white but jaundiced by cigar smoke. 'Please sit.' He left the window and sat down on an ostentatious chair with a high carved back. It created the illusion of two eagles perched on his shoulders.

'I would like to interview one of your employees,' said Rheinhardt. 'I do not know his name but I do have a description. He is a young man in his late twenties or early thirties. He has black hair and blue eyes.'

Schopp nodded.

Rheinhardt expected him to speak but a peculiarity of his manner delayed his response by a few uneasy seconds.

'You must mean Herr Sprenger. Markus Sprenger.'

'In what capacity does he work here?'

'He is an undertaker. But he has also made himself very useful to Doctor Profanter – our embalmer.'

'Useful?'

Again, the response was delayed.

'He prepares Doctor Profanter's instruments and assists him when he arrives.'

'When did Herr Sprenger start working for Schopp and Sons?'

'He commenced work here about a year ago. Before then, I believe he was employed by Concordia. He came to us with excellent references.'

Schopp's delivery was disconcerting. It was as though his sense of time deviated from everyone else's.

'Where is he now?' asked Rheinhardt.

'I don't know exactly. I'll call Wiesner.'

'If it's not too much trouble, Herr Schopp, I would be most grateful if it was *you* who helped us to find him.'

Schopp shrugged and rose from his chair.

'Herr Wiesner is perfectly capable.'

'With respect, Herr Schopp . . .' Rheinhardt gestured towards the door.

'Very well. This way, please.'

The corridor outside led past a series of offices, some of which were occupied by middle-aged men attending to paperwork. Herr Schopp asked them if they had seen Herr Sprenger, but none of them had. A larger room, filled with coffins and smelling of sawdust and varnish, was empty. The morgue was also deserted.

Herr Schopp consulted his pocket watch. He stared at its face for an inordinate period of time before saying: 'I'm sorry, Inspector Rheinhardt. It is five minutes past five. He must have gone home.'

'Do you have his address?'

'Wiesner will get it for you.'

As they retraced their way down the corridor Rheinhardt was conscious of the sphinxes on their pedestals. They were close cousins of the sphinxes in the garden of the Belvedere Palace, with wings, braided hair and breastplates. He remembered the discovery of Cäcilie Roster's body, and how, overcome with despair, he had begged one of the great stone beasts for assistance. It was absurd – and he knew it. But he could not quell the conviction that his entreaty had been heard.

CHAPTER 47

Sprenger's apartment block was located on one of the side roads between the Hoher Markt and the Danube canal. On entering the building Haussmann was about to ascend the stairs when Rheinhardt restrained him. His assistant looked puzzled.

'The concierge,' said Rheinhardt. 'I want to talk to the concierge first. You wait here.'

Rheinhardt found the concierge's quarters further down the hall. A nameplate read *Herr Adolf Kolowrat, Hausmeister* and beneath this was an electric bell. Rheinhardt pressed it and shortly after the door was opened by a middle-aged man holding a meerschaum pipe.

'Herr Kolowrat?'

'Yes.'

'Inspector Rheinhardt. Security office. May we come in?'

The concierge led Rheinhardt and Liebermann into a shabby little parlour.

'Please take a seat, inspector.'

Rheinhardt declined. 'I would like to ask you some questions about one of your tenants: Herr Sprenger.'

'Herr Sprenger? Yes. First floor.'

'Do you know if he's in?'

'Yes. I passed him on the stairs a few minutes ago. He's just back from work.'

Somewhere in the building a door slammed shut. Rheinhardt and Liebermann exchanged glances.

'Herr Kolowrat, can you remember what time Herr Sprenger returned on Sunday night?'

The concierge looked uncomfortable. Most apartment blocks in Vienna were locked by ten o'clock, obliging latecomers to wake the concierge and pay an admittance fee – the *Sperrgeld*. Kolowrat exhaled, producing a cloud of dense smoke, the acrid fragrance of which was not unlike burning leaves. His response to Rheinhardt's question was hesitant: 'Herr Sprenger returned . . . very late.'

'How late?'

'I'm not sure. I didn't check the time. I just let him in and then went back to bed.'

'Was it after midnight?'

'Very probably.'

'How was he acting?'

'I'm sorry?'

'His behaviour . . . was he, for example, agitated?'

Kolowrat bit the stem of his pipe, revealing his yellow teeth.

'No. I wouldn't say that.'

'Did he look dishevelled?'

'No. He looked perfectly respectable.'

'Does Herr Sprenger often return late?'

'He's a young man,' said Kolowrat, smiling indulgently and raising his hands. 'Yes, he often comes back after I've locked up. But he never returns drunk – not like some. And he's always very respectful,' the concierge paused before adding, 'and *generous.*'

Rheinhardt lowered his chin – a curt acknowledgement that he understood Kolowrat's meaning.

'Where do you think Herr Sprenger goes – when he returns late?'

The concierge glanced at Liebermann.

'Where *all* young men go.'

Rheinhardt adopted a more severe expression. The concierge, responding to Rheinhardt's disapproval, took the pipe from his mouth and corrected his posture.

'Has he ever returned with a woman?'

'No.'

'Has he ever mentioned a woman by name?'

'With respect, inspector, we do not talk of such things. I let him in, we discuss the weather, he gives me ten hellers – sometimes twelve – then I go back to bed and he goes upstairs.'

Rheinhardt thanked Herr Kolowrat for his assistance and as they were leaving pressed a one-krone coin into the concierge's palm.

'At last,' Rheinhardt whispered to Liebermann. 'We have him!'

'Well,' Liebermann cautioned. 'The evidence is

certainly mounting. But we cannot be sure – as yet.'

'I beg to differ,' said Rheinhardt.

'Policeman's intuition?'

Rheinhardt smiled.

'Something like that.' Rheinhardt was not inclined to mention his desperate appeal to the Belvedere sphinx or his peculiar conviction that some nameless force was now working to their advantage. 'You know,' Rheinhardt continued, 'for weeks I have been eager to confront this monster. I have thought of little else. But now the time has arrived . . .' Rheinhardt abandoned the sentence and shook his head. 'I must confess to being more than a little apprehensive.'

'You would be a very peculiar fellow if it were otherwise, Oskar.'

They joined Haussmann and walked up the stairs to the first floor. In a metal frame screwed below the knocker of a painted door was a card on which the name *Herr Markus Sprenger* was written.

'Gentlemen: are you ready?' whispered Rheinhardt.

Liebermann and Haussmann nodded.

Rheinhardt took a deep breath, lifted the knocker, and let it fall.

Footsteps . . .

Time seemed to slow, intensifying expectation.

A bolt disengaged and the door swung open.

Eyes . . .

This was Liebermann's first impression.

Eyes like stained glass – a dark, luminous blue. The blue of cathedral windows and lapis lazuli, made even more arresting by their appearance beneath a shock of jet-black hair. Sprenger was clean-shaven and strikingly handsome, with well-defined features that recapitulated the physical perfection of sculpture – an impression that was reinforced by the pallor of his unblemished marmoreal skin. He stood, studying his visitors with detached interest.

'Herr Sprenger?' said Rheinhardt.

'Yes.'

'I am Detective Inspector Rheinhardt.' He produced his identification but Sprenger did not look at it. 'This is my assistant, Haussmann, and my colleague, Herr Doctor Liebermann.'

'You wish to speak with *me*?' Sprenger sounded mildly surprised.

'Yes.'

'What about – may I ask?'

'Perhaps, Herr Sprenger, it might be better if we continued this conversation in private?'

'Yes, of course. This way, please.'

Rheinhardt and his two companions followed Sprenger down the hallway and he admitted them into a reading room. The shelves of a substantial bookcase sagged beneath the weight of a well-stocked library. Every available space in the bookcase had been used up – additional volumes had been inserted horizontally above the vertical spines of others. Some architectural prints hung on the walls and heavy half-drawn curtains created a sombre, shadowy atmosphere. There were only two places to sit.

'Please . . .' said Sprenger, gesturing towards an old chesterfield. He pulled a chair from beneath a table and offered it to Liebermann and Haussmann.

'My associates are happy to stand,' said Rheinhardt. Sprenger sat down in front of his portly guest. 'We have just come from the premises of Schopp and Sons.'

'Is that so?'

'Where you have been employed for the past year?'

'Indeed.'

'You are an undertaker.'

'That is correct.'

Rheinhardt smiled.

'Herr Schopp speaks very highly of you.'

'I always try to do my best.'

'He told us that the references supplied by your previous employer were excellent.'

'That would be Herr Hanl. He was very kind.'

'You enjoyed working at Concordia?'

'Very much so.'

'Then why did you leave?'

'The position that I took at Schopp and Sons – my present position – was a more senior post.'

'And more remunerative, no doubt?'

'Yes – although money was not my *only* consideration.'

While Rheinhardt continued to engage Sprenger in conversation about his work, Liebermann edged closer to the bookcase. He scrutinised the titles: *The Egyptian Book of the Dead*, *Roman Gods*, *Athens and Sparta*, *Greece and the Hellenistic World*. Below these academic works were several collections of folk-tales, and among these, a copy of the *Tristan* of Gottfried von Strassburg.

Across the hallway, Liebermann spied an open door. Through it he saw a wardrobe and an iron bedstead. He signalled to Rheinhardt that he should keep Sprenger talking, and nudged Haussmann forward to create a diversion. Liebermann crept across the hallway and entered Sprenger's bedroom. A frock coat had been thrown onto the eiderdown. The fabric emitted a smell with which Liebermann was very familiar: carbolic. On the washstand he found a porcelain bowl and next to it a collection of bottles. Liebermann crouched down and read the labels. They were mostly colognes; however, two of the bottles seemed out of place. One contained slaked lime and the other lead oxide. He might easily have failed to recognise their significance had he not also noticed as he stood up the dark, gritty streaks that ribbed the inner surface of the bowl.

Hair dye, thought Liebermann.

A second and more significant realisation followed immediately after.

'Forgive me,' Sprenger's muffled voice floated

across hallway. 'But I am unclear as to why you are here, inspector. Am I to understand that you are conducting an investigation and that you believe I might be able to help?'

Liebermann re-entered the reading room and, catching Rheinhardt's eye, nodded.

The inspector changed position, shifting his weight to the left.

'Herr Sprenger, can you tell me what you were doing on Sunday night?'

'I was out.'

'Where did you go?'

'Well, if you must know . . .' Sprenger raked his hand through his hair. 'I fell into conversation with a Galician woman and she invited me back to her room in Spittelberg.'

Mention of the red-light district obviated further explanation.

'I see,' said Rheinhardt. 'Would you be able to identify the woman and the house?'

'I don't know about that. I regret to say that I'd been drinking.'

'Really? That surprises me.'

'Why?'

'Because Herr Kolowrat told us that when you returned on Sunday you were sober.'

'You've spoken to him?' Alertness turned to indifference. Sprenger shrugged. 'Then he was mistaken.'

'You may be wondering', said Rheinhardt, 'why it is that my assistant and I are accompanied by

300

a doctor. The reason is quite straightforward. He is here to examine you.'

'What?'

Liebermann stepped forward.

'Only a superficial examination,' said Rheinhardt. 'He needs to take a look at your torso.'

'But why?'

'Herr Sprenger,' said Liebermann, employing the commanding tone of a medical professor, 'Would you please stand and remove your shirt?'

The undertaker did not move.

'I am obliged to inform you,' said Rheinhardt, 'that failure to cooperate with the security office is a very serious offence.'

Sprenger produced a loud sigh, stood up, and deftly unfastened the buttons of his shirt with one hand. Then he removed the garment and laid it over the back of his chair.

'Herr Sprenger,' said Liebermann, 'your back is covered in scratches.'

'I know. What of it?'

'Some of them are very deep.'

Sprenger flashed an angry glance at Rheinhardt. 'Look, inspector, what's the purpose of this?'

Rheinhardt joined Liebermann.

'How did you get these injuries, Herr Sprenger?'

'It was the woman – the Galician woman on Sunday night. She went wild.'

'These injuries were not sustained on Sunday,' said Liebermann. 'I'd say they were sustained earlier. About two weeks ago.'

301

'Well, that's easily explained. I often go to Spittelberg.'

Rheinhardt raised his eyebrows: 'Do all of the women you have relations with go *wild*, Herr Sprenger?'

'It's not uncommon, inspector. May I get dressed?'

Rheinhardt crossed to the window and drew the curtains aside to let more light in.

'Does the name Bathild Babel mean anything to you?'

'No.'

'What about Adele Zeiler?'

Sprenger paused before answering: 'Yes, I do know that name. She was murdered. I read about it in the newspapers.'

'And what about Selma Wirth and Cäcilie Roster – do those names mean anything to you?'

Sprenger picked up his shirt.

'Cäcilie Roster was a singer. She was murdered too.'

'On Sunday night.'

'Oh, I see. You suspect me?' Sprenger laughed. 'That's ridiculous. You have the wrong man, inspector. I'm sorry.'

Sprenger fastened the buttons of his shirt.

Liebermann coughed to attract his attention: 'Do you dye your hair, Herr Sprenger?'

Sprenger rolled his eyes.

'As it happens – yes, I do.'

'Why?'

'Why do you think, Herr doctor? Why do most men dye their hair? I'm going grey.'

'Would you be so kind as to open your mouth?'

The unexpected request made Rheinhardt turn around sharply.

'What?' asked Sprenger.

'Open your mouth wide – and pull your lower lip down.' Liebermann demonstrated by tugging at his own lip. 'Like this.'

Sprenger copied him.

'Thank you,' said Liebermann. 'You are not going grey, Herr Sprenger. You are a young man. Further, you have been dyeing your hair black for many years. You started long before greyness would have been an issue. No, Herr Sprenger, you do not dye your hair because you are going grey. You dye your hair for a quite different reason. The fact that you dye your hair black – the opposite of your natural blond – provides us, I believe, with some indication as to why you do it. By dyeing your hair black you distance yourself from the realm of day and associate yourself with the night. It is symbolic – is it not? Black is the colour of mourning, the colour of death. And death has special significance for you.'

Sprenger did not move. Although his stare was fixed on Liebermann's his expression was oddly vacant, as though he, Sprenger, had retreated into himself. It was therefore something of a shock when Liebermann felt Sprenger's fist slam into his stomach. The blow was powerful and lifted him off his feet. Liebermann was propelled backwards and landed awkwardly on Rheinhardt. The pain was excruciating and Liebermann was blinded by the tears which filled his eyes. The next thing he saw was Haussmann, curled up on the floor and with blood pouring through the fingers that covered his face. Sprenger was no longer there.

CHAPTER 48

Liebermann pitched himself at the door. He felt a pang of guilt – the moral traction of his Hippocratic obligation – as he leapt past Haussmann's writhing body. Yet he was not delayed by his conscience. The imperative of catching Sprenger was sufficiently powerful to negate all other considerations, including that of his own safety.

At the end of the hallway Sprenger was opening a small window.

'Max, get down!' Rheinhardt shouted, aiming his pistol.

Liebermann threw himself on the floor.

A shot rang out.

Sprenger was still moving and showed considerable athleticism as he slipped beneath the sash.

Liebermann scrambled to his feet and followed, but he found the window less easy to negotiate than he had expected. He was dimly aware of Rheinhardt's approach and guessed that the inspector would have some difficulty squeezing through the narrow gap. Rolling over the windowsill, Liebermann landed on a cast-iron platform which formed part of a fire escape. The whole structure shook as Sprenger made his descent.

When Liebermann reached the ground he found himself in an alley separating two apartment blocks. Sprenger had interposed a distance of some twenty metres between them and was only a few strides from the exit and the streets beyond.

Another shot.

Sprenger veered off to the right and disappeared from view.

Liebermann heard Rheinhardt cursing. The expletive bounced off the opposite wall and sounded like the voice of an enraged god. Liebermann continued his pursuit, his feet pounding the cobbles until he was disgorged into a dilapidated backstreet. He caught sight of Sprenger, who was heading north towards the Danube canal. Sprenger's punch had left a bolus of pain in Liebermann's stomach. The young doctor was finding it more and more difficult to breathe, his chest ached and his limbs felt heavy.

The distance between them was widening.

Don't give up . . .

Don't give up . . .

This repeated exhortation created an insistent beat which he willed his legs to keep time with. It was like self-hypnosis. Liebermann became less aware of his surroundings and the world shrank, becoming nothing but the rhythm of his running, the pain in his gut, and Sprenger's receding shirtsleeves.

They spilled out onto the busy thoroughfare of Franz-Josefs-Kai: people, carriages – the general hubbub of the Ring – the sound of a barrel organ and the smell of sausages on a brazier. Across the canal Liebermann could see the public baths. He persevered, pushing himself to the limits of endurance. Sprenger was eclipsed by some pedestrians and then appeared again, running in the road with the traffic. Liebermann's spirits plummeted when he saw Sprenger getting on a tram. A bell sounded over the din, and Liebermann watched in despair as the vehicle moved away. He clenched his fist and shook it at the sky. Then he noticed something that made him start. There was a tram parked next to him, an 'L'. Liebermann looked at Sprenger's tram – also an 'L'. He jumped on board and addressed the driver: 'My name is Liebermann. I am an honorary agent of the security office. There is a dangerous and wanted man travelling on the tram ahead and by the authority invested in me by His Majesty the Emperor I command you to follow it.'

The driver was not convinced of Liebermann's authenticity and, having previously observed him venting his frustration and anger at the clouds, said flatly: 'Are you mad?'

'Quite the contrary – I'm a psychiatrist.' Liebermann removed one of his visiting cards from his coat pocket and flashed it in the driver's face. 'There! You see? Doctor Max Liebermann. Now, if you do not proceed this instant you must expect to find yourself before a magistrate tomorrow, explaining why you chose to obstruct the course of justice!'

Liebermann's florid (and disingenuous) threat had the desired effect. The anxious-looking man rang the bell and the tram rolled forward.

'Thank you,' said Liebermann. There were now at least three carriages between Sprenger's tram and his own. 'Can't you go any faster?'

'I can, but—'

'Then do it!'

The tram shuddered and began to accelerate. Liebermann glanced at the seated passengers, who were watching him with wide eyes and amazed expressions. He bowed – not wishing to seem discourteous as well as insane – and returned his attention to the road. Once again the driver rang the bell. The carriages dispersed and they gathered momentum.

'Excellent!'

Liebermann felt someone tapping his shoulder.

He turned to discover the conductor, his right arm stretched out and his palm open.

'Your fare, sir?'

Liebermann looked into the man's dead eyes and saw the end of Austria-Hungary. An empire that produced so many bureaucrats and petty officials would never survive the new century. Here was a man who had been instructed to take fares and that was what he intended to do, whatever the circumstance. Liebermann sensed all the others behind him, a great army of automata with grand titles and flamboyant uniforms, operating in every stratum of society – and was too exhausted to argue. He gave the conductor a coin and accepted his ticket.

Sprenger's tram turned off Franz-Josefs-Kai and began its transit across the Danube canal. Liebermann grabbed a support to stop himself from falling as they careered around the same section of track. Through the window Liebermann noticed a steamboat, eructating smoke from a long funnel and tugging two barges. It was heading east, churning the grey-green water and leaving a frothy trail. The slow, almost imperceptible, passage of the flotilla was oddly calming.

On the other side of the bridge Sprenger's tram came to a halt. As the people waiting at the stop converged around the open platforms, Liebermann caught sight of Sprenger's shirt-sleeves in the throng. The undertaker made no attempt to run and was threading his way in an unhurried manner through the crowd.

Liebermann jumped off before his tram stopped and walked briskly around the press of bodies. He emerged on the other side to see Sprenger no more than ten metres away. Unfortunately, it was also at that precise moment that Sprenger chose to check if he was being followed. On recognising Liebermann, the undertaker immediately took off again.

The brief respite on the tram had done

Liebermann a great deal of good. He had recovered his breath and the pain in his stomach was no longer quite so distracting. Indeed, he seemed to be catching up with Sprenger.

The undertaker disappeared around a corner and Liebermann followed, skidding on the pavement which was slippery with squashed fruit. A number of barrows were parked at the kerb and costermongers were shouting the prices of apples and apricots. Just ahead, some Hassidic Jews were descending the steps of a synagogue.

Liebermann shouted: 'Stop that man!'

The Hassidim froze but did nothing.

'Stop him!' Liebermann tried again. None of them were prepared to stand in the undertaker's way.

Sprenger dashed past the synagogue and entered one of the buildings on the same side of the road. Liebermann was so close by now that he could almost touch him. Inside was an empty, lightless vestibule, with a broad staircase curving upwards. Liebermann chased Sprenger up the stairs, across a landing, and down a hallway. At the end of the hallway Sprenger tried one of the doors, violently shaking the handle. It was locked. Behind him was a window. There was no escape. He stood, his hands by his side, looking at Liebermann.

The sound of their breathing was loud and ragged. Liebermann drew the back of his hand across his forehead to wipe off the perspiration. He considered shouting for help but knew that he couldn't count on anybody's assistance. The tenants would probably be as reluctant to get involved as the Hassidim had been. Liebermann was aware of voices but they did not seem to be coming from anywhere inside the building, which was eerily quiet.

'You must come with me to the Grosse Sperlgasse police station,' said Liebermann.

Sprenger shook his head.

'I don't think so, Herr doctor.' His blue eyes caught the soft light and flashed brightly. 'You're not armed – are you?' Liebermann did not answer. 'No. It was the inspector who had the gun.'

'You can't get away, Herr Sprenger.'

'Perhaps not . . .'

A faint smile.

'If you accompany me to Grosse Sperlgasse . . .'

'Spare me!' The smile vanished. 'Spare me the horse-trading and the empty bargaining! I will hang, Herr doctor. Whether I am docile and come with you like a lamb – or whether I skin you alive with my penknife.'

Liebermann was not confident that he could better Sprenger if he was forced to defend himself. His courage deserted him: his racing heart felt swollen in his chest, his mouth, dry.

'I was right – wasn't I?' His voice sounded thin. 'Death is significant to you.'

'Death is significant to everyone, Herr doctor. You should appreciate that more than most, by virtue of your profession. Death cures all diseases!'

'No. I mean personally significant.' Sprenger's gaze was steady. 'Death *excites* you?'

The undertaker tilted his head and, ignoring Liebermann's question, asked one of his own.

'What did you see in my mouth?'

'A possible defence.'

'What?'

'A *legal* defence. Something that might save you from the gallows: you must have noticed it yourself?'

'Speak plainly, Herr doctor.'

'The bluish line that runs along your gums. It is a sign.'

'Of what?'

'Lead poisoning. You dye your hair with lead oxide – it has damaged your brain. You are not responsible for your actions. A judge would have to take such evidence into consideration before passing sentence.'

Sprenger laughed.

'I can assure you that I am completely responsible for my actions. I know exactly what I have done.'

'You may think that, Herr Sprenger.'

'I believe I have made my position quite clear with respect to bargains.'

'Then you *will* hang.'

'Perhaps . . .' Sprenger took a step forward. Liebermann's muscles tensed. 'I would rather face an executioner than spend the rest of my life in a prison cell or – even worse – an asylum for the criminally insane.'

Sprenger took another step.

'Stay where you are.'

'Are you frightened of me, Herr doctor?'

Liebermann considered his response carefully.

'Yes. I am frightened of you.'

Sprenger sighed.

'"Night is the other half of life, and the better half."' It was a quotation from *Wilhelm Meister's Apprenticeship*.

'Are you fond of Goethe?' Liebermann asked. The question sounded weak – a transparent attempt to engage Sprenger and stall his advance.

The undertaker did not reply. His eyes were fixed on Liebermann. His expression was intense and focused.

Voices – laughter – the sound of cutlery.

Where is it coming from?

Sprenger came forward again. Liebermann raised his hands and took a step backwards.

'Herr Sprenger. I really must insist that you stay where you are.'

'"Night is the other half of life, and the better half,"' Sprenger repeated. His voice was a whisper. Liebermann saw the undertaker's lips moving, but he produced no sound. He was repeating the sentence to himself, again and again.

Suddenly, Sprenger turned on his heels – and ran for the window.

Liebermann cried out: 'No!'

Sprenger's body shattered the glass and dropped from view. When the tinkling had subsided, there was a piercing scream. Liebermann rushed down the hallway. Immediately below the window, hanging from the exterior of the building, was a striped awning. A man dressed in a white shirt and black tails – a waiter – was kneeling beside Sprenger's body.

Liebermann hurried down the stairs and out into the street. He sprinted towards the coffee house. The people who had been sitting at the tables outside were standing up and looking at Sprenger, aghast. A woman with a large floral hat was sobbing against the shoulder of a male companion.

'I'm a doctor,' said Liebermann, dropping to his knees and clutching Sprenger's wrist. At first he thought he was imagining it, the sluggish, feeble beat. But it was definitely there. Sprenger had survived the fall.

CHAPTER 49

Rheinhardt was sitting in Liebermann's office at the General Hospital feeling tired and extremely hungry. He took the Luger pistol from his pocket and studied its construction: the long barrel, the crescent trigger and elegant handgrip.

A perfect example of the gun manufacturer's craft.

Yet even with such a finely balanced weapon he had missed Sprenger – *twice.*

Rheinhardt did not feel shame when he reflected on his inadequate marksmanship but rather a sense of relief, for he knew that if he had hit his mark he would – at that moment – be feeling quite different. He would not be looking forward to his bed, the warmth of his wife's body, and a swift descent into untroubled, restorative sleep. Instead, he would be contemplating the night ahead with trepidation: a long night, sitting in the darkness, smoking and ruminating – wrestling with his conscience. Liebermann often spoke of unconscious motivation. Had some hidden part of his mind interfered with his aim? He was too weary to tackle such an esoteric question. His stomach was gurgling and for Rheinhardt hunger precluded thought. The feeling of emptiness, the nagging hollow at the very centre of his being, was too distracting. He put the Luger back into his pocket and wondered if he would be able to get to Café Eiles before it closed.

Rheinhardt opened one of Liebermann's drawers and examined the contents: a formulary, a pen and a stethoscope.

But no biscuits . . .

The door opened and Liebermann entered.

'What are you doing?'

'Looking for something to eat.'

'Well, you won't find anything in there. This may come as a surprise to you, Oskar, but not everyone keeps a store of *Linzer biscotten* among their work things.'

Rheinhardt closed the drawer and leaned back in his chair.

'Well?'

'His condition is stable.'

'Will he live?'

'Professor Bieler is very optimistic.'

'I suppose that qualifies as good news.' Rheinhardt folded his arms across his stomach. 'The people of Vienna would have felt cheated if Sprenger had succeeded in his bid to evade justice.'

'They might still be denied.'

'You are thinking of the lead oxide . . .'

'It is something the court must consider.'

'Surely, Max, you cannot believe that Sprenger

316

was driven to perform his atrocities by his hair dye! Not every individual unfortunate enough to suffer from lead poisoning then takes it upon himself to kill for sexual gratification!'

'The brain is complex – and poisons may have effects that vary from individual to individual. It is not inconceivable.'

'Are there any other cases similar to Sprenger's that you know of?'

'No. However, there are some historians who have posited a theory that the Roman Empire fell not because of the incursion of the barbarian hordes but because of a generalised insanity resulting from the widespread use of lead pipes and kitchenware. I suspect that the foundations of Sprenger's thanatophilia were laid in his childhood and that the lead poisoning exacerbated his existing psychopathology. If so, then the poisoning might represent a mitigating factor. I would be more than happy to prepare a medical report.'

Rheinhardt narrowed his eyes.

'I think you're pleased to have him here.'

'I wouldn't say *pleased*, exactly.'

'What, then? You are not *dis*pleased.'

'I am grateful that I have been afforded an opportunity to satisfy my professional curiosity.'

'Psychiatrists,' said Rheinhardt, shaking his head. 'At what point do you baulk at the study of perversity and madness? Do you never think that some things are so dreadful – so appalling – that they should simply be left alone?'

'It is always better to understand than not.'

The inspector had heard Liebermann's pithy dictum many times before.

'Are you so sure?' Rheinhardt looked troubled. 'Sometimes I wonder whether some minds are so deranged that nothing useful can come out of their study. Krafft-Ebing's *Psychopathia Sexualis* has sold in thousands of copies and because it is a scientific work respectable gentlemen read it without scruple. Yet do they really read those cases – page after page of horror, sickness, and moral degeneracy – to improve their understanding of mental illness? I think not. They read the *Psychopathia Sexualis* because it is sensational and it arouses in them a dubious prurient excitement.'

There was an uncomfortable silence.

Rheinhardt ventured an appeasing smile. He realised that he might have gone too far.

'I'm sorry, Max: I am tired and hungry. You are a peculiar breed – you psychiatrists – but invaluable, nevertheless.'

Liebermann inclined his head.

'What do you want to do about Erstweiler?'

The sentence was delivered with a certain frosty reserve.

'Good heavens! Erstweiler! Our trip out to Simmering feels like ancient history!'

'I'll be seeing him again tomorrow morning. Perhaps you should be here.'

'Ten-thirty? Would that be convenient?'

'It would indeed.'

318

Rheinhardt stood up and slapped a heavy hand on Liebermann's shoulder.

'Well done, Max. You're a courageous fellow.' The young doctor shrugged. 'Could I interest you in a late dinner at Café Eiles?'

Liebermann returned Rheinhardt's smile.

'I was about to suggest something very similar myself.'

CHAPTER 50

Kristina was sitting at her dressing table, inspecting her face in the mirror. A thin line had appeared which she had never noticed before, a hairline crack curving around her mouth. When her expression was neutral the mark was insignificant, as subtle as the craquelure in varnish. Indeed, she had to tilt her head in the light to see it. But if she smiled the line deepened.

Perhaps she had been laughing too much lately? Perhaps this was the cost of happiness? When she was younger, there had been very little to laugh about and her skin had been taut and smooth. She had been wrong – and more than a little naive – to assume that success and contentment would come without complications.

The house was silent. Her husband Heinz had not yet returned. The old general was dying, and the good doctor was doing all that he could to make the war hero's last hours as comfortable as possible. Heinz was a good man. She did not like keeping things from him, but in this particular instance there really was no alternative.

I'll do it now, she thought. *Get it over with.*

Kristina rose from her dressing table and crossed to the wall on which Czeschka's Ashputtel lithographs were hanging.

Her mind went back to the day when the detective from the security office had come to question her. She remembered the young doctor who had accompanied him. What was it he had said? Something about the lithographs being very fitting, given her occupation. He had made her quite anxious by standing so close.

Kristina followed the wall, pausing to consider each tableau. It was like participating in the fairy-tale equivalent of the *Via Crucis*: the stepsisters, Ashputtel by the wishing tree, the handsome Prince. The final lithograph was a portrait of Ashputtel with a white dove perched on her shoulder. An inscription below the image read *'For she is the true one'*. Kristina pulled the bottom of the frame away from the wall and caught two sheets of paper as they fell from their place of concealment.

The first was a drawing of a naked girl lying on a divan. Her legs were parted, exposing her sex. She was wearing black stockings which were too large and had slipped down her skinny thighs. The collapsed silk had been executed with exquisite precision. A small but distinctive oval mole below the girl's belly button had not escaped the artist's meticulous eye.

The second drawing was of the same girl standing

with a companion of roughly the same age. They were both naked and wore sulky expressions. Again, the oval mole was clearly visible.

Kristina stared at the images for some time and a few tears trickled down her cheeks. She wiped them away with the sleeve of her kimono and, bracing herself, crossed over to the enamel stove. She crouched down and opened the door in its base, releasing a blast of heat.

A complex set of emotions stayed her hand.

It felt very wrong to be burning art. Of course, the artist's choice of subject matter was questionable but there was no denying his talent. And more importantly still, by proceeding with this barbarous act she felt that she was – in a sense – doing violence to herself.

Such considerations had made it impossible for her to destroy the drawings when she had first acquired them. Instead of doing what was necessary she had stupidly hidden them behind the lithograph of Ashputtel and the white dove. What if the young doctor had touched the frame – and the drawings had fallen to the floor? She could not afford to be sentimental.

Kristina posted the first drawing into the stove. She watched the paper blacken, curl and then burst into flames. Something close to grief tightened her chest and her breath became laboured as she watched the image of the girl turning to ashes. Curiously, the bottom right-hand corner of the drawing resisted ignition, managing by some accident of physics to preserve its existence for a few more seconds more.

Kristina read the signature: *Rainmayr*.

The paper turned from yellow to brown and then shrivelled to nothing.

CHAPTER 51

'Herr doctor, I am concerned that we are not making very much progress,' said Erstweiler.

Liebermann looked down at his supine patient and after a brief pause replied: 'I am sorry that you are dissatisfied.'

'My condition,' Erstweiler continued, 'or, rather, the natural state of anxiety that arises from my unusual *situation* remains unchanged. I cannot sleep, my bowels are still loose – and every moment of the day I live in dread of *his* appearance. You will forgive me, I hope, for questioning the efficacy of this treatment of yours. What did you call it?'

'Psychoanalysis.'

'None of the other patients are receiving it.'

'No. It's new.'

'The modern world is too enamoured of novelty. Just because something is new does not mean that it is better.' Erstweiler was clearly depressed and showing the irritability so typical of patients whose mood was low. 'Perhaps the time has come, Herr doctor, to try something different. What about hydrotherapy?'

'I do not think hydrotherapy will be very helpful.'

'Why not? It helped that chap who kept on shouting about the Hungarians coming. When he returned to the ward after hydrotherapy he was much better.'

'I do not think hydrotherapy is the appropriate treatment for *your* condition.'

'What condition?' Erstweiler raised his arms and let them fall heavily on the rest bed. 'I have seen my doppelgänger . . . and if I see him again that will probably be the end of me. I am tired of all this talking, Herr doctor.'

'Then perhaps you should try listening. Psychoanalysis is a listening cure as well as a talking one. It demands that I – for the most part – listen to you. But sometimes you must listen to me. I have been thinking about your dream, Herr Erstweiler, the dream of the English fairy story.'

'What of it, Herr doctor? It was only a dream!' Erstweiler sighed – exhausted by his own impatience.

'Dreams,' said Liebermann, 'are shaped by processes in the mind that obey certain laws or principles. If one is conversant with those principles it is possible to interpret dreams. Dreams are the royal road to the unconscious.'

'The unconscious?'

'That greater part of the mind – ordinarily inaccessible – wherein can be discovered the answers to the most puzzling questions about human experience: in your case,' Liebermann clapped his hands together lightly, 'why it is that you have hallucinations of a double. It is my belief that the cause of your hallucinations is a set of memories buried in your unconscious. And your dream gives us some indication as to what those memories relate to.'

Erstweiler was about to speak, but before he could raise a further objection Liebermann added: 'Allow me to explain.'

The young doctor leaned forward on his chair.

'The language of dreams is symbolic; however, symbols, as they appear in dreams, usually possess features in common with the object or person they are supposed to represent. Thus, by studying these correspondences a dream can be made intelligible. Now, let us consider the content of your English fairy-tale dream, beginning with the most important element, the *pivot* around which the narrative turns.'

'I'm not sure I understand what you're getting at.'

'Do you remember the title of the fairy story? What did Frau Middleton call it?'

'I think she called it *Jack and the Beanstalk*.'

'So the defining image of the story is . . .'

'The beanstalk?

'That is correct.'

Erstweiler looked perplexed.

'You think it *means* something? The beanstalk?'

'I do.'

'Well – perhaps you'd care to enlighten me.'

'Think of it as an object with features – some of which are shared with other things.'

Erstweiler made some grumbling noises and then said: 'A beanstalk is long . . . and it grows.'

'Excellent. Remember also that you described the beanstalk *rising up.*'

'You think that's significant?'

'Very much so. Come now, Herr Erstweiler, apply yourself. What is long and rises up? What grows and stands *erect*?'

Erstweiler's eyes opened wide.

'Herr doctor – am I understanding you correctly? Are you implying . . .'

'Yes?'

'Are you implying that the beanstalk in my dream represents the male reproductive organ?'

'I am indeed. Your dream is – fundamentally – a sexual dream. It is about sexual longing and a forbidden wish fulfilled.'

'Herr doctor, this is ludicrous!' Erstweiler sneered. 'My dream is a recollection of a story told to me when I was a child. A story for *children*! How on earth could it be sexual?'

'The unconscious often finds expression by appropriating innocent material. Some memories – particularly if they are disturbing – are only permitted to enter awareness during sleep after donning a disguise. The more innocent the disguise, the more likely it is that the memories will find expression in a dream. Now, let us remind ourselves of the narrative: the boy – whose part you took in the dream – climbs up the beanstalk and discovers a castle on a cloud. In the castle is a goose who lays golden eggs, which belongs to an ogre. The boy steals the goose, but is pursued. On reaching the ground, the boy chops down the beanstalk and the ogre falls to his death.'

'Herr doctor,' said Erstweiler. 'I am finding this conversation somewhat confusing . . .'

Liebermann ignored his patient's objection.

'We must delay consideration of the cloud for a short while and consider next the castle. Enclosed spaces – such as boxes, cases, chests, rooms, houses – and large buildings – are often symbolic of the uterus.'

'Herr doctor, I asked you to convince me of my own insanity. But you seem determined to accomplish the very opposite. I find myself doubting *your* mental stability.'

'A fact,' Liebermann continued with blithe indifference, 'which is underscored by the presence of the goose, whose golden eggs signal fertility.'

'Herr doctor . . .' Erstweiler's fingers gripped his hospital gown.

'Let us proceed,' Liebermann pressed on, 'to the proprietor of the castle. In my opinion, the ogre conflates two *real* individuals. Your father, whose ogre-like behaviour once caused you so much distress on top of the Stephansdom – a location, please note, that brought you close to the *clouds*. And Bozidar Kolinsky – who, like your father, was a brute.'

'Bozidar Kolinsky,' whispered Erstweiler. His grip tightened and the blood drained from his knuckles.

'Indeed.' Liebermann sat back in his chair and watched the beads of perspiration forming on Erstweiler's forehead. 'In your dream, the ogre owned the goose. Now, consider *this*, Herr Erstweiler: over whom did Bozidar Kolinsky have an exclusive right of possession, by legal contract and in the sight of God?'

'Frau Milena.'

'Ergo . . .'

'Frau Milena is the goose?'

'And not just any goose – but a goose capable of laying golden eggs. I recall you saying that Herr Kolinsky was a miser . . .'

'Herr doctor.' Erstweiler swallowed. 'I don't feel well. My heart.' He rested his palm on his chest. 'I can feel it racing. Please, Herr doctor.'

'We are almost finished.' Liebermann touched his patient's shoulder. 'I hope that I have succeeded in persuading you that your dream was not as innocent as it first seems and that the characters therein correspond with real persons. But what of the story? Does the narrative itself correspond with actual events?'

'My heart!'

'Again, in my opinion, this is almost certainly the case, and I would propose the following: you fell in love with Frau Milena – and grew to hate her husband, Bozidar Kolinsky. It was unfair, wasn't it? That an uncouth, brutish man should be married to someone so young and beautiful. Frau Milena seduced you – and together you *hatched* a plan. You would kill Bozidar Kolinsky, Frau Milena would inherit his property, take his miser's horde, and you would both be able to—'

'No, no, no . . .' Erstweiler sat bolt upright and looked at the door. 'Stop this! *He*'s coming – I can feel it.'

'The boy in the English fairy story killed the ogre with an axe. He chopped the beanstalk down – an image which also conveniently suggests castration – just as you, presumably, chopped down Bozidar Kolinsky. It would not have been difficult if he was drunk. And I must suppose you did so with great vigour, drawing on a store of anger and resentment formerly reserved for your father. Each blow was an assertion of your new-found potency.'

Erstweiler called out: 'No, no . . . please, Herr doctor. Do something.'

'When it was dark, you dragged Bozidar Kolinsky down to the basement and hacked his body into little pieces. There are many places in Simmering where one can easily dispose of small packages: factory incinerators, the Neustadter canal . . .'

Erstweiler screamed: a loud, tormented wail.

Rheinhardt appeared in the doorway.

'Is everything all right?'

'Oh, dear God!' cried Erstweiler. 'I told you he

was real . . . Can't you see him? I am finished . . . finished!'

Erstweiler clutched his chest, his eyes rolled, and he fell back onto the rest bed. His arm stuck out at an awkward angle.

'Good God, Max,' said Rheinhardt. 'Aren't you going to do anything?'

Liebermann rose from his chair and lifted Erstweiler's wrist.

'No one has ever died of hallucinations, Oskar. There is no need to worry. His heart is racing, but he is in no great danger.'

'What happened?'

'Exactly what I thought would happen. I confronted him with the truth, and his psyche divided. His mind was not robust enough to survive the trauma of killing a man in cold blood: memories of that dreadful murderous night could not be integrated with earlier memories and were subsequently projected onto a hallucinatory alter ego – his doppelgänger.'

'He cannot remember what he did?'

'The memories of that night exist in his unconscious; however, whenever Erstweiler is reminded of his crime the anxiety and guilt become intolerable, and the memories are disowned – externalised.'

'Will he remember now – when he wakes?'

'I don't know. We'll have to wait and see; however, he has just had a pitiless and uncompromising encounter with the truth and there is a good chance that his defences have been shattered.'

Erstweiler groaned. He turned his head to the side and a thin plumb line of clear saliva dropped from the corner of his mouth.

'What I don't understand,' said Rheinhardt, 'is why his accomplice ran off, leaving her house behind and presumably whatever monies Herr Kolinsky had saved. I mean to say, it rather defeats the object of the exercise. Presumably the plan was to report Herr Kolinsky missing to the police and in due course they intended to embark on a new life together. They just might have got away with it!'

'The answer is quite straightforward,' Liebermann responded. 'Frau Milena, like Herr Erstweiler, was not a natural wrongdoer. She would never have been able to kill her husband unassisted: she needed someone to do it for her. Even so, complicity was not enough to dilute her guilt. It must have risen up, unexpected, and crashed around her like a great wave of horror and misery. She could not cope, and in a state of extreme distress she sought relief by interposing as much distance as she could between herself and the scene of her crime.'

'Where do you think she is?'

'Who knows?'

'I wonder when she left.'

'That question I think I can answer. Her departure would have coincided with the onset of Erstweiler's illness. The two are linked. One can imagine the poor fellow, waking up, reaching out across the empty bed, no longer able to benefit from the sweet, soothing balm of confederacy. He would have risen that morning and stood in the fierce heat of his own conscience. And – more importantly – he would have been aware that he stood there alone. When he looked at himself in the shaving mirror he would have seen not Norbert Erstweiler, warehouse clerical officer, but the repugnant face of a murderer. Thus, the idea of the doppelgänger insinuated itself into his mind and sank into the seedbed of imagination that is the unconscious.'

Rheinhardt tapped Erstweiler on the cheeks with the palm of his hand.

'Herr Erstweiler . . .' The man groaned. His eyelids flickered – showing only the whites – and then closed again. 'He looks delirious.'

'He's in shock, that's all.'

Rheinhardt sat down in Liebermann's chair.

'If he remembers – when he wakes – will we be able to get a confession out of him?'

'I expect so.'

'This is all very extraordinary.'

Liebermann smiled.

'Yes, it is.' Then, remembering their previous brittle exchange, when Rheinhardt had questioned the propriety of probing the darkest regions of the mind, Liebermann added: 'Psychiatry has its uses.' He could not resist a final sharp reiteration of his belief in the sanctity of *all* knowledge, however unpalatable. 'It is always better to know than not to know. One would be foolish to enter hell with a sputtering candle when a fiery torch was close to hand.'

'Touché, my friend,' laughed Rheinhardt. 'Touché!'

CHAPTER 52

Liebermann walked down the hospital corridor in a way that betrayed his eagerness. His stride was long and his expression earnest. In due course he came to a room that was guarded by a constable. The officer bowed and clicked his heels.

'Anything to report?' asked Liebermann.

The constable shook his head.

Liebermann knocked on the door. There was no reply.

He knocked again.

'Perhaps he's asleep,' said the constable.

'When was the last time you took a look at him?'

'About half an hour ago.'

'Was he asleep then?'

'No. He was just staring into space.' The constable shivered. 'Those eyes . . . they go right through you.'

'Thank you, constable.'

Liebermann turned the handle and entered the room. Sprenger was sitting up in bed. One of his legs was encased in plaster and his left arm was supported by a sling. Some blood had seeped through the bandage wrapped around his head. His gaze was locked on a fixed point on an imaginary horizon.

'Good afternoon, Herr Sprenger,' said Liebermann. The young doctor pulled a chair up beside the bed and sat down. 'I hope you are feeling better today.'

Sprenger did not move.

'If you are in pain, then I do hope you will say so. I have spoken to Nurse Egger who informs me that you have not requested any medication. This is most unusual given the severity of your injuries and I suspect that you are suffering in silence. It is perfectly reasonable – and acceptable – for you to request pain relief.'

Liebermann allowed a lengthy pause before continuing.

'Do you know who I am, Herr Sprenger?'

The young doctor stood up and waved a hand in front of Sprenger's face.

Not even a blink.

Liebermann wondered whether Sprenger's condition was in fact more serious than he or Professor Bieler had appreciated. The undertaker's impassive mien and uncanny stillness suggested brain damage.

'Can you hear me, Herr Sprenger?'

Liebermann took Sprenger's pulse, which was normal. He then produced a small mirror and directed light into Sprenger's eyes. The pupils shrank. Sprenger's breathing was slow and regular.

The young doctor sighed, crossed to the window, and gripped the iron bars. He looked down on an empty courtyard.

'Elective mutism,' he said flatly. 'You are perfectly capable of speaking to me. You are just choosing not to.'

Outside in the corridor a trolley rattled past. The constable called out. Although it was not possible to hear his exact words, the tone of his voice was clearly playful. A coquettish contralto laugh followed. There were a few more exchanges, and the rattle of the trolley faded.

Liebermann sat down again.

'I would like you to speak to me. I would like you to say whatever comes into your mind, without any attempt to censor the flow of ideas and images.'

Time passed.

'Do you dream, Herr Sprenger?

The undertaker turned his head slowly and looked directly at Liebermann. His eyes gathered in the light and shone like sapphires.

'"Night is the other half of life, and the better half."'

Liebermann sat up.

'What does that mean to you – that quote?'

Sprenger turned away again.

After a few minutes, Liebermann stood and prepared a syringe. He took Sprenger's right arm and carefully administered some analgesic.

'That should help,' said Liebermann. 'You must

337

get into the habit of asking for morphium when you need it.'

Liebermann put the syringe away and lifted his bag onto the bed.

'I would like to understand your . . .' Liebermann searched for the right word and, finding none suitable, settled on the neutral 'objectives.' He reached into his bag and removed a notebook and pencil. He placed them on Sprenger's bedside cabinet. 'I'm leaving some writing materials. Just here – in easy reach. When you are feeling stronger, I would like you to consider writing a history. *Your* history.' Liebermann closed his bag and snapped the hasp shut. 'For the moment, however, you should rest. I will try to visit you every day.'

CHAPTER 53

What was it like? Communion?

How clumsy language is. How completely void of meaning. Imagine this: for it is the position in which I find myself. Imagine a parrot, placed before some great wonder of the ancient world – the pyramids or the Acropolis. And now imagine a blind man, attempting to comprehend the majesty of these buildings, by listening only to the report given to him by the bird. I squawk – chirrup – and shriek. Whistle and yawp. And you can listen, but to what end?

Have you ever known ecstasy, Herr doctor? If you are like other men – and I have no reason to think otherwise – you will most probably seek to answer that question with recourse to some *carnal* memory. For millennia, poets have misappropriated the language of mysticism to describe the gross, the bestial. You will remember the moment in which you swooned and became nothing but sensation – and I must smile. That you could mistake animal rutting followed by a spasm in the groin for *ecstasy* reveals the poverty of your experience: the pleasure of a pig rolling about in its own filth! Ecstasy is not to be found in the farm-yard! You do not find ecstasy buried in a midden heap!

When She came to collect Adele Zeiler, we were united.

What was it like?

What is it like to transcend the limitations of the body?

What is it like to feel time and space dissolving into nothingness?

What is it like to feel fire instead of blood in one's veins?

What is it like to watch worlds collide and explode?

What is it like to drink stars from the mouth of heaven?

What is it like to kiss the face of eternity?

Oh, to be sheltered – once again – in the sanctuary of those great wings, which close around the soul with the tenderness of a mother suckling her newborn child!

Words: hopeless words.

You will never – can never – understand.

When it was over there was darkness and the play of gentian. The light gradually faded until a final smudge of violet phosphorescence flickered before extinction. I was back in this world. The Zeiler girl was empty: a husk. It was cold and I felt unwell. I picked myself up and left the Volksgarten, and as I trudged through those empty streets I think I knew – even then – that it would not stop there.

The next day I did not go to work. I sent a message saying I was ill. But, in truth, I was wretched with longing. The communion had inflamed my desire, not quenched it. I wanted Her more than ever.

Fortunately I had already made the acquaintance of the shop girl, Fräulein Babel. She was a capricious, whimsical child, and occasionally showed me small kindnesses that I found quite touching. Even so, the pity that she aroused in me found no significant purchase. Every night, I dreamed of those wings – and the solace of Her embrace.

PART IV

ASHPUTTEL

CHAPTER 54

Although Rheinhardt and Liebermann had communicated by telephone, they had not seen each other in person for over a week. They began their evening's music-making with some of Hugo Wolf's Goethe settings, the highlight of which was a particularly boisterous rendition of *Was in der Schenke waren heute* – 'What a commotion in the Inn.' Liebermann attacked the keys of the Bösendorfer with furious, gleeful violence, while Rheinhardt sang the melody as loud as his vocal cords would allow. Such was their relief at reaching the end of the song without a single error that they both laughed. As the evening progressed, their choices became more subdued and they finished their programme with four introspective lieder by Brahms. The last of these, *Die Mainacht* – 'May Night' – was performed with great amplitude of feeling. For Liebermann, the words of Ludwig Hölty's poetry seemed to find an uncanny echo in the testament that he was about to show his friend:

When, O smiling vision that shines through
    my soul

Like the red of dawn, shall I find you
   here on earth?
And the lonely tear
Quivers more ardently down my cheek.

They entered the smoking room and sat opposite the fireplace. Liebermann had positioned Sprenger's notebook on the table between the two chairs.

'Is this it?' asked Rheinhardt.

'Yes.'

Rheinhardt picked up the notebook and fanned through the pages.

'He's still not speaking,' said Liebermann, 'but over the last two weeks he has been complying with my request. He has been writing an account of his history and instalments have been arriving daily. Progress has been slow, probably because of the morphium he is given to relieve pain; however, it is just as likely that the medication has served to facilitate his disclosures – breaking down his internal resistances. Even though Sprenger refuses to engage in conversation, I have been treating him like any other patient. After he completes each new chapter, I then read it in his presence and reflect aloud on its content. What you have in your hands is a brief but extraordinary biography. It details Sprenger's life, from his birth to the murder of Cäcilie Roster.'

'Shall I read it now?'

'Yes, it won't take long.'

Liebermann poured some brandy and offered Rheinhardt a cigar. After turning only a few pages Rheinhardt exclaimed: 'Griesser! His assumed identity is the name of his old schoolteacher!'

'Indeed. Now read the next paragraph.'

Rheinhardt brought the notebook closer to his nose.

'An amateur archaeologist . . .'

'I visited the Natural History Museum and spoke to the archivist. He was able to find the schoolteacher's original letter addressed to the Museum director.'

'Remarkable. Where was it sent from?'

'Kluneberg – a tiny mountain village in Styria'.

Rheinhardt continued reading, grumbling to himself, occasionally muttering a single word such as 'madness', 'astonishing' or 'fiend', while Liebermann swirled his brandy and smoked. The atmosphere in the room became pungent and hazy. When Rheinhardt had finished, he closed the notebook and turned to Liebermann. He opened his mouth as if to speak, then stopped and filled his cheeks with air. Shaking his head, he said: 'Insane. He is completely insane!'

'I agree. But there is an underlying logic to his madness that makes it – in a sense – comprehensible.'

'Can we believe everything that he has written here?'

'He may have embellished certain episodes from his early childhood, but for the most part I think he has given a faithful account of his life. The existence of the schoolteacher's letter gives us a strong indication that Sprenger is telling the truth.'

Rheinhardt took a cigar.

'You were right – he's a . . . what did you call him?'

'A *thanatophile*,' said Liebermann, relishing each syllable. 'Yes, I *was* right, although I must confess my use of the term was little more than a naming exercise – yet another example of how we doctors create a strong impression of erudition by seasoning our German with Latin and Greek! I had no idea why or how Sprenger might have come to associate the instant of another's death with sexual gratification.'

'And you do now? I'm not sure I do – even after reading this . . .' Rheinhardt tapped the cover of the notebook before adding '. . . bizarre deposition.'

'You will remember our discussion of the Sophocles syndrome, in relation to Erstweiler?'

'I do . . .' Rheinhardt waved his cigar in the air '. . . vaguely.'

'Then you will forgive me for repeating myself, because if you do not understand the Sophocles syndrome you will not understand Sprenger.'

'But you mentioned it in relation to Erstweiler.'

'Indeed, the syndrome elucidates the behaviour of both men. Professor Freud has posited a general phenomenon of early childhood, characterised by love of the mother and jealousy – perhaps even hate – of the father. Our two cases, Erstweiler and

Sprenger, represent extreme examples of what can happen when Oedipal feelings are *unresolved*. In the case of Sprenger, the emphasis has fallen on love of the mother, whereas in the case of Erstweiler, the emphasis has fallen on hate of the father.'

'I would not dispute the notion that all children love their mothers,' said Rheinhardt. 'That is self-evident. Moreover, it is also self-evident that one must grow up, and that growing up involves becoming more independent. Therefore, the intense love that one feels for one's mother during early childhood must go through certain changes: which is what I believe you are referring to when you talk of feelings being *resolved*. All of this I am happy to accept; however, I have a strong suspicion that when you refer to *love of the mother*, you don't mean *that* kind of love. Your allusion to Sophocles' Oedipus suggests something altogether less innocent, less natural.'

'Natural? Perhaps it is natural for the human infant to have a presentiment of adult feelings. Perhaps this first great attachment to the mother is a form of rehearsal for future intimacies.'

'If so, then it is a rehearsal relevant to only half the population! How does Oedipus's situation translate with respect to the female child? As a father of two daughters I would be most interested to know.'

'I am not sure that Professor Freud has given that question much consideration.'

Rheinhardt harrumphed and drew on his cigar, producing a flotilla of smoke clouds.

Liebermann ignored Rheinhardt's disapproval and continued with his explanation: 'Sprenger's mother died in childbirth and absence – as we know – increases yearning. So it was that Sprenger's love for his mother was intensified and his overestimation of her beauty – encouraged by his father's insistence that she was an angel – was never tested against a fallible reality of flesh and blood. His longing knew no bounds. Idealisation was transformed into idolatry. In his childish mind, his father's encomium became a psychological truth. She was not *like* an angel, she *was* an angel – with wings – the undeniable fact of their existence being supported by photographic evidence! Any young boy, bereft of his mother, would pine for her, want her back again. But Sprenger, knowing that he had been the cause of her death, desired her return with a depth of feeling that is difficult for us to appreciate. The notion of reunion offered the prospect of absolution: freedom from the guilt associated with his first – and most terrible – sin.'

The young doctor paused to take a sip of his brandy.

'Sprenger mentions *communing* with his mother's image,' Liebermann continued. 'It is worth noting that in our culture the idea of communing arises mostly in two contexts: the mystical and the carnal. We *commune* with God and we *commune* with

350

lovers. Thus we can conclude that, even when Sprenger was very young, *thanatos* and *eros* were drawing closer together in his unconscious. I would also direct your attention to the fact that Sprenger's father seems to have been jealous of his son's *communing*. On discovering his son holding his wife's photograph, we learn that he snatched the picture away. For young Sprenger, it must have been like being found *in flagrante delicto.*'

Rheinhardt raised his eyebrows.

Liebermann was unperturbed: 'Sprenger's precocious interest in death – as evinced by his desire to see the mummies in Vienna's Natural History Museum – was merely symptomatic of his desire to be reunited with his mother. I also wonder if oblivion held some attraction for him, because it suggests a corresponding state – or non-state – before birth, the oblivion of the womb in which the unborn child is not only close to its mother but symbiotically joined.'

Liebermann lit himself another cigar.

'I will summarise: firstly, all male infants experience feelings towards their mothers which presage the sensual longings of maturity; secondly, in Sprenger, these feelings were magnified by his peculiar circumstances; thirdly, Sprenger wished to be reunited with his mother; and, finally, Sprenger's mother became "idealised" as an angelic being. These four factors – taken together – represent the cornerstones of Sprenger's psychopathology.'

Satisfied with the first part of his exposition, Liebermann allowed himself a brief pause during which he enjoyed the woody flavours of his cigar. Rheinhardt waited patiently.

'It is not difficult,' said Liebermann, stirring, 'to see how Sprenger learned to find corpses *desirable*. His nocturnal auto-erotic activities were undertaken while holding his breath and keeping very still – something he did initially to avoid waking his father. In due course, stillness became eroticised and incorporated into exploratory play with the village girls. When he saw Netti and Gerda in their caskets – *perfectly still* – he became acquainted with a level of arousal more intense than anything that he had experienced before. Thus Sprenger's sexual interest was diverted by small degrees from its natural course to a most irregular destination. If Sprenger's sexual development had progressed in the context of an otherwise normal life, he would have been no different to any of Krafft-Ebing's necrophiliacs. But this was not the case. His sexual development occurred against the remarkable background I have already described. This combination raised him above the ranks of common deviancy. With the strengthening of his libido, his desire for communion with his mother gained urgency; however, even in Sprenger's disturbed mind the universal taboo against incest necessitated a defensive transformation. To make such an ambition acceptable, his mother – already equipped with

352

wings – became the Angel of Death. It was a meta-morphosis that required little effort, and his fevered imagination supplied him with appropriate hallucinations: subtle intimations, auras of violet light, and the winged figure herself . . .'

Rheinhardt stubbed out his cigar.

'Are you proposing,' said Rheinhardt, his cheeks aglow with indignation, 'that Sprenger killed women to satisfy an infantile wish to have inter-course with his *mother*?'

'Ultimately – yes.'

'I'm sorry, Max, this time . . .' Rheinhardt shook his head. 'This time you have followed your mentor into a quagmire. I have the greatest respect for Professor Freud, but—'

'Oskar, how can you doubt it!' Liebermann cried. 'When Sprenger writes of his visit to the Cathedral of Notre Dame in Paris he mentions the portal reliefs. His attention was captured by Mary depicted not as Mother of God but as the bride of Christ. Do you not see? That was the turning point. Soon after, he resolved to summon the Angel of Death by commiting a murder. The portal inspired him to summon *his* bride. Mother and bride become one in his unconscious.' Liebermann reached over and impudently snatched the notebook from Rheinhardt's lap. 'And what about this?' He flicked through the pages with quick, impatient movements. '*Oh, to be sheltered – once again – in the sanctuary of those great wings, which close around the soul with the tenderness*

353

of a mother suckling her newborn child? That is how Sprenger describes communing with the Angel of Death! Does that not strike you as odd? That he chooses to compare one of the most terrifying personifications in mythology to a mother suckling her newborn child!'

Rheinhardt offered a concessionary tilt of the head.

'Yes, I must admit: that is a most peculiar sentiment to express – given the nature of the being he is describing.'

A lengthy silence ensued, during which Liebermann continued turning pages, intermittently pausing to reread certain passages. Rheinhardt observed his friend, the intensity of his expression and the stubborn set of his jaw.

'This is interesting,' said Liebermann, his voice sounding distant and absorbed. 'Sprenger says that he was fond of Fräulein Babel. There was something about her that moved him to pity. Do you remember when we were at Fräulein Babel's apartment? And I suggested that the perpetrator might have left the door open because he wanted to be caught. I think this passage confirms my hypothesis. Some residue of conscience was rebelling against his psychopathology and the effects of the toxin in his brain.'

'Ah, yes,' said Rheinhardt, his full baritone suddenly sounding abnormally loud. 'I wanted to ask you about that. You have hitherto given me the impression that the lead oxide was very significant. Yet now you seem to be placing much greater stress on Sprenger's Oedipal inclinations and his early sexual development.'

'Both are important,' Liebermann replied. 'Sprenger's longing for his mother, his auto-erotic behaviour, his exploratory games with the village girls, his exposure to the caskets, and his necrophilia in adulthood *all* contributed to his illness. But his wish to commune with the Angel of Death might have remained a wish, and only a wish, had it not been for the lead oxide. It is possible that the poison, over many years, accumulated in those parts of the brain that mediate inhibition. Without inhibitory functioning there was nothing to stop him – and fantasy became reality.'

The two men fell silent and a significant interval of time passed. Somewhere in the building a cello was playing. The notes teased at the limits of audition, suggesting – but never quite becoming – a recognisable melody. Eventually, Liebermann turned towards his friend and said: 'I think we should consider one other factor that has contributed to Sprenger's unique presentation.'

'Oh?' said Rheinhardt, blinking as he emerged from the closed world of his private cogitations.

'Us,' said Liebermann.

'I beg your pardon?'

'Us: me – you – all of us – we Viennese. We are utterly preoccupied with sex and death. The signs of this preoccupation are everywhere: in our theatres, art galleries, opera houses, and concert halls. Consider Klimt's seductresses, or the funeral marches that director Mahler puts in his symphonies. The good people of Vienna are flocking to the opera house in order to see the new production of *Tristan and Isolde*: a story in which – tellingly – the potions of love and death are confused. Young rakes are always having affairs which end with a demand for satisfaction. What begins in the bedroom progresses inexorably to the grave: prostitutes on the Graben and suicides reported daily in the newspapers – Professor Freud, who has shown us that even a dream of flying is libidinous – Krafft-Ebing – Schnitzler's promiscuous shop girls – the overblown pomp and macabre ceremony of our funerals – and syphilis, our national disease – always there to remind us of our dual obsession: sex and death. Sick bodies produce symptoms – and the sick body of our society has produced Sprenger!'

Rheinhardt grunted into his brandy glass.

'You seem to be making an appeal for clemency on Sprenger's behalf. Let us not forget those poor women: Fräuleins Zeiler, Babel, Wirth and Roster.' Rheinhardt put down his brandy glass and pulled at his lower lip. 'Just a moment . . .' His eyes widened. 'Sprenger doesn't mention Fräulein Wirth.'

'I was wondering how long it would take you to realise that.'

Two furrows appeared on Rheinhardt's forehead.

'Why doesn't he mention Selma Wirth?'

'He doesn't mention Selma Wirth – because he has no idea who she is.'

'What do you mean?'

'He didn't kill her.'

'How can you say that?'

Liebermann lifted the notebook and held it up in the air like a fervent preacher wielding his Bible: 'What Sprenger has written in here is entirely coherent. One couldn't fabricate such a history. A fabricated history would be full of anomalies and wouldn't make sense psychologically. He has not baulked at admitting the murders of Fräuleins Zeiler, Babel and Roster, so why should he baulk at admitting to the murder of Fräulein Wirth?'

'Could the omission of Fräulein Wirth be a failure of memory? You said he is being given morphium.'

'No, Oskar. Sprenger never knew her. She was killed with a dagger, not a hatpin. We should have given this inconsistency more thought, afforded it greater significance.' Liebermann allowed his words to register and waited for the alarm to show in Rheinhardt's eyes, before adding: 'Fräulein Wirth's murderer is still at large.'

'Dear God,' said Rheinhardt, picking up his glass again. Liebermann poured him another brandy. The inspector swung his head back and dispensed with the contents like a shot of schnapps. He coughed and repeated: 'Dear God.' Rheinhardt turned the empty glass in his hand: 'What now? Where do we begin?'

'Frau Vogl?' Liebermann ventured.

'Yes, and Fräulein Wirth's neighbour, Frau Lachkovics. Perhaps they will be able to remember some new detail. The neighbour's daughter – Jana – was a simple child. I doubt that she will be able to help us more than she already has.'

'When we questioned Frau Vogl she mentioned seeing a man wearing a bowler hat waiting in the courtyard outside Fräulein Wirth's apartment.'

'She did indeed.'

'And Frau Vogl believed that Frau Wirth was seeing someone – a lover.'

'It was only a suspicion and if the gentleman wearing the bowler hat was Frau Wirth's lover why would he have been loitering in the courtyard?'

'A good question: to which the answer might be that he was waiting in the courtyard in order to observe the arrival of Frau Vogl.'

'To what end?'

Liebermann shrugged.

'I don't know.'

It was obvious to Rheinhardt that his friend had had an idea but was not eager to share it. The inspector, slightly irritated by Liebermann's evasiveness, voiced his own train of thought.

'There was also the landlord's agent,' said Rheinhardt. 'Shevchenko. I'll talk to him again. Fräulein Wirth had fallen behind with her rent. Frau Lachkovics said that her neighbour was in debt because she was always spending money on doctors.'

'Doctors . . .' Liebermann repeated. Then, playing a five-finger exercise on Sprenger's notebook, he added: 'Fräulein Wirth had a *consultation* with Doctor Vogl.' The word 'consultation' sagged under a weight of innuendo.

Rheinhardt spoke sofly: 'What are you suggesting?'

'When we left the Vogls' house I couldn't help feeling that there was something—'

'Wrong,' Rheinhardt cut in. 'I know, Max. But you didn't succeed in winning me over to that view.'

'What if there had been some impropriety?'

'Between Vogl and Wirth?'

'Yes.'

'Well, Vogl wouldn't have killed Wirth to ensure her silence – if that's what you're thinking – even if exposure would have meant the end of his marriage. A man in Vogl's position wouldn't take such a risk. Besides, Frau Vogl is a striking, handsome woman – is she not? It seems unlikely that Vogl would have chosen to pursue his wife's lame friend. What are we to suppose – that while Vogl was examining her wasted leg he was overcome with passion?'

'She could have seduced him. She could have offered him particular *favours* – to which men are partial and for which women commonly express distaste.'

'And why would she have done that?'

'To spite Frau Vogl.'

'Frau Vogl was Frau Wirth's friend.'

'A beautiful, healthy, talented, successful friend – feted by society and loved by her husband. One could grow to resent such a friend if one was a lame laundry worker.'

Rheinhardt considered Liebermann's proposal and shook his head.

'No . . . you are wrong.'

Liebermann smiled.

'I might be wrong – but not *very* wrong.'

'What are you doing tomorrow?'

'Actually, I'm having the day off.'

'Then I hope,' said Rheinhardt, 'you haven't arranged to do anything important.'

CHAPTER 55

Liebermann and Rheinhardt met mid-morning for coffee and proceeded directly to Frau Vogl's salon. On entering, they found the vestibule empty. They waited a few moments to be received but no one came to greet them.

'What do we do now?' asked Rheinhardt. Liebermann pointed to an electric bell push mounted on the wall and pressed it.

A faint ringing emanated from somewhere within the building.

In due course, the door at the rear of the vestibule opened and a young woman with blonde hair entered. They both recognised her from their visit to Frau Vogl's house.

'Inspector,' said the young woman.

'Fräulein,' Rheinhardt responded, bowing.

'Was Madame expecting you? She didn't say—'

'No,' Rheinhardt cut in. 'Frau Vogl wasn't expecting me; however, I would be most grateful if she would spare us a few minutes of her valuable time.'

'What shall I tell her?'

'That I wish to speak with her.'

'In connection with . . . ?'

'A matter of utmost importance.'

'Madame is upstairs with the machinists. I'll let her know that you're here.' Then she curtsied and excused herself. The sound of her footsteps – remarkably heavy for a young woman – could be heard as she made her ascent.

Several minutes later the figure of Kristina Vogl appeared in the doorway. She was wearing a blue dress which complemented her eyes and her dark hair had been skilfully arranged in a bouffant wave. A few loose strands hung down past her ears: a hint of dishabille which softened her features and carried with it a suggestion of the bedroom. Above her heart was a large brooch. It was square-shaped, partitioned into quadrants by a silver cross, and each of these quadrants was filled with colourful semi-precious stones.

'Inspector,' Kristina said warmly. 'What a surprise.' She advanced and offered Rheinhardt her hand, which he took and kissed. When he lifted his head, he took a step backwards, as if he could not tolerate standing so close to such a radiant being.

'Frau Vogl,' he said, unable to conceal his admiration.

'May I get you some refreshment, inspector? Some tea, perhaps?'

'No, thank you.'

Kristina addressed her assistant: 'Wanda, is the reception room ready?'

'Yes, madame,' replied the young woman.

'We'll continue when I've finished with Inspector Rheinhardt and Doctor Liebermann. Run along now.' Liebermann was surprised that Frau Vogl could remember his name – particularly as she had not taken the trouble to acknowledge his presence. 'This way, please, gentlemen.'

She led them to a large room which so overwhelmed the young doctor that he found himself surveying his surroundings in a state of blissful enchantment. Being a devotee of all things modern he was almost incapacitated by the white lacquered walls and the long mirrors, the glass lamps and the elegant simplicity of the furniture. The cuboid table looked very much like the one he had purchased for his smoking room.

'Beautiful,' said Liebermann. 'Is the decor by Moser?'

'Moser and Hoffmann: if you are interested, there are some examples of their jewellery-work displayed in the vitrine.' Liebermann looked through the tilted window at the treasures displayed within. His attention was immediately captured by a bracelet, made from coral salamanders. 'Please,' the hostess continued. 'Do sit down, inspector.'

Rheinhardt waited for Kristina to settle before lowering himself onto one of the hoop-backed chairs.

'Herr doctor . . .' said Rheinhardt, looking up at his friend. 'Would you care to join us?'

'Of course,' said Liebermann, a little embarrassed. 'My apologies.'

With some difficulty, he pulled himself away from the vitrine. Taking one of the vacant places, he addressed Frau Vogl: 'Delightful. I am very fond of Moser. I have a table just like this one.'

'By Moser?'

'Yes.'

Kristina's expression showed that she was impressed; however, she did not enccourage Liebermann to elaborate. Instead, she turned to face Rheinhardt.

'Inspector, I must congratulate you. When I saw the headline on the front page of the *Wiener Zeitung* . . . well, you cannot imagine my relief. My dear husband was so worried for my safety he would not let me leave the house without an escort! It is wonderful to be free of fear once again.'

'Frau Vogl, you are most kind, but I did not catch Sprenger alone. Much of the credit for his capture must go to my colleague here – Doctor Liebermann – who, for professional reasons, prefers his police activities to remain unreported in the newspapers.'

Kristina glanced at Liebermann, somewhat uneasily.

'You wanted to speak to me concerning a matter of *utmost* importance. I presume it has something to do with poor Selma.'

'Yes,' said Rheinhardt. 'That is correct. There are some aspects of Fräulein Wirth's circumstances which require clarification. You may be able to help us.'

'Oh?'

'You will recall that during our prior interview, you suggested that Fräulein Wirth might have found an admirer.'

'I . . .' Kristina hesitated and shook her head. 'I really don't know. I pitied Selma. Her life was never easy and she seemed to be the recipient of more than her fair share of bad luck. I was always hoping that she would meet someone. I think in my eagerness to see her happily married I rashly overestimated the significance of the small changes I observed in her dress and manner.'

'Frau Vogl,' Liebermann ventured. 'What were these small changes?'

'Oh,' Kristina replied. 'I can't remember, precisely. She smiled more: I suppose one would say she was . . . I don't know, more *girlish*.'

'And her dress?' Liebermann pressed.

'What about it?'

'How was it different?'

'She had bought a new . . . no.' Kristina looked flustered. 'No. She looked more groomed – that's all . . .'

Rheinhardt leaned forward in his chair.

'Frau Vogl, you said that you saw a man waiting outside Fräulein Wirth's apartment.'

Kristina looked confused – but then, quite suddenly, her face brightened with recognition.

'Yes, that's right: a man with a bowler hat.'

'Please, Frau Vogl. Think very carefully. Can you remember anything else about him?'

'No. He was just . . . a man.'

'Is it possible that this gentleman could have been Fräulein Wirth's admirer?'

'Inspector, on reflection, I do not think that Selma had an admirer.'

'But, let us assume – for argument's sake – that your early suspicions were correct. Is it at all *conceivable* that the gentleman who you saw might have been Fräulein Wirth's lover?'

'I couldn't possibly say.' A note of irritation had crept into her voice. 'With respect, inspector, I don't understand why you're asking me these questions. What difference does it make if this man *was* or *wasn't* Selma's lover? Indeed, what difference does it make if she *did* or *didn't* have a lover at all?'

Rheinhardt leaned forward.

'I regret to say that the answer to these questions may be of considerable importance, Frau Vogl, because we now have good reason to believe that Markus Sprenger did not kill Selma Wirth.'

Frau Vogl's expression hardened.

'What?'

'I am sorry. I appreciate that you will find this news most distressing.'

Kristina breathed deeply and her bosom rose and fell.

'I don't understand. What are you saying, inspector?' The pitch of her voice rose hysterically.

'Sprenger . . . it was in *all* the newspapers. Markus Sprenger.'

'I am afraid that some new evidence has come to light.'

'New evidence?'

'Yes,' said Rheinhardt. He did not reveal more, even though Kristina's expression communicated an urgent appeal for more information. Some moments passed before she straightened her back and recovered her composure. 'Do you think then,' she said in a lower, more controlled register, 'that I am still in danger?'

'Possibly,' said Rheinhardt.

Kristina raised a trembling hand to her temple.

'Oh, this is dreadful. Quite dreadful. Are you sure, inspector? Are you sure it was not Sprenger?'

Rheinhardt nodded solemnly.

'Frau Vogl, we are very much in need of your help. Think very carefully. Did Fräulein Wirth give you any reason to worry about her safety? Did she say anything that might be pertinent?'

Kristina looked from Rheinhardt to Liebermann – and back again.

'Yes.' The word was tentative, experimental. 'Yes, she may have . . .'

Rheinhardt took out his notebook and pencil.

'Please . . .'

'Selma despised the landlord's agent.'

'Shevchenko?'

'Was that his name? I only knew him as the *landlord's agent*.'

'Why did she despise him?'

'She said he was ill-mannered – uncouth – an animal – and . . .' Kristina touched her colourful brooch as if the stones were magical and might endow her with the strength to continue. 'I think he once presented her with an obscene proposition.'

'I am afraid you must be specific, Frau Vogl.'

'He offered to cancel her debt, if she . . .'

'Submitted to him,' Rheinhardt offered helpfully.

'Yes. If she submitted to him.'

'I see.'

Rheinhardt made a few notes.

'Frau Vogl,' said Liebermann. 'You say that you *think* Shevchenko made an obscene proposition. Why *think*? Surely, if Fräulein Wirth told you this, it is not speculative.'

'I'm sorry . . . The agent *did* make such a proposition. Yes.'

'Selma told you this?' asked Rheinhardt.

'Yes. She did.'

The inspector bit the end of his pencil: 'Frau Vogl. Why did you not mention this before?'

'It had slipped my mind. You must understand – this conversation – we had it almost a year ago. And Selma never referred to it again. I naturally assumed that after Selma had refused him the landlord's agent had refrained from making further advances. Nor did I imagine that Shev – . . . Shev – . . .'

'Shevchenko,' said Rheinhardt.

368

'That Shevchenko would perhaps – one day – force himself upon her. If I had thought such a thing I would have demanded she leave the apartment – whatever she said, however she objected – and made appropriate provision.'

Rheinhardt looked up from his notebook. Liebermann sighed as he saw the flame of admiration reignite behind his friend's melancholy eyes.

They found a coffee house close to the cathedral.

'I'm going to telephone Haussmann,' said Rheinhardt. 'I'll get him to locate Shevchenko and call me back here if he has any success.'

Rheinhardt went to find the telephone booth and on his return Liebermann saw his friend talking to the head waiter. A few coins changed hands and the waiter bowed obsequiously.

'Ah,' said Rheinhardt, delighted to see that their order had arrived. 'I've been looking forward to this.' He sipped his Türkische and cut through the plum flan with the edge of his fork. It was a generous portion: a slab of moist pastry, covered in crescents of purple fruit and sprinkled with icing sugar. He chewed slowly to prolong his first moments of pleasure. 'Excellent. What did you order?' He looked at Liebermann's nondescript white wedge.

'Cheesecake,' said Liebermann.

Rheinhardt shrugged, took another sip of his coffee and resumed eating. When he had consumed roughly half of his flan he remembered his companion and said: 'Well. What did you think?'

Liebermann stirred his Schwarzer and stared into his cup as if the answer he should give was written on the spiral of light brown froth.

'Something isn't right.'

Rheinhardt stopped chewing.

'You thought she was, what? Lying?'

Liebermann put down his spoon.

'From the moment she saw you, she seemed anxious to disarm you. She offered her hand, flattered you, and smiled like a coquette.'

'Perhaps she saw in my person an admirable figure of manhood – and was unable to contain herself.'

Rheinhardt smiled into Liebermann's surly visage.

The young doctor considered his friend's remark and proceeded as if it had never been made.

'She said that Selma Wirth had looked different and was about to say that Wirth had bought a new dress; then, on remembering that Wirth was in no position to make such a purchase she changed her mind and opted for an innocuous comment concerning the woman's grooming habits.'

'You are not a psychic, Max. That is pure supposition.'

'She seemed bemused when you first mentiond the man with the bowler hat, and I strongly suspect that this was because she had only the faintest recollection of having claimed to have seen him.

When you announced that Wirth's killer was still at large, her reaction was most interesting: she was more concerned about how you had come to that conclusion than her own safety: and when you pressed her for more information concerning Fräulein Wirth's circumstances, she seemed to pluck the Shevchenko incident out of the air. The way she was speaking sounded to me like . . . like an improvisation. Particularly when she pretended that she couldn't remember his name. In fact, she has a very good memory for names.' Liebermann picked up his fork but the utensil halted before reaching its destination. 'Frau Vogl said that Wirth had told her about Shevchenko's proposition almost a year ago – without the slightest hesitation. Most people, when recalling an event in the past, pause or slow down so that they can calculate the time that has elapsed. The absence of a pause suggests that no calculation was necessary.'

'Which means?'

'Contrary to appearances, she had already given the matter of Shevchenko's indecent proposal much consideration, or . . .'

'What?'

'She was making it all up.'

Rheinhardt pushed the remains of his plum flan around the edge of his plate.

'You know, Max, I am in danger of being persuaded.'

The inspector finished his cake and took some cigars from his pocket. He gave one to Liebermann, lit it, and then lit his own. Liebermann turned his head and gazed out of the window. Rheinhardt wanted to ask his friend what he was thinking but knew there would be little point. The young doctor had retreated into himself.

If Rheinhardt *had* asked the question and Liebermann had responded candidly, the answer would have taken Rheinhardt by surprise. Indeed, it would have shocked him. For at that precise moment Liebermann was thinking of Miss Lydgate inserting her fingers into Bathild Babel's sex. This image – which had previously disturbed Liebermann – was suddenly no longer prurient, but expressive of certain possibilities . . .

They smoked their cigars in silence and passed the next hour in desultory conversation. The only topic which moved them to fluency was the music of Karl Goldmark – in particular, the early songs, and his opera *Die Königin von Saba*. In due course the head waiter came to their table. He bowed low and said: 'Inspector, your assistant is on the telephone.'

CHAPTER 56

S hevchenko's office was in a room above a piano shop which seemed to attract a very accomplished clientele. Bursts of Beethoven – played with great power and ferocity – rose up through the floorboards. The music created a curious tension in Liebermann's fingers. They began to twitch sympathetically. It was as if the spirit of Beethoven's violent genius had stormed his brain and taken possession of his nervous system. Liebermann locked his hands together, fearing that he might be compelled to shadow the *presto agitato* of the C sharp minor Sonata on an imaginary keyboard.

The remains of Shevchenko's midday meal had not been cleared. An apple core had turned brown and the inedible skin of a sausage – crumpled and semi-transparent – resembled the sloughed-off hide of a snake. A smear of bright yellow mustard contributed an incongruous splash of colour to this otherwise moribund still life. Liebermann was overcome by a sense of bathos. The mundane trappings of Shevchenko's routine – scraps on a plate – underscored the gulf that separated high art from the necessities of material existence. It seemed to the young doctor that the music which filled the air was arriving from another universe, a place entirely free from corruption, decay and corporeal imperfections.

They had been in Shevchenko's office for approximately ten minutes.

After introducing Liebermann, Rheinhardt had explained the purpose of their visit. Shevchenko had listened impassively. Indeed, his expression had verged on indifference.

Liebermann found that he could not look at the Ruthenian without feeling slightly nauseous. The man's hair was greasy, his beard untrimmed, and dirt had accumulated beneath his fingernails. He wore a frock coat, the material of which had become shiny in places through excessive wear. He also seemed to give off an unpleasant odour, similar to the sour smell that Liebermann associated with geriatric wards – an unpleasant blend of stale perspiration with ammonia.

'Well, inspector,' said Shevchenko. 'I'm sorry to hear that the man who killed Fräulein Wirth is still free – naturally. But I'm afraid you're wasting your time talking to me. I've already told you all that I know about Fräulein Wirth.'

Rheinhardt leaned forward.

'When we last spoke, Herr Shevchenko, you said that Fräulein Wirth hadn't paid her rent for months.'

'Yes. She was always a bad payer. And she would

give me such excuses.' Shevchenko shook his head. 'Such weak excuses.'

A few bars of the slow movement from the *Waldstein Sonata* wafted up from below.

'It must be difficult for you to work up here,' said Rheinhardt.

'Why do you say that?'

'The music! Don't you find it distracting?'

Shevchenko shrugged.

'It doesn't bother me.'

Rheinhardt leaned back and his chair creaked loudly.

'Tell me, Herr Shevchenko. How would you describe your relations with Fräulein Wirth?'

'Relations? What do you mean by *relations*?'

'Did you get on?'

'It's not my job to get on with tenants, Herr inspector. I collect rents. A rent collector is never very popular.'

'But, within reason, would you describe your relations with Fräulein Wirth as good?'

Shevchenko paused to consider the question before answering: 'As good as they could be, given my responsibilities.'

'She was not an unattractive woman – Fräulein Wirth.' Shevchenko shrugged again. 'Did you find her attractive?'

The Ruthenian's eyes narrowed. He grunted and said: 'What are you getting at, inspector? I am a plain-speaking man and would prefer it if you came directly to the point.'

'Did you offer Fräulein Wirth exemption from the payment of rental arrears in exchange for sexual favours?'

The Ruthenian's right eyebrow rose by a fraction. 'Who told you that?'

'A friend of the deceased.'

'The neighbour? What's her name? Lenkiewicz? No – Lachkovics! That's it – was it Frau Lachkovics?'

'It was not Frau Lachkovics.'

'Then who? I have a right to know.' Shevchenko held Rheinhardt's gaze for a few moments, then sighed and looked away. 'You have been misinformed, inspector.'

'You did not find Fräulein Wirth attractive?'

'No, inspector. I didn't.' Shevchenko lifted his head and looked directly at Rheinhardt. 'When was I supposed to have made this proposal?'

'Some time ago. A year – perhaps . . .'

The opening bars of the *Pathetique Sonata* added melodrama to the exchange.

'About a year ago,' Shevchenko repeated. He paused and counted his fingers while whispering the months of the year. 'Actually, inspector, a proposal of that nature was made at that time. But it wasn't me who made it.'

The music stopped abruptly, mid-phrase.

'Would you care to elaborate?'

'I am not a man to sully the reputation of the dead. The poor woman is in her grave.'

'Herr Shevchenko, am I understanding you

correctly? Fräulein Wirth offered *you* sexual favours in exchange for financial assistance?'

The Ruthenian placed his hand in his frock coat and took out a leather wallet that opened up like a book. He held it out so that Rheinhardt and Liebermann could see inside. It contained a photograph of a woman and an image of Jesus Christ ascending up to heaven in a cone of light. 'Frau Shevchenko,' said the rent collector. 'We were married for twenty-five years. God didn't choose to bless us with children – we only had each other. I never so much as looked at another woman my whole life – and haven't since Frau Shevchenko died.' The opening chords of the *Pathetique* sounded again. 'She died about a year ago: a terrible illness, a wasting disease. Pain, vomiting, blood in the bedpan – and lots of it. I would work all day and be up all night nursing her. Sometimes the priest or one of the nuns would come and I'd get a couple of hours' sleep, but no more. The doctors couldn't do anything for her.'

At that moment the pianist below began an airy waltz, in which a repeated discordant semitone was employed to humorous effect. The change in mood was jarring.

'Do you really think that under those circumstances,' Shevchenko continued, 'I would be seeking an arrangement – of the kind you suggest – with Fräulein Wirth?'

Rheinhardt and Liebermann were silent. The waltz petered out.

Shevchenko looked at the image of his wife for a moment before putting it back in his pocket. His knuckle went to his right eye and his attempt to collect the tear that was waiting to fall did not succeed.

Liebermann felt a pang of regret. He had judged Shevchenko unkindly. The man's lack of self-care had an obvious cause: profound grief. He was simply biding his time, waiting for death and a much longed-for reunion with his wife.

'I am sorry to have troubled you, Herr Shevchenko,' said Rheinhardt very softly, rising from his chair.

The Ruthenian nodded.

Rheinhardt and Liebermann crossed the floor, their footsteps coinciding uncomfortably with the beat of a jolly German dance tune.

CHAPTER 57

Frau Lachkovics's apartment was empty. Liebermann and Rheinhardt waited for her to return, smoking in the courtyard, and when Rheinhardt's stomach began to emit gurgling sounds it was decided that they should repair to a local beer cellar. They found a welcoming establishment and spent the next hour enjoying well-cooked *tafelspitz* – boiled beef – served with fried potatoes, apple horseradish and chive sauce. The meal was washed down with several steins of *Edelweiss*. Fortified by the wholesome fare and the cordial properties of the liquor, they marched back to Frau Lachkovics's apartment and were relieved to find the windows brightly illuminated.

The two men were admitted into a humble parlour where Jana, Frau Lachkovics's daughter, sat silently on a wicker chair in the corner. Rheinhardt introduced Liebermann and was surprised by Frau Lachkovics's response. She became agitated – her gaze oscillating anxiously between Jana and Liebermann. It appeared to Rheinhardt that Frau Lachkovics had jumped to an erroneous conclusion: that he had brought a doctor with him to examine Jana, with the intention of getting her admitted into a hospital. Rheinhardt was moved by a wave of pity.

'Frau Lachkovics,' said the inspector, reaching out and gently touching the woman's sleeve. 'Herr Doctor Liebermann is my colleague. He is not here to act in a medical capacity.'

The woman sighed: a release of tension.

She motioned as if to speak – but an idea seemed to rise up in her mind which robbed her of confidence.

'Frau Lachkovics?' Rheinhardt inquired.

She shook her head: 'Please sit.'

Rheinhardt and Liebermann were obliged to share the narrow space between the arms of a small sofa. They found themselves squeezed together, and no amount of shifting, wriggling or turning eased their compression.

'You were out earlier,' said Rheinhardt to Frau Lachkovics, withdrawing his elbow from beneath Liebermann's arm.

'Yes,' replied Frau Lachkovics, drawing up a stool. 'I'm sorry, we were in Ottakring. My mother . . . you remember – I told you I have an elderly mother?'

'Indeed.'

Frau Lachkovics adjusted the drop of her skirt as she sat down.

'The tram was late – I don't know why. Did you send a message? If I had known then—'

Rheinhardt cut in: 'Please do not fret on our account, Frau Lachkovics, your late return afforded us an opportunity to enjoy the splendid *tafelspitz* served at the Trinklied.' He gestured vaguely towards the street. 'Frau Lachkovics, I have some more questions I would like to ask you in connection with Fräulein Wirth.' Frau Lachkovics did not raise any objection.

The arrest of Markus Sprenger had been discussed interminably at the laundry; however, knowledge of his arrest did not embolden her to ask Rheinhardt why he had come back again to ask more questions. She passively accepted the policeman's authority.

'Frau Lachkovics,' Rheinhardt continued, 'are you quite certain that Fräulein Wirth did not have any gentlemen friends?'

'I cannot be absolutely sure. But I think it very unlikely. You see, we saw a great deal of each other. We would walk to the laundry together in the morning and return together at the end of the day. And I always knew when Selma had visitors. You can hear people knocking on her door from here. The walls are thin. I never saw any gentlemen arriving, apart from Herr Shevchenko, the landlord's agent. I saw Selma's friend Frau Vogl and some other girls from the laundry, Christa and Steffi – but never any men. Besides, if she *had* met someone, I'm sure she would have said something. It was in her nature to share personal things. She was never reticent.'

'About the time when Fräulein Wirth . . .'
Rheinhardt glanced at the girl in the corner and
searched for a diplomatic turn of phrase. 'About
the time when Fräulein Wirth met with her sad
end, do you recall ever seeing any strangers
loitering in the courtyard?'

'No.'

'A man wearing a bowler hat and a long coat?'

'I do not recall seeing any strangers.'

'But what about any gentlemen answering to
that particular description?'

'A bowler hat and long coat? There are many
men who dress like that.'

'Indeed,' Rheinhardt altered his position: 'You
mentioned Herr Shevchenko . . .'

Frau Lachkovics frowned.

'Yes?'

'Has he always behaved . . . correctly?'

'I don't understand . . .'

'Always shown you the proper respect that a lady
is entitled to expect from a gentleman?' The
woman looked at Rheinhardt blankly. 'I am sorry,'
Rheinhardt continued, 'but I must ask you an
indelicate question. Did Herr Shevchenko ever
proposition you? Did he ever make an unwelcome
amorous advance?'

'Herr Shevchenko! Good heavens, no!'

Frau Lachkovics's cheeks became luminous and
a hectic flush travelled down her neck.

'I am sorry, madam, but I am obliged to ask
you yet another indelicate question. Did Herr

382

Shevchenko – to your knowledge – ever proposition Fräulein Wirth?'

The flush intensified.

'No, no . . .'

'Would Fräulein Wirth have told you – do you think – if he had?'

Frau Lachkovics paused before answering. Rheinhardt could see that she was giving his question serious consideration.

'Yes,' she said finally. 'Yes, I think she would. Herr Shevchenko is not that sort of man. His only concern is collecting rents. He never makes small talk, never dallies. He just collects the rent and leaves. Most of the tenants around here don't like him. It's true: he never smiles and he can be abrupt and surly. But I do not think he is a bad man – rather someone who is sad and lonely.'

The wicker chair creaked as the girl in the corner stood up. She crossed the floor and stood behind her mother. Frau Lachkovics turned and smiled.

'Jana?'

The girl did not respond. Instead, she fixed her stare on Rheinhardt. Her gaze was purposeful, yet her expression remained disconcertingly void. Her lineaments gave no clue as to the nature of her personality, her mood or what she might be thinking. She raised her arm. In her hand she was holding a book.

'Can I keep this,' she said in a dull monotone, 'now that she is dead?'

'I beg your pardon?' said Rheinhardt.

'Jana!' exclaimed Frau Lachkovics, tugging the girl's skirt sharply to express her disapproval. The admonishment had no effect.

'Now that Selma is dead,' Jana continued, 'can I keep her books?'

'Selma gave you that?' said Rheinhardt.

'Yes.'

Rheinhardt extricated himself from the sofa and rose to take the volume from the girl's hand. He examined the spine and discovered it was a collection of children's stories.

'There's another one in the kitchen,' said Jana.

Rheinhardt fanned through the pages. Some illustrations flashed out from the blur of text. Suddenly the fluttering came to a halt at a point where a little ticket had been inserted. Rheinhardt pulled it out, studied the print, and then said to Frau Lachkovics: 'Is this yours?'

'No.'

'What is it?' asked Liebermann.

'A ticket for one of the luggage lockers at the Südbahnhof.'

The ensuing silence was broken by Jana.

'Well – can I keep the books?'

'You can keep the books,' said Rheinhardt, 'if I can keep this ticket.'

CHAPTER 58

Heinz Vogl entered his wife's bedroom. It was not very late and he was surprised to find that she had retired so early. Indeed, he felt a little indignant and persuaded himself that, if she was asleep, waking her could be justified.

'My dear?' he called. The eiderdown undulated as she turned to face him.

'I'm still awake,' she said, somewhat redundantly. Vogl advanced along the wedge of light that infiltrated Kristina's room from his own. He sat on the edge of the bed. 'What time is it?' she asked, blinking up at him.

'Ten o'clock – or thereabouts.'

'How was your meeting?'

'It went well enough. Professor Raich was in favour of appointing Mitterwallner – but Professor Lischka and that fool Kinigader objected. Fortunately, I was able to persuade Salvenmoser to vote with us and in the end the outcome was satisfactory. But it was a tiring, frustrating process, and I fear that the discussion – which became quite heated – will leave an atmosphere of ill feeling in some quarters. The air will have to be cleared in due course.'

Vogl reached out and touched Kristina's cheek. 'What is it, my dear?'

'Do you remember the police inspector – Rheinhardt – and his colleague Liebermann?'

'Yes, of course.'

'They came to the salon today.'

'Really? What did they want?'

'They said that they have acquired some more evidence and that the man whom they caught – Sprenger – the man who was supposed to have killed Selma, well, now it seems he didn't kill her after all.'

'Oh, my dear, that is terrible news. You are still in danger.' Vogl lifted his wife's limp hand to his lips and kissed her fingers, each one in turn. 'I hope you didn't come home on your own.' Kristina did not reply. 'You did? Oh, my dear – you must be more careful. You cannot afford to take such risks. Not now.'

'I cannot go on living like this,' Kristina whispered. The tone of her voice was curious, almost strangulated. Her eyes became glassy as the tears welled up.

Vogl gathered her into his arms, and rocked her backwards and forwards.

'My poor darling . . . do not cry. Inspector Rheinhardt managed to catch Sprenger – and I'm sure he'll catch whoever was responsible for poor Selma's murder, eventually. It's only a matter of time.'

These words – intended to be comforting – seemed to have the very opposite effect. Vogl felt his wife's body becoming tense in his arms as the tears washed down her face.

CHAPTER 59

The cab came to a halt outside the Südbahnhof, joining a line of parked carriages. The two men stepped down onto the expansive forecourt. While Rheinhardt paid the driver, Liebermann admired the architecture. It was a perfect example of Viennese ostentation. He might have been looking up at the façade of any of the great European opera houses rather than at a train station. Its grandiosity made him smile and although he was a committed modernist the sheer bravado of the structure's vaulting ambition made him quietly proud to call Vienna his home. The building boasted five entrance portals above which sat a tier of arched windows and a further row of oblong windows. A terracotta tympanum enlivened the massive pediment, each corner of which supported a majestic classical figure. Sphinxes could be seen on the roofs of the two wings which flanked the façade, and each of these wings possessed pediments of their own.

'Impressive, isn't it?' said Rheinhardt, joining his friend. 'But now isn't the time . . .'

He slapped a hand on Liebermann's back and the impact of the good-natured whack propelled the young doctor forward.

The interior of the Südbahnhof was as magnificent as the exterior. Rheinhardt and Liebermann entered a vast hallway dominated by a grand staircase that rose and divided below a balustraded gallery. The floor was illuminated by rows of spherical gas lamps mounted on tall posts of intricately worked iron and yet more flickering globes floated beneath the ceiling, the detail of which was almost invisible on account of its lofty elevation.

Although it was almost eleven o' clock the station was still very busy. The late train from Trieste had just arrived and a crowd of people were hurrying across the concourse. A dark-skinned gentleman wearing a djellaba, fez and soft yellow slippers passed, accompanied by a porter dragging a gilded chest on a trolley. Following close behind him were a group of extraordinarily noisy Italian women, and some Austrian businessmen who clearly thought that 'ladies' should conduct themselves with greater decorum in a public place. A whistle sounded and somewhere a jet of steam was expelled. The air smelt of coal dust and oil.

Rheinhardt and Liebermann struggled through the stream of human traffic and made their way to the luggage lockers. They presented Fräulein Wirth's ticket to the clerk and, after making an entry in his ledger, he gave them a key in return.

Each of the lockers was numbered, and they

found number one hundred and six at the end of the first row. Rheinhardt crouched down. Before he turned the key he glanced up at his friend.

'I am reluctant to open it up for fear of being disappointed.' The bolt sounded and Rheinhardt eased the door open. 'Yes, there's something inside.' The inspector reached in and took out a cylinder of rolled-up paper and some postcards. He rose and turned the first photographic image towards Liebermann.

It showed two young girls – naked. Their bodies were barely pubescent and they stood, rather awkwardly, in front of a floral backdrop. They affected interest in a horned figurine that had been placed on a stand. The second photographic image showed the same two girls sprawled on a rug, and the third showed them kissing.

Liebermann took the postcards and studied them closely. He picked out the first again and tilted it to capture more light.

'This girl – the one with the birthmark on her stomach . . .'

Rheinhardt glanced at the naked model and then back at Liebermann.

'She looks . . .' He hesistated before adding: 'Familiar.'

'Yes, that's what I was thinking.'

'It can't be – surely not.'

'I think it is . . . and I strongly suspect that her companion is Selma Wirth.'

Liebermann turned the card over to see if he

could find out where it had been printed. But there was no information of that kind. Rheinhardt began unrolling the cylinder of paper. He discovered that he was holding a very accomplished but extremely distasteful pencil sketch: two girls – clearly the same girls – lying side by side, their legs spread apart. One of them was wearing black stockings while the other was entirely nude.

Rheinhardt recognised the style: the emaciated bodies, the mass of baroque detail where their young thighs met. The signature confirmed his initial suspicion.

'What on earth is going on?' he asked Liebermann, pointing to the cursive scrawl in the lower right-hand corner.

CHAPTER 60

Rainmayr stood in the centre of his studio, admiring his own sketch.

'Well, well,' he said to Rheinhardt. 'Wherever did you get this from?' It's not bad really. There are a few things I'd do differently today. The perspective is a little uninteresting and the faces are somewhat dull – but it's perfectly acceptable. Of course, I could get the same effect with less effort these days.'

'When did you make this sketch?'

Rainmayr shook his head: 'Oh, I couldn't say exactly. It must have been over twenty years ago.' He made a knocking sound on the roof of his mouth with his tongue, before adding: 'No, more than that, most probably: twenty-five, perhaps?'

'Who did you sell it to?'

'I can't remember, inspector. I've done so many sketches like this. But you must tell me, where did you get it from?'

'Herr Rainmayr, do you recall the names of these young models?'

'No, it was too long ago.'

'Do you remember anything about them?'

'I do,' said Rainmayr. Then, correcting himself, he added. 'I mean, I don't. No.'

Rheinhardt glanced at Liebermann. The inspector had become as sensitive as any analyst to the small and telling errors of speech described by Professor Freud. Liebermann nodded, confirming that the slip was significant.

Rainmayr noticed that something had passed between the two men and added nervously: 'They were street girls. I don't know how many street girls have worked for me over the years – hundreds. You can't expect me to remember every single one of them.'

'Herr Rainmayr,' said Liebermann. 'You know very well who these girls are.'

The artist laid the sketch down on his table and looked across the room at Liebermann: 'No, I don't. I honestly can't remember.'

'With respect,' said Rheinhardt, 'I have found Doctor Liebermann to be very good at determining whether or not people are telling the truth.'

'What? He can read minds?'

Liebermann shrugged, as if to say: *as good as*.

'Then maybe he should do a turn at Ronacher's,' said the artist, smiling. 'They're looking for some new acts.'

Rheinhardt circled the easel and considered Rainmayr's unfinished painting. It was typical of the artist's work: a young woman with wasted limbs, small breasts, and exposed pudendum. Rheinhardt focused his attention on the girl's eyes.

He searched for the person within but found no evidence of occupation. It was as though her soul had departed. The emptiness was chilling.

'Herr Rainmayr, if you do not cooperate I will be returning this evening accompanied by my assistant and three constables. We will confiscate all of your work, you will be tried and you will spend many months in jail. Well, Herr Rainmayr? Are you going to cooperate, or are you going to put your trust in those powerful patrons of yours – gentlemen who I am confident will offer you little assistance at the first sign of trouble?'

'You cannot intimidate me, Rheinhardt,' Rainmayr sneered.

'Good day, then,' Rheinhardt replied, bowing curtly. He marched towards the door, inviting Liebermann to follow.

'No – wait,' Rainmayr called out. His voice had become thin and attenuated. The artist picked up a solitary cigarette from among the detritus on his table. Then he rummaged, without success, for some matches.

Rheinhardt offered him a light.

'There. Now, who are they?'

Rainmayr drew on the cigarette and shook his head. 'This girl here is Selma Wirth.' He pointed at one of the reclining nudes depicted in his sketch. 'You are already familiar with that name, of course. Like poor Adele Zeiler – one of Sprenger's victims.' He shook his head again. 'I couldn't believe it when I first read of Selma's murder – and so soon after Adele's. Two of them! It was like being jinxed. I was worried that you would discover that Wirth had also been one of my models once, albeit a long time ago, and make a connection. You will appreciate that I did not want to find myself arrested on suspicion of committing a double murder.'

'Were you still acquainted with Selma Wirth?'

'No.' Rainmayr blew smoke out through his nostrils. 'About a year ago we ran into each other by chance in a coffee house. We spoke briefly, but it wasn't a very agreeable exchange. She asked me for money – which I didn't have. She was bitter and quite rude as it happens.'

'Why do you think that was?'

'I have no idea and I didn't stay long enough to find out. Apart from that one occasion, the last time I saw her would have been over twenty years ago. When she was sixteen or seventeen.'

Rheinhardt pointed to the other reclining nude. 'And this girl? Who is she?'

Rainmayr grimaced and was evidently struggling to resolve some inner quandary. He sighed and said quietly: 'Hofler. Erika Hofler.'

Liebermann stepped forward.

'Herr Rainmayr, you are lying.'

The artist threw an evil look at the young doctor. 'Not such a great mind-reader after all. You had me fooled for a minute.'

Rheinhardt raised his hand to stop Liebermann's riposte and said: 'Go on, Herr Rainmayr.'

'Erika Hofler,' Rainmayr continued. 'A pretty one: I liked her a great deal. She was different from the others. She actually showed an interest in my work and asked questions about colour and form. When she wasn't modelling she wouldn't just lounge around being cheeky, she'd pick up one of my books. I'd catch her reading Vasari's *Lives* or Cellini. She wanted to learn, so I gave her some lessons and she wasn't at all bad. The other girls resented her, of course. They were jealous.'

The artist took a few more drags from his cigarette and stubbed it out on a plate.

'She had it hard, young Erika. Her father was a brute. He drank heavily and flogged his wife and children with a strap. I can still remember the marks those beatings left.' Rainmayr traced some lines in the air. 'Once, I did a study of Erika's wounds for a client.' Rainmayr's eyes glazed over as he recreated the image in his mind. 'Hofler eventually drank himself to death, which was a good thing in some ways but not in others. Frau Hofler didn't have much money when Hofler was alive, but after he was gone . . .' Rainmayr showed his palms. 'The money I paid Erika was all they had. There was a younger sister, too: Mona, a beautiful little girl, but always sickly. She couldn't run without coughing up blood. One of the bad winters finished her off. The charity doctors did what they could. It wasn't enough.' Rainmayr shook his head. 'She needed to see a specialist. Poor Erika was devastated. And Frau Hofler . . . well, what can one say. Something happened to her head.' Rainmayr screwed his finger against his temple. 'They put her away in one of the institutions.'

'How did Erika survive?'

'I supported her for a while, but eventually she stopped modelling and found other ways of making money—'

'Prostitution?' Rheinhardt cut in.

'You know how it is, inspector.' Rainmayr picked up one of his brushes and began to clean it with a rag. 'Three years ago I was invited to an exhibition: and there she was – Erika Hofler. She was calling herself Kristina Feuerstein. She'd become a respected couturière. She'd worked in the big fashion houses of Paris and on her return to Vienna mixed with the secessionists.'

'Did you speak to her?'

'Yes.'

'And she recognised you?'

'Of course.'

'What did you talk about?'

'We talked about art, inspector.' Rainmayr dropped the clean paintbrush into the groove on his easel. 'I don't have to say any more, do I, inspector? I'm sure you know enough now for your purposes.'

'Why do you feel obliged to protect Frau Vogl? We *are* speaking about Frau Vogl – aren't we?'

'I don't feel *obliged*, inspector.'

'All right: why do you *want* to then?'

'She started off as a street girl and now she enjoys the society of countesses. I admire her. You think I'm some kind of monster, like Sprenger. You are quite wrong. I have my own code of conduct which might be different to yours – but it is a code of conduct nevertheless. Erika has managed to put her past behind her. Well, Good luck to her. She was my little favourite . . .'

As Rainmayr said the word *favourite* the cast of his countenance altered. There was something about his expression that made Rheinhardt think of the gentleman he had observed in the play-ground. He saw again the man's hungry eyes locked on his daughter Mitzi as she ascended the climbing frame.

'What happned to Frau Hofler?' asked Liebermann.

The artist shrugged.

'How should I know?'

CHAPTER 61

Kristina dismissed her assistant and offered Rheinhardt and Liebermann chairs. They were gathered, once again, in the modernist reception room of House Vogl. A sketchbook lay open on the cuboid table, showing a female figure in a shapeless 'reform' kaftan, her arms raised above her head and the wide, loose sleeves collapsed into generous folds around her narrow shoulders. Kristina remarked that she had not anticipated the pleasure of their company again so soon, and as she spoke Liebermann noticed how she brushed Rheinhardt's hand – ever so gently – with her own. It was a quick and subtle manoeuvre that might easily have been missed had he not been studying the couturière as closely as he would a patient.

'Now, inspector' she said, her facial muscles tensing to revive her wilting smile, 'how may I help?'

Rheinhardt looked weary.

'Some items have come into our possession which I would like you to examine.'

'Items?'

'Yes.' Rheinhardt opened his holdall and took out the postcards. 'Some images of young women: formerly the property of Fräulein Wirth. I am obliged to forewarn you that they represent examples of a low art produced for gentlemen of questionable character.'

He handed Kristina the postcards and she placed them on her lap. As soon as she registered the first tableau – the two girls standing awkwardly in front of the floral backdrop – she was clearly shaken. A pulse became visible on her long neck. She struggled to manufacture an impression of disinterested bewilderment.

'Inspector.' She made a supplicating gesture, showing her palms. 'I don't know what to say . . .'

'Where do you think Fräulein Wirth got these from?'

'They must have been left in her apartment by a gentleman.'

'We did not find them in her apartment.'

The couturière swallowed.

'Where, then?'

'In a luggage locker at the Südbahnhof.'

Kristina repeated her gesture of supplication.

'Perhaps she intended to sell them. Poor Selma had very little money.'

'Frau Vogl, look closely – if you will – at that first image. Do you recognise those girls?'

Kristina ran her fingers along the edge of the uppermost card.

'See how worn it is,' she replied. 'Isn't it very

400

old – this postcard? I'm afraid I don't recognise them – no – how could I?'

Liebermann leaned forward.

'Ashputtel.'

Kristina Vogl turned to face the young doctor. Her expression demonstrated that she welcomed his interjection, even though it was utterly incomprehensible.

'I beg your pardon?'

'Ashputtel – the story – as depicted in the lithographs hanging on your bedroom wall: last month, when Inspector Rheinhardt and I came to your house, I made some comments concerning the lithographs and your profession. How fitting – I said – that a couturière should have a special liking for a story in which so many dresses appear. You said that this had never before occurred to you.'

Kristina smiled but the delivery of her response was mildly indignant.

'I purchased those lithographs because I like the artist's style, not because the story of Ashputtel has dresses in it!'

'Indeed. And we must also suppose that sometimes you are so impressed by the cut of a new dress out of Paris that you see only the inventive lines and nothing else – not even the fabric. Naturally, some things are attended to at the expense of others. But the issue here is *what things and why?*'

'With respect, Herr doctor, I am finding it exceedingly difficult to grasp your meaning.'

'Then let me speak more plainly. You did not fully appreciate that the story of Ashputtel features dresses, because there is another dimension to the Ashputtel narrative that – in your mind – is afforded priority of interest.'

'Is there?'

'Ashputtel tells the story of a girl who is despised by her stepsisters but who struggles against poverty and adversity and is finally rewarded with the hand of a prince.'

Kristina's features hardened. She did not respond to the young doctor, but turned instead to Rheinhardt and held out the postcards: 'Please – take these back. I am sorry I cannot help you.'

'But you haven't looked at all of them,' said Rheinhardt.

'I cannot help you,' Kristina insisted.

'Then perhaps you would be willing to consider another image?' Rheinhardt removed Rainmayr's sketch from his holdall. Pointing at the reclining figure of Erika Hofler, he added: 'This girl . . . does she not seem familiar to you? Notice, she has a birthmark, just here.' Rheinhardt touched his own stomach. 'It would be very easy to identify her – even if she has now grown to adulthood.'

The room became very still.

Kristina stared at Rainmayr's sketch. She did so for an inordinate amount of time and then, quite suddenly, jerked away as if wrenching her head out from between the plates of a vice. Rheinhardt was about to speak but Liebermann stopped him with an admonitory frown. Tears were imminent. He could *feel* them coming. As a consequence of sitting – year after year – with lachrymose patients, he had developed an uncanny sense of when people were about to cry.

The couturière's shoulders began to shake and when she looked up the tears were streaming down her cheeks.

'It's me,' she said. 'The girl. It's me – but you know that already . . .' Rheinhardt found a handkerchief in his pocket, a crisp square of linen, which he handed to the sobbing woman.

'And the other girl is . . .' He invited Kristina to complete the sentence.

'Selma.' Kristina blew her nose and dabbed the handkerchief against her skin. 'There it is, then! You have discovered my secret. I am a fraud!'

'You are not a fraud, Frau Vogl,' said Rheinhardt. 'You are a lady possessed of a very considerable talent.'

'Talent!' she repeated, spitting out the word as if it tasted of bile. 'Yes, I may have talent but I am not, as you say, a *lady*. I am this girl.' She flicked the sketch with her hand and the violence of her abrupt movement created a tear in the paper.

'Erika Hofler,' said Rheinhardt.

The sound of her real name made Kristina start.

'How do you know?' Her gaze fell on the cursive scrawl that occupied the bottom right-hand corner

403

of the sketch. 'Rainmayr. You've spoken to Rainmayr?'

'Yes, we have.'

'He gave his word! He promised never to betray me.'

'Herr Rainmayr only revealed your true identity under duress,' said Rheinhardt. 'He would not have done so otherwise.'

Kristina raised her chin and, recovering her composure, asked: 'What do you intend to do now that you have found me out? Tell the newspapers? My husband?'

Rheinhardt shook his head.

'No. We intend to do neither of those things.'

The couturière looked puzzled.

'Frau Vogl,' said Liebermann, 'when we were here yesterday, you said that Herr Shevchenko – the landlord's agent – made Fräulein Wirth an indecent proposal. That wasn't quite true, was it?'

'I told you what I could remember.'

'Well, none of us have a perfect memory – although your powers of recollection in this instance are not really relevant. You see, I believe that what you told *us* yesterday was a wilful distortion of something that Fräulein Wirth told *you*.'

'I really don't know what you're talking about.'

'Fräulein Wirth confessed to you that her financial situation was so dire she was contemplating offering herself to Shevchenko.'

'That is an absurd thing to say, Herr doctor. She despised Shevchenko.'

'One must suppose she hoped to make you feel guilty.'

'To what end?'

'To increase the likelihood of you giving her money.'

'Selma did not need to make me feel guilty, Herr doctor. I was happy to give her financial assistance. The problem was getting her to accept it.'

'On the contrary. You resented giving her anything.'

'How dare you say that!'

'You thought it wise to offer Selma inducements to ensure that she would be discreet concerning your common history and she accepted your pecuniary gifts without scruple. Indeed, her ready acceptance was tinged with an air of entitlement. She *expected* you to give her money. On those occasions when you did not give her money she became manipulative, demanding. Even so, you were able to cope with this situation. She could be pacified with medical consultations and therapies of modest expense and the strained fiction of your friendship was yet sustainable. But when the opening of this fine fashion house was reported widely in the press and your name appeared in the columns of the society pages – alongside those of counts and countesses – the disparity of your circumstances became too much for poor Selma to bear. You were Rainmayr's favourite when this sketch was made, and now you had become a favourite of the great and good of Vienna. Bad

feelings boiled up inside her: envy, resentment –
intensified by her infirmity. What did she say to
you? How did she justify her excessive requests?
*You can afford it, you are wealthy? And are we not
old friends?* And when you finally said *no*, that
was when things became deeply unpleasant. It was
then that Selma Wirth informed you of these items
– the sketch, the postcards – items that might
easily fall into the wrong hands.

'Something had to be done. You had read about
the murders of Fräulein Zeiler and Fräulein Babel
in the newspapers. Everyone in the city was talking
about the Volksgarten fiend – his heinous crimes
– and the fact that the police were sure he would
strike again.'

'What *exactly*, Herr doctor, are you accusing
me of?'

'Your old comrade had become a liability – one
you could ill afford to tolerate.'

The tears began to flow again, but on this occasion Liebermann suspected artifice. Kristina stole
a glance at Rheinhardt to gauge his mood.

'Of course I wanted her out of my life,' said the
couturière, unfolding the neat square of linen and
shaking it in the air. She buried her face in the
handkerchief. 'She had the means – and the will
– to destroy everything that I had worked for.'
Liebermann noted with satisfaction that the
couturière had already rejected the idea of chal-
lenging the accuracy of his version of events. 'You
have no appreciation, Herr doctor, of what

difficulties I have had to overcome. No understanding of what I have had to go through in order to escape a wretched and degrading existence. How could you understand? You who have enjoyed – no doubt – every advantage available to a man of your class. Of course I wanted to be rid of her – this poisonous, covetous creature. But I did not kill her, if that is what you are insinuating. How could it have been me? Dear God, the woman was *used* by a man! It said so in the *Tagblatt*, the *Zeitung*, the *Neue Freie Presse*. She was *taken* by a man!'

Neither Rheinhardt nor Liebermann responded to her outburst. Kristina sighed, wiped away her tears, and nodded – as if she had suddenly been supplied with a very important piece of information.

'I see,' she said softly, continuing the agitated head movement. 'You think that I paid someone? Do you *really* think I would risk being blackmailed again? Do you *really* think I would risk being blackmailed over a murder? I would have to be insane!'

'I do not think you paid someone,' said Liebermann

'Then what *do* you think?' Kristina straightened her back and pushed her bust forward. The movement seemed calculated to emphasise her gender. It gave Liebermann even more confidence.

'I could not help noticing,' said Liebermann, 'that you and your husband sleep in separate rooms. A very practical arrangement favoured by many doctors and their spouses. Your husband must often arrive home late, and on returning he can attend to his toilet before retiring without disturbing your sleep. However, this choice also reveals a logistical feature of your conjugal relations. You must go to your husband or he must come to you.'

'Inspector!' cried Kristina. 'This is not proper. These are private matters. I will not sit here and be insulted. You cannot allow this man to—'

'Please,' said Rheinhardt firmly. 'Allow Doctor Liebermann to continue.'

'On the evening of the sixteenth of April,' said Liebermann, 'you visited Fräulein Wirth. She showed you some postcards and sketches – just like the ones Inspector Rheinhardt showed you today. We must suppose that they were a recent acquisition, otherwise you would have known of their existence somewhat earlier. I fancy she came across them by chance in one of the junk shops on Wiebliger Strasse. You arranged to return much later the same evening in order to buy the images from her – for what I imagine must have been a substantial sum.' Liebermann sat back in his chair and pulled at his chin. 'I do not know whether you hatched your plan on the way home or whether an opportunity arose for intimacy with your husband – an opportunity that served as inspiration. You did, however, make love to him, and subsequently went back to your bedroom taking that part of his being essential to your purpose. You expelled his vital fluid and poured it into a syringe taken from your husband's study. I cannot say exactly how events transpired on your return to Fräulein Wirth's apartment. Here I must speculate. Did you stab Fräulein Wirth directly? I don't think so: the knife was too well placed. Perhaps you arrived with some chloral hydrate – also taken from your husband's study – which you poured into a drink? Once she was unconscious, it would have been considerably easier for you to insert the knife between Fräulein Wirth's ribs and inject your husband's semen into her person. Of course, you had no idea that there were more images. No idea that Fräulein Wirth had intended to extort even more money from your purse.'

Kristina Vogl stared at Liebermann. The handkerchief fell from her hands and she clasped her stomach as if suddenly afficted by gastric pain.

'You do not know how I have suffered . . . to get all this . . . you do not know what this means to me.' The couturière looked around the reception room, her eyes glistening. 'You do not know what a woman like me must do.' She bent over as if the pain in her stomach was becoming more intense. 'And now you're going to take it all away.' Turning to Rheinhardt she smiled – a peculiar smile that made her look innocent and girlish. When she spoke again, her voice was equally juvenile: she sounded like a lost child. 'Will I be hanged, inspector?'

Rheinhardt stood up and walked to the vitrine. His step was ponderous and he was breathing heavily – a series of linked sighs. He looked through the tilted glass at the colourful jewellery, the semi-precious stones and salamander bracelet, but he did not reply.

CHAPTER 62

Liebermann was seated in a box just to the right of the opera-house stage. The stalls were almost full and he glanced anxiously at his wristwatch.

Where was Rheinhardt?

An extraordinarily large chandelier hung down from the ornate ceiling. It consisted of two rings of light (a smaller circle floating above a much larger one) from which thousands of adamantine crystals were suspended. The Emperor's box was dark, but beneath it the standing enclosure was crowded: military personnel and civilians kept apart by a bronze pole. Directly below, the finely dressed patrons were making more noise than usual, excited by the promise of a revolutionary production. A strikingly beautiful young woman dressed in blue velvet and pearls was gliding down the central aisle, accompanied on either side by Hussars. In the middle of the front row, two gentlemen dressed in the uniform of Court officials were taking their places next to a gentleman who was possibly the German Ambassador.

Liebermann heard the door opening and turned

to see Rheinhardt making an awkward entrance – struggling to part the red drapes. He was clutching a bag of pralines. The inspector blustered into the box and sat down next to his friend.

'I'm so sorry. I got rather delayed . . . something I had to sort out for tomorrow morning.'

'Oh?'

Rheinhardt dismissed the inquiry with a hand gesture.

'I have some news.'

'Concerning?

'Frau Milena. The Czech police have arrested her.'

'When did that happen?'

'Last night. She had adopted a false identity and was living in a village close to the Bavarian border.'

'How did they find her?'

'They didn't – she found them.'

'She gave herself up?'

'Yes: made a full confession.' Rheinhardt opened the bag and invited Liebermann to take a praline. The young doctor chose a white crenellated sphere dusted with cocoa the colour of ochre. He bit the chocolate in half and examined the interior, which was black and pitted with tiny pieces of crushed almond. The chocolate melted in his mouth, releasing a delicate blend of coffee and oranges. 'Good?' continued Rheinhardt. 'They should be – I got them from the shop downstairs and they were prohibitively expensive.' The inspector selected a praline covered in toasted coconut. He began chewing, closed his eyes and produced a groan of deep satisfaction. After which he added: 'She's being brought back to Vienna in the morning.'

'Guilt – I suppose.'

'What?'

'That is why she gave herself up. Guilt. Like Erstweiler, her mental constitution was not strong enough to survive the emotional consequences of her own crime. When she and Erstweiler killed Bozidar Kolinsky, in a way they also killed themselves.'

Rheinhardt nodded in agreement. He took a second praline, the sweetness of which seemed to render him incapable of speech: an almost idiotic smile played around his lips. In due course he came to his senses and said: 'So – *Tristan and Isolde* – thank you so much for getting tickets.'

'Well, a celebration was in order, surely – and I thought the themes apposite.'

'The reviews have been stupendous! The dawn of a new epoch in the history of opera – so they say.'

'I am most eager to see Roller's sets. Apparently, his work is richly symbolic. Everything he incorporates has meaning – even the colours and small decorative details. In this respect he's a little like a psychoanalyst . . .'

They continued talking about the production's excellent reviews until the orchestra finished tuning up, the lights dimmed, and the wiry frame of director Mahler appeared on the podium.

The prelude was exquisite, emerging naturally from the preceding moment of silence and repeatedly dissolving into mute lacunae before rising in a great wave of sound which – when it broke – created an indefinable yearning, the physicality of which united the audience in a collective and audible sigh. Mahler's genius made the score entirely transparent, a slow tempo encouraging the ear to savour every melodic line and nuance. He was like some great anatomist, wielding his baton like a scalpel, revealing mysteries that had hitherto remained beyond the reach of human comprehension.

When the curtain rose, Liebermann found himself looking down on the deck of a ship, the rigging of which stretched out towards the audience. But this was no ordinary vessel: the sea that it had crossed was not the body of water separating Ireland from Cornwall but the deeper and less fathomable ocean of the unconscious. This vessel had sailed straight out of a dream. Liebermann noticed that the deck was strewn with curious objects: a gold chest shaped like a reliquary, a couch marked with pagan carvings, and sumptuous brocaded cushions.

Unfortunately, with the arrival of the singers, the music changed – and the spell which had up to that point held Liebermann in thrall lost some of its potency. Although Liebermann was highly appreciative of Wagner's orchestral writing, he frequently found the composer's declarative vocal parts less impressive. Be that as it may, Liebermann was still able to enjoy the performance by focusing his attention on the statuesque figure of Anna von Mildenburg, who made an arresting Isolde. The great soprano was dressed entirely in silver-grey and wore a collar piece encrusted with semi-precious stones in a geometrical arrangement. It reminded Liebermann of Frau Vogl's brooch . . .

During the first interval the two friends went outside to smoke cigars. They stood under the loggia talking about the performance and watching the carriages and trams rolling around the Ringstrasse.

'How is Haussmann?' Liebermann asked, suddenly recalling the last time he'd seen him: the poor boy writhing around on Sprenger's floor.

'I am pleased to report that he is fully recovered. In fact, he'll be helping me with a little police business tomorrow morning.'

A beggar approached holding out a tin cup. As he advanced towards them a uniformed steward came out from behind the doors, waving his hands in the air: 'Go on, away with you! Leave these gentlemen alone!'

Rheinhardt gestured for the steward to stand back, and dropped a coin in the cup.

'Get yourself something warm to drink.'

The beggar bowed, touched the tin to his forehead, and shuffled off.

'You shouldn't encourage them, sir,' said the steward.

'No,' Rheinhardt replied. 'Perhaps not . . .'

When the curtain rose for the second act the stage was bathed in violet light: a garden, on a hot summer's evening. An arched doorway and steep marble staircase led up to the keep of a fairytale castle that was partly obscured by trees. The battlements of the castle were glowing with a soft pink hallucinatory luminescence. Beyond a low wall, decked with lilacs, violets and white roses, the garden sloped down to a glittering moonlit sea. The entire scene was constructed beneath a sky shimmering with thousands of stars. The effect was truly magical.

This, then, was the setting for the introduction of the idea of *Liebestod* – the love death – Wagner's metaphysical conflation of desiring and oblivion. The orchestra surged, ecstatic and sublime, and the two lovers, Tristan and Isolde, sang of a need for each other so deep, so profound, that it would necessarily require their utter annihilation as individuals to be fulfilled.

– *Thus might we die, undivided*
– *One for ever without end*
– *Never waking*
– *Never fearing*
– *Embraced namelessly in love*

The voices of Erik Schmedes and Anna von Mildenburg were so full of passion and power that Liebermann felt something catch close to his heart.

Again and again the lovers sang of their longing to be free of the world, the bliss of non-existence, and the heady pleasures of communion with the night: the effect was completely overwhelming.

Mildenburg's voice soared above the turbulent orchestra.

– *Let me die.*

And Liebermann too wanted to die – in love – and to *kiss the face of eternity . . .*

It was in all of them, this insane obsession with sex and death. They were all sick: Sprenger, Erstweiler, Rainmayr, Wagner, Mahler, Schmedes and von Mildenburg. And yes, he – Max Liebermann – had to include himself at the end of this list. He was just as afflicted with the very same madness.

What was wrong with the German soul?

Why were love and death so intermingled in the German imagination?

Liebermann glanced across at Rheinhardt and saw that his cheeks were streaked with tears.

We Viennese, thought Liebermann to himself. *What will become of us?*

CHAPTER 63

Rainmayr was awakened by a loud banging sound. As he surfaced from a pleasant dream of rising above Vienna in a hot-air balloon, the artist realised that someone was bashing on his door. He rolled off the mattress and called out: 'Who is it? What do you want?'

He did not get a reply.

Swearing under his breath, Rainmayr pulled his kaftan over his head and crossed to the window. Outside, he saw an empty cart. From his vantage point he couldn't see who it belonged to.

The banging became more violent.

'All right, all right – I'm coming!' Rainmayr shouted.

When he opened the door, he was surprised to see Inspector Rheinhardt, together with a smartly dressed young man and two constables.

'Inspector Rheinhardt? What on earth do you think—'

The artist stepped out of the way as Rheinhardt marched purposefully into the studio, followed by his companions. Rheinhardt made a sweeping gesture and the constables began to pick up Rainmayr's sketches and canvases.

'No!' shouted Rainmayr. He turned on Rheinhardt. 'You said you wouldn't do this!'

'I changed my mind,' Rheinhardt replied. Then, taking a step closer to Rainmayr, he continued: 'I have consulted the state prosecutor and the case against you is very strong. You are charged with possessing indecent images and with the seduction of young women below the legal age of consent. Possessing and supplying erotica is a serious offence which carries a maximum penalty of six months' hard labour. The seduction of minors – you will appreciate – carries a more severe penalty.'

'The seduction of minors! You have no proof.'

'I'm afraid I do. Your friend the actor – you know, the one who lives over there.' Rheinhardt pointed towards the window. 'He did not require a very large incentive to provide us with a statement.' Rheinhardt smiled and patted his coat pocket.

Rainmayr watched as the constables lifted his unfinished canvas from the easel. The officer carried it out through the door and there was a crashing sound as he threw it onto the cart.

'You lied to me! You said you wouldn't do this!'

'Herr Rainmayr . . . you may think me immoral, but I can assure you that I have a code of conduct which my conscience does not allow me to breach. It may not be a moral code that you share – but it is a moral code nevertheless. A man with your strong views on the nature of morality must surely understand this. Come, now – get dressed. There is much that we must do today.'

CHAPTER 64

The secure hospital was silent but for the sound of the warden's footsteps as he made his midnight inspection of the upper floors of the east wing. Occasionally, Herr Trommler would stop outside a cell door, gently ease the viewing panel aside and peer through the grille at the occupant within. Most of the incarcerated men slept like babies. Very occasionally, he would see a candle flame and the hunched back of someone writing. Some of the men fancied themselves as poets and composed verses into the night. The warden had read some of their work and was surprised by its naivety – lyrical ballads about maidens and heroes.

A curious screeching drew Trommler towards one of the cell doors. He hadn't ascertained yet whether Sprenger was a sleeper or a poet. Until now, the new admission had behaved very much like a sleeper.

The warden slid the viewing panel aside.

Sprenger was standing in the middle of the cell, arms outstretched. He was gazing up at the moon through a small barred window. Shafts of silver light angled through the opening and illuminated Sprenger's body. He was naked, his clothes folded neatly on the bed. The screeching sound emanated from something which Sprenger held tightly in his right hand.

Trommler recoiled in horror when he realised that Sprenger was squeezing the life out of a plump rat. His horror turned to disgust when Sprenger convulsed and Trommler heard the smack of vital fluids spilling onto the concrete floor.

Trommler banged on the door and directed his flashlight into the cell.

Sprenger turned around slowly. He was still tumescent. Dropping the dead rat, he acknowledged Trommler with glistening, bloody fingers.

'Night is the other half of life, and the better half,' said Sprenger, smiling. The flashlight faded, but the smile impressed itself indelibly in the ineffable substance of Trommler's soul. It was destined to reappear in his nightmares.

CHAPTER 65

'**S**omething for you from Inspector Rheinhardt,' said Liebermann, handing the parcel to Amelia Lydgate.

'For me?

'Yes. With gratitude for your assistance.'

The Englishwoman looked bemused.

'But it is I who owe a debt to Inspector Rheinhardt. It was he who permitted me to attend Professor Mathias's autopsies and I have profited greatly from my association with the professor.'

'It is Inspector Rheinhardt's opinion that your contribution to the investigation was significant and should therefore be rewarded.'

Amelia blushed, placed the parcel on her gateleg table and stroked the wrapping paper.

'Well? Aren't you going to open it?'

'I will. But first, forgive my discourtesy, some tea? I must make you some tea. Please, do take a seat.'

Amelia excused herself and Liebermann sat down. He looked around, registering the various features of the familiar room: the blue vase with its unvarying choice of white blooms, books of Latin and Greek, the journals of Amelia's grandfather Ludwig Buchbinder and, hanging on the wall, three mezzotint views of her homeland: the Royal Greenwich Observatory, the great cathedral of St Paul's and a pastoral scene under which was written the words *The Heath from the South Front of Kenwood House, Hampstead.*

It had been over a month since Liebermann had visited the opera house with Rheinhardt, but as he waited for Amelia's return his auditory imagination spontaneously recreated the glorious strains of the love duet from Tristan and Isolde. Once again he heard the voices of Erik Schmedes and Anna von Mildenburg. Beneath their declarations of love the orchestra heaved and swelled.

The inner music fragmented as the creaking stairs forewarned Liebermann of Amelia's arrival. She entered the room and placed a tray of tea things on the table next to Rheinhardt's gift. After pouring Liebermann a cup of Earl Grey tea and offering him a *vanillerkipferl* biscuit, she picked up the parcel and squeezed its surface. Something soft was contained inside.

'Open it,' said Liebermann.

Amelia's hesitancy – her embarrassment – was affecting.

The habitual intensity of her expression was interrupted by a brief smile. Amelia tugged at the yellow bow and carefully unfolded the wrapping paper. The movement revealed some brightly coloured fabric inside. Lifting it up, she allowed the material to unfurl.

'Oh,' she gasped. 'It's . . . beautiful.'

'A reform dress from House Wolnik,' said Liebermann, sipping his tea. 'After her arrest, Frau Vogl transferred the deeds of her salon to her assistant Wanda Wolnik who, it seems, has a talent for design equal to her mentor's.'

Amelia stroked the material and blinked at her guest.

'How did Inspector Rheinhardt know that I . . . ?'

'He had a little help from his wife, who knows about such things – and I may have said something or other,' Liebermann answered.

'Thank you,' said Amelia. A vertical crease appeared on her forehead. 'I will write a note to Inspector Rheinhardt and his wife. It is a gift I will treasure.'

'And wear – I hope,' said Liebermann.

Amelia held the dress up against her body.

'Oh, it's so beautiful,' she repeated.

'Why don't you try it on?' Liebermann suggested.

Again – the briefest flickering smile.

'If you wouldn't mind . . .'

'Of course not.'

Amelia left the room.

She was gone for some time. Liebermann finished his tea, ate a biscuit, and flicked through a textbook on blood diseases. The subject matter did not interest him much and he abandoned its study in favour of further consideration of the mezzotints.

In due course Amelia returned.

He heard her saying: 'It fits perfectly' before she made her appearance.

The garment hung loosely from her shoulders and undulated as she stepped into the room. It was cut from a material of the richest red, covered with a repeated circular gold motif. These colours found corresponding tones in Amelia's russet and copper hair, which she had unpinned.

Liebermann had always found reform dresses unflattering – but now he was persuaded otherwise. This was how a modern woman should be dressed: unconstrained, unfettered – free to inhale the air of a new century.

Amelia turned a full circle, creating a ripple of brilliance on the fabric.

She was like the high priestess of some ancient mystery cult, a primal power, enigmatic and ineffable. Hygeia. Her femininity was at once alluring and also a little frightening.

It was clear that she had discarded her corset and Liebermann became acutely aware of the proximity of her nude form just beneath the fabric. His thoughts misted and he was troubled by ghostly images of pale flesh. Once again, the love duet sounded in his mind and he was overcome with a yearning so strong that it was as if he had been mortally wounded and his life blood was ebbing away.

> *– One for ever without end*
> *– Never waking*
> *– Never fearing*
> *– Embraced namelessly in love*

Amelia Lydgate stopped revolving. She fixed him with her pewter eyes.
'More tea?' she asked.
The spell was broken.